GO FAST

GO EAST

GO FAST

ROD HUMPHRIS

a Simon Ellice story

First published in Great Britain in 2019 by Rat's Tales

Rat's Tales Publishing 6-7 Queen Street Bath, BA1 1HE

10 9 8 7 6 5 4 3 2 1

Book design by Laura R. Molnar
Printed and bound in Great Britain by T J International

Illustrations Copyright © Laura R. Molnar & James Nunn, 2019

A CIP catalogue record for this book is available from the British Library

ISBN: 978-0-9935761-9-5

The paper this book is printed on is certified by the (c) 1996 Forest Stewardship Council A.C. (FSC). It is ancient-forest friendly. The printer holds FSC chain of custody SGS-COC-2061

CONTENTS

To Sarah

1

NOTTAMBULO

Neither the sea, nor those of us who work upon it, know anything of early or late; there is only the right time, or the wrong time.

Soumaiya brought me strong coffee and ruffled my hair and then pinched me until I pushed her off. I stood under the shower for a bit, working at the cracks in the marble with my toes, and then let her dry me on the balcony with the breeze blowing gently in from the sea. The city was quiet and the buildings were exhaling the heat of the day. The cat came down from the roof and twined herself about my legs. When I had finished getting ready Soumaiya sat on the bed and watched me go. She has a way of looking at me from under her long lashes that is very sad.

I took an old smock; it can be colder than you expect out at sea, and got into the front of the old Peugeot beside Musty. Martin was in the back, quiet as always.

"Good evening, boss, how are you today?" Musty said.

Musty talks too much when he is scared. I don't permit this, so Martin and I bear down on him with our silence and he has learned to keep quiet until we are on the way back. Later I will make some casual remark to him, to release him, and he will overflow with words like water bubbling out of a fountain.

"You all right, Martin?" I said.

"Ja, boss. I'm okay," he said, and his voice sounded okay.

"No drink?"

"No drink."

"Good."

We went down through the streets of the old town which were only just wide enough for the small car. It was claustrophobic in there, with the constant winding about, and the ancient houses looming above. I had my .38 resting on my thigh, for whatever good that might do, and I'm sure Martin did too. We came out onto the sea-front road and sped up. The trunks of the palm trees flashed past rhythmically for a bit and then we slowed to make the turn into the docks. I lifted a hand to the two gendarmes by the gates, leaning on their car smoking. They waved back.

Tony, Happiness and Pete were there before us with the two white pickups. They smoked and cradled their Kalashnikovs, looking relaxed. Three more pieces of human flotsam, or maybe jetsam, washed up on this alien shore.

"Evening, all," I said.

"Evening, boss," they said. I didn't hear anything I didn't like in their voices so I turned my attention to the boat.

Nottambulo, my baby, she looked big and powerful on the oily black water, as she always does in the harbour. She would seem a lot smaller out to sea. We loaded her by heaving the bales hand to hand from the pickups to the boat, my crew catching them and packing them down in the way I like. They are heavy as each one is weighted to sink. We lashed them down under netting and straps. Pete stood slightly to one side keeping a constant watch on the surrounding warehouses and docks, and I had an eye out to seaward. I checked all the things that should be checked: fuel, guns and chocolate, and started one engine.

I love it when those engines come to life. They burble away quietly to themselves and all the potential that is in them is right there in that deep, quiet sound.

Tony threw over our painter and I backed us out from the quay. I raised a hand to the three on the dock in goodbye and dismissal, put her into forward gear and spun the wheel. We slid out past the massive stone blocks of the harbour wall on tick-over and then I pushed the throttle a little so that she rose in the water, but still with only a low rumble from the engine. The water in the lagoon was almost completely flat and the entrance to the sea came up very fast as it always does. I held over to the right of the channel so that I could turn into the slight swell that I knew would be waiting for us as we came out.

I kept her on only one engine until we had turned the headland and then pushed the buttons for two, three and four, eased the levers forward, turned off the riding lights and we became a flat black arrow screaming across a flat black sea, only the passing howl of the engines and the short, white track of our wake marking our way.

When we had dropped the faint, dark mass of the land astern I turned to put the pole star on the other bow.

Musty scanned the airwaves with headphones to the radio. Mustapha Ben Berri, he was a kid on the make in Beirut who got caught offering coke near a school by the wrong kind of Muslims and only got away because their van got t-boned at a junction. He ran to the docks, jumped a ship and ended up with us. Lucky really, kids like him are use once and throw away round here, but I like him and he is good in the boat, so he has a place to be for a while.

Martin had the big glasses and searched the horizon, quarter by quarter with his quiet blue eyes. He speaks slow and not often but he thinks quickly. He's heavy set and strong with it, blond and blue eyed, from Scandinavia somewhere. He hasn't volunteered any personal information so I haven't asked. I trust him though, at least until the fourth beer. The first time I saw him drop a shot of vodka into his glass I didn't know what was coming and got a sprung rib. Since then I keep out of the way and get the local gendarmes to hang about nearby and wait until someone screams. Martin gets a night in the cells, they get to punch and kick a blond, blue eyed European, but not too hard, and of course they get paid. He always seems quite happy, peaceful even, the morning after.

The wind picked up and a small chop bucked the boat, enough to test the lashings on the cargo, but the screws bit down into the water and we made good time. It was not yet two in the morning, still five hours of darkness ahead, the dead of night.

At nearly eighty knots we should be the fastest thing on the face of the water and have a radar signature like a rabbit in a field of corn. Only a helicopter would be able to catch us and she'd have to find us first; the sea, even the Alboran Sea, which is what the western end of the Mediterranean is called, is a big place.

I stood with my feet apart, one hand on the binnacle, and the other lightly holding the wheel, feeling the tone of the water and coaxing her into the rhythm of it so that she didn't bounce any more than I could help. It has a sweet, out of time quality, racing this amazing boat through the dark of the moon; I sink into it like a dream and everything is moving very fast and everything is also very still. The miles passed under our keel and I was well into that place, reading the water, reacting without conscious thought, my eyes more on the stars than the compass, a little high on our speed.

We raised the trawler a bit after three, just where she was supposed to be. First one, rather dim, riding light at the masthead, then the glow from the wheelhouse, and finally her dark bulk against the stars. I eased down to a bare ten knots and circled behind her, keeping our distance. *Canaillas* was there in rust- streaked lettering on her transom. We were down wind and I could smell the fishiness of her.

"Ready?" I said.

"Ja, boss," Martin said.

"I'm ready too, boss," Musty said.

On board the trawler a door slammed and someone waved. I put the helm hard over, throttled back and let our momentum carry us closer. Martin and Musty squatted low, ready to reach for the cargo straps. They also had AKs laid ready to hand on the thwarts, set to auto with safetys off, just in case.

"Ola, Nottambulo," a voice called.

"Ola, Canaillas," I answered. "Is that you Jans?" I called.

"Yes. Yes, it is me." It sounded like Jans and was about Jans's size and shape.

"How's the tuna?" I shouted.

"Not bad, caught a few last week," Jans said. Jans doesn't fish for tuna and despises those who do.

I pushed the throttle levers full up. The engines roared and the screws thrashed the water into foam, we began to pick up way, but very slowly.

There was the sharp sound of a single shot and Jans fell forward into the sea. A man stepped out from behind the wheelhouse and began shouting orders in Spanish. Floodlights came on at the masthead, throwing hard white light about. Automatic fire started from near the bow and from the wheelhouse. Martin returned fire at the lights but we hit our own wake coming back at us and his aim went high. Musty was concentrating his fire on the wheelhouse and I heard glass breaking. Someone started screaming and then stopped. I held the wheel and kept us turning. The screws were gripping better now and we were moving away. Some of their fire was hitting the boat.

It was hard to stay at the helm waiting for the bullets to hit me. I locked my hands onto the wheel to keep me there. Over the engines I heard the dry, splintery sounds of them hitting woodwork and glass-fibre, the sharp whack of them going into the cargo and the crisp and wet sound of them going into muscle and bone. I straightened her up and decided that we must be out of the range of their lights. I jinked her right and then back so that we were no longer on the line that they knew. Their fire was still coming but none of it was hitting us now. I made myself relax my grip on the wheel a bit. There was a smell of blood but no smell of petrol. I spoke to the others but they didn't answer me.

When we were completely clear of them I backed the engines down to idle, put her in neutral and went to have a look. I knew that Musty was gone as soon as I shone the torch on him. He had slumped back against the bales, more or less upright and facing me. I couldn't see any blood but I could see his eyes; only the dead look at you that way. Martin was lying in the scuppers breathing wetly. I saw where the holes in his smock were and left him be.

I found the pole star, put it behind us and got back up to speed. Martin died quietly after about an hour; I didn't know when exactly. At one time I could still just see the movement of his laboured breathing, a bit later I couldn't. From that point on he was just a shape in the darkness.

I drove on with the two dead men for company under the swinging stars. There was no good feeling now and I felt tired and sick as the adrenaline washed out of me. It was hard to remember to check the horizon. I kept looking at Musty, and he kept looking at me. We didn't talk.

When I had raised the light on the Cap de Trois Fourches, and the darkness around it had thickened so that I could tell it was land, I stopped the boat and turned off the engines. I put them over the side, Martin with the main anchor and Musty with the kedge, tied to their feet. They went off with barely a ripple into the black water, and when they were gone, they were completely and instantly gone, and that was that.

I sat on the thwart and listened to the silence. There was the slap of the small waves against the side of the boat and the engines ticked occasionally as they started to cool. I took a few deep breaths and shook myself, like a dog shakes, trying to get rid of the tension. When I stopped, my body carried on trembling by itself. I couldn't stop it so I didn't try. The sea was very big and very black. I didn't like that so I stopped thinking about it and ate a piece of chocolate.

I checked the well and found that we were taking on water. When we were moving the holes would be above the water, when we stopped and settled back down, we began to sink.

I started the engines, switched on the pumps and turned west of the Cape, away from the entrance to the lagoon, away from home. There are a few small beaches below the cliffs on that side that have no access by land. It was the best I could think of. By the time I let her nose touch the sand of one of them, there was a faint lightening in the western sky, a reflection from the beginning of the sunrise in the east, hidden from me by the land.

I jumped out with the painter and waded ashore. There was nothing to tie it to and the anchors were no longer available so I wound it round a large stone and jammed that into a fissure in the rocks. The water in the small bay was quite calm so it would be okay. She lay there with her nose on the sand like a big black arrow saying, 'here it is, this is the place'. At least it was dark in there under the cliffs and she would be hard to see against the blackness.

I worked hard for the next hour or so, getting the cargo ashore. I had to pull her in twice as the weight came out of her and she floated off. It was hard to throw the bales clear of the water but I got most of them ashore without any damage. There was no obvious place to hide them so I packed them behind boulders, and threw a few bits of driftwood and some dried seaweed over them. It wasn't good but it would have to do.

I pumped out a bit more water, but not much. I was wet up to the shoulders from wading out to get back on board and when I stopped the heavy work, I started to get cold. I remembered that Martin usually brought a thermos of coffee, found it in the scuppers and drank it. It helped a lot. I fetched the painter, scrambled back on board for the last time and backed her out.

I thought about creeping round under the cliffs but decided that it was too risky. My sleek, black rocket ship looked well enough in the lagoon amongst the other playthings but here in the wild, rugged, empty coast, where only local fishermen go, she looked like a visitor from space. I reluctantly put her nose to sea again and headed out to put the cape, and anyone watching from it, over the horizon. It was galling not to be able to use her full power, but doing eighty knots in the black of night was one thing, in the revealing daylight, another. Apart from that, although I had set out with more than a tonne of fuel in the reinforced tanks, there was not much left now.

By the time I had looped round and entered the lagoon from the east, the day was past early and into morning. Normally I would go into the pontoon but the distance out to our mooring would help to hide the damage. The heat from the sun caught up with me as I slowed and I began to sweat. I hooked her up and waved to Asif, who had seen me. He started down towards the pontoon, to come out to me in a tender, but I dove in and swam for it. The cold water broke the spell that had been on me and I began to shake again. I took a hold of myself so that I could talk to him.

"Ki daayra, boss?" he said. "Where are the others?"

"We had a little trouble. They are gone."

"Enna lillah wa enna elaihe Rajioun. Is she all right, boss?" Asif is the old fellow who looks after Nottambulo for me; he loves her as much as I do.

"She needs a clean and a bit of temporary glassing, Asif. I've left the pump on but she needs to come out."

"I will see to it immediately."

"I'll need her again tonight, I'm afraid."

"Inshallah."

I pushed my hands over my head to get rid of the worst of the water, wrang out my shirt and tied it round my waist. I wanted a beer, and then probably another beer. I crossed the road and went under the arch of bougainvillea into the garden bar of the Hotel Rif. I waved to Ali and dropped into a chair under the fronds of a banana. He's a good waiter and he came over quickly with a long, cold beer on a tray. He waited while I poured most of it down and then held the cold glass against my forehead for a moment.

"How are you, Simon?" he said.

"Better, Ali. Thank you."

"Shall I fetch another one, Simon?"

"Yes, I think that's a very good idea." I leant back and closed my eyes. "And then a taxi please, Ali."

When he had gone I took my phone out of its waterproof case and turned it on. Time to share the bad news. Time to phone Guy.

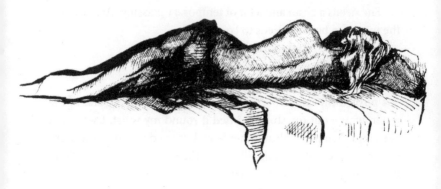

2

SAM

I lay face down on the sheets and they became sweaty and wrinkled. It wasn't sleep exactly and it wasn't satisfying, but it was better than nothing. Soumaiya lay beside me for a while and I held onto her. She put a gentle hand on my shoulder at the time I told her to wake me and I pulled myself out of it and stood under the shower for the third time that day. She took her clothes off and came into the shower too so that she could wash me. The water was completely cold by now, or at least as cold as it ever gets here, and that, and more strong coffee helped clear my head a bit. I sat on the balcony, letting water evaporate off me while I drank the coffee. She put a towel over my lap, so that none of the neighbours would be offended, and gently rubbed my hair dry.

It was time to face the world again, so I put on some clean trousers and a fresh shirt and went out into the hot, dirty streets to get my car. I keep it, an old Lincoln Continental with a bonnet like a pool table, in Azooz the mechanic's yard a couple of blocks away. There was an old Land Rover parked in front of it so I gave a whistle and called out, "Hey, Azooz."

"Who wants Azooz?" a voice called out from under a Hilux.

"Simon wants Azooz," I said.

"Oh it's you, Simon, peace be with you," he said, getting out from under in a hurry. "You, you son of a wet fart, get the keys to that piece of shit and move it now, or I will hang you up by your worthless testicles," he said in Arabic to one of the boys hanging about the yard.

"Thanks," I said.

"Your noble car honours us with its presence. It is like I keep a shark in my swimming pool. No one will ever piss in it while it sleeps here," he said.

"You have a swimming pool, Azooz?" I said.

"Sadly no, I barely even have a shower," he said. I believed him.

I took the back way, the way past our emporium of delights. That is to say the nasty concrete building where we store, and from which we sell, the heavy black resin which is our stock in trade. It's in the wasteland of squalor that sits between the old town and the countryside beyond, a place where men sit around doing nothing much and children play in the dirt. The two white Hilux were parked outside and three men were sitting on cheap plastic chairs, playing cards on a cheap plastic table, under a tattered stripy awning; Tony and two locals, Karim and Romeo. They each had a beer and a half smoked cigarette. There were no customers at the moment.

I got out and said, "Well?"

"Not bad," Tony said. "Two and a half keys, about."

"Okay. I want you and Happiness and Pete here at nine. You two as well."

I stuck my nose inside to see that all was well. It was, apart from the smell, of course.

The road up to the house goes between two buildings and seems to just stop against the hillside. It doesn't, it winds left and right across the face of the slope until it gets to the top, but you can't see that from below. There are a few passing places but not many and no clearly defined edge. I kept the old bus away from the edge. There are a couple of crumpled wrecks at the bottom that have had all the useful bits taken off them long ago. There is another road, but it goes the long way round and only the nervous use it. Sometimes I am one of them.

Once over the shoulder of the hill it all gets a lot nicer; this is where the rich people live. The old town, the harbour and the lagoon are laid out beneath you and look very good. Even the slums don't look so bad and you can't smell them from up here. The road is more or less level and amazingly, has good tarmac on it. The houses are well spread out and have spacious gardens and swimming pools. Guy and Zara's house is the fourth one in, next to the mayor's. They have a good sized staff compound, out of sight behind the tennis courts, and the guard by the gate who waved me in, discreetly lowered his assault rifle as he recognised me, but that's not unusual up there.

I left the Lincoln in a space under the big canopy where the family's cars sleep while not wanted. It lowered the tone appreciably. I went through the arch of bougainvillea to the pool and the outside bar area. The sun was a huge ball hanging low in the west and the light was soft and had the underwater feeling of evening. The side of the house blazed orange, caught in its last rays, and the shadows of the poolside furniture were long across the terrace.

They were there, where they usually were at this time of day, on the big comfortable high-backed cane chairs in the leafy, green shade of the vine that grows over the pergola. Guy with his endless, very dilute, scotch and soda and Zara with her much more serious gin and tonic. Guy pretends to drink but Zara does it properly.

He was sitting with the European papers spread about him. Zara was in a languid pose as usual, leaning forward over the table to display her improbable cleavage. She is thin and her skin hangs a little as if she has dried out within it. She was holding her glass up and looking at me over it. Her nails, which were as real as her breasts, were dark purple.

"Missed you again then, darling? How many times is that?" she said.

"Leave the boy alone, it's not his fault. Want a beer?" Guy said, raising a hand and clicking his fingers. "Beer," he said to the young man who ran over from his lurking place near the bar.

"And more ice," Zara said.

"The bullets don't seem to like you, do they," Guy said.

"You should see the binnacle," I said.

"I've heard. You stayed at the wheel?"

"I had a choice?"

"Well, you saved your own life and the cargo."

"Assuming we get it back."

"I think we will. Anyway, you did what you could, the rest is, as they say, in the lap of the gods."

The boy returned with beer and ice.

"Fuck'm, my boy, fuck'm," Guy said, raing his glass to me.

"Fuck'm," I said, raising my glass and taking a swallow.

I looked at Guy, looking at me with his glittering black eyes, and he looked right back at me. He has the face of Lord Lucan and the eyes of a snake and he wears his hair too long, and dyes it. There's a small black cobra in the mountains here that's pretty similar, though probably nicer.

"Good old Simon," he said. "What would I do without you?"

"Some work, I suppose," I said.

"Do you think the gods look after smugglers?" Zara said.

"I think the gods look after those who look after themselves," Guy said, "And I expect, so does Simon."

"I do. I don't know why Martin and Musty died and I didn't, but I'm grateful it was that way not the other," I said.

"Life is precious and beautiful. Well my life is precious, if only she were beautiful," Guy said, laughing.

"You think I'm beautiful don't you, Simon?" Zara said.

"I think you two should leave me out of your domestic. I'm getting used to people shooting at me, but there are limits to what I can take," I said.

"Coward."

"Coward, he ain't. I take it that you need some more crew?" Guy said.

"Not going to give it up then, darling? Save your lovely skin while you can? Take the money and run?" Zara said.

"Sweetpea, stop baiting the boy or I will shut you in the pool-house. If it weren't him it would be me. Is that what you want?"

"Yes, love of my life, that's what exactly what I want."

"Excuse her, Simon, she's a little drunk."

"No I'm not."

"Yes, you are. You're small and you're a drunk."

"Very funny. I'm not small." She lifted one breast in each hand as if that were the only measure of size that mattered.

"I meant mentally, darling," Guy said.

"You're in a bad mood tonight, Zara," I said.

"So would you be, darling. You'll see."

"Anyway, crew. Like who?" I said, deciding to let that one go.

"What about that greasy Genoese? Tony something?" Guy said.

"Alleppo. He's handy about boats but he fancies my job."

"So take him anyway. What about the munt?"

"Happy's all right but the sea scares him."

"So?"

"So, it makes him a lot less useful on a boat."

"He'll get used to it. Do him good."

"Okay, I'll take him tonight and we'll see."

"Pete?"

"He's basically Tony-lite but without any knowledge of boats."

"What am I doing employing such a bunch of fuckwits?"

"Don't ask me, you hired them."

"What about one of the rag-heads?"

"Don't know them very well. I'll have a look at them and see what I think."

"I can get you a line up of ten to choose from if you want."

"I know."

"Do you know what you want?"

"I want two men I know and trust who are good at the job," I said.

"I'm sure you do. Just imagine what a shambles this was before you got here," he said.

"I should've driven a harder bargain," I said.

"Too late now, old son. At least you get to sit at the feet of the master and learn the ways of the tao."

"You just said it was a shambles."

"Yeah, but it was a brilliant shambles. Anyway, you're earning more money every month than your old man earns in a year. So that isn't so bad, is it?"

"Yes, but now I can guess what you're earning, can't I?"

"Hey, it's my town. I had to kill a lot of fuckwits to get to this position. And look what I got for it." He pointed at Zara and grinned wickedly.

"C'mon, darling. Kill the old bastard and have me instead," Zara said. "You know you want to. I'll teach you things you can't imagine. Come in the house with me now and I'll give you a taster."

"You do know Guy is sitting right there, don't you?" I said.

"He doesn't mind," she said.

"I don't really," Guy said.

"Do you two not realise that I've led a sheltered life? They don't do this kind of thing in the home counties much," I said.

"Yes, they do," Guy said. "I should know."

"Oh, fuck, here we go," Zara said.

I followed her gaze towards the house. A girl in a swimming costume came out of it and walked towards us. We all watched her do it.

"This is Sam, my daughter. Simon Ellice," Guy said, watching us.

"Hello, Simon." She pushed her sunglasses up onto her head so that I could see her clear iron-grey eyes. "I'm very pleased to meet you," she said, offering me a hand.

"Hello, Sam. I'm pleased to meet you too," I said, taking it. Her hair, still damp from swimming, was thick and fair, to her shoulders. She was younger than me by a year or two, maybe.

"Dad's been telling me about you," she said.

"Well, he didn't tell me about you. Where've you been all this time?"

"Oh, learning to walk about with a pole up my arse." She took her hand back and sat down on the chair beside mine.

"She means finishing school, in Switzerland," Guy said. "It was bloody expensive and doesn't seem to have done much good."

"I can give you a polite brush off in three languages and tell you to fuck off in five, that's got to come in handy." She raised a slim, tanned arm and beckoned to the boy. "Would you like another beer, Simon?" she said.

"Thank you," I said, feeling I'd been offered more than beer.

"Watch her, darling," Zara said. "She's not as nice as she looks."

"Don't speak, Auntie, your dewlap wobbles," Sam said.

Zara held her neck with one hand and lifted her glass to her mouth with the other.

"I didn't know you had any children, Guy," I said.

"She might not be mine," he said.

"Oh, I'm pretty sure I am," Sam said.

"These things happen along the way sometimes, I'm not sure how." Guy said.

"Don't be crude, Daddy. You've got the most amazing boat apparently, Nott something?" she said, turning to me.

"Nottambulo, it means nighthawk," I said.

"Nottambulo." She savoured the word. "Dad says you've taken over all the deliveries and you're practically running the show nowadays."

"I didn't mean to, it just happened that way," I said.

"Well you're clearly very good at it and he's very grateful," she said.

"He must have forgotten to mention it," I said, looking at Guy.

"I do disburse a little small change now and again," he said.

"Well, isn't that generous of you."

"I know, but anything to help out an old pal's boy."

"Old pal? You didn't say that. Who?" Sam said.

"Didn't I? My old mate Teddy. Edmund Ellice. A man of Whitehall corridors and unimpeachable rectitude. Husband of the delightful Helen and, as it happens, Simon's father."

"That rings a bell. Have I met him?" Sam said.

"No, and I don't suppose you will either, sweetheart. We're off his Christmas card list since I took up this line of work."

"And almost everyone else's. So, the pater disapproves?" she said, turning back to me.

"We don't seem to be speaking at the moment," I said.

"I'm not surprised. I wonder what I'd have to do to stop father speaking to me?"

"Taking up moral rectitude would do it, I think," I said.

"What is moral recti-whatever?" Zara said.

"In Teddy's case, something to do with his bottom I expect," Guy said. "Or possibly other peoples," he added. "You've heard of a rectal thermometer?"

"I don't think you should do that, Sam, whatever it is," Zara said.

"Don't worry, Auntie, I won't. So, can I have a ride in your boat, Simon?"

"Sure, if you like."

"Great, is it time for me to go and change?" Sam said.

"Yes, go do that," Guy said.

"Are you going out for the evening?" I said.

"Yes, I am. You're going back for that hash and I'm coming with you."

"Are you?" I said.

"You said you needed some crew," Guy said.

"See, I told you," Zara said. "Not as nice as she looks."

"I may not be nice, but I am a lady," Sam said, and got up. She placed her beer bottle on her head and walked off across the terrace to the house with it balanced there. We all watched her go.

"I used to have an arse like that," Zara said.

"No you didn't," Guy said.

"Is she really…" I said.

"Yes," Guy said.

"Supposing…"

"Just bring her back alive. If she can't look after herself, that's her problem."

We wound on down the hill, the headlights disappearing off into the void one moment and then sliding back onto the cliff face the next. The young woman in the passenger seat looked down at the appalling drop with apparent equanimity. She had changed into dark jeans, a dark top and sturdy boots and tied her hair back. The change made her look businesslike but didn't detract from her loveliness one bit.

We got to the bottom safely and the road straightened out and we entered the squalor of the slums.

"Funny, I don't remember this," she said.

"So, how long have you been away?" I said.

"Nearly two years. A lot seems to have changed."

"I didn't know finishing school was that long."

"I was a slow learner."

"Didn't you come back in the holidays?"

"It all seems smaller and dirtier, but I remember the smells."

"Here we are." I pulled up outside the storehouse and got out. The Peugeot had joined the two Hilux and the whole gang of them were there, sitting about or leaning on the cars.

"Very salubrious," Sam said. We went over to the men. They weren't looking at me.

"Evening, boys. This is Miss Samantha, she's joining us tonight," I said. They carried on looking at her in ways that were variously curious and predatory. "Say hello to Miss Samantha, boys."

"Hello, Miss Samantha," they chorused, followed by more than one dirty laugh.

"Right, Tony, Happiness, you come with us. Romeo and Karim, you stay behind and look after the shop. The rest of you be at the dock at three. Got it?"

There were nods and smiles all round.

"Well, come on then." I got back in the car and started her up. Sam got in beside me and the other two got in the back. The springs sagged a bit as Happy sat down.

"Good evening, Miss Samantha. It's a pleasure to have such a beautiful woman with us. My name is Anthony Aleppo, from Genoa, pleased to meet you." He had moved forward into the gap between the front seats and was holding out his hand for her to shake.

"Leave it, Tony," I said.

"Okay, well, I was only wishing to be friendly." He sat back in his seat, in no way abashed.

Asif met us at the pontoon, smiling. Nottambulo was tied up near the end.

"She'll be okay, Simon," he said.

"She's beautiful," Sam said, standing by the edge and having a good look at her.

Asif and I climbed in and he showed me what he had done. It would do fine for now. I patted his shoulder in thanks.

"All ready to go?" I said.

"All ready, Simon."

I checked anyway.

"Come aboard then," I said to the others.

Tony made to help Sam but she ignored him and jumped gracefully in. She moved about the boat as if she was used to boats.

"I can't swim," Happiness said, looking anxiously at the dark water.

"Then don't. Sit down all of you and don't move until I tell you to," I said.

Asif let us go and I got on with taking her out. When we had settled into a steady twenty knots crossing the lagoon I took a look at my crew. Happy was looking at the bottom of the boat, Tony was looking at the girl, she was looking where we were going. She seemed completely at ease and was letting her body ride comfortably with the movement of the boat. At least she wasn't going to be any trouble in that way.

I reached into the locker behind me and got out some hardware. I keep four Kalashnikovs on board; they are cheap, easy to get hold of and very reliable. These four belonged to the boat, three for use and one for spare, I clean them myself and they don't leave the boat. I tossed one each to Happiness and Tony.

"And me," Sam said, holding out a hand. She looked calm and serious, and as if being passed an AK was quite normal for her.

What the hell, I threw one gently to her. It's not necessarily a good idea to throw these things unless you are sure they will be caught, but I keep them with the chamber empty so I took the risk. She caught it easily and checked it over as if it was quite familiar to her. I passed out two spare magazines each. I fill them myself too.

When I opened her up, Happiness's knuckles went as near white as they could go and Sam's face got a big grin on it. She had her chin up and was leaning into our speed, willing us on. Her hair was threatening to come loose from its rubber band but she didn't care. She was a fine sight.

"How fast?" she shouted back to me. I told her.

"Fucking amazing! Can I drive?"

"No."

There was no need for any evasion and no shortage of fuel this time so we went straight there. I found the place without any trouble and, as Asif had replaced the anchors, I dropped the main one off the stern as we went in. We would use it to pull us off if necessary; the additional weight of the cargo would hold us down onto the beach. I sent Happiness over the bow with the kedge. He landed into less than a foot of water and went thankfully back to dry land.

"I'm going to go in and help Happy bring it out. Tony, you catch it and stow it as we throw it up. Sam, you watch our back." I pointed to the narrow opening to the sea. "We won't be long but if anyone had seen us and if they have the legs to reach us in time, this is the point where we're vulnerable."

"Aye, aye, skip," she said, grinning at me and settling onto the bench seat at the stern, her AK up and ready.

It was still there. A lot of flies had settled on it for some reason and they buzzed about in the light of my torch. We shooed them off and began to get it out. It was an awkward spot, too tight for two, so I threw them over the rocks to the big Nigerian who caught them easily and stacked them on the sand. There didn't seem to be nearly as many of them now that there were two of us doing it.

I thought I heard a sound from the boat as I heaved the last one over. "Everything okay?" I called out.

"No problem," Sam's voice called back.

We ran them out to the boat, wading in beside her, waist deep, and passing them up. It was about two tonnes, that's a lot of hash, but as a load for two fit young men to move about, it's nothing. It was Sam who received them, not Tony. She took them easily, taking a good hold with both hands and lifting them cleanly. I decided not to ask where Tony was. When we had finished I sent Happy back aboard first and brought the kedge myself.

The load was neatly stowed and Sam and Happy had almost finished putting the netting over it and tightening the straps. Tony was lying in the bilge unconscious; I assumed he was unconscious not dead. He looked as though he would be missing several teeth whatever happened and the butt of Sam's AK needed cleaning. I didn't really care either way.

"Sorry about that," she said.

"No problem," I said.

I started her up and made us all stand right aft. One good heave from Happy and we slid off. Time to go home.

I let Sam drive for a bit on the way back. No one but me and Asif ever drive the boat, but I let her drive anyway. She did it well.

I considered dropping Tony over the side but decided that he was more useful as he was. Anyway the chandlery would be running out of anchors.

When we got to the quay the men were waiting for us with the pickups, backed up to the edge ready. Asif had brought my car and was waiting there too. He tied us up and came aboard. He, Happiness and I, threw the bales out to the others and they loaded up. Pete stood by, keeping a good look out. Sam knelt in the bows with her AK out of sight and kept watch too. You didn't have to tell this girl what to do.

"Where's Tony?" Pete asked. I didn't answer him but carried on working. He shrugged and went back to his job.

When we had finished I called two of them over and pointed to Tony. "Put that in the boot of the Peugeot, and if it wakes up and lives let me know," I said. One of them whistled through his teeth in surprise. Tony didn't stir as they moved him. Happy would tell the others about it and it would do no harm.

Pete came over to me and said, "What happened to Tony? He looks bad. We should get him to hospital."

"Whatever happened to him, he brought on himself. Don't bother yourself about it," I said.

"We need him. He's a good man. I'll take him myself when we're done."

"No you won't."

"What do you mean? Why …"

People generally expect to build up to a fight but I've learned not to bother with all that. I stepped in while he was still busy expressing himself and hit him hard in the solar plexus. He bent over, holding himself and trying to breathe. Some snot dribbled out of his nose. Now that I had plenty of time I took careful aim at his jaw - I didn't want to hurt my hand, and laid him out backwards.

"One more for the boot, Happy," I said.

"Yes, boss," he said, grinning.

"Okay, Asif, you can take her now. You know what to do," I said.

"I have her, Simon, leave it to me." The old man backed her skilfully out and took her away, back towards her mooring.

I made the Peugeot lead the way and Sam and I followed in my car. This wasn't strictly necessary, but I'd had quite enough of this load and I was going to see it safely back to the store, and then forget about it for a while. The streets were almost empty;

this town being a port, never sleeps completely. Two men cruising slowly about in a police car waved at us and I waved back.

We were quiet in the car, enjoying the moment.

"Phew," she breathed out and stretched. "That was fun. I love your boat, Simon."

"Good. You're turning out to be a bit of a surprise yourself."

"Amazingly, I'm really glad to be back. I thought it would be boring, being here again, but I don't think it's going to be. Maybe this isn't such a bad life after all."

"I didn't think it was so good last night, but maybe I do now. Did you grow up here?"

"In the holidays. I've mainly been at schools in the UK, Dad's not big on parenting. I thought I'd be here for a few weeks and then go travelling or something, but now I think I might stay for a while."

"Good. So, they did a course on the common assault rifles of the world in Switzerland?"

"Oh, that's Dad. He's always been very good about letting me play with his toys. We used to go out and practise together since I could lift a .22. I think it's his idea of being a good father."

"Now you say it, I don't know why I asked."

"You've got a flat in town?"

"Yes."

"Is it nice?"

"I like it."

We sat on the bonnet of the Lincoln while they put it all away. No need to take a turn now. When it was all done we got back in and I swung the old car around.

"Shall I take you home, Miss Wealden?" I said.

"Only if you want to," she said.

We left the car at Azooz's and walked through the empty streets. Under one of the arched passages I drew her to me and we kissed, experimentally at first and then harder. We pulled ourselves apart and went on, not talking but very aware of each other.

I held the door for her, shut it behind us and kicked off my shoes in the hall. She unlaced her boots and then prowled quickly about, looking at the flat. I waited in the big front room that looks out over the city. She came in and stood in front of me.

"Nice," she said.

"Glad you approve."

She stepped into me and I held her hard against me and we kissed some more. Although slim, she was strong. Almost at once it was urgently necessary that we undress so we separated just long enough to rip our clothes off and then sank onto the soft rug together.

Later, when our skins were cooling in the slight breeze from the open doors onto the balcony, I picked her up and carried her to the comfort of the big bed. We began again there, more slowly this time, and, liberated from the first overwhelming need, worked ourselves up to such a height that afterwards we lay exhausted in a slippery pool of our shared sweat, dazed, and in my case, panting slightly.

We moved apart so that we could cool down and sleep. I let myself dive down into the deep, soft, blue water of sleep with the same abandon with which I had just given myself to the girl beside me, and some of the stored tension within me washed away.

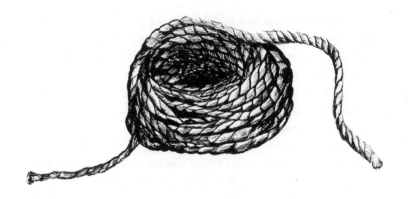

3

FISHING

In the morning, not early, I woke and sat up, carefully so that I wouldn't disturb her. She was as beautiful in sleep as in waking. I leant back against the carved wooden headboard and looked at my familiar bedroom. There were motes of dust dancing in the golden shaft of light streaming through the open doorway and I watched them for a while.

Sensing my wakefulness or waking of her own accord she stretched, yawned and sat up. She went from sleep to waking easily and immediately and was completely present.

"Morning," I said.

"Morning. That was a good sleep. Got any coffee?"

"Should have."

Half way to the door I remembered Soumaiya. I took a light dressing gown from the back of the door and put it on.

She was in the kitchen wearing a long dress and a headscarf instead of her usual jeans and t-shirt. She kept her eyes down and wouldn't look at me.

"I will bring you coffee," she said.

"I can take it," I said. There was a tray with two cups on it, waiting.

"I will bring it," she said.

"I'm here now," I said.

"No, I will bring it. It is my job," she said.

I went back to the bedroom and sat on the bed. Sam was sitting up with the sheet pulled up to her lap and one of my books on the history of the Rif open on her legs.

"I want to go up into the hills," she said. "Has Dad still got the farm and the horses?"

"Yes, he has."

Soumaiya brought the coffee in and put it on the table on my side of the bed. She kept her eyes down and withdrew.

"Your house girl?" Sam said.

"Yes. Came with the flat," I said.

"What's her name?"

"Soumaiya."

"She's very pretty."

She drank the coffee and she read bits of the book. I sat beside her on the bed and drank coffee and thought about things, mainly her.

"This is quite interesting," she said. "Isn't it funny how sometimes you don't notice really cool things that were there all along."

"You mean the Rif mountain range. Home of the Berbers and source of the black gold?" I said.

"Yes."

"The word Berber is from the same root as barbarian. They're originally a Nordic race that got stranded here by the tides of history. Our local Vikings," I said.

"So it says. I want to go there now."

"Have you not been?"

"No. Apart from teaching me to shoot, Dad wouldn't let me do much that was interesting. No trips into the interior. Said he'd be too tempted to sell me. I don't think he ever completely trusted his men either."

"I wouldn't. You'd command quite a reasonable price."

"How much?"

"I think I could get about quarter of a tonne for you. Possibly with the baggage animals thrown in. Would be more, of course, if you were a virgin."

"I am a virgin."

"Are you sure?"

"What's it to you?"

"Put that book down and I'll show you."

"Oh, will you?" She put the book down.

I showed her, but I shut the door first this time.

Afterwards we stood in the shower and had a wash and then had breakfast on the balcony. She wore my dressing gown and received Soumaiya's service as her natural due. It occurred to me that my small collection of side arms and other toys were lying oiled and ready in the drawers in my study.

"What about you then, Simon Ellice? Tell me everything about yourself, immediately."

"Everything?"

"Yes, everything."

"Okay. My name is Simon Ellice but most people call me Si. I am the only son of Edmund and Helen Ellice of Aldermark in Hampshire. I'm currently earning my living running hash from Morocco to Europe for your father."

"How come?"

"You mean generally or specifically?"

"Both."

"It's a good question. I've been thinking about that myself. I was bored; at least, that was part of it anyway. I'd done a year of ocean racing and had had enough of it. I was home and I didn't know what to do with myself and then Dad and I had a fight."

"You killed him?"

"I mean a row. Just words."

"Of course. Why? What about?"

"Me. I was supposed to get a job. A proper job. Like him. Something involving suits and desks and living in London."

"Fuck. At least I don't have that problem with Dad."

"No. I thought I wanted to do something more with boats. He told me if I did I would always be poor and he wouldn't support me. It got my back up a bit and we had words."

"You decided to prove him wrong?"

"Yes, I knew about go-fast boats, or cigarette boats, that's what they call them in the States, and I saw an article about them one day and thought I could do better. So I did. I have. I borrowed some money from one of my father's off-shore accounts and had her built to my design in Italy. I've given the money back since but we're not speaking."

"You don't sound like you mind too much."

"We never really got on. Not that I ever saw much of him, what with being away at school and him always working."

"It's hard to imagine them being friends."

"My father and yours?"

"Yes."

"They were pretty close at one time. University and afterwards. And Mum as well. I've seen the photos."

"So that's why here."

"Rather than any of the other dealers along this coast? Yes, family connections."

"That's quite cool. I feel like we almost know each other."

"If Guy hadn't gone beyond the pale I expect we would've."

"And now here you are, out of bounds yourself."

"Only temporarily I hope. I want to be able to return to the real world sometime. I've no reason to think that anyone back home knows what I do for a living but I'll spend a bit of time somewhere else doing something safe and innocent before I go back. In the meantime I'm sure it's driving Dad mad."

"What about your mother?"

"She doesn't care what I do. We keep in touch by phone. She keeps talking about visiting but she hasn't so far. I'm not sure she should, but she'll do whatever she wants as always, I'm sure."

"Why shouldn't she visit?"

"Dad would go mental for one thing. There's a lot of history between them. Her and Guy and Ed. I don't know what Guy did but it must've been something big."

"More than likely. Would it matter if he did? Your dad. Go mental, I mean."

"I don't know. Guy's right when he said rectitude; he really cares about the forms of things. But for all that, I don't know. I don't even know what he does. Not really. But I'm pretty sure he's not just a civil servant. Sometimes he seems to know things you wouldn't think he would know."

"Like what?"

"When I said why I left The Rifles he looked at me like he knew what I wasn't saying."

"I thought you must've been in the army. Dad wouldn't let me. Was it good?"

"Sandhurst was okay but I didn't get on with regular army life."

"Got bored and got into trouble?"

"In essence, yes."

"Happens to me all the time."

"Okay, your turn," I said. "Tell me about you."

"What do you want to know?"

"I don't know. Do you have a mother?"

"I don't think so. I've asked Dad but he doesn't always tell the same story."

"Do you mind much?"

"About not having a mother or Dad lying to me?"

"Both, I suppose."

"I don't know if I mind not having a mother. I've never had one so I don't know what I've missed. I never think about it."

"And Guy lying to you?"

"I don't think he really lies as such. It's more that truth as a concept is something that passed him by. He doesn't mean anything by it, it's just the way he is. Some people are just like that."

"That's true. I suppose there've been a few Zaras over the years?"

"One or two."

"None who mattered?"

"To me? Fuck no. They come, they go."

"Guy gets bored of them?"

"Sometimes. This one seems to be unusually persistent."

"They do seem to have a sick sort of synchronicity about them, don't they, Guy and Zara."

"It won't last."

"So, it was just you and Guy then? Living up there on the hill. Your childhood."

"Apart from a few schools."

"And uni?"

"Sort of."

"Got bored…"

"…and got kicked out. Yes."

"Could happen to anyone."

I looked into her eyes and she looked into mine and I smiled and she smiled back and the whole damn world that didn't understand us could go hang.

"It wasn't always like this," she said. "The money and the lifestyle, I mean. We've sat down at night with our backs against a wall and no chance of sleep a few times, me and Dad."

"I can imagine," I said.

"It was a brutal thing, getting the town. And then it was keeping it and that's not much easier."

"Nor likely to ever be so."

"No but I've never seen him looking so relaxed as now. I think it's because of you."

"I've never seen him look anything else."

"That's because you don't know him. I think he trusts you."

"That's hard to believe."

"I know, I'm probably imagining it. How long do you plan to stay?"

"Don't really know. Not long. I'll earn a bit more cash and see how I feel. I hope I'll have the sense to get out before it's too late."

"Before they find out back home?"

"No, before someone kills me."

"Is that likely?"

"It's getting more likely. When I built Nottambulo I did too good a job in a way. I've made something that just can't be beat. Your dad owns the Sûreté and the Gendarmerie in Nador so we're pretty safe loading up, and once we're at sea no one can catch us. Unlike the other methods we haven't lost a load yet," I touched the table to ward off bad luck.

"Only just."

"Exactly. Only just. Word has got about."

"What are the other firms doing?"

"Same as always: hiding it in containers, small fishing vessels, yachts, people whatever."

"And now they all want a go-fast boat instead?"

"They do. And why buy one, if you can, which you can't easily, when you can steal one, if you can. She's guarded round the clock and I'm very careful what dark alleys I walk into. It can't go on like this forever."

"I see that. Where'll you go, when you go?"

"Don't know, Greece probably. I could slip back to the yard in Italy, have the old girl re-sprayed and the cargo bay turned into accommodation, and then head off to the islands for a bit of relaxation."

"That sounds like fun. When the time comes, I might ask for a ride."

"Who knows, when the time comes, I might offer you one." We clinked coffee cups on the idea. I wondered if Soumaiya could hear us from the kitchen.

"If I ever meet your father I'm going to thank him for pissing you off," she said.

"I might just do the same," I said.

"What's the plan for the day then?"

"I know what my plan is but I'm not sure where you fit into it."

"Didn't I just sign on as crew?

"Did you? I got distracted."

"I did. I intend to come with you and do what you do."

"Do you?"

"Yes."

"And if you get in the way, or get hurt or killed?"

"Then I do."

"As long as we understand each other."

"We do."

"Okay then. Get dressed and choose something from the top drawer of the cabinet in the study. We'll leave in a few minutes."

"Yes, boss."

We walked through the hot, dirty, busy streets to get the car. Sam only had the clothes that she had had from the night before and I could see that she was hot in them, but they hid the slim .32 hammerless that she had chosen well enough.

She looked about at the scene and the people with interest. "They used to come up to me and try to sell me things," she said.

"Not while you're with me," I said.

"I see."

"This is Azooz. Hey, Azooz, how are you today? This is Miss Samantha. She's allowed to use my car, okay."

Azooz exchanged a few remarks with me sotto voce and then he went up to Sam, gently took her hand and said, "Greetings, Miss Samantha, my life is complete now that I have met you, I and all my slaves wait to serve you."

"Thank you, Azooz, that's good to know," she said.

"You can drive. Might as well get used to it," I said, and got into the old bus.

When we had pulled out of the yard - she got the hang of the car quickly enough - she said, "What were you two talking about back there?"

"He said if I got bored of you he would like to buy you. I said you owned me not the other way round. He said I'd been out in the sun too long again. I said you were Guy's daughter and then he understood."

"So I own you? I haven't owned anyone before."

"That I don't believe."

"Why do you keep your car there, not outside your flat?"

"They watch it twenty four hours a day and make sure no one puts anything underneath it."

"Really? That's interesting. Where're we going by the way?"

"Back to the store. Turn right at the water."

I made a call on my mobile and Hamza arrived on his little moped as we pulled up outside the low concrete building. Karim was dealing to a small queue at the plastic table and Happy was sitting by the door cradling a mug of sweet tea and keeping watch from behind mirrored shades. His personal AK was leaning against the wall beside him. A big CCTV camera bolted to the corner of the roof sent grainy images to a monitor above the massive old safe inside.

"Go and help Karim," I said to Sam. "Karim, explain what you're doing will you."

"Yes, boss."

"Over here, Hamy. Pull up a chair."

Hamza and I sat under the old acacia, to one side. He was in his early twenties, thin as a reed and as sharp as the teeth of a barracuda. He might look poor but that was just part of his trade.

"Good morning, Simon. How may I assist you today?" he said.

"I'm sure you know."

"I commiserate you on the loss of Mr Martin. Mustapha not so much. I can get you another Mustapha tomorrow if you want."

"I know, Hamy. I'm okay for the moment. Do you know who I need to find?"

"I regret, I do not. I could ask around for you if you would like. How badly would you like to know?"

"Quite badly. Half a kilo maybe."

As well as being a man who could find things out Hamza had a few girls who sold to tourists straight off the boats.

"So little for the life of two of your best men?"

We bargained back and forth for a bit, mainly out of habit and politeness and then shook hands on it.

"Good. I will text you as soon as I can. It may be a few days."

"Tonight would be better."

"You have no patience, Simon."

"I know."

Hamza got back on his bike and put-putted away. I went over to see how Sam was getting on. They had nearly got through the queue of small time dealers who came each morning to get what they would sell to the tourists.

"I can't believe how cheap we're selling this stuff. This is thousands of pounds worth in Basle." She held up a block of kif wrapped in cling film.

"How would you know that then?" I said.

"I take an interest in the family business."

"Do you? You wait till you see what the producers get for that. I'll bet you've paid more for a coffee. Good morning, Mr Alwas. How are you today? This is Miss Samantha who has joined our team."

"How lovely to meet you, Mr Alwas. Can I get anything for you?" Sam said.

I could see the man visibly stick out his chest and pull his stomach in. It didn't make much difference.

"Mr Alwas is an important businessman from Imzouren and he always honours us with a substantial purchase. Will I have them bring you a whole block from our meagre stores?" I said.

"Ah, yes. Oh, why not. Thank you, that would be very kind of you."

"Karim." I snapped my fingers and Karim went quickly to fetch a kilo block from the pile on the table inside.

"If you will excuse us, Mr Alwas, I must take Miss Samantha to see Mr Guy now."

"Oh, of course. Do please give my kindest regards to Mr Guy."

"He will be very happy to receive them."

We got back in the car. It was hot now so I turned the aircon on. I decided to drive this time.

"Surely this is the wrong way," Sam said.

"Force of habit. I don't tell anyone where I'm going. We're off to the boat yard. I have to see my baby and make sure we can have her back for tonight."

The yard was busy from the increasing arrival of pleasure craft into the lagoon but they always had a space for us. Nottambulo was up on a cradle by herself in a shed to one side. Asif was with her, as I knew he would be. She looked huge out of the water.

"Hi, Asif, how's it going?"

"Good morning, Simon. Come see. I show you." He led us forward to where two lean young men, stripped to the waist and covered in dust, where sanding off his temporary glass-fibre repair to one of the bullet holes in the hull, one of them holding an air sander and the other sucking away the dust with a vacuum hose.

"Come and look at this," I said to Sam.

"That's steel," she said, having a close look.

"Stainless steel. Tougher than glass-fibre and lighter for its strength too. They'll have welded that up, ground it flat and got two coats of radar absorbing paint on it by this evening. Won't they, Asif?"

"I will be watching them while they do. The work will not pause for a second."

"Why the funny shape?" Sam said, running her hand over a section of the hull.

"Those grooves entrain air under the keel. At speed we move along on a cushion of bubbles," I said.

"Entrain, eh?"

"Oh yes."

"You're a boat geek."

"I am a boat geek."

We walked on to where another team were working on another hole and then climbed a ladder to inspect the topside. Here more men were cleaning back the glass-fibre topcoat around holes in the binnacle and in the covers over the fuel tanks and the engine housings.

"These will be filled with resin, glassed over and sanded back tonight too. See the fuel tanks? More stainless with a jacket of Kevlar and then glass-fibre on top."

"You were at the wheel when this happened?" Sam said, inspecting the damage to the binnacle.

"Yes."

"Bloody hell, you were lucky."

"Yes. Have a look at these." Asif and I lifted one of the engine cowlings. "These are four V8 Mercurys, two pairs linked in series, each pair driving through one shaft. There's a clutch between each pair so that I can start them independently and those are super-cavitating props back there."

"You don't say." She bent down over the nearest one and stroked its gleaming inlet manifold. Asif looked scandalised. "Now can we get out of here? I'm dying of heat in these clothes."

"Okay. Time we went to see the old man. Asif, I'll meet you at the pontoon at ten. Have her fuelled and ready. Okay?"

"No problem, Simon."

We got back in the car, got going and I put the aircon on full. The temperature had gone up ten degrees in the last hour and the sunlight had got the hazy quality it gets when it's going to be hot.

"Hey, don't do that," I said. Sam was in the process of pulling her top over her head. "Drugs, guns, slaves we can do. Murder, torture, no problem. Naked female flesh in public we can't do."

"Seriously?"

"Seriously. Wait till we get to the house."

"How about this?" She wriggled out of her jeans instead. "Mind that truck."

"Where the fuck did you come from?" I said.

"Somewhere cooler than this, that's for sure." She put her head in the blast from the aircon and pulled down the neck of her top so that the air went down it. I concentrated on the road and put my foot down.

"This is nice," she said. She was playing with the Colt Pocket Hammerless that she had chosen. "Ah, ha. That's what I want."

She put down the window a couple of inches and before I had realised what she was up to, took a shot at a passing road sign.

"Got it!"

"If you do that again, you're going to have to walk."

"Live a little, can't you." She replaced the round in the magazine from some loose ones that she had in a pocket of her jeans and leant back against the seat. She stayed quiet until we got there, occasionally drumming on the dashboard to express her happiness. This suited me; I had things to think about too.

"Hello darlings. What's he like then, sweetie, any good?" Zara said.

She and Guy were having breakfast on the terrace at the table under the pergola. There was a bottle of gin in an ice bucket next to her.

"Morning, Auntie. Didn't you sleep well? You look a little haggard," Sam said.

"Shut up you two," Guy said. "Boy. More coffee." He raised his voice to a young man who was standing sweating in the sun by the house. "Wait." The man stopped in his tracks. Guy turned to me.

"Bacon, scrambled, toast, coffee," I said, loud enough for the man to hear me.

"Same for me," Sam said. "I'm going to change." She walked into the house and we three watched her go, as we had before.

"Well?" Guy said.

"Well what?"

"How did you get on? The hash. You know; what we do for a living."

"Oh yes. Got it all back. The boat'll be ready for tonight."

"Good. How did my daughter do?"

"Very well."

"Good."

"Tony tried it on and she hit him in the head with the butt of an AK. More than once. He'll live."

"I doubt it. She's useful then?"

"Yes, very. She says she's signed on as crew. Has she?"

"Don't see why not. How was the munt?"

"Better than I expected."

"Good, that's sorted then."

"I suppose it is."

Sam came back out of the house in a bikini. She dove into the pool, swam its length and back again with an easy crawl and pulled herself out at the end. She got to her feet, put her head back and used her two hands to sweep the water out of her hair.

"Shame they're starting to sag already," Zara said. They weren't though. Not at all.

"That's better," Sam said, taking a chair. "What's the plan then?"

"You and I have a little job to do and then this evening we're off for a boat ride," Guy said.

"You coming too?" I said.

"I've just decided I am." The old bastard was smiling again.

"Oh, goody," Sam said. "In which case I think I'll have a siesta after breakfast. I'm quite shagged out." She looked at Zara over her coffee cup, daring her to say something.

When I got back to my flat Soumaiya was making bread in the kitchen. She was still wearing all those clothes. She is slim and quiet and has the gentle eyes of a gazelle. She turned to me and stood there waiting, with her eyes down, for me to say what I wanted.

"Hi, Soumy, how're you doing?" I said.

"It does not matter how I am doing."

"It does to me."

"What would you like me to do for you?"

"Oh, I don't know."

"I am here to meet your needs. Whatever you say I will do. I can cook you some lunch if you would like. Tell me what you want."

"Okay, Soumaiya, I'd like some lunch please."

"Thank you. I will make you some lunch." She turned her back to me and started working.

I went into the front room and lay on the couch. The cat dropped onto the balcony and came in. She jumped up onto my belly and started kneading it with her paws. I took her by the scruff of the neck and shook her gently and then stroked her hard. She lay down and started purring and washing herself. I let my head go back and watched the slowly turning blades of the fan.

Soumaiya put a tray with some couscous and tagine down on the table near me and gave a little cough. It was dark outside and the cat had gone.

When I had woken up enough to realise that I was hungry, I ate. It was very good and I finished it all and wiped the plate with some bread. She took that tray away and bought another with coffee. I drank it and went into the shower for a bit. She didn't come to wash me, so I had to wash myself.

When I got out of the shower she brought me fresh clothes and stood waiting. "Soumaiya," I said softly, but she kept her eyes down and wouldn't look at me. I picked up my favourite .38 and a spare magazine from the drawer and set out for the night's work.

It seemed like everyone on the street scuttled away from me as I walked. They all kept their heads down and turned aside. I wanted to tell Azooz to get me a different car but he wasn't in the yard so I looked at one of his boys. The boy raised his eyes to the office with the greasy bed in it over the workshop and unconsciously put his hand over his bottom.

"Never mind," I said, and got into the Lincoln. There was the empty shell casing from Sam's .32 on the floor. I threw it out of the window and the boy caught it.

Asif was sitting on a chair at the landward end of the pontoon when I got there and Nottambulo gleamed blackly at the other end of it.

"All ready?" I said.

"All ready, boss." He got off the chair for me but I didn't want it so he stood there. I walked up the pontoon and back again. Every now and again a car cruised along the boulevard, mainly taxis hoping for a fare, the sound of their tyres on the tarmac loud in the still air. The lights from the garden of the Hotel Rif shone up into the tall palms planted at regular intervals along the front. It was still warm from the heat of the day and I quite fancied a cold beer but now was not the time.

Happiness arrived in a Hilux and showed us his very white teeth in his very black face. "I don't like this business with boats," he said.

"You want to quit?" I said.

"I'm just saying," he said.

"Well don't."

He and Asif exchanged a look. I walked up the pontoon and back again. And then again.

My phone rang. It was Hamy. "The man I think you want is Arkiba," he said.

"Arkiba is a place not a man," I said.

"Yes, Arkiba. Mochadem Djout of Arkiba, or rather one of his sons."

"You sure?"

"Did I ever let you down?"

"Not yet. Thanks Hamy." I hung up.

Guy's white Range Rover arrived at speed and stopped in the space that's usually kept clear in front of the entrance to the pontoon. Sam got out of the driver's side. She was in working clothes again, a dark shirt, jeans and the same heavy boots. She looked as good in them as she had before.

"Evening, captain. Crew reporting for duty, sir," she said, offering me a smart salute and a radiant smile.

"Think you can find room for an old man?" Guy said, joining us. He looked damn happy too, and not that old.

"Come on then," I said, and led the way. Sam skipped up beside me and took my arm in hers.

"Aren't you pleased to see me?" she said.

"Of course I am, but we're working now. Come on, Happy."

"How're we doing for rope?" Guy asked.

"Plenty in the stern locker."

"Good. Heavy things?"

"Huh?"

"Weights. You know."

"Bugger. No."

"Unlike you to forget something, Simon. Happiness, perhaps you and Asif could find something?" Guy said.

"Right away, boss." He made the planks shake as he ran.

"I'd forgotten how big this thing is. I'm glad we didn't have to get another one. Perhaps you would like to show Sam how she works?" Guy said.

"Oh, yes please," Sam said.

We climbed aboard and Guy sat on the big bench seat at the back and watched as I talked Sam through checking the tanks, opening the fuel lines and starting number one engine. She was about to push the button for number three when I grabbed her hand.

"No. Only one for now."

"Why?"

"One is enough to take us out."

"But two would be more fun."

"You can have fun some other time. Right now, one engine will do."

"Children, children. Sam, this is work not play so do as you're told."

"Yes, Father." She didn't seem put out.

"Good now where's that munt? I want to get on with this."

The big man ran back down the pontoon with a holdall swinging from one hand. I nearly dropped it when he swung it over the side to me. I heaved it into the scuppers and let it lie.

"All right then. Happy, you get in and sit down. Sam you get the painter in and then get those fenders aboard," I said.

"Yes, boss," they said, and did as they were told. I eased her out backwards and then put her into forward gear and off we went.

"You can take her," I said to Sam. "No more than twenty knots inside the lagoon. Keep to the right of the channel and turn into the breakers on the bar. If you make Happiness crap himself you can clean up the mess. If you break her you will walk home."

"Aye, aye captain." I went back and sat next to Guy.

"You got a grip of your crew, old son?" he said.

"I'll cope," I said.

"Got to run a tight ship you know."

"Fuck off."

"Whatever you say, old thing."

"You do realise that she might get killed doing this?"

"So might we all, so might we all. Let her have her fun. Might as well get some work out of her. Recoup some of the expenses."

"Your call I suppose."

"It in't her that usually has the problem in my experience. We'll see."

"Sam," I shouted over the howl of the engines, "Take her up to eighty, no more. Course, due north for now."

She raised a thumb in acknowledgement.

"The radio or the binoculars?" I said to Guy.

"Can't he do it? he said.

"Take a look." I pointed to the figure sitting down in the bottom of the boat holding onto the cargo straps for dear life.

"Airwaves then," he said.

I passed him the headphones. He tied his long hair, which was flying about in the wind of our speed, in a rubber band and put them on, plugged them into the set which was beside him and began to turn the dial. I took the heavy binoculars from their place in the binnacle locker, braced my feet against the planks on the floor and let my upper body move with the boat. It was hard work keeping them steady but it got easier after a while.

We saw, or heard, a few fishing vessels, a couple of small oil tankers coming up from the canal, and a fine twenty five metre ketch inbound, but nothing we cared about. I gave Sam a new course after about an hour and a bare three hours after we had set out we were creeping up on the wrong side of the harbour break-water at Adra on the Spanish coast.

The lights from the dock threw a black shadow on the water and I got onto the rocks by feel as much as by sight. I put the line round a rock and pulled her in hard, squeezing the fender. Happy left some skin on the rocks and sucked his hand but Guy jumped ashore nimbly enough. I threw the rope back aboard and Sam backed her out into the darkness.

We walked out from behind a warehouse into the orange light from the lamp posts and headed into the town, just three guys off a ship going for drink. We chose a shabby bar in a side street. I had a strega with the others while the barman fetched us an unlicensed taxi. I made the driver drop us off a few streets from Jan's house and we walked the rest of the way.

"You going to keep watch then, Happy?" Guy said.

"Sure, boss," he said, and faded into the darkness.

I knocked on the door. It was late for house calls, even for Spain, but Camilla was up. "Ola, Camilla."

"Ola, Simon. Ola, Mr Guy. I thought you would come. Come in. Come in. You can leave us, Belinda."

A big, comfortable woman all in black got herself out of a chair with some difficulty, nodded to us and left. Camilla, Guy and I sat at the kitchen table and she poured brandy for us.

"Jans."

"Jans."

"Jans." We clinked glasses.

"I'm sorry Camilla," I said.

"I'm sorry too," she said, looking at her glass.

"Do you know who?" Guy said.

"Ah, Jans. He always made light of it but we both knew this could happen. I have two sons without a father now. They want to work the boat. Teordoro is only fifteen. It is not easy growing up these days."

"Jans was a very good man to deal with. I'll miss him," I said.

"Do you know how much a funeral costs here?" she said.

"A lot, I know. You have Jans to bury? They found him?"

"Yes, they found him. Down by Castell del Ferro. It will be tomorrow afternoon. Did you know I used to work the boat with him when we were first married?"

"No."

"That was on Babosa. At least Canaillas is paid for now."

"We must find them. Whoever it was."

"Yes, I know." She looked even more sad.

We didn't say anything more for a bit and we drank our brandies. She looked at my face as if hoping to find some answer there. And then at Guy. Perhaps she did.

"Okay, Mr Guy. This is what you need." She took a small folded piece of paper from her sleeve and gave it to him. "He was the boys' second cousin but he is no family now. You can do what you must."

"I am sorry," I said.

"I am sorry too, Camilla," Guy said.

"Yes, and I am sorry as well. As I say, it is hard growing up. I will be their father now. What do I need to know?" she said.

"What do you need to know?" I said.

"To meet Nottambulo," she said.

"You?" I said.

"Yes me. There are bills to be paid."

"That's very good. Have you pen and paper?" Guy said.

She got them but he indicated me, so I took them and I wrote down a number and slid it across to her. She looked at it, puzzled.

"It will be like this. Read it backwards. Place, time, date. No spaces. If there is company go six miles south and four west-south-west." I drew a line in the air. "If there's still a problem, go the same but backwards. East-south-east. I will find you. Okay?"

"Okay."

"It'll come on this." Guy passed her a cheap mobile phone and a charger. "Turn it on once a day for ten minutes and then turn it off. If you have a problem you can text to the number saved in the phone. Okay?"

"Okay, Mr Guy, Simon. I will be there."

"Okay. Hasta luego. We have work to do." He pressed a bundle of 500 Euro dollars into her hand.

"Hasta luego, Guy, Hasta luego, Simon."

I shut the door quietly behind us and we went. Happy re- materialised beside us. It wasn't that far back to the town so we walked this time and went into a different bar.

I ordered coffee and another taxi. Guy sat down with an old man who looked up hopefully over a draughts board. They began a game. Happy sat down and watched, trying not to take up too much space. I stood at the bar. The coffee was good and I was thinking of ordering more when the taxi pulled up.

"Finish up, Father, we have a tide to catch," I said to Guy.

"There are no tides in the Mediterranean, young man," the old man said.

"The young are very stupid," Guy said.

"Is this one your son too?" the old man said, pointing at Happiness and grinning.

"No, he is my slave," Guy said.

Guy sat in the front of the taxi and chatted with the driver in Spanish. The man told him all about where he lived and what his wife was like and his children. When we got to the quiet street in Almeria he put his gun into the man's face and tucked a 50 Euro note into his shirt pocket and said, "Nice to meet you Rolando. Maybe I'll look you up sometime. What did you do tonight?"

"Senor?"

"Think carefully. What did you do tonight?"

"I sat in my car in Adra, Senor. Not many fares tonight. Very quiet night. Didn't see anyone. Didn't go anywhere."

"Good. Well done, Rolando. Hasta luego."

A man came out from the back of the house, gave us a knowing look and walked on quickly. There was a light coming from a low room at the end of the garden and the sound of pop music playing quietly. We walked silently up the path and fitted silencers. I had a good look at the door.

Guy took one side and I the other. "Ready?" I said in a low voice. They nodded. "Go."

Happiness put his boot against the door near the hinges with an explosive kick and the whole thing fell inwards. We followed it fast. One of them started to reach for a shotgun that was lying on the bench, but I had time to hit him in the face with my left hand, and he sat and held his nose instead. The other two just stared at the muzzles of the guns facing them and didn't move.

"Which one of you is Victor?" I said.

Two of them flicked their eyes at the one I'd hit.

"Good. You two must come with us also but we do not need to hurt you unless we have to. Understand?" They nodded enthusiastically.

We cuffed them together in a chain and put them in the back of the old Peugeot that was standing on the drive. Guy and I collected up a few kilos of this and that, put the shotgun and some handguns into a convenient holdall and put it in the boot. Happy added some AKs and an old Model L that he found in a cupboard at the back. Another customer turned up but he ran away quickly when he saw Happy.

It was a bit of a squeeze getting Happy into the back with them but we made them pile up a bit. Guy sat in the front. I drove us sedately back to Adra and parked in shadow by the docks. It was dead quiet, not even a cat moving. I walked to the end of the mole and shone my torch out to sea. Sam answered my signal with a single flash from hers.

She backed Nottambulo very neatly in by the ladder and we chased them onto her and followed ourselves quickly and quietly with the spoils. Sam had us moving the instant my foot hit the deck and we were away into the black darkness. I clicked another cuff onto the hand of one and an eyebolt in the load bay just in case. Victor was looking wildly about but the other two were accepting the situation fairly calmly.

We made a good few miles until we had sunk the lights of the town and then Guy said, "Shall we do this?"

"Might as well." I told Sam to bring her down to a stop and found the flask of coffee that Asif had put in the binnacle locker for me. I poured each of them a plastic mugful and we went forward to look at our captives.

"Here." I passed Happiness the keys. "Let's have a look at Mr Victor."

He brought the man up in front of us, pinned by his grip on each arm. The young Spaniard had a wide brutal face and such dark irises to his eyes that they seemed black.

Guy looked into his face with interest. "Hello, Victor, my name is Guy. What is it we want to know, Simon?"

"We want to know who he's been dealing with, which growers or dealers, and what his arrangements with them are."

"There we go, that's what we want to know. Would you care to tell us? No. Thought not. Over to you, man of knots."

I bound his wrists together with a figure of eight that would tighten and not slip.

"Over he goes, Happy, take it up slow, Sam. Don't want to pull him apart," I said.

We towed him up to more or less full speed, kept him at that for a while and then slowed down to see what had happened. At eighty knots he was skating across the sea like it was a hard surface, which to him it must have been. He was alive but not conscious so we put him in the bilges and carried on towards home.

Guy had a play with Victor's phone and downloaded its contents onto a small laptop. I stood at the wheel with Sam and kept lookout, Happy concentrated on a section of the engine cowling.

"You're getting the feel of her," I said in Sam's ear.

"I am, aren't I. I wish I could have come with you though."

"Maybe next time. But who would drive the boat? I had a man called Martin who would do that for me, but these guys shot him." I pointed to the three young Spaniards.

"I think he's coming round."

She was right, he was. We sat him up and slapped him a bit to get his attention.

"Hey, Victor, how're you doing?" Guy said. "You don't look so great. Would you like to tell us what we want to know now, or would you like to go back in?" The brutish face stared back at him with fear, but also stubbornness. "What's the name of the person you are intending to buy from in the Rif?" There was no response. "Good for you, old son. It's no fun if you give in too easily. In he goes, lads."

We slung him over the stern of the boat and Sam took us back up to speed.

"Not so long this time. Don't want to waste too much time waiting for him to come round," Guy said.

We had slowed down almost to a walk and he was thrashing about, trying not to drown when he suddenly disappeared. Happy and I pulled on the rope and he popped back up. We pulled him back aboard and discovered that there was a sizeable piece missing from one of his calves.

"We seem to be fishing," Guy said. "Let's put him back in and see if it happens again."

"Parar! Parar! I will tell you. I will tell you," the man said.

"Oh, okay, if you want to. So what were you guys up to then?" Guy said.

"My leg. I am bleeding."

"Tell me what I want to know or go back in."

"Okay, okay. We were going to take this boat from you and use it from this side. We have a pick-up in Ras Kebdana. We planned to load up at the Red Beach, go meet Jans to bring it in and come back in empty ourselves."

"But Jans wouldn't," I said.

"No, Jans wouldn't."

"How did you make him come to the meeting?"

"His son, Angelo. We put Angelo on Canaillas and made him."

"Who was going to sell to you from the Rif?" Guy said.

"Afra. His name is Afra."

"Afra who?" I said.

"Jout, something like that."

"Afra Saliba, second son of Mochadem Djout," Guy said.

"You know?" I said.

"Of course I know. Right then, thank you, Victor, that was very helpful. Now I'm going to ask you to promise never to do anything like this again. You promise?" Guy said.

Victor nodded vehemently. "I promise."

"Good. So now you drink some coffee and we will put a tourniquet on your leg and then you can make a phone call for me. After that we will take you back to Spain, yes? Good."

His two friends encouraged him, I poured him a mug of coffee and put a lot of sugar in it. Now that he had given in he was no more trouble. He didn't really seem to understand what had happened to his leg, I don't think it can have started to hurt yet, but that wasn't going to matter. Guy showed Sam and me his phone. He had stored a number under the name 'Afra'.

"What a fuckwit," he said under his breath.

Guy coached him for a bit and made him practise. I wrote the important place names and the time and date on a piece of cardboard in felt pen to help him. He couldn't hold the phone because his hands had lost their feeling from the rope so Guy dialled for him and held the phone to his ear. We got a sleepy voice on the other end cursing us in Tashelheit and then Arabic and then Spanish, but he recognised Victor and the quantity of the order got his attention. He tried to argue the price up but Guy shook his head and Victor held out for the going rate. The deal was done and the exchange arranged. Guy disconnected the call.

"Well done, Victor. I think we should cut you in for a little bit of this," he said. Victor looked pleased, so did his companions. "Okay, Sam, you can turn us around and take us back to Adra now. Simon, I think we should set those two free now, don't you?"

"Okay, I'll just get the keys."

I went to Sam at the wheel and said, "Can I borrow back that .32 for a minute? I don't want to make a mess."

"I could…"

"What?"

"Never mind." She offered me her bum and I slid the little gun out from under the waistband of her jeans and put it in my trouser pocket.

"If you two lean forward, I'm going to come behind you and un- cuff you," I said. They did so and I put a bullet through the brain- stem of each of them in such quick succession that they hit the deck almost simultaneously.

Victor looked confused for a moment and then his attention was drawn to his chest where he saw the dark wooden haft of a knife protruding from it, just over his heart. His eyes went out and his head dropped forward. Guy slowly withdrew his blade and wiped it on the man's shirt.

"You lot can clear up. Is there any coffee left?" he said.

Sam stayed at the wheel all the way back. She seemed tireless. Asif looked surprised when she guided Nottambulo gently into the side of the pontoon. I threw him the painter and stepped off with the stern line in my hand.

"I'm going home for a nap. Come up about lunch time," Guy said to me, and walked off to the waiting Range Rover.

Happy got into the Hilux, waved, yawned and departed.

"Fancy a beer?" Sam said. "I need to wind down a bit before I go to bed."

We crossed the road to the Rif hotel. It was just beginning to get light and it was cool and lovely in the garden. I kicked the youngster in whites who was asleep on one of the loungers by the pool and said, "Two beers, quick."

"And two towels," Sam said. She peeled her clothes off and dove cleanly through the still surface of the water and did a breast-stroke along the bottom of the pool. The boy came back, put a tray with two tall glasses of beer on a table and looked around for Sam to give her the towels draped over his arm. Her head broke the surface and he was about to speak when he saw that she was naked. He dropped the towels and ran away.

"Something I said?" She grinned up at me.

It looked too good, so I took a mouthful of beer to get rid of the taste of coffee and cordite and joined her.

She tried to drown me, probably in fun, but I got hold of one of her feet and lifted it up until she took hold of me in such a way that I had to let it back down again. We horsed about for a bit and then got out and sat in the towels drinking our beers.

"This is so much more fun than I thought it would be," she said.

"I'm amazed that Guy's letting you do this," I said.

"It's very sweet of him."

"You don't find the killing a problem?"

"If you're Guy's daughter, you get used to it."

"I felt pretty rough my first time but it's amazing how quickly you adapt, isn't it?"

"Has to happen to us all, allegedly."

"So they say. It might happen to us rather sooner than most if we keep doing this though."

"Maybe. That was very neat, the way you dispatched those two. I shall study you, Mr Ellice."

"You seem to be a quick learner, Miss Wealden."

"Why thank you, master." She got up and came and sat on my lap facing me and unpeeled her towel. "What do you fancy doing next, then?"

"Er…" I seemed to be having trouble making a sentence.

"Can't you think of anything?" she wriggled about a bit.

"I think we should go back to my flat. Now," I said, grabbing hold of her and lifting her off my lap while it was still possible to do so.

4

FEEDING THE BIRDS

"I'm going to get that girl to make us some coffee," Sam said.

I woke up enough to grab hold of her wrist, "Wait," I said, "I'll do it."

"Let go. All I want is some coffee. It's what she's for isn't it?"

"Just be nice to her, okay."

"Or what?"

"I don't know. Or I won't sleep with you."

"That's okay, I'll find someone else, perhaps someone with a bigger prick."

She took my dressing gown and went out of the room. I had a look to check that she wasn't serious about that and lay back and stared at the ceiling. The last few days had been rather busy and I didn't feel much like leaping out of bed.

"I should think Happy would be a good bet," she said, coming back in. "Coffee on the balcony if you want it. Come on, things to do. I need to go shopping."

"Shopping?" I sat up and had a good stretch. I supposed I would get up, I could always go back to bed later. She had my dressing gown on so I wrapped a towel round myself and went out to the balcony. The sounds of the day coming up from the city seemed distant and irrelevant to the three of us up here in my lovely flat.

"Yes, shopping. Don't you have work to do?"

"No. Yes. Later. What are you, my boss now?"

"Don't know, I'm thinking about it. How do you get promotion around here?"

"Kill the person you want to replace, I suppose."

"That what you did?" She passed me a cup full of strong black coffee.

"Sort of."

"Andy? "

"That's right. You knew him?"

"I sort of fancied him I think. It was a while ago. He was quite cute in a way as I remember."

"If you say so."

"I do. What happened?"

"He was Guy's main man. All I wanted to do was drive the boat and leave the rest to him but he wouldn't leave it be; kept giving me instructions like he was my boss. One day he wanted me to come with him into the hills on a buying trip and I thought he wanted to talk, but he tried to kill me. That's why I ended up being involved with the buying and all the rest of it. It was hard to say no after I'd just killed him."

"That's not quite what happened."

"What do you mean?"

"He was drinking too much so Dad poured a bottle of scotch

down him and told him you'd asked permission to bump him off. He told me all about it."

"What a bastard."

"Isn't he."

We drank our coffee in silence for a bit.

"Why did you ask if you already knew?" I said.

"Just wondered what you'd say."

"Oh."

"It doesn't matter anyway, about Andy I mean. You're the boat man. All this would be fucked without you and that boat. Wouldn't it?"

"Yup. In Europe hash is worth real money, here it's just an agricultural commodity. Getting it there is the only game that counts, and that's what I do."

"Exactly. So if I were to replace you, say, just for the sake of argument, I'd need to…" she held up a hand and started checking the items of on her fingers, "Before I bumped you off I'd need to… handle Nottambulo - I can do that; handle the men - I'm working on that one; - handle the business up in the hills. That's next."

"I appreciate the warning. Do you want my job or Guy's?"

"It wouldn't make any difference. Neither actually; I just want to have a little fun, that's all. I'm going to have some fun this afternoon."

"Doing what, in particular?"

"I'm not going to tell you."

"Oh for fuck's sake. Order some breakfast. I'm going for a shower. No don't, I'll do it."

I found Soumaiya in the kitchen. She was still dressed like a good Muslim woman and she looked sorry for me. I didn't understand why at the time. I asked her to make some scrambled eggs in my politest Arabic and went for a wash.

"I'm going to need some help shopping," Sam said, over the eggs, "and I don't think you'll do."

"I wasn't going to offer."

"Soumaiya, come here a moment."

"Be nice to her."

"I want her to help me, what do you think I'm going to do?"

"I've no idea."

Soumaiya stood before us, looking at the table, waiting.

"You speak good English don't you, Soumaiya?" Sam said.

"Simon has taught me to speak English, and I have taught him some Tashelheit," Soumaiya said.

"Good. I need your help to buy clothes today. Can you be ready in ten minutes?"

Soumaiya looked at me, I shrugged my shoulders, she lowered her eyes again and said, "I am ready now."

"Good. Bye, honey," Sam said, kissing me on the cheek, "missing you already."

I looked over the railing of the balcony and watched them go down the street, Sam leading and Soumaiya following behind like the slave that in fact is what she is, though I hadn't been in the habit of thinking her so. The cat dropped off the roof and came to say hello to me.

I finished the coffee and went out too. I stopped at the store as usual. Romeo was dealing and Happy was sitting by the door looking dangerous with his bulging muscles, mirror shades and the AK propped against the wall next to him. I went over and took the seat beside him. He didn't move or say anything.

"You awake, Happy?"

"So, so."

"What's wrong, been up all night?"

"Hah, very funny."

"You want to be a boat man?"

"Huh?"

"You did all right last night, and the night before. There's a place on my crew, if you want it."

"Who else?"

"You, me and Sam."

"Miss Samantha?"

"Yes."

"Okay."

"Okay, you'll do it?"

"Yes."

"Good. Now you're mine I'll send someone else to do this shit job and you can get some sleep."

"That's good."

"By the way, what happened to Tony?"

"Tony dead," he said.

"Ah, well," I said.

I went up to the house. Guy was in his study but the door was open so I went in. It was the room of a man who doesn't care about comfort much. White walls, metal filing cabinets and a lot of tech. He was watching the monitor that showed the cameras at the store. The real cameras I mean, not the old one you can see.

"That Romeo is a lazy fuck," he said.

"He certainly is."

"No concept of customer service at all."

"Happy's on my crew."

"Told you."

"I've sent Pete to do his job so he can get some sleep."

"Whatever." He led the way out and shut and locked the door.

I followed him to the terrace via the bar. Zara was idly flicking through a copy of Country Life.

"What do you think about this?" she said, showing me a picture of an over-stuffed leather sofa that looked like it belonged in someone's idea of a gentleman's club from the century before the last one.

"I'm not sure it would go with the house," I said.

"Ignore her, Simon, she's bored."

"I am bored. It's living in this useless bloody country. You can't buy anything except plastic furniture and hash."

"No, we can't live in Mayfair, and if you ask again I'll swap you in for a newer model," Guy said.

"Perhaps I should come out with you on your lovely boat, Simon. Will you take me out for a ride?"

"I think the boy's got as much of that going on as he can handle," Guy said. "Besides why would he want you when he can have her?"

"That's not very nice. You fancy me don't you, Simon?"

"Of course I do, Zara, but Guy would kill me if I even thought about it."

"No I wouldn't, help yourself. Might cheer her up a bit."

"I couldn't. It'd feel all wrong, I'd be thinking of you all the time."

"I don't mind," Guy said.

"I do," I said.

"She's probably not much good in bed. What's she like, Simon? A bit inexperienced I expect?"

"Do you think we could talk about something else. Like maybe getting ready for this afternoon."

"No need, it's all taken care of," Guy said.

"How can it possibly all be taken care of? Who by?"

"By me and my girl, of course."

"Really? By you and Sam?"

"She's persuaded me to let her join in the fun and games. I wouldn't before but she's grown up a lot recently and I've changed my mind. I've sent her ahead to see to the horses. We'll catch her up later."

"But, you're going to… She might have to…"

"I know. Just relax and don't worry about it. Have a little lunch with me and then we'll go for a drive."

"Okay, if you say so."

"I do."

Later that afternoon I raised my field glasses, rested my elbows on a rock and had a good look down over the ledge at the pass below me. Nothing to see. I looked at a few rocks and they looked like rocks. I let my attention diffuse, as one does when tracking, looking for the thing that doesn't fit. Nothing. I was definitely in the right place so there was nothing I could do about it.

This wasn't very comfortable so I sat up and leant back against a relatively smooth bit of the cliff face; it was warm from the sun. I looked up into the cloudless blue sky until it ceased to be blue and became that pale no-colour with no name. There was no shade up here and I had not thought to bring water. I like being up in the mountains; they change the perspective of things, generally for the better. They're uncomplicated and unequivocal. I understand why the ancient Romans believed the gods lived in the mountains.

A lizard came out from a crack and hung on the face of the rock looking at me. For a while I didn't move and neither did he, then a lammergeier appeared, wheeling silently above, lifted by the air rising up the face of the Ametek, and then side-slipped away out of sight again. When I looked back, the lizard had gone.

A few hundred feet below me lay the pass that led down to Mesbar and eventually the coast. The path itself was barely distinguishable on the stony ground; just a hint of a line winding between the boulders.

I pulled out the old paperback copy of *The Long Goodbye* that I had stuck down the back of my trousers next to my .38 and stretched out my legs. I held the book so that my peripheral vision included the killing ground below, and read for a while. The sun strengthened, the shadows retreated slowly under the rocks and the stone that I was sitting on got harder. The lizard reappeared without me noticing him arrive. In the book Marlowe sat in a bar and drank a long, cold highball. Lucky bastard.

"What do you think, Bud, are they there?" I said to the lizard. He stayed where he was but didn't answer me.

There was a flicker of movement down there. I folded a corner to mark my place, put the book down and settled down beside the TAC-50, which was sitting on its little legs, pointing out across the valley like a sinister black finger. I lifted it, tucked the butt into my shoulder and used the scope to have a look. It was almost as good as the binoculars.

A caravan of mounted men and pack animals nodded into view from the hidden ground on the far side of the pass. They toiled up to the ridge and their leader paused to shade his eyes and scan the way down. His horse twitched its ears forward and back and snorted at the void before it. The man kicked it on and then settled back into the saddle and let his body sway loosely as it started to pick its way delicately downwards. He held the reins against the pommel in one hand and the other cradled an assault rifle against his thigh. I put the crosshairs on his chest and rested my index finger on the trigger.

There were six in all. Well mounted on small, tough horses which could do this all day and would make the best of any grazing, however poor. The men were a lot like their horses, lean and tough looking. Apart from their headscarves, some of which may once have been white or blue, they wore dusty red and orange tunics and trousers; the same tones and shades as the landscape around them. A string of six mules, each one tied to the next, made up the centre of the group. They carried uniform square bales wrapped in coarse hessian, twelve in all. One of them kicked at a fly on his belly without breaking step. Unlike the horses, they let their heads hang and accepted their fate.

The last man came over the ridge and started down. The group was bunching up as the leading animals were slowed by the steepness of the path. Behind them, on the far slope something moved and a straight line, which was a gun barrel, became visible. Now I could see that the rifle was attached to a man shrouded in sandy rock-coloured cloths.

"Ah ha," I said to no one in particular.

The lead horse stopped and his rider fell forward out of the saddle. He hit the ground like a dropped sack and didn't move. The sound of the shot floated up to me, and was followed by another and then many more. Four men under camouflage, waiting, still and silent among the rocks, one behind, one in front and one to each side, shot and killed five of the men in the first few seconds. The track became a bedlam of plunging horses. The mules, feet planted and showing the whites of their eyes, tried to back up. The last man got his horse round and, lying low on its back, raced for the top of the pass. I swung the heavy rifle to get a bead on him but a searching shot from below brought the animal down before I could get to him. It pinned him to the ground and thrashed madly, unable to get to its feet. The man tried desperately to get his leg out from under it and beat at it with his fists, but it was dying and could not get up.

Two of the men calmed the horses, started to check that the dead were dead and begin to search them. The third stood to one side watching. The fourth climbed back up to the struggling man and horse. He shot the horse and then the man and then turned to face up towards me. He unwound his headscarf and a mass of fair hair came free. It was Sam. She waved to me, though I doubt if she could see me, so I stood up and waved back.

I sat down and began to pack the sniper's rifle back into its case. Down on the pass Sam pulled a long knife from her boot and turned back to the dead man. The lammergeier returned and began to circle, waiting for its turn.

It was hard going, getting back down from the high place with the weight of the big gun on my back, and I was sweating when I let myself down off the last rock face onto the slope of scree and boulder. I had to move carefully so that I didn't start any rocks bounding down onto the horses below.

I looked back up at the buttress of bare rock I had just come down. Above it at least twenty of the massive birds were circling now.

The horses whinnied gently and tossed their heads when I got back to them. I tightened their girths, strapped the rifle case to one and mounted the other. I didn't bother to lead the pack animal, it would follow along anyway. I pushed on as fast as I could, given the uneven nature of the ground, as I had to skirt the shoulder of the Ametek before I could turn back to join the dirt road that wound up towards the pass and rejoin the others. It was good to be on a horse by myself riding through the mountains. When I got to the track I moved up into a fast canter and arrived at the place where we'd left the vehicles in a satisfactory cloud of dust. We had come in two of the big Toyotas, each with a horse box behind and Guy's white Range Rover and they were tucked in under a group of cedars to one side of the road.

The birds had disappeared from the sky and the caravan of horses and mules was just coming into view out of the fold of land that hid the beginning of the path up to the pass.

I handed the horses to Habib the horsemaster, threw the TAC-50 into the boot of the Range Rover, took a bottle of water from the cooler and then sat on a flat rock in the shade to watch them arrive.

Sam was leading. Now I saw what she'd meant by shopping. She had discarded her camouflage, her head was bare, her mane of fair hair flowing about her shoulders, but other than that she was an Arabian prince. She had a black sirwal, like trousers but looser, that suit riding so well, tucked into her boots. Above that was a simple, dark maroon tunic and over all a jet-black bisht, or cloak, heavily embroidered with gold thread. At her belt was the gleam of the traditional silver dagger.

She sat her horse with the ease of complete confidence and the AK-47 slung across her back in no way detracted from the look. There was light in her eyes and laughter bubbling up out of her.

She jumped off her horse, threw her arms around me and kissed me, and then did a little dance in the dust.

"You having a good day then?" I said, grinning in spite of myself, for her joy was irresistible.

"I'll say I am. Dad said we'd be feeding the birds and I didn't get it, but I do now. Not a shot fired, not by any of them I mean. Isn't that good? I got that one that tried to run, did you see?"

"Yes, I saw. A fine shot. No need for me up there at all."

"Well, you know Dad, he likes to make certain. Don't you, Dad?" Karim led one half of the string of baggage animals to one side, followed by Happy with the rest, and Guy bringing up the rear, walked his horse up to us. He sat a little slouched with his gun resting across the pommel. He looked very relaxed, but then he almost always does.

"Don't I what?" he said.

"Like to be sure," Sam said.

"Always. You must have made good time to beat us back. See anything at all?"

"Nothing but the birds," I said.

"Good. Now, Daughter, you can earn your pleasures. I'm driving back with Simon. You can see the load safely back to the store and help Habib get all these animals away to the farm. Think you can manage that?"

For an instant a flicker of anger flashed across her face and was gone.

"Yes, Daddy, I think I can manage that."

"Good. Here, Happiness." He tossed his AK to the big man who caught it with a grin, "She's the boss, understand?"

"Yes, boss."

I could see that this brightened Sam up.

"Don't be long. I'll see you at the house. Ready?" This to me.

"Sure."

Normally I would have been the one packing and sorting, or at least supervising the packing and sorting. I wasn't sure how I felt about the change. Or about what I'd witnessed that afternoon. As I got into the passenger side of the car I took the .38 from out of my waistband, but not my book; I'd left it up on the rocks above the pass. Bugger.

Guy drove fast and well, letting the heavy car slide on the corners a bit just for the fun of it, and raising a lot of dust. He must be as old as my father but he doesn't look that old and he doesn't drive old. I could tell that he was having a good day. The rattle of the stones abruptly stopped and became a steady hum as we hit the tarmac. He put his foot down and we flew back towards Nador.

"Has she killed many people?" I said.

"You shocked, old son?"

"Maybe a bit."

"Okay for the men but not the girls, huh?"

"Something like that."

"She in't just for decoration you know. She's a working girl now and she's my daughter. What did you expect?"

"Hey, I get that. Just let me catch up, will you."

"Well, don't be too slow about it."

"I'll do my best. I take it one of those lads was one of the chief's sons?" I said, changing the subject.

"I'm assuming so."

"Has he got any left?"

"One, I think."

"He won't be pleased."

"He started it."

"That's true."

"It's the way of these people, you know that. There's feuds still going on up there that started centuries ago. If I did anything less they'd think I was a pussy."

"I know."

"Any hint of weakness and all the bribe money in the world won't keep Nador in my hands."

"I know."

Guy drifted onto the gravel skirt of the road to overtake a lorry on the wrong side. A boy pulled at his goat to get it out of the way. We missed it by at least a couple of inches. At this speed we'd be back in Nador in less than an hour.

"I wanted to talk to you," he said.

"I guessed."

"Between you and me, it's you and Nottambulo that have made the difference recently. In the year you've been here. For better and for worse."

"What do you mean?"

"I haven't told you this before, but we're shipping more than three times what we used to, and thanks to you, we haven't lost a load yet. I used to reckon on losing about one in five with the containers. Less than that with the lorry but that was much smaller loads. If I'd known, I wouldn't have agreed to such a high percentage."

"At three times the volume, I don't think you're losing out," I said.

"I'm not saying I am."

"So you're not tempted to get your own boat and replace me with Sam then? She seems to be thinking that way."

"You should know. No, my daughter, my lovely daughter, is, how shall I put it, easily bored. She's having fun right now, but when this gets routine, forget it. That's why I don't mind her taking part at the moment; I'll be there with her, or you will, and in a while she'll get bored with it and stop."

"You trust me to look after her? I'm flattered."

"You know what they call you?"

"Who? I didn't know they called me anything."

"The locals. Simon SarSour. Do you know what SarSour means?"

"No."

"Cockroach."

"Oh."

"Ever tried to kill a cockroach?"

"Of course."

"You have to hit it pretty hard."

"I suppose you do."

"And there's another thing I bet you haven't noticed."

"What?"

"You and Sam work very well together, I've been watching. Like you've known each other a lot longer than you have. You automatically cover each other's backs and the men are very careful around you when you're together. It's interesting."

"I hadn't noticed."

"And that's interesting in itself."

"Is it?"

"I know she doesn't look it, but she's pretty tough. I've learned over the years to trust her to look after herself. It's usually the other people who get hurt."

"You said that before."

"Probably. So what I'm saying is, go on doing what you're doing for as long as you want and make a lot of money. And when you begin to feel like you've had enough, let me know and I'll either try to buy Nottambulo off you or get you to help me come by another. Okay?"

"Okay."

"Good. This is what I do and I'm going to keep right on doing it until I want to do something else but I know it's not the same for you, or her. Get me?"

"I think so."

"If you've had enough and you want to go and she wants to go too, that's not a problem, okay? You're good for her. You get me?"

"I think so. I'm not sure she's good for me."

"That's your problem." He grinned at me.

"Hm."

"Anyway, I wanted to do this today with my girl, just her and me. Tomorrow, why don't the three of us go and see the old man up in the hills together? What do you say? Like a family day out."

I looked at him.

"You know what I mean," he said.

"Okay," I said. "I think I could handle another ride up into the hills. Count me in."

"After that I'm going to let you two do most of the work until she gets bored, or you decide to call it a day. Okay?"

"Okay."

"Good, that's settled."

Guy stopped the Range Rover in front of the car-port and we got out. A servant appeared to re-fuel and clean it.

"Why don't you stick around for a bit. Have a swim. Sam'll be back in a bit. I must go to the office but I'll meet you by the pool for a drink shortly. Okay?"

"Okay."

I wandered thoughtfully off to the pool. I washed the sweat and dust of the day off myself in the outside shower, helped myself to a pair of trunks from the pile and swam for a bit. It's a good pool, pretty big for a private house, even in this neighbourhood, and it doesn't get used much so it's always fresh. Like everything else there, Guy had it kept immaculately clean. I swam lengths fast enough to work on my fitness for a bit and then floated on my back, looking up at the empty sky, while I got my breath back. It was like being nowhere. With the water supporting me from underneath and the blank sky above me, I could be just a body, just a spirit. No past, no future, no needs or desires, no problems.

I took a big breath, rolled down into the water and swam to the bottom. I turned on my back, facing up and blew a small stream of bubbles until my lungs were completely empty, then put my legs underneath me and pushed myself explosively up to the surface. I took a breath and swam slowly to the side and got out.

"You looked very relaxed there," Zara said from one of the pool-side loungers.

"I long ago worked out that I'm very unlikely to come to any harm while I'm in the water. It would make a mess of the pool," I said, and lay down on the next lounger.

"Ha, very good. You're quite right. Careful, I might jump you."

"No you won't, you can't use me to wind Guy up while he's not around."

"Don't you believe it, he's always around, or watching. Trouble is, I think he really wouldn't mind."

"Let's not find out, shall we."

"Shame."

"The pool boy is quite pretty."

"He won't, I tried. Too scared."

"I don't blame him, no offence."

"None taken. Drink?"

"Thanks. A beer."

She raised a languid arm and clicked her fingers. The boy ran over for the order.

When he had brought a tall glass of golden liquid, with the glass already sweating, for me, and more of the makings of G and T for Zara I raised my glass to her and said, "Cheers."

"Back at you, Mr Ellice." She lowered the level in her glass and sighed. She makes her drinks about fifty-fifty and uses a tall glass.

"I'll say one thing for you, if life were a drinking competition you'd be a champion," I said.

"You mean it isn't? Well, almost everyone's good at something and I just happen to be good at this." She gave another demonstration with obvious satisfaction. "It's a gift I never take for granted. If it weren't for this I'd become a nuisance and Guy would have me taken out into the desert," she waved an arm to indicate the massive dry hinterland of the African continent. "Just keep the juice coming and I'm your good-time girl with the perfect breasts." She raised her chest and gave them a little shake to emphasise the point.

"Very nice."

"I bet you wish that girl had a pair like these."

"I think there's room for variety."

"Thinks she's action woman, that one."

"You think she isn't?"

"What I think about her isn't fit for your delicate ears, sweetheart, but I'll tell you, I think she's trouble. And if you think she gives a flying fuck about you, you're wrong. She doesn't and never will."

"She's a great fuck by the way, and I'd sooner have her watching my back on a job than any of the others," I said.

"You just think I'm jealous because she's younger than me and likes playing with guns."

"You sound jealous."

"Perhaps I am, but that doesn't mean I'm wrong."

"Doesn't mean you're right, either."

"What really gets me is the way Guy looks at her. Like he respects her."

"So? Why shouldn't he?"

"You don't get it do you? Who else does he respect then? Go on name someone?"

I tried thinking about that and didn't like what I thought.

"He finds people useful or convenient and that's about it. She's the same and that's why he respects her," she said.

"Don't we all?"

She took a long drink and settled back on the lounger. "Yes, you're right, we're all just a fucking convenience to one another in the end. Or, in my case, a non-fucking convenience. Just promise me one thing?"

"What?"

"If you decide to leave, fuck me before you tell him."

"You're a very strange woman. Don't you think about anything else?"

"Soft furnishings. Mainly I think about sex and soft furnishings."

Guy appeared and we all moved to the table under the pergola. I joined him in some of the contents of the scotch bottle. The day began to become evening in the beautiful way it does there. Zara flicked through Homes and Gardens and Guy spread out a bundle of newspapers and began to pick through them. I watched the sun slipping softly down towards the horizon and thought about Sam.

One of the Land Cruisers pulled up to the gate, followed by a white Hilux and they were let in.

"Ah, good," Guy said, and put down his paper.

A slim Arab came through the archway and approached us with the total assurance of someone used to instant obedience from all those around him. He had a black keffiyeh arranged as a shemagh, covering the head and most of the face, and a black bisht heavily embroidered with gold thread flowed about him as he walked. I involuntarily thought about where I'd left my gun, and then remembered. Happy and Karim appeared. Happy was carrying a large wicker basket.

"Put that on the grass, it may leak," Guy said.

Sam uncovered her head. She looked radiant. She strode up to us and made her report. "All good, boss. No problems. Last load of horses on the way to the farm now, put the bales in the store, Karim says it's good stuff, and here we are."

The men stood respectfully behind her.

"Good. Well done." Guy pulled two fat bundles of notes out from under the newspapers and tossed them to her. She took them and threw them accurately, one each, to the men who caught them and examined them with big grins.

"Okay?" Sam said.

They all nodded.

"Good. Happy, you be here at ten tomorrow. If you get drunk and are late I will find you. Even if you are dead I will find you. Understand?" she said.

"Yes, Oya."

"Good. Off you go."

"Yes, boss." They didn't look to me or Guy for confirmation, they just went.

"What a brilliant day," Sam said, sitting down. "That's what I came here for."

"Glad you like it, sweetheart," Guy said.

"Want a drink, Oya?" I said.

"Fuck yes."

"What is an Oya?" I said, passing her three fingers of scotch with a little ice.

"Warrior goddess of the Yoruba," Sam said, "apparently. I'm assuming it's a compliment."

"What's a Yoruba?" Zara said.

"Happy's a Yoruba," I said.

"Funny, I thought he was Nigerian," Zara said.

"Well, they say you learn something new everyday," Guy said, with a malicious smile.

"What's that on your arm, dear?" Zara said.

"Oh, I missed some," Sam said, looking. "I had a quick wash in a stream on the way down."

"I'd say it suits you," Guy said. "Both the name and the decoration."

"I'd say so too," she said, with immense complacency, smiling at us all. "I feel like I've found my vocation at last."

"What's in the basket?" Zara said.

"A present for Mochadem Djout," Guy said.

"The heads of six of his men, including one of his sons," I said.

"You sick bastards," Zara said.

"We're going to deliver them to him tomorrow," Sam said. "Are we going to eat soon? I'm hungry."

Guy snapped his fingers and the boy ran up. "Supper," he said. "Something good and don't be long."

"Have we got any decent champagne around here?" Sam said.

"Bound to have," Guy said.

"Well, get it cooling. I'm going for a wash and brush up."

"You heard her," Guy said to the boy.

"Four bottles." She held up some fingers. "Why don't you come and scrub my back?" she said to me, stretching and moving her thighs against each other.

"That's not very subtle, dear," Zara said.

"It is, for me, Auntie," Sam said. "Up to you," she said to me, rising and leaving. I watched her go.

"Bitch on heat," Zara said.

Guy was looking at me, enjoying the situation. "You might as well," he said.

I decided that sitting there wasn't going to be any better than not sitting there, so I got up and followed her. I found her in the guest quarters. She was already naked and there was more blood on her than I had realised. It had run down inside her sleeves.

She saw me looking and said, "Ever fucked a girl covered in other men's blood?"

"Not as I remember."

"Well, here's your chance."

When she had finished with me, and I had finished with her, which didn't take long, she was already half way there, we stood under the shower and I scrubbed her back and washed away the blood from her arms and sides.

"That's better, I needed that," she said.

"Glad to be of service."

"Go on out, I'll be there in a moment."

I wasn't entirely comfortable about the reception I was going to get from the others so I stood by the doorway for a bit looking at the scene. All the pieces of it were the usual pieces, but the feeling wasn't the same. The golden light of the lowering sun was cheap and vulgar and the sweet scent of the jasmine hid an undertone of decay. Or maybe it was just me.

"Hey, Si." She came up behind me, put an arm around my waist and leant against me. She'd put on slacks and loose top. "Let's you and me go and drink some of that champagne, shall we?"

"Okay, Oya," I said.

"Hey, I am what I am. Okay?" She seemed to have caught my mood.

I pulled her round in front of me so that I could see her properly. She looked back at me, fearlessly.

"You're very beautiful," I said.

"But not as nice as you thought I was?" she said.

"What does nice mean anyway?"

"Don't ask me."

"You are what you are, and I am what I am."

"Can't argue with that."

"Better drink some champagne then," I said.

"Bloody good plan, Si."

We walked out together, arm in arm, round the pool, which glowed in its own limpid light, and there was an ice-bucket with champagne in it on the table.

Guy wasn't at the table but Zara was. We pulled a pair of chairs close to each other and sat down.

"That didn't take long," Zara said.

"Stop it," I said.

"Be nice, Auntie," Sam said.

"They really are heads," Zara said, indicating the basket, "I went to have a look."

"Yes, they really are," I said.

"You lot are unbelievable. How can you like killing people?"

"Who said we like it?" I said.

"They do," Zara said.

"Shall we drink that champagne then, or are we just going to look at it?" Sam said.

I thumbed the cork off, shooting it into the pool, and filled glasses.

"Well, my children," Guy said, rejoining us and accepting a glass. "Here's to the trade."

"Dark nights and no more Spaniards," I said.

"Days like today," Sam said.

"Fuck you all," Zara said.

5

A LONG SHOT

I woke up in my own bed, alone. It was very quiet.

"Soumy," I called out, "coffee."

Nothing. I got out of bed and went to look. Everything was as it should be but she wasn't there. I poured myself a glass of water, put on my dressing gown, opened the curtains and sat on the balcony. It was early enough to still be cool. People were going about their business below me.

I drank the water and put the glass down. I was still thirsty.

"Sou…" I started.

"Bugger!"

I got up and went into the kitchen. I picked up the big coffee percolator, looked at it and put it back down. I opened some cupboards. There must be some coffee somewhere but I couldn't see it. I refilled my glass at the tap and went and sat back down.

I got up again, went to the bookcase and tried to find a book. There didn't seem to be any I wanted. I pulled out a few and took them back to where I was sitting. I opened *Sick Heart River* by John Buchan, tried to read the first page and then put it down. I walked round the room twice and then stood on the balcony looking out at the city. Two old women were having a loud conversation below me, and their voices carried up to me. They sounded raucous and happy.

I went into the shower and turned the water on. It came through warm enough so I stood under it and started to wash myself. There was the sound of a key in the door and the door shutting. I turned the water off and went to see.

Soumaiya was in the kitchen putting shopping away. She was wearing the Muslim getup as usual.

"Where've you been? I wanted some coffee," I said.

"I've been buying coffee. You are making the floor wet," she said.

I went back to the shower.

When I came out there was the smell of coffee and the sounds of cooking coming from the kitchen.

"Come and sit with me while I eat," I said, when she brought bacon and eggs and toast to the table.

"Okay," she said, and sat down with her hands folded in her lap and a look of resignation on her face.

"I know almost nothing about you," I said.

"That is because you have never asked. There is not much to know."

"Tell me now. Where're you from?"

"My village is in the south, near Tiznit."

"Why did you leave?"

"My brother made a mistake with a delivery of kif. The package was lost. I was the price for his life. He is dead anyway, now, but I am here."

"Can you not go back?"

"You know the answer to that."

"I'm sorry, you're right, I do know. Did Guy buy you?"

"No, I was a gift. A small gift from our local chief to the famous Mr Guy."

"What do you want? What would you do if you were free?"

"That is an unkind question. I am not free."

"I didn't mean it to be."

"I know. I am in danger already. I have learnt English from you and I have got used to the freedom that you have given me. I don't wear this only because it is wrong that you should see me, but also because I must try to become a dutiful woman again. I should not be speaking to you; a good house girl would not be sitting at a table talking to a man, almost like an equal."

"Why must you? You're my house girl and you know I like you as you are. Were."

"I am not your house girl. I am Mr Guy's best house girl for the use of his best man, Simon SarSour. Sometime, sometime soon I think, you will be gone and I will be given to someone else."

"Why do you think I'll be gone?"

She shrugged. "Good things come to an end. I knew it was the end when you brought her here. Now let me go and clean the kitchen and make you something to take for your lunch."

"Lunch?"

"You told me to make you a packed lunch when you came in last night, and to wake you at eight."

"Oh."

I got dressed and went into my study. It's my thinking space and has useful things in drawers and on shelves. I have a small but well cared for collection of side-arms and a few knives in one drawer; bomb making equipment in another. I keep detonators, but not explosives in the flat; there are reference sections on international law enforcement, particularly as it relates to drug smuggling; several languages including, Spanish, French, Arabic and Tashelheit; and lots of maps. I also have a laptop in one corner which I use for access to the internet.

I refreshed the edge of my flat-handled knife and strapped it to my right calf under my trousers, checked that my phone was charged and that there were no messages, emptied the magazine of my .38, looked down the barrel, reloaded, put one in the breech and topped up the magazine. The cat sat on the other chair and washed herself while I did this. When I was ready, I got up to go and so did she.

"Good luck, Simon," Soumaiya said, handing me a cloth bag with sandwiches and a bottle of water.

"Thank you," I managed to snatch a kiss as I took them from her. She pushed me away but I don't think she minded.

Up at the house I found father and daughter at the back the compound playing with the TAC-50.

"Just getting my eye in," he said.

"I don't understand how Dad can be better at this than me," Sam said. She was on a mat on the ground with the big bolt action to her shoulder. She settled into it, let out a breath and there was the crash of the shot. I'd forgotten just how loud the thing was. The recoil visibly shifted her back on the mat.

"Where'd that go?"

"Six inches low and about the same left," Guy said, and passed me the binoculars.

One of the house boys was on the slope of the far hill with a metal dustbin and a pot of paint. He put a bit of paint on the hole the last round made in the bin and scuttled back away from it. He looked worried.

"One more and then it's my turn," Guy said.

"Okay, Dad," Sam worked the bolt and settled down again. I watched the black cross that had been painted on the bin through the binoculars. It must have been about three quarters of a mile away. The air was still and the visibility perfect.

The crash came again and a tiny black hole appeared top right.

"Top right," I said, "about six inches."

"Bugger."

"Let me show you how it's done," Guy said, and took Sam's place.

He snapped out the magazine and loaded in the five massive, half inch rounds from a box beside him, replaced it and worked the action.

"Let me see," Sam said, holding out her hand. I passed her the binoculars.

There came the shattering crash again.

"Bastard," Sam said. "Do that again."

"I will." Guy said.

This time I put my hands over my ears. I could still feel the punch of it in my body though.

"Hah! Two inches left," Sam said.

Guy worked the bolt and tried again.

"Bang on," she said.

"That's good enough for now," Guy said, sitting back on his heels. "We'd better load up and get going."

"I'll go and change," Sam said.

"You going in fancy dress then?" I said.

"Damn right. If I go to the trouble of shopping, I'm not going to waste it."

"Oh, hang on, I almost forgot," Guy said, and lay back down to the gun.

There was the sound of the shot and he got to his feet. "That boy was bothering Zara," he said. "Sam, if you're going to change, go and hurry up."

"Really?" I said.

"Well, he won't be doing it again," Sam said, lowering the binoculars.

"Simon, will you pack this up. I'll meet you by the cars in ten minutes."

"Yes, boss," we said in unison.

I found Happy at the back of the big white Toyota. He was putting the heads into canvas saddlebags.

"Having fun?" I said.

"Not really." He picked the last one up by its hair and dropped it in. I could smell them from where I was standing.

"Here you are, pack this too, will you." I put the TAC-50 in its case in the back of the truck.

"Can't you?" he said.

"Problem?" I said very softly, holding his eye and being very, very still inside and very ready.

"No boss," he said with a sigh, "I will pack it for you."

"Thank you." I walked off to one side and sniffed the jasmine that was climbing up the supports of the car-port. At no point did I turn away from the big Nigerian so much that I couldn't see what he was doing.

"Here I am," Sam said, tripping lightly up in her costume.

"Oya," Happy said, getting up from kneeling over his work. "You look like a princess."

"Thank you, Happy. I feel like a princess, or a prince, I'm not sure. Are we ready?"

"I believe so," Guy said, joining us. He had a map, two-way communication equipment in a metal case and a bag of sandwiches. "Sam, you can drive."

Happy and I got in the back. Guy sat in the front with Sam and off we went.

"You all right in the back there, Simon?" Guy said.

"Why shouldn't I be?"

"Got enough leg room?"

"Plenty thanks."

"Good."

Sam was in great spirits and she and Guy talked about all kinds of subjects, mainly involving guns. I chipped in occasionally and Happy told us a bit about some Nigerian practices with scaffold tubes and string that made even Guy seem quite civilised. We picked up a huge horse-box with four horses in it from Guy's farm near Ait Hiddra and pushed on.

We took the road south and the traffic became less, then turned west on the little used road that would eventually peter out not far from Arkiba. South again was the main east–west highway which had made these roads almost completely empty, apart from local traffic. We were now not far from our destination but approaching it from behind. Guy studied the map and his hand-held GPS and guided us for a few miles up a road that was no more than a track. We passed a few deserted houses and eventually stopped when it ran out completely. There were the remains of a shepherd's hut and a stream tumbling down the hill, and above us the mountains rose into patches of low cloud interspersed with bright sunshine.

We got the horses out and offered them some water and nose-bags of oats. Sam looked at each of the horses and scratched their withers and offered them a hand to sniff. She led one to one side, hitched it to the trailer and started going through the pile of saddles looking for the best fit.

"You having that one, then?" I said.

"Seems like the best one to me."

"I'm sure it is. See these others?"

"Yes."

"They need saddles too."

"So?"

"So we're going to look for the best fit across the four. The best fit overall. You can wait to be a princess until we get to the village."

"I'm having this saddle."

"We'll see. Help me saddle the others."

She slipped a bridle onto her horse and adjusted it to her satisfaction, tightened the girth and got on. Next moment she was cantering up the path out of sight. I stood there looking at where she had gone.

"You'd better get those horses ready, Si," Guy said.

"If that was anyone but her, I'd shoot her when she comes back round the bend," I said.

"If the moon were made of cheese…"

"I know."

When the rest of us were mounted up she reappeared round the bend at a collected trot, looking completely unrepentant, and joined us.

Happy had a suitably chunky mount and had the saddlebags with the heads festooned about him. I had the TAC-50 in its case strapped crosswise behind me. Guy had the communication equipment. Happy and I also had AKs with broad leather straps across our shoulders. We each had packets of sandwiches and a bottle of water. Not Sam of course, hers were still in the truck and could stay there as far as I was concerned.

"These clothes are perfect for riding and this fellow is all right," she patted the horse's neck.

"Glad you approve," I said.

"Right, follow me you lot," Guy said, and led us out.

Happy was okay on a horse, but not at the same standard as the rest of us, so I took up the rear where I could keep an eye on him. The path, which was only wide enough for single file, wound up into a belt of Moroccan cedars. It was going to where the stream came from but took a more circuitous route to get there, crossing and re-crossing it, as it did so. The light under the trees was calm and soft and the air smelt lovely; the sound of the water throwing itself down the mountain was cheerful and my spirits lifted. It was good to be on a horse too. Sam looked amazing with her cloak flowing around her. She sat her horse like she was born on one.

When we cleared the tree-line the land was bare and dry. The mountain sloped steeply up into the clouds and when we were on the path up to the pass we were very exposed. Guy stopped us before we went over and made Sam put her shemagh on so that only her eyes were visible. From then on she led the way under his quietly spoken direction.

As we began to come down again we came into the terraces. The amount of work that has gone into these over the centuries has to be seen to be believed. Each one has been hacked by hand out of the mountainside and irrigated by its own water channel that branches off the main one. The men plough with mules and then the women plant and tend the crops. When the plants are full grown they are taller than those who tend them; the Berbers are not a big race on the whole. The contrast between the soft emerald luxuriance of the kif terraces and the hard dry land around them is intense. The smell is pretty amazing too.

We were in Mochadem Djout's land now and could expect to meet his people. Sure enough, not much further down we disturbed a group of women who were taking a break from their labour. They were sitting in the shade of a plum tree talking and chewing the hard bread that they take into the fields with them. I think they must have heard the sound of our horses and assumed that we were their men visiting. There were quick, hissed warnings and three or four young children disappeared into the forest of kif plants. The women looked at us with curiosity and fear.

I called out a polite greeting in Tashelheit and we carried on past them.

"Won't they phone ahead?" Happy said.

"They'll be lucky to have some cheese with their bread, never mind a phone. The men wouldn't let them," I said.

"I discovered long ago that for a villager in the Rif, visiting the next-door village is like visiting another country and visiting the next one again is like visiting the moon. They tend not to get out much. I managed to pay half the going rate for three years on the strength of it once. Must have been three tonnes at least," Guy said.

"This is the bled as-siba," Sam said.

"The what?" Happy said.

"I've been reading up on it. The land of insolence. Never conquered, but never included either. Left behind. Not really in this century, nor in the last either. That's why I'm wearing this get up," Sam said. "Apart from the fact that I look amazing in it."

"It's beginning to change now. The increasing demand for kif is drawing the city boys deeper and deeper into the mountains, looking to develop the supply and cut out rivals. Used to be, they would deal in the markets for a few hundred kilos but now they come up into the hills looking for tonnes," Guy said. "I like to think I innovated the practice."

We wound down the slope and up the next one. The cultivation looked well organised and was more extensive than I'd expected. Here and there were patches of food crops, tomatoes, potatoes, squash and beans of several kinds. We passed more workers, including children. They looked scared but replied to my greetings in their own language with a reserved respectfulness. They looked at Sam with great curiosity.

"I leave you here. Pause a minute and let's sort out comms," Guy said when we came to a fork in the path.

He and Sam dismounted and stood under an olive tree together. She unwound her keffiyeh, put on an earpiece and throat-mic, and wound it back on. Guy tapped the radio in his hand, she nodded. "Hang on," he said. He loped off to one side and spoke into the radio. Sam clearly answered him as he laughed and rejoined us.

"Good," he said, "that's sorted. Over that ridge is the valley of Arkiba and the village. You go left and down, I'm going right and up. Give me a half hour head start and then go down. Don't get between me and anything you want me to shoot."

I transferred the TAC-50 to his saddle and off he went. We eased our horses girths and sat down under the olive tree. Happy and I got out our sandwiches.

"What about me?" Sam said.

"What about you?" I said.

"Don't I get any?"

"Did you bring any?"

"You know I didn't. Give me some of yours."

"No."

"That's petty."

"I don't care."

"Here you are, Miss," Happy said, passing one of his.

"Thank you, Happy. I'm glad to see someone around here knows how to be a gentleman."

A lizard came out from under a rock and we watched it move in darts from place to place. Sam threw a stone at it but missed.

"You scared it," she said.

"Sorry," I said.

"Careful, or I'll point at you when we're down there."

"How's that going to help?"

"It'll make me feel good."

"Well, do it if you want."

"I think it's time to go down," Happy said, looking at his big gold wristwatch.

He was right. When we came over the ridge we could see the small village below. The Berbers don't waste a wall once it's been built; they invariably build on to what they already have. Villages become a cluster of buildings with none of them really separate from the others. They use local stone, earth, sometimes mixed with concrete and the terracotta tiles are a very similar colour too, so the effect is more as if their houses have grown out of the land than been built on it.

Not entirely in this case though. Something that looked as if it one day aspired to be a villa had been roughed out in concrete blocks, slightly apart from the main cluster of houses.

"Signs of wealth," I said.

"I wonder who paid for that?" Sam said.

"I don't believe it was us."

"Is it me, or does that look like a newish Merc down there?"

"You could be right."

We were passing more people now and they included a group of men hacking a new terrace out of the side of the hill. We didn't deign to notice them but I'm sure one of them was hunting in the pockets of his jellaba for a phone as we passed. Bloody amazing if there was a signal though.

There must have been, as sure enough, a few minutes later there were signs of activity down at the village, men were running from house to house and several assembled in the clear space that did duty as the village square. We rode our horses steadily downwards with complete unconcern, outwardly at least, Sam leading and Happy and I following like good servants. Quite a few of the men assembling down there seemed to be carrying, or leaning on, rifles of various kinds. The regular beat of the women pounding the dried leaves and flower heads stopped and many scarf-covered heads appeared at the small windows of one of the larger buildings.

"Ready?" I said.

"Ready," Sam said.

We crossed the bridge and advanced into the space. Happy and I moved up, one each side of her but still fractionally behind. There must have been fifteen men in front of us, most of them armed. Sam rode unhesitatingly towards them and stopped facing the centre of the group.

"I seek Mochadem Djout," she said in passable Arabic with a strong voice. I translated into Tashelheit as best as I could.

"I am he," a man said in accented Arabic, stepping forward. His face, under a startlingly blue keffiyeh, was deeply lined and as brown as walnut. He had small black eyes and the mouth under his large, hooked nose had only a few stumps of teeth. He was looking at Sam with evident confusion. "May I ask who addresses me?" he said in the polite form.

"Samantha Jane Wealdon, first daughter of Guy Wealdon of Nador, addresses you."

There was a lot of muttering from the crowd. The old man was studying her carefully and then gave me and Happy the same treatment. I could hear some of the men behind him saying "It's a woman!"

"Silence," he said to the men around him. "May I ask what brings you to my door?"

"Trouble, Mochadem. I regret that trouble brings me to your door. As is universally known, all kif that passes through Nador does so only with the blessing of my father who is the amghar n-ufilla of all such trade there. I am here to return the heads of some dogs who dared to disobey him in this matter and obtain restitution for their disrespect."

Her words, or rather my translation of them, caused an outbreak of shouting and gesticulation amongst them, all of it angry.

In the midst of the tumult two men in white jellabas were having an urgent private conversation. One of them was a plump man in his thirties with a thick black moustache crawling across his lip. The other had the hood of his jellaba up instead of wearing a keffiyeh and wore dark sunglasses so there wasn't much of his face to be seen. He had shiny black shoes peeking out from under the hem of his jellaba instead of sandals.

"Do you see the one with the black shoes?" I said quietly to Sam.

"I do," she said, without turning her head.

The plump one moved forward and spoke into the ear of the mochadem. The old man appeared to give a grudging consent.

The younger man faced Sam and said in English, "What stupidity is this? You, an English girl, come here dressed up like a cheap hustler from the Jamal f'na. What do you think we are, a bunch of savages? Go while you are still alive and tell your father that his day is over. Arkiba sells to whoever it chooses and Nador is a free port."

I translated for the benefit of the crowd. There were general nods and signs of approval. The mochadem looked pleased.

"You think so? Ask Afra," Sam said, and gestured to Happy, who tossed the saddlebags down in front of the chief.

"Afra," the old man said, and the word was taken up by the others. He stooped down and opened one of the bags. His face hardened as he saw what was inside. He went from bag to bag until he found the head of his son. He lifted it gently out and looked at it. "Afra," he said again, and there was a sigh in the crowd behind him.

"You did this?" he said to Sam.

"With my own hands, Mochadem, and I will do the same to anyone who disputes my father's right to Nador," she said.

"You will not leave here," the plump man said, taking an AK from the man nearest him, "and I will make you beg for death, you stupid English whore."

"Don't move," I said under my breath to Happy, who was looking like he might.

"Arkiba," Sam said to the mochadem. "You have a bad spirit amongst you who teaches your son to be a fool. That man there." she pointed at the man with sunglasses and shiny shoes. Everyone turned to look at him.

There was a big, wet sort of sound, that we all felt as much as heard, and he more or less dissolved into a thing of cloth and pulp that slowly slumped to the ground and began to make a pool of blood. In the far, far distance I heard the faint crack of a rifle, but only because I was listening for it.

Everyone looked at Sam. "If you wish to kill me, you may try," she said to the chief's son, spreading her arms, offering herself. He dropped the AK and started backing away. The other men tried not to let him get behind them.

"Fool," the old man said to him. "You are as stupid as a woman. Get out of my sight."

"Arkiba," Sam said, "it grieved my father to kill your son. He sends his sincere condolences and hopes that this can be the end of the matter between us. It would please him if he could purchase your entire crop for the next year coming and for all the years following. He begs me to tell you that if you have any enemies you care to mention he would be honoured to kill them for you as a token of his esteem."

The chief looked at the bloody mess on the ground and then turned to Sam and said, "If Allah wills it, let it be so, amghar n-ufilla Wealden. I have no more sons to spare for this. Let me keep the poor weak thing I have."

"Peace be upon your house, Mochadem Djout. We will leave you to your mourning."

We turned our horses and walked back over the bridge and started up the path. Behind us the women came out of the houses and joined the men, and the wailing began.

"I want to talk to you," Sam said, back at the house as Guy disappeared behind the jasmine on the car-port.

"I'm listening."

"No, properly. Somewhere else. Is there a decent restaurant in town? Have supper with me. Please."

"I'm cleaning my guns."

"Listen," she pulled me behind the big truck, where no one could see us and put her arms around me, "I'm sorry. I know I can be a bitch sometimes. Have supper with me."

"Okay."

"Good. I'll go and change."

"I'll meet you by the pool." I picked up the TAC-50 in its case and followed Guy. He was putting maps and comms. away in his office.

"Where d'you want this?" I said.

"Isn't that a nice toy. Leave it there, I'll put it away later. Fancy a drink?"

"Sure."

"Where's that girl? I suppose she'll drink more of my champagne. Probably want something from you too, eh?" He locked the door and we went to the terrace bar.

"Did you leave her behind?" Zara said from her place at the table.

"I should've taken you as a gift for the old fellow," Guy said.

"Why didn't you?"

"I've gotten so used to you sitting in that chair that I forgot you can actually walk about."

"I can walk about fine. I just don't have anywhere to go."

"Can you ride?" I said.

"Don't know. I expect so."

"No, we didn't leave her behind, she did rather well I thought. I couldn't hear or see as much as you, Si?"

"Did you hear him call her amghar n-ufilla?"

"No I didn't. Head chief? That's not a word you hear much nowadays."

"He's an old man and still thinks in the old ways. I think you've just been promoted by association with your daughter."

"She's quite a girl, isn't she?"

"She certainly is," I said, looking towards the house. The other two followed my gaze. Sam came out onto the terrace wearing a long black evening dress. She had put her hair up and had diamonds at her ears and throat. She moved in that way that only a few women can. None of us could take our eyes off her.

"Got a date with the prince have you, darling?" Zara said.

"Simon's taking me out for dinner. Do I look okay?" she said to me.

"Not too bad," I said.

"Good."

"I'm not quite your equal in sartorial elegance though." I had on my usual loose khaki trousers and a shirt which had been worn to start with and had acquired a certain amount of dirt and horse hair during the day. "Shall I go home and change and pick you up in half an hour or so?"

"I don't mind if you don't. I'd rather go now."

"I don't mind at all. Let's go along to the Riby. Will you excuse us?"

"Go. Take tomorrow off if you want, I don't need either of you 'til Monday," Guy said.

I led Sam to the cars and opened the passenger door of my old Lincoln for her.

"Madam," I said, handing her in.

"Thank you, sir."

"You do look astonishingly beautiful by the way," I said.

"Good, I wanted to look my best tonight."

I took us out on the road along the crest of the ridge. It would eventually lead the long way back to Nador but for now it was still the place where the rich had their residences. We passed a few white painted faux Moroccan and Californian-style villas and turned inland onto a side road. This climbed a little further to the highest part of the escarpment and stopped at the Ksar tn Rbbi.

"Wow, that's nice," Sam said. "I'd forgotten."

"The castle of people meeting. Or something like that," I said. The ancient red sandstone was catching fire in the evening sunlight.

We parked and walked through the archway of bougainvillea onto a short avenue of date palms that led to the castle. It wasn't huge as castles go but the starkly square towers made of massive blocks of stone with only a few small square windows high up were impressive enough. A smartly dressed Arab in a perfectly white jellaba and red fez welcomed us at the massive arched doorway. He looked at Sam with great respect but at me with confusion and embarrassment.

"I am so sorry, sir. I'm afraid that the Ksar tn Rbbi has a dress code. We ask our guests to be a little more formally dressed than you are, sir."

"Don't worry," I said. "We'll have a drink on the terrace while you go and find Robbie."

"I'm sorry sir, I can't let you in."

"Well, I'm coming in so you will have to stop me, if you can." I took Sam's arm and we walked through the archway and into the courtyard. The doorman fluttered about in front of us for a moment and then ran off to get help.

"This is lovely," Sam said, looking around her.

"They show you a hard face on the outside and keep the best inside," I said.

The courtyard was a garden full of soft delicate leaves and flowers and the gentle music of water cascading from fountains. The air was cool and scented with jasmine and hibiscus, and it was a garden room of many small rooms; each more enticing than the last. I followed Sam about, enjoying her enjoyment. She trailed her hand in a glass-clear mosaic pool, disturbing the fat, lazy koi only slightly and patted the head of a noble hunting dog, one of a pair who guarded the way into a tiled recess, scattered about with cushions and roofed by the spreading fronds of the surrounding date palms.

She pulled me to her and we kissed for a moment and then she was off again. I followed her through another arch out onto the terrace. The view was as good as it could well be. The land fell away in front of us, down to the town below and beyond it, the sea. It was one of those evenings when the haze of the day evaporates to leave for a while a bright, sparkling clarity before the sun begins to dip. The clean curve of the breakwater separated the turquoise lagoon from the dark blue Mediterranean beyond.

"That's Melilla," I said, pointing to a cluster of lights to the north. "And that is Africa," I said, pointing inland.

"Those are camp fires?"

"They are. There are men with camels, bedding down for the night down there just as they have done since there were camels and men. Not so very far that way the desert begins."

"Si, this is just what I wanted tonight, thank you."

"You're welcome. Ah, here's Robbie."

"Oh, it's you," a slender Scot with floppy ginger hair and a sallow complexion joined us. He was followed by the doorman.

"May I introduce Robbie Anderson, or Robbie of the Riby as we know him, this is Miss Samantha Wealdon."

"Welcome to the Castle Rbbi Miss Wealdon, I'm sad to see that you're keeping such sorry company, shall I have him removed?"

"I'd like to see you try," I said.

"Call me Sam, please. What a wonderful place you have here, Robbie, I may call you Robbie?"

"You may indeed."

"Thank you."

"It's a reasonably fair spot for such a hot, barbarian land. Can I show you to a table," he snapped his fingers for a waiter, "some champagne? A cocktail?"

He pulled a high-backed chair out for her at one of the half-dozen round tables, with perfect white tablecloths, that lined the edge of the terrace.

"Let's have both. I'll have a manhattan to start with please."

"Me too, and put a bottle of your Ruinart on ice for us," I said.

"I could find you a clean shirt too."

"The lady likes me as I am."

"Do you really?" he said.

"Actually, I do," Sam said, looking at me with her head on one side.

"At the Riby, whatever you want, you may have," Robbie said, bowing and departing.

"We go fishing in Nottambulo together sometimes," I said. "I've tried to get him to work for us but he's stubbornly straight."

"Perhaps I should try."

"Perhaps you should."

Our waiter brought a pair of manhattans in frosted glasses and a plate of thin slices of toast, some with caviar, some with hummus, some with salsa verde.

"Cheers."

"Cheers."

We gently touched glasses and drank.

"Ah," she sighed, "that's very nice."

"This is a not a bad way to end the day."

"It was a good day. For me, it was another good day."

"You've done a lot in the last few days."

"Yes, I have haven't I. With you. I wonder what we'll do tomorrow. Perhaps you'll take me fishing?"

"Do you like fishing?"

"I might do, I'm not sure. I liked the fishing that we did with that Spaniard."

"It's a bit like that except, usually, no one dies and hopefully you get something nice to eat."

"I might like it because I'm with you."

"Really?"

"Yes, of course."

"Even though I was angry with you when you wouldn't help with the horses today?"

"Oh, that. I've forgiven you for that."

"You've forgiven me? What if I haven't forgiven you?"

"You're here aren't you?"

"If it'd been anyone but you, I'd have shot you on the spot. Disobedience is a black and white issue for me."

"I know, but I expect if I'd been anyone but me, I wouldn't have done it, so that's all right."

"And I think you're doing something bad to Happy. He nearly picked a fight with me this morning."

"Happy's very sweet. I let him carry things for me."

"Well, don't get him killed."

"You're very nice but you do worry too much."

"It's the worrying that keeps me alive."

A waiter turned up with champagne and menus. I took the bottle from him and did the honours.

"Mr Robbie's compliments, and he says if there's anything that you want that's not on the menu, please ask," he said.

"Excellent, let's order now, I'm hungry," Sam said.

"Some of your chicken bastila for a start," I said.

"I'm feeling quite carnivorous," Sam said.

"And some of the quick lamb, some couscous, vegetables, oh, and bring us a bowl each of harira while it's cooking. Ask Robbie to look out a decent bottle of burgundy to go with the lamb, will you?"

"Yes, sir. Right away, sir."

"Many people in tonight?"

"We are full, as usual, sir. They are just bringing out another table now."

It was true, two men carried out a table and put it on the end, to make up for the one we had annexed. Men in jellabas, some with the rope agal on their keffiyeh that is more common among Arabs than Moroccans, and also in well cut western suits, and women in evening dresses, though none to touch Sam for looks, began to arrive. They all glanced at us with curiosity but turned away out of politeness.

"There'll be a few discreet questions asked about us tonight," I said.

"I never thought about it before, but I'll soon become someone here, won't I? If this carries on."

"Sam Wealden, beautiful but deadly. Daughter of the famous Guy, enforcer for the family firm. Perhaps he'll change his letter-head to Wealden and Daughter."

"He has a letter-head?"

"Not to my knowledge."

"I've been… travelling for a long time. Not belonging. Do you belong, Simon SarSour?"

"Here? No, not here. Don't know where though. You?"

"I belong… I belong… on the back of a horse winding up into the mountains. I belong far out to sea in Nottambulo. I belong in your bed. Sometimes."

"You've only known me five days."

"Four."

"It feels longer."

"I feel like I've known you for ever, I don't know why."

"Perhaps it's because we've been doing such intense things together."

"Perhaps."

Our food came and it was as good as I expected, which was very good indeed. The sun made its graceful exit and they brought lamps which flickered beautifully in the still air. The noise of others talking around us was very pleasant. Sam ate with enthusiasm and enjoyment and I did too. We did justice to the bottle of burgundy when it came and the evening slipped into night. The lights of a tanker heading for the straights of Gibraltar tracked slowly across the horizon.

I moved my chair round to her side of the table so that we could both watch it and put my arm around her shoulder. We sipped old brandy and the waiters began clearing away the other tables around us.

"What are you thinking, Si?" she said, leaning into me.

"I was thinking that I'm very glad you turned up. What were you thinking?"

"I was thinking that you can take me home to bed now, if you'd like."

She kissed Robbie, finishing her conquest of him, I scribbled my name on the bill and we did just that.

6

ARE YOU LOOKING AT ME?

In the morning she bounced out of bed while I was still trying to decide if I wanted to be awake yet and got Soumaiya making coffee while she had a shower.

"Mind if I borrow your car?" she said, coming back in, towelling her hair with one hand and holding her coffee with the other.

"I'll need it later. Why don't I give you a lift?" I said.

"Don't worry, I'll be fine."

"Suit yourself, what're you up to today?"

"I might give Dad a hand with the accounts."

"Does he let you do that?"

"Oh, yes."

"But do you like doing accounts?"

"No."

"But you do them anyway?"

"No, I just said that."

"Oh."

She pulled on her jeans and tied her hair back with an elastic band.

"Well, I suppose I'll see you later," I said.

"'Spect so." She pulled a top over her head, picked her .32 off the dressing table and left the room. The front door slammed.

"Bloody hell. Soumaiya," Soumaiya put her head round the door, "coffee."

She brought me coffee.

"She's gone?" I said.

"Yes, thank goodness."

"Don't be like that."

She looked at me again as if she was sorry for me.

"May I have some breakfast please, Soumy?"

"Yes, Simon, I will cook it for you now."

I drank some coffee and tried to wake up. My phone rang. It wasn't Sam, it was my mother.

"Hi, darling," she said.

"Hi, Mum," I said.

"What are you up to, darling?"

"At the moment or in general?"

"Either. I don't mind."

"I'm still working for Guy, if that's what you're wondering. Right now, I'm drinking some coffee. How're you, Mum?"

"I'm okay, darling. A little bored perhaps."

"Mum you're always a little bored. How's Dad?"

"He's fine, darling. Just fine. Well, I mustn't keep you. I'll phone again soon."

"Mum…"

"Yes, darling?"

"Was there something you wanted?"

"No, darling. Nothing in particular."

"Oh. Okay…"

"Bye, darling."

"Okay… Bye, Mum."

She disconnected and I stood there staring at the wall.

"What's wrong, Si?" Soumy said, and I realised that she was standing next to me with a tray of food.

"Women are another species. You know that?" I said.

"Yes, Si," she said, looking sorry for me again and passing me the tray.

When I got there, my car wasn't in Azooz's yard. I shouted a bit and he appeared in a hurry.

"That strange girl took it," he said. "You did say she could."

"So I did. Azooz…"

"Yes, Simon."

"Lend me a car of some kind, will you?"

"Of course, Simon."

I picked Robbie up at the Riby in a battered, old, purple Fiat and we started back down the hill.

"Has this thing got any brakes?" he said, holding onto the door handle and trying not to look down.

"Not so as you'd notice."

Asif had my girl ready and waiting at the end of the pontoon and he'd brought our rods and a bucket of bait. I thanked him, told him we would be back at about dark and we pootled out towards the breakwater.

"So, you and the lovely Sam then?" Robbie said, sitting with a box of lures on his lap and making up a wire trace.

"Who knows."

"You look pretty good together."

"Thanks," I said. "I think."

We spent the morning trolling along the outside of the break-water. We both had a few horse-mackerel, Robbie picked up a nice amberjack which gave him a good fight and I had a medium sized barracuda. When it got on to be lunchtime we wound in and I took her up to speed and headed for the Islas Chararinas, which are little more than three large chunks of rock sticking out of the sea near Ras Kebdana.

We picked a likely spot in the lee of a steep cliff, dropped the hook and each let down ledger rigs with big chunks of the half rotten squid and mackerel that Asif had put in the bait bucket. I pulled in a bucket of sea water so that we could wash the stuff off our hands and we opened beers and got out the sandwiches.

"I should give this up, go home, settle down and get married," Robbie said, putting his feet up on a thwart and taking a long pull at his beer.

"Should you?"

"I should."

"Fair enough. Marry whom exactly?"

"I don't know, Fatima maybe, or Kenza, or Menena."

"Are there any of the chambermaids you aren't sleeping with?"

"No, but..."

"You've got a bite."

"Have I? Oh yes, so I have." He lifted the rod out of its holder and let the line run for a moment and then struck. The rod bent and stayed bent and the reel screamed as whatever it was ran off line. "I think I've got into a young bullock," he said.

I reeled in the other line and got the anchor up as fast as I could, but it was no good. We saw a triangular dorsal fin break the surface a hundred yards away and then the line went slack.

"Black tip, I think," I said.

"Bugger. Why weren't we using decent gear?"

"Don't blame me. How was I to know you were going to get into a shark with a weedy little bait like that?"

"I want to come back with proper stuff and try again now."

"We can I suppose. What do you want to do now?"

"Let's put on a couple of those big jet-heads and go and look for some dorado or a tuna."

"Okay, I'm game."

We checked our lines for damage and I cut the last few meters of mine off, just in case, and tied on the big shiny lures. I put Nottam-bulo into gear and headed out to sea. Robbie stood up looking for any signs of birds diving or floating debris.

We spent the afternoon hunting about over several square miles of the Western Med and very good fun it was. We didn't catch anything but we might have. I looked at my watch and discovered that the sun wasn't lying; it was getting late.

"Do you want to stay here until the last minute and then race back, or leave now and go at trolling speed?" I said.

"Trolling speed for me, and pass me another beer, if you will."

I got one for myself too and we sat at the back while the engines burbled away taking us home.

"That's better, I think I was feeling a little tense when we came out," I said, stretching and having a great big yawn.

"Me too. I'll miss this if something happens to you."

"I thought you were going to give it up and go home."

"I am."

"But maybe not today?"

"Maybe not. Shall we wander along to the bar for a swift one when we get in?"

"Are you buying?"

"Surely I got them last time."

"Would you like to walk the last bit?"

"Okay, I'm buying."

"Then I'm drinking."

We handed Nottambulo and our catch over to Asif's safe keeping and walked over the road.

I quite like the bar in the Hotel Rif. It's big and cool and has many private areas where you can sit and drink a beer and read a book or meet a friend. It's also the one bar in the whole of Nador where everyone will be at some time or another. I like to have an idea of who's about so I hang out there from time to time when I feel like it. Or, if he's not working, get a bit drunk with Robbie.

"Bar or table?" I said to Robbie as we walked in.

"Henry," he said.

"Table," I said.

Henry is one of those Englishmen who you seem to find washed up in most tropical ports; as English as hell but down on the place and probably not fit to actually live there. He has the kind of squint that makes him hard to talk to; you never know which eye to look at, and if you do talk to him, he'll be sure to tell you all about the idea he's working on that will make him rich. The current one was an oceanographic research vessel which also had accommodation for tourists and which the Moroccan government was sure to finance when he just finished the plans and showed them to his friend Abdul in the ministry. The two things about him that aren't complete fantasy however, are his capacity to accept drinks without feeling the need to reciprocate, and that he knows at least as much about everyone and their business as they do. I don't mind talking to him now and again, but not too often.

We chose a table with comfortable rattan chairs off to one side from where we could see the entrance and also watch what was happening at the bar. I gave Ali a low whistle as he passed and he came to an exaggerated stop and attended us.

"Evening, Ali," I said.

"Good evening, Mr Simon, and, Mr Robbie."

"Two beers please, Ali. Mr Robbie is buying."

"Truly?" Ali said, his eyes twinkling with mirth.

"You may put them on my tab, Ali," Robbie said gravely.

"But you don't have a tab, Mr Robbie," Ali said.

"Don't I? I'm sure I do."

"No, Mr Robbie. Do you not remember?"

"Hang on, I remember something."

"We tossed for our tabs and I lost," I said. "I think we'd had a few."

"It's coming back. Go on."

"And you said, 'Cancel my tab, Ali, from now on I will pay as I go'. It was your Easter resolution."

"So it was."

"Excuse me gentlemen, I will go and fetch you two beers," Ali said, and suited his actions to his words.

"Did you really pay off my tab?" Robbie said.

"And my own."

"That's amazing. I haven't set foot in here debt free since the first day I arrived. That's something to celebrate. Was it much?"

"Enough to feed you and me at the Riby for a week."

"That much?"

"Yes."

"Thanks, Si."

"You won it."

Ali placed two foaming glasses of beer in front of us and gave Robbie a little slip of folded paper on a small silver tray. Robbie looked at it absently.

"Well, pay the man," I said.

"Ah." He patted his pockets helplessly. "I seem to have come out without my wallet."

"You don't say."

"Will you put it on my tab, Ali?"

"I already have, Mr Robbie," Ali said.

"Cheers," I said, holding up my glass.

"Cheers," he said, clinking his against mine.

We drank and then settled back in our chairs to have a good look at the room.

"I suppose it's just my nature, that's all," Robbie said. "Who's that talking to old Henry?"

"I was asking myself that. They were talking about us a minute ago."

"I sometimes wonder at myself being seen with you."

The man sitting on the bar stool beside Henry wasn't easy to place. He was lean and looked slightly dissolute, like a journalist or a gambler, but there was also a sharpness about him. He was pale, like someone only just arrived but wore his tropical suit like he was very used to it.

"Well, I'm sure he's got the whole story about both of us by now. He probably knows things about us that we don't even know ourselves," I said.

"If he buggers off I might go and ask old Henry about him, tit for tat," Robbie said.

"Those fellows over there are new in town too aren't they?" I said.

"Those six in the loud shirts?"

"Yes, them."

"Look like oil workers to me. Don't suppose we'll see them up at the Riby."

"Maybe."

"You just looked at your phone again, you expecting a text from anyone? The lovely Sam by any chance?"

"Not particularly."

"No plans for this evening then?"

"I might get an early night."

"I'll get some more refreshment coming along then, shall I?"

"Okay."

We sank a couple more beers. More people came in and the atmosphere livened up. Ali and his team of young men, smart in their whites, moved swiftly among the tables delivering drinks and then food. Some of the newcomers stopped to speak to Robbie and me, more him than me. The Riby has such a status that even the wealthiest are more than happy to be known to its manager. Everyone with half a brain knows who I am and what I do, but then several of the stately gentlemen in well cut suits who paused to speak to us receive a monthly delivery from our storehouse. They just nodded to me, politely acknowledging me but not wishing to know me personally. This rather suits me than otherwise; Robbie has to make small talk with all kinds of people, it's part of his job, I'm glad I don't.

I left him talking to the trophy wife of one of the local hotel owners and took my beer over to the bar where Henry was, for the moment, alone.

"Evening Henry, can I buy you a drink?" I said.

"That would be very civil of you, my boy. I'll have another Tom Collins if Elio knows where Ali keeps the decent gin."

The slim, doe-eyed young man behind the bar smiled a secret smile, pulled an unlabelled bottle out from under the counter and shot a hefty measure into a glass.

"That's my boy. I suppose you want to know who that gentleman was who was asking about you."

"Was he only asking about me?"

"No, no, but I got the feeling that it was you he was most interested in."

"Well?"

"A freelance journo if you believe that. Doing a piece on the younger generation of expats. Not the workers of the world but the well-heeled dropouts of Europe and America who end up in unlikely places, like this."

"I take it you didn't entirely believe him?"

"Journalist maybe, but not doing something so vague, I don't think. I'm expecting to read in my copy of the Sunday Times that the casual playboy that we all thought we knew so well was actually a hardened criminal of some kind."

"Very funny."

"Unless you've got some interesting family connections perhaps? I know you try to hide it dear boy, but that accent of yours isn't from the local comp, is it? Where did you say you went to school?"

"I didn't. What's my family got to do with anything?"

"Don't ask me, sport. I know nothing about anything."

"Did he give a name, say where he's staying?"

"Couldn't say. For some reason it didn't occur to me to ask him."

"Well, thanks Henry, you're a good sort whatever they say. What's your name, Elio, another drink for my friend. Make it a long one, will you?"

"Oh, that's very decent of you, Simon. Are you joining me?" he indicated my nearly empty glass.

"Thanks, but I must go and rescue Robbie from that harridan."

The woman in question was the same petite and lovely wife of the local businessman. I held up two fingers to Ali as he scuttled past me and sat down next to Robbie.

"Evening, Mrs Murr, can I offer you a drink?" I said.

"No thank you, I must join my friends." She looked a little startled and shot Robbie a quick look before retreating.

"Did you have to? I was enjoying that," Robbie said.

"And you think I live dangerously. I'm hungry. Do you want a burger?"

"A burger?"

"Yes, the food of the common man. They also do chips."

"Oh, all right then and my glass seems to be empty."

"Taken care of. I put it on your tab."

"Very sensible. What did old Henry have to say?"

"Not much. Journalist possibly, interested in me, definitely."

"I shall start a scrap book and keep cuttings. When I'm old I shall sit at the bar and tell stories of how I knew you in the old days before they caught and hanged you."

"I don't think they do hanging much anymore."

"I expect they do around here."

"You might be right. I think I'd better have a chat with him, whoever he is."

"You think Henry gave you the full goods? It's not like him to say so little, even if he has to make it up."

"I know. Ah ha, speaking of which. Order me a burger will you, I'm just going to the loo."

I caught up with Henry and followed him through the swing doors. We were alone with the porcelain so I spun him round and pushed him fairly gently up against the wall. He gave a little squeak and said, "What, Si? What?"

"You're holding out on me, Henry. That's not nice," I said.

I dropped my hands and stepped back half a pace but kept eye contact. He carefully straightened his tie.

"What's his name?" I said.

"Bill Smith. His name is Bill Smith." He looked at the floor.

"Really?"

"That's what he said."

"Staying?"

"Here."

"What else?"

"He asked what you did."

"And you told him."

"Everyone knows." He looked up at me defiantly.

"What else?"

"He asked if any of your family ever came out to visit you."

"What else?"

"Nothing. That's it, I swear."

"Let's hope so. If you find out anything else, you might want to mention it to me. Don't you think? You don't have to, but you might want to. Eh?"

"I suppose I might," he said.

"Good. Thanks, Henry," I said, and left him to it.

I returned to Robbie and my beer. He was looking wistfully at the group of women that contained Mrs Murr.

"You were a long time," he said.

"Probably the first signs of prostate cancer," I said.

"Don't say that."

"Well don't make stupid remarks."

"I prefer not to know what you get up to. This bar is a sacred place and shouldn't be profaned by any of your antisocial activities. Did you learn anything?"

"He's staying here. I'll go and have a chat with him sometime soon. Did you order some food?"

"I did, and if I'm not mistaken, here it comes."

He was right. Ali arrived bearing a loaded tray and a mournful expression.

"Don't look like that, Ali," I said.

"I can't help it, I'm affected by these things," he said. "He looks frightened."

"Come off it. I didn't touch him. Worse things happen here every Saturday night."

"I don't work Saturday nights."

"Yes you do."

"I only work when everyone is nice."

"Ali, the only one in the whole room who's nice is you, and Robbie a little bit. Tell me someone who is nice, go on, see if you can."

"Mrs Murr is quite nice," Robbie said.

"I don't mean in that way."

"Those men are nice." Ali pointed to the group of men in loud shirts.

"How do you know? I bet they aren't all nice."

"They buy drinks and keep quiet even when you can see that they want to have a party. That's nice."

"That is nice. Perhaps they have to stay sober for some reason."

"What reason can anyone possibly have for staying sober at this time of day?" Robbie said.

"You're always sober when you're at work," I said.

"That's what you think. Anyway so are you."

"They're waiting for their boss," Ali said.

"How do you know that?" I said.

"Because he's just arrived. Excuse me, gentlemen." He slid off swiftly to wait on the new arrival.

The man, who was walking straight towards the group with an undeviating step, must have commanded a deal of their respect, as several of them nearly got to their feet. He motioned them to sit and accepted the place vacated for him by one of their number. Perhaps in his late forties, he wore casual clothes and had a thick head of salt and pepper hair but there was an indefinable essence of the military about him.

"You get a lot of that. Ex forces chaps working in oil out here. Probably on the way to Libya. You can always tell," Robbie said.

"We don't know they're in oil," I said.

"No, but do we care?"

"Probably not."

"On the other hand there is something I do care about,"

"Apart from Mrs Murr?"

"Apart from Mrs Murr."

"What?"

"My glass is empty and I'm pretty sure it's your round."

To his credit Henry reappeared at the bar. I told Ali to give him a large one on me; he wouldn't forgive me in a hurry, but if he drank it, and he would, it would help to keep him off balance. I stayed on, drinking steadily with Robbie. We moved on to whiskey and I got a bottle for the table. It was an enjoyable evening but I couldn't let myself go, there was too much on my mind.

One of the handy things about having a bottle on the table is that you can be always refilling your glass and drinking from it without consuming more than you wish. I'm not saying that I was sober, but when the crowd began to thin out and there was a feeling of it beginning to be late, I wasn't as drunk as I probably looked. Certainly not as drunk as Robbie.

"Seriously, Si. You should get out, you know? Do you know that? It's not safe, what you do. You're a decent fellow. Well mostly. I'm not saying you don't have your dark side, but then I suppose we all do. You know what?"

"No, what?"

"I'd be sad. I would. Very. Honestly."

"Sad if something happened to me?"

"Exactly. So think about it will you? Think about it for me."

"Shall we get a taxi?"

"You're avoiding the subject."

"No I'm not." I made a sign to Ali and he nodded and spoke to one of his minions who ran off to the front of the building.

"You should settle down. Get the lovely Sam pregnant and buy a farm."

"Robbie, if you say that to me again I may have to hit you."

"Got to choose one woman and settle down. Has to happen sometime. I'm thinking of asking Mrs Murr out."

"Don't do that."

"Lovely woman, where is she? Perhaps she would like a drink."

"She's long gone and it's time we were too."

"You know what the trouble with you is, Si? The trouble with you is, for all you're such a hard bastard, you spend most of your time doing what other people want. Have you noticed that?"

"Robbie."

"What?"

"Shut up."

I decanted him into the taxi that pulled up outside. I gave the driver a little more than the fare, made sure he'd had a good look at my face so that he would know who was paying him, and told him in Arabic to get my friend safely back to the Riby. Another car pulled up behind his but I decided that it would be nicer to walk back so I wandered up the sea-front under the palms.

The evening breeze had died away to nothing and the water was glassy and slick. The boats riding at their moorings were sitting on their reflections and some had seabirds sleeping along their railings. I shook myself a little to dispel the effects of the alcohol and clear my head, and bounced gently on my toes as I walked. It was a perfect temperature; I like the heat but after a hot day the coolness of the night is delightful. Money and friends and lovers and excitement and all kinds of things are good, but to be alive and whole and walk along the seashore and smell the smell of the sea and just be, is also very good.

A car came slowly up the road and passed me. It was the same car that had been at the Rif. There was only the driver in it - he must be giving up for the night.

There were one or two men about. You always find some of those who have got too close to the ever-present hash, sleeping, or begging, along the waterfront at night. During they day the gendarmes chase them away, out of sight, but at night they emerge and form knots to throw dice and share a pipe. They are cowed beings who bother no one.

There are parts of the town which look modern, have wide streets, concrete buildings, pavements, things like that, but this town has been a place of trade and habitation and fishing since the Romans knew it as part of Carthage. Longer, probably. You only have to turn a corner or two and behind the smart facades you find the old buildings huddled together, leaning against each other as if they might fall down without that support. The streets are often only wide enough for two women carrying baskets to pass, and arches often span the small gap here and there, so that it is impossible to know where one building begins and the next ends. My flat is in a section like this. It's on rising ground a bit back in from the sea and I have a view, albeit narrowed by the other buildings, of the waterfront in the distance.

I was going to go all the way along the front and then turn in but I decided to cut the corner and navigate through the streets instead. At this late hour the silence was deep and I could hear my own feet clearly on the cobbles. I practiced being silent, rolling my feet gently onto the ground, and my night-sight began to improve as I went into the blacker darkness. The thin moon which had only recently risen was out of sight below the buildings but glimpses of Orion, who was hunting out above the sea, gave me my bearings as I turned left or right as the mood took me, for there was no going straight in there.

I may have heard stealthy footsteps behind me, or I may not. I felt that feeling of my back anticipating a bullet and shivered for an instant. I stood back in a doorway and waited, wishing that I'd picked up a gun when I left the house. Nothing happened, nothing at all.

When I'd got bored of this, which didn't take long, I went on, this time faster and with a deliberately undisguised step. High time I went to bed and stopped messing about. I soon picked up my street, followed it like an old friend to my door and let myself in. I didn't bother to hit the switch - the hard, artificial light would have been unpleasant - but climbed the stairs by feel and opened the door to the flat with my key. Soumaiya had left a small lamp on in the hall, as she always does when I'm out at night. Her door was shut.

I went into the kitchen and pulled the cord for the small light that lives under the cupboard. There was some warmish coffee in the pot on the stove so I poured it into a cup and went up onto the roof to drink it.

All the houses here have flat roofs and they are part of the house, at least if you have the top flat, which I do. I've lain there many times with Soumaiya, sometimes with the cat, looking up at the stars. There is a balcony of masonry, to about waist height, and if you are below that you are quite private. I sat in a deck-chair and listened to the almost-silence of the sleeping city and looked out over the other roofs. The coffee was a bit stewed and very bitter, so I took tiny sips, but I liked it nonetheless. It was nice to be in my own place and to feel secure.

I was just beginning a yawn and stretch when I thought I saw a movement on the roof opposite. I stifled the yawn and tried to look at the place with my peripheral vision. It was probably a cat.

But it hadn't been the movement of a cat. Perhaps someone sleeping up there. But they would be invisible below their balustrade. Keeping low I went down to my study and took my night-vision glasses out of their drawer by feel, as much so that I could forget it and go to sleep, as out of any real curiosity.

The unearthly clarity of the image showed me two men on the roof opposite. One of them was dressed like a local and was squatting patiently on the surface of the roof. The other, who was sitting on a plastic chair, was looking at me through what I took to be night vision glasses, his elbows resting on the parapet. It was the thin man from the bar at the Hotel Rif. He was still for a bit and then he shrugged his shoulders and lifting a hand, waved to me.

I looked at him a bit more and at the other man, so that I would know them again, and went down to bed. My bed wasn't empty. A sleepy grunt greeted me as I slid under the sheet and two arms took hold of me. It was Sam.

7

UNDER A THIN MOON

Sam and I had breakfast on the roof the next morning. The opposite roof was empty but the shutters on the window below had been folded back. I didn't tell her about the watcher in the night. She looked amazing with her hair all tousled and half asleep on a cheap plastic chair, cradling a cup of coffee with her elbows on the cheap plastic table, wearing my too-big dressing gown. I must get her one, or get another one.

"You were back late," she said.

"I would've been back earlier if I'd known you were in my bed. How did you get in?"

"I phoned Soumaiya."

"She has a phone?"

"Of course she has, I found it in her bag ages ago. Guess what?"

"What?"

"I've brought some clothes and hung them up in the wardrobe with yours."

"Have you? That sounds good to me."

"Good. Your girl didn't like it though."

"It'll be fine, don't worry about it."

"I won't. The moon's late, isn't it?"

It was hanging like a ghost of itself on the horizon, about to disappear.

"Oh, swear not by the moon, the inconstant moon, lest thy love prove likewise variable, or something like that," I said. "It was just rising when I came in, whenever that was."

"Here am I barely awake and you're quoting Shakespeare at me. That is Shakespeare, isn't it?"

"Romeo and Juliet. But soft. What light through yonder window breaks? It is the East and Samantha is the sun. I did it at school and a few bits stuck."

"You're in a funny mood this morning."

"No I'm not. Anyway, by rights it should be me with the hangover. Do you want to go back to bed?"

"Haven't you had enough of me?"

"How could I possibly have enough of you? You stole my car, by the way. Did you put it back?"

"I'm hungry."

"You're always hungry. What about my car?"

"Who cares about cars?"

"I care about my car. Where is it?"

"I don't know."

"Are you telling me you got blind drunk and left it somewhere?"

"No. I just forget that's all. It'll come back to me."

"So what did you get up to yesterday?"

"I went up to the farm and took one of the horses out for a ride."

"By yourself?"

"Yes, why not?"

"No reason."

Soumaiya arrived with a tray of khlea and eggs and more coffee and served us.

"What is this shit? I don't want this," Sam said.

"Try it, it's good."

"I said, I don't want it." She tossed the plate over the parapet. I heard it hit the street below.

I made a small motion with my head to Soumaiya and she quickly withdrew.

"More coffee?" I poured some for her and myself and started eating my breakfast. It was very good.

"Tell her to make me some eggs and toast," she said.

"No," I said.

She got up to go to the stairwell. I intercepted her and spun her round to face me.

"Your br…" I started and then had to parry a vicious punch to the throat and then a kick to the groin. I stepped in and managed to get a grip of one of her arms. She tried to bite me and knee me but I kept pushing her back and managed to trip her and force her down onto the floor. I used my weight to hold her there. The towel round my waist had come off and her dressing gown had flown open so we were effectively naked with me pinning her arms and lying on top of her.

She spat in my face but I didn't much mind that. I held her there, letting her feel the strength of my grip and looking into her raging eyes. It must have hurt but she showed no sign of it. There was a sheen of sweat on her skin and her hair had some of the red dust from the stonework in it. She looked very wild and very beautiful and I wasn't sure that I recognised the girl I'd known up to then.

After a bit, the struggling of her legs underneath me became something different, and I couldn't help responding though I was still angry. She softened and pushed herself into me. I eased my grip and then carefully let go. She put her hand up to my head and pulled me down to her, not to bite me this time but to kiss me, fiercely. We made love, if you can call it that, fast and hard and when her small screams had echoed back from the masonry around us I got off her and discovered that there was blood running down my side.

I told Soumaiya to go to her room and shut the door and then dragged Sam, who was now quiet and submissive, down into the flat and into the shower.

When we were clean I fetched gauze and ointment and made her dress the deep scratches from her nails in my side and back, and then rubbed ointment into the grazes on the backs of her arms, buttocks and back.

When we were dressed I picked up her .32 from the bedside table, removed the magazine and the shell from the chamber and tucked it into the waistband of my trousers. My un-tucked shirt hid it adequately. In my study I opened a drawer with the many small partitions, took out the key labelled 'Rif' and put it in my pocket. I made her precede me down the stairs to the street. She didn't say anything at all. A small yellow dog was hunting in the cracks between the cobbles for scraps of her breakfast.

After a bit, when we were out of the building and walking on the streets, she seemed to come back to herself. Her posture changed in some subtle way and when she spoke it was in the voice that I knew.

"Ow," she said, moving her shoulders gingerly, "you hurt me."

"Not as much as you hurt me."

"Where are we going?" She put her arm through mine.

"Well, since my car is apparently lost, we're walking down to the pontoon to pick up another one."

"And after that?"

"After that, I'm taking you home."

The exercise and the sunshine made me feel more normal and by the time we got to the Hotel Rif I had recovered some of my good humour.

"I'm hungry," Sam said.

"Go and get some breakfast then. I'll join you shortly," I said, following her up the steps. The man called Bill Smith was drinking coffee and reading a paper at one of the tables in the bar. I turned towards reception instead of going in.

There was no one in reception except Anas, so I offered him a casual handshake with a 20 Euro bill in it and said, "Chap called Bill Smith?"

He looked down at the bill, held below the level of the counter and said, "210."

I don't trust the lifts there so I took the stairs. 210 was at the end of the corridor on the corner of the building, views of the sea and a balcony. I knocked, just in case. No answer. The door surrendered to my key with no problems. When I first came to Nador I had lived in the Rif, and one quiet night, while the staff were sharing a pipe by the pool, I had hopped over the counter and swapped my room key for the master key that they kept behind the till.

There was a copy of Dr Zhivago on the bedside table, two tropical suits and some shirts hung up in the wardrobe, a phone charger, shaving and washing things, underpants, socks. The empty suitcase didn't seem to have any secret compartments. There was nothing hidden in the cistern of the loo, under the mattress, underneath the drawers in the dressing table or the bedside table, or behind the picture of a sunset in the desert hanging on the wall.

When I flicked through the pages of the book a fine hair fell out. I didn't know which page it had come from so I didn't bother putting it back.

When I got back downstairs to the bar Sam was sharing a table with the man. They both had coffee and she was tackling a good approximation of the full English. I joined them.

"Morning," I said, taking a seat and having a good look at the chap. He seemed a bit younger close up. He returned my inspection ounce for ounce with shrewd, good humoured eyes. He seemed pleased with the situation.

"Good morning, Mr Ellice, would you like some coffee?" he said, holding up a hand.

"I imagine Ali is on his way," I said. Not a very rash assumption given that I'd exchanged signals with him as I'd passed the bar.

"This is Bill," Sam said. "He offered to keep me company as you'd deserted me. He says he's a journo."

"How do you do." We shook hands. His rather fine hand was stronger than it looked.

Ali arrived, looking a little worried, and poured me some coffee. He topped up the cups of the others, put the pot down and left without a word.

Bill took a sip of his coffee without taking his eyes off me. I did the same.

"But you're not convinced though? That he's a journalist," I said.

"He could be. He's been telling me stories about the excesses of some of the Arab oil princes he's been interviewing. He's promised to introduce me to some of them."

"Have you found any oil princes in Nador, Bill?" I said.

"Sadly no. I suspect that most of the wealth here comes from the drugs trade."

"Really? So are you looking for drug princes instead, if there are such things?"

"I suppose I am. I was rather thinking that you might be that very thing yourself, Mr Ellice."

"Call me Simon, please. You really shouldn't believe anything Henry tells you, you know. He probably also told you that the Moroccan government department for marine research is funding a vessel that he's building, didn't he?"

"As a matter of fact, he did."

"There is no such department and never has been. And I am not a drug prince, nor even a princeling. If you ask about, you will find that everyone who's been here for more than a week has had a story of some kind told about them by old Henry. We regard him as a harmless eccentric as long as no one takes him too seriously."

"I do apologise. Clearly my journalistic enthusiasm for a story has got the better of my good sense. What do you do, may I ask?"

"Certainly. Very little at the moment, I'm afraid. I've been bumming about in the Med and I've got sort of stuck here for the moment. I suppose I shall have to think about a career soon but until the trust fund runs out I can't seem to find the motivation."

"Nice work if you can get it."

"What can I say." I gave a deprecating shrug. "I think we should make a move, Sam, if you can bring yourself to abandon your plate." She was wiping up the last few crumbs of scrambled egg with a piece of bread.

"Coming." She took a gulp of coffee and stood up.

"It's been a pleasure to meet you Miss Wealden." Bill got to his feet and offered her his hand.

"Likewise." She gave it a brief shake and returned his smile.

"Maybe I'll see you about, Simon."

"It could easily happen, I'm not hard to find. Say hello to Henry for me when he comes in."

"Will do."

Sam and I crossed the road and walked along to where Asif was sitting on a plastic chair, patiently mending a net. Nottambulo lay out at her mooring amongst the various gin palaces, ocean going yachts and sundry craft that littered the lagoon. She looked like a wolf amongst sheep.

"Sabah el kheer, Asif. How are you today?"

"Ana bekhair. Shokran, Simon. Your little car is safe." He tossed the keys to me.

"Shame, I was hoping someone would steal it."

"No one will steal from you, Simon, but I think you should get a better car."

"So do I, Asif."

I led the way to the little car and got in. Sam got in the other side and pulled a face.

"Let's hope you recover your memory soon, I'm losing my credibility here."

"What's that smell?" she said.

"Probably best not to know."

It was touch and go whether the tiny engine would get us up the hill, but it did. The guard at the gate smiled as he let us in. I put it next to Guy's white Range Rover and walked through the archway towards the pool. Sam followed me listlessly and turned off to go into the house. Guy and Zara were in their usual chairs doing their usual things.

"Well, here's love's young dream. Shagged out yet?" Zara said.

"Pretty much, thanks for asking," I said. "How about you?"

"Morning Si. Want a beer?" Guy said, putting down his paper.

"Maybe not yet. Went out with Robbie last night."

"Coffee?"

"Tea actually, thanks."

"Weakling," Zara said.

"Nonsense, the boy is just keeping himself fit, that's all. He's one of the workers of the world."

"I am?"

"Absolutely."

The houseboy ran over in response to Guy's upraised hand and received an order of tea for me and more ice for Zara.

"Was that my daughter I just saw disappearing into the house?" Guy said.

"Pretty much."

"You don't seem completely sure?"

"Have you any idea where my car is? She borrowed it yesterday and says she's forgotten where she left it."

"Why don't you go and have a crack at the new houseboy darling?" Guy said to Zara. "I need to talk to Simon."

"I would but he's even uglier than you."

"Just piss off, will you?"

"Why didn't you say so?"

"I just did, didn't I?"

"I'll be in the bath with a razor if you need me." She waved at the houseboy to pick up her little collection of ice-bucket, lemon slices and tonic and follow her, and wandered languidly off to a lounger at the other end of the pool with her magazine.

"So?" I said, when she had gone.

"Ah, yes. Just between the two of us, my lovely daughter had a bit of a wild day yesterday. She went up into the hills near Beni Ahmed and got chased away by some of the locals. Luckily she took the munt with her and he got her back in one piece. Or she got him. Either way, I'm afraid your car is in a ravine over there somewhere."

"She told me she went for a ride alone. Chased why, exactly?"

"Apparently she shot a goat, or someone, or something, don't ask me why."

"What do you mean, or someone?"

"Don't ask me. She doesn't always tell the truth, you know."

"I had noticed. Perhaps she wanted them to chase her."

"That may have been it. Anyway there's a Hilux they came back in at Azooz's if you want it, or tell him to get you something else and send the bill to me. Sorry about that."

"I was thinking of a change anyway."

"Good. And there's something else. What do you think about the moon?"

"Sam was on about the moon this morning. It's still in its first quarter and it rises late at the moment. You want to make that delivery."

"I mentioned it to her, yes. Yes, I do. We're behind hand and Camilla is willing if you are."

"If it were to be done, let it be done quickly."

"Quite so. Good man. Tonight then?"

"The moon's only getting fatter."

"True, true. You'll take the princess?"

"Will she be good?"

"Feel free to throw her overboard if she isn't."

"I think I'd have to throw Happy over first."

"Rather you than me. As we're a bit short handed at the moment, I'll bring the stuff to the dock for you myself. What time would you like it there?"

"We'll go a bit early, say eleven."

"Right oh. Here, pick a spot will you?" He slid some of the papers aside to reveal a sea-chart. I deliberated and then put my finger on a point somewhat to the east of our last rendezvous. "Good." He scribbled the coordinates on the edge of the paper twice, tore one off and gave it to me. "I'll go and let her know now so that she has plenty of time to be there. Let them know if you want any lunch or anything."

"I think I may go home for a brief nap. Why don't you bring Sam and Happy down with you and I'll meet you there?"

"Will do." He left me in sole possession of the table and went off to his office. Zara looked at me over her magazine from the far side of the pool and gave me a little wave.

I wandered over to her and said, "How long have you known that girl?"

"Same time as you, sweetie. You're looking a bit rough this morning."

"Thanks, I can't handle my drink like you can. Why did you say she's trouble? What do you know that I don't?"

"Nothing, darling, just look with your eyes not your prick."

"Uh," I grunted and started to leave.

"Oh, sweetie."

"What?"

"Did you know that no one has ever left Guy. Left working for him, I mean."

"What do you mean?"

"Just what I say, darling. No one has ever left. They've only ever disappeared. Think about it, why don't you."

"Thanks."

I drove the little car back down into town and into Azooz's yard. Amongst the fleet of vehicles there was a reasonably new Hilux so I went to have a look at it. The bullet holes in the driver's side door looked like they'd happened very recently and presumably whatever one of Azooz's young boys was trying so hard to get out of the upholstery wasn't strawberry jam. Must be the one.

I'd been thinking that I wanted a different car but I hadn't got as far as thinking about what. I supposed the Hilux would do. At least it had the benefit of being anonymous, without the bullet holes anyway. I wandered into the workshop and saw two pairs of legs sticking out from under an old Jag.

"Hey, Azooz, leave that boy alone and talk to me a moment," I said.

"He is holding my spanner," a voice came from under the car.

"I am sure he is, now come on out."

"Okay, okay, I come. Oh it is you, Simon, if I had known I would not have let this unworthy car detain me for a second." He stood up and wiped his hands on his overalls.

"So you've forgotten my voice, Azooz? How can that be?"

"It is hard to hear well from under a car, Simon. How can I serve you?" He looked away from me towards the ground, and then up at the sky, and then at the Hilux behind me.

"You can patch and spray that and put new plates on it for tomorrow noon." I indicated it with a thumb.

"I will try, Simon. Who knows, it may be possible." He offered me a shrug, expressive of the mysterious way of things.

I thought about that for a moment and then I said, "Azooz, you are right as always. If Allah wills it, it will be so. For all we know this is my day to die, or maybe yours. But if I make it through the day, and you do too, I will see you tomorrow."

"Do not speak of death so lightly, Simon, may Allah protect us, I am not ready to die."

"I think we should all be ready to die, how else are we to live?"

"Carefully, I think."

"Oh, and, Azooz, there is another thing."

"What other thing is there, Simon?"

"I just want to thank you, Azooz. You have been a loyal friend to me. You have cared for my car for all these months and kept it safe. It is good to know that in this imperfect world there is the possibility of trust between two men. Thank you." I held out my hand.

It was impossible for him to refuse me so he wiped his hand on his overalls again and accepted my grasp. That meant that he had no choice but to meet my eye. He didn't seem to like what he saw there.

I gave him a carefree wave as I ambled out of the yard and headed towards home. When I had turned two corners, instead of going home, I cut off down one of the narrow alleys, lengthened my stride and headed back towards the jetty and the Hotel Rif.

Asif was leaning against the inevitable pile of fishing nets, taking forty winks. His shuttle was lying on his lap and his battered straw hat was tilted down to shade his eyes. He looked very peaceful and I envied him his ease.

He's a man of some status in his world, which is the ancient, enduring, unchanging world of the inshore fisherman. His sons work the family's boats most of the time now but he still takes one out when I don't need him. He cares for Nottambulo and mends nets for his family and others and watches patiently. I happen to know that his second wife is a pretty young thing and I believe that there is another crop of children coming along behind the first. What I pay him should feed and clothe them more easily than fishing ever would. I regard it as money well spent.

I sat down on the warm stonework and looked down into the clear water below. Not far from me were a group of boys watching big floats made of discarded bits of polystyrene and tape attached to hand-lines. The floats drew my eye; once you're a fisherman it's hard not to watch a float, any float.

"Ahlan wa sahlan, Simon. I do not believe they will catch anything today," Asif said, pushing up the brim of his hat with a finger.

"Ahlan, Asif. I thought you were asleep."

"Just resting my eyes. Mirko has his eyes open for me. He is a good watcher, like his father." He indicated the group of boys with a slight nod of his head.

"How many sons do you have, Asif?"

"That is a good question." He held up the fingers of his left hand one by one as he thought of them and then two fingers of his right hand. "I have seven sons, Simon, and good boys they are on the whole though none of them have the skill of fishing like their father." He smiled at this in satisfaction.

"How many daughters?"

"Not so many, thanks be to Allah." He didn't bother to count them.

"Asif, someone, a ferenji, is watching me. Thin, usually wears a suit, about my height, seems to be staying at the Rif."

"I know the man. He has a hungry look like a street dog. He walked along the front looking at the boats with big glasses half an hour ago."

"We're going out tonight. Early; about eleven. I think he may be watching us."

"The moon is still a sickly thing but there will be no cloud tonight. It is good that you go before she has risen. Will I bring her to the dock at the half hour before?"

"No, I will meet you here and take her over myself. Have her ready at ten for me, and, Asif, I have a favour to ask you."

"It is already given many times over, name it."

"I would like a good pair of eyes on the roof of the old library, the tall building back from the docks, you know the one?"

"I know the one."

"Good. From there you can see the place where we load her and also you can see the roofs of the dock sheds. I will come in from here and wait until Mr Guy and the cargo arrive. If there is a light on the roof of the library I will turn away, but if there is not I will come in. Is it agreed?"

"It is agreed. I will send Jony with my own glasses after the sun has set one hour. Also if anything looks wrong he will write to me and I will phone you." He proudly extracted his mobile phone from a pocket of his robe and held it up so I could see it. I nodded approvingly.

"But if the airwaves should be unreliable, I will look for the light anyway," I said.

"If there is any danger to be seen there will be a light. I will see to it."

"Asif, you bring me peace of mind. Now I must go. I will be here when it is time."

"Bettawfeeq, Simon."

"And to you my friend."

As I rose and turned back towards the hotel the old man extracted his big plastic glasses from another pocket, perched them on his nose and pushed experimentally at the buttons on the phone. One of the boys passed his line to a friend and went over to help him. Presumably he was the one called Mirko.

The bar was fairly empty, it now being somewhat after lunch. Henry was in his usual place so I wandered over to him and said, "Morning, Henry."

He flinched slightly and said, "Good afternoon, Simon, you seem to be in here a lot at the moment."

"I do, don't I? Have you seen Ali?"

"I think he's shagging one of the boys in the pantry."

The Moroccan Arabs have a pretty even-handed way of approaching sex but I thought this was unlikely so I opened the pantry door and looked in. Ali was standing over two young men with a clip-board as they counted cutlery in trays on the shelves.

"Got a minute, Ali?" I said.

He looked harassed but said, "Of course, Simon, would you care to come in?"

"Perhaps we could wander off towards the pool?"

"Certainly. You, attend Mr Henry, you, water the palms. We will finish this later. After you, Simon." He followed me out into the sunshine.

"You and I have known each other quite a long time, Ali, haven't we? About a year anyway."

"This sounds very serious, Simon, are you going to proposition me?"

"No, I'm going to ask you a question. I think you know as much about what goes on in this town as anyone, more than most."

"I like to think that that is so, yes. What is your question?"

"An unusual thing happened to me earlier. Azooz, you know Azooz the mechanic?"

"A dirty man of unspeakable habits, but a reasonable mechanic I believe. I know him, yes?"

"He was almost rude to me, Ali."

"Was he indeed?"

"People aren't often rude to me, Ali."

"No, they are not rude to you, and for very good and sufficient reasons."

"Do you know why this may have been, Ali? Could it have something to do with this Bill Smith do you think?"

"He is a flick. I have seen his kind before."

"I agree. He has someone working for him," I described the other man on the roof, "and maybe others. Do you know who, by any chance?"

"I do not." He hesitated. "I am a barman and I am always neutral in the affairs of my customers, but because you paid off Mr Robbie's bill I will find out, if I can."

"Thank you, Ali. I thought you would. But be careful, won't you? I do not know what all this means but it must mean something."

"Pah! I do not care for that thin thing. He is nothing in my opinion. It is those others I worry about. If it was them, I would say no."

"What others?"

"You saw them last night. Colourful shirts."

"Oh, them. I thought you liked them."

"I have changed my mind. Because of the man with the wrong haircut."

"What do you mean, the wrong haircut?"

"Is it not obvious? He is a man who should have a short haircut like a soldier; he is a soldier, anyone can see that; but he does not. It is wrong."

"Oh. Is my haircut okay, Ali?"

"If you can call it a haircut, yes, but you are not a soldier."

"That's true. Thank you, Ali."

"You are welcome, Simon."

I'd had enough walking so I took a cab back to the flat. Soumaiya brought me some couscous and salad and then I lay down on the big bed. It still smelt of Sam. I thought I had too much on my mind to sleep but I was wrong. I woke slowly and luxuriously from a refreshing sleep as the muezzin was calling out for the prayer at nightfall. I spent an hour in my study with my toys, cleaning and oiling and sharpening. It's a very restful occupation and helps with thinking, wonderfully. When I had packed a small holdall with a few bits and pieces I connected to the internet and checked the balance at my bank in Zurich. It was as it should be.

"Simon." Soumaiya put her head through the door. This was unusual.

"Hi, Soumy. Are you okay?" I said.

"I would be better if that woman didn't exist but it is not that."

"Sometimes I think I would be too. What is it?"

"In the market one of the women looked at me like she was sorry for me and another was rude to me."

"That's interesting."

"I think something is wrong, Simon."

"Yes, Soumy, so do I."

"Well, what are you going to do about it?"

"I don't know."

We had supper, that is to say I ate and she watched me, and then coffee. There was no hurry and we were quiet and I told her about what it's like out at sea, which I had never done before for some reason, and I told her about the thin, hungry looking man called Bill, which seemed to help make the situation clearer in my mind and then I had a shower and changed into dark clothes. She brought me a warm top and watched me leave with her sad eyes, just as she always does.

There was no companionable car journey with my crew now. The street was empty, so I slipped out of the door quietly and immediately turned into a side-street. My favourite .38 was loose in my waistband and I was rested, alert and as ready as I could be.

All of which turned out to be quite unnecessary as my walk to the jetty was completely uneventful. It's easy to feel a bit of a fool when you take precautions that turn out to be not needed, but it's better to be a live fool than a dead one, or so I tell myself anyway.

I felt a bit exposed crossing the road; there's no hiding on that wide, bare tarmac but the relative darkness of the jetty took me in and I felt better as I headed towards the water. There was no wind, and, as Asif had predicted, no cloud, the stars shone down with no mercy and seemed to shimmer as they do on such nights. Asif shared my mood, not surprisingly, and greeted me in silence.

"All is ready?" I said.

"All is ready."

I checked the things that I always check and Asif watched, taking no offence, and then I started number one. The deep rumble had its true effect on me and I felt more ready and more like myself.

"Okay, Asif. I'm ready."

"Allah be with you, Simon. I will see you later."

"Inshalla."

He stepped nimbly ashore and threw aboard the lines. I made them fast, stowed the fenders and then eased the lever forward. We rode up in the water and became a thing of the sea, not the land. I started the other engines, though I left them on tick-over, clutches disengaged, they were ready. I got out an AK and made sure it was ready too.

It only took a few minutes to get to the docks. I slowed her down to a walking pace and then down to a stop while I was still out in the deepwater channel. She lost her way and settled back into the water. The dock was a clear space under the orange sodium lights. Nothing moved on it, not even a scavenging dog. The faces of the dock sheds were lit but their roofs were in darkness and the buildings rising up behind were a darker darkness again. I could discern their shape where the rooflines interrupted the stars. There was no light on the old library.

I had started to search the area with my glasses when the two Hilux turned the corner of the sheds followed by the white Range Rover. The cars pulled up near the water in line. Guy got out and stood leaning against the big car, looking out to sea. He saw me and waved. Sam came round to stand beside him and waved too.

I moved the lever and went in smartly to join them. Sam caught the painter as I threw it, passed it round a bollard and sent it back to me. Happy's big white teeth grinned at me and he caught the stern line naturally and easily. Perhaps he was becoming some kind of sailor.

Sam jumped down from the dock and wrapped her arms around me.

"Sorry, I was a bit funny earlier. I'm ready for work now, captain."

"Good," I said.

Happy lifted the bales out of the pickup and lobbed them easily down to me. I passed them to Sam who stowed them as well as I could have done myself. She and I spread the netting over them and tightened it down. It's a good thing to do something with some- one who is as good at it as you are and who's working with you. Guy stood above us with an AK cradled easily in his arms. Romeo watched from the other side of a pickup.

"Come on then, Happy," I said.

"Coming, my captain," he said, and jumped down unhesitatingly.

"Bon voyage, my children, I shall see you tomorrow," Guy said. He tossed his rifle into the back of the car and climbed in.

I released the bow line, Sam did the stern and I said to her, "Go on then, you can take her."

"Aye, aye, skip."

Happy sat down on the seats before the binnacle and held on. I lifted my glasses, braced myself and had a good look at the receding dock. There was no light on the top of the library building but there was something, a head and shoulders against the sky, no two, Jony and a friend presumably. There were no gendarmes by the gates, which was unusual. I watched the pickup and the Range Rover leave; their tail lights were bright in the lens. I scanned along the roofline of the dock sheds. There was a blip near the northern end. I steadied on it, it looked like a man, a man holding glasses and looking at me. Perhaps I was imagining it. Already it was too late, too far, to see. I put the glasses back in the bag and paid attention to where we were going.

"See anything?" Sam said.

"Nothing that looks like a problem," I said.

She took us out over the lumpy water at the entrance to the lagoon without any fuss and let in another engine as we settled into the better water without me saying so.

"Head for Melilla," I said.

"Really?"

"Yes, and leave the riding lights on, no more than forty knots."

"Aye, aye Skip."

"That's skipper, to you."

"Aye, aye, skipper."

"That's better." I stood behind her and put my hands on her hips. She pushed her bottom back into me. I was beginning to feel okay with her again.

As we approached the proper port that is Melilla we passed outside a small container ship, doused our lights and went hard about into the darkness. Its radar shadow would shield us from the most sophisticated equipment, should there be any about.

"You've done this before," Sam said.

"I may have done. Take her up to eighty and look out for any shipping in the distance. If we hit the wash of anything big we'll go flying."

"Yes, boss."

"Happy, you're on the radio."

"I am?" he said.

I made him come aft and showed him how to work the kit. Before long he was holding the headphones hard against his ear with one hand and turning the dial with the other, which is to say that he wasn't holding on with either hand. That done, I got out the binoculars and took watch myself. It occurred to me that it was odd that I wasn't driving, but she was doing it as well as I could have, so why not let her?

We jinked about the Med a bit and approached our destination as the moon showed the tip of its horn over the horizon. There were the lights of several fishing vessels floating serenely on the smooth water so we skirted them at a distance that should make the sound of our passing no more than a distant whisper and locked onto the one lying separate from the others.

I took the helm now and Sam and Happy assumed their positions by the cargo with AKs at the ready. I came in to her dead on the bow and we read the rust-streaked lettering. *Canaillas*, she was. Camilla stood out on the fore-hatch and pulled off her cap and shook out her long hair. One man and two young lads watched us from the deck as we slowed and turned to come up alongside. They had their hands where we could see them, which showed that Camilla understood.

"Ola, Canaillas," I called out.

"Ola, Nottamulo," she called back.

"How are the tuna?" I said.

"Fuck the tuna," she shouted in a fair imitation of Jans.

"Good to see you, Canaillas. Permission to come alongside?"

"Come on in, Simon. We are ready."

It was good to have Happy's extra strength as we lie a lot lower than the trawler and it takes a good, well timed, heave to get the bales cleanly up and onto her deck. He made easy work of it and the man and two lads formed a chain to get them down into the hold quickly. Camilla and I watched as they did so. Sam kept a lookout out to sea.

"Okay, Camilla?" I called, as Happy heaved the last bale.

"Hasta Luego, Simon."

"Hasta Luego." I spun the wheel and took her back up smoothly to twenty knots.

"That went well," Sam said, coming up beside me.

"That was what it should be."

"Want me to take her?"

"I'll have her for a bit, you take the glasses."

"Yes, boss."

I gave myself a good long spell at the wheel, just because I wanted to. The moonlight increased the visibility a lot and helped me read the water so I pushed her up almost to top speed, not because there was any need but because I could. Sam stood with one hand on the coaming and the other sweeping the heavy glasses along the horizon, her hair flying out behind her and her body moving easily with the boat. She had a fine, keen, wholesome look, like a hunting dog who senses game.

I turned my head to check on Happy. He caught the movement, flashed me a smile and then returned to his work.

"Sam," I shouted, turning back. She turned to me, looking the question, ready to do whatever I wanted. "Coffee," I said. She smiled and nodded and reached into the binnacle cupboard, pressing unselfconsciously against me as she did so. She poured us each a plastic mug full and passed them round.

"Cheers." We raised our mugs to each other, sharing the moment with simple delight. Whatever complications there might be on land, on the water we seemed to have become a crew.

8

DIRTY WORK

We crossed the bar in the early hours and took a wide loop back
in to our mooring. Sam picked it up with a boathook and made
us fast. The little tender put-putted out to us with Asif at the tiller.

"Hey, Happy," I said.

"Yes, boss?"

"If you're becoming a sailor, I'd better teach you some knots."

"I'd like that. Am I becoming a sailor?"

"Seems like it to me. You go back with Asif first, we don't want
to overload the tender. Ready?"

"Ready, boss."

It was all a bit precarious, but he got in without tipping her up,
and Asif got him safely back to the jetty. Sam and I stood with our
arms around each other watching.

"Well?" I said.

"All well, I'd say. Let's go home to bed," she said.

"Okay," I said. "Let's."

I patted the old girl as we left her, thanking her for the ride and looked back at her over Asif's shoulder as we motored in. I'd put a lot of thought into her and she had repaid me many, many times over.

Asif had an immobile, unhappy look on his face so I passed Sam my bag and said I'd meet her at the end.

"What's wrong, Asif?" I said, when we were alone.

"Jony has not come back." He waved the mobile phone about helplessly as if it was at fault.

"Is it possible that he took a friend with him? I thought I saw two heads on the library roof."

"It is possible, but why would he?"

"To help pass the time perhaps. Okay, take care of the boat and fill her up, I will go and look. If he is stoned or asleep with a girl in his arms, I will beat him for you."

"Thank you, Simon."

"No problem." I rejoined Sam and Happy who were waiting quietly by the road. Sam yawned and stretched and Happy caught it and yawned too. "Ready, boss?"

"I wish. No, I've a job to do. Happy, will you take Sam home please? I mean back up the hill."

"Sure, boss."

"Why? I want to sleep with you," Sam said.

"Sorry, I have work to do. I will come and find you in the morning. Actually I mean in the afternoon, this is the morning."

"What work? I'll come and help."

"I have to find a boy, that's all. Now go."

"Why?"

"Because I have to." I raised my hand to stop a passing taxi, took my bag from Sam and got in. They watched me go.

My driver had a fat spliff hanging from the fingers of one hand and drove very slowly. When I made him stop just past the docks he smiled absently at me and palmed a note without looking at it. I watched him turn and cruise back down the strip and then walked back along towards the building that is known as the old library.

I don't know if it ever was a library, seems unlikely, but now it's the home of some of the more tenuous and less reputable shipping offices of the port. Some Victorian empire builder built it and added a Dutch style edifice of swooping masonry on the top which raises it above the level of the surrounding buildings. Presumably that was the idea at the time.

I put a round into the chamber of my .38 and trod softly into the alley, barely wider than my shoulders, which leads behind the row of buildings. I couldn't see what I was treading on but I could smell it. If I had known, I would have put on some heavy boots when I left the house instead of my usual trainers. When I came out into the slightly wider alleyway behind, a couple of rats ran away from me and sat under the row of bins watching me. One of the bins had been wheeled under the fire-escape, which either meant that someone was up there now, or that they hadn't bothered to move the bin back after they left.

The bin was full and heavy enough not to move much when I scrambled up onto it, so I got onto the cast iron work without any noise. I could tell that someone had been before me as some of whatever was on the ground had been left on the rungs by their feet. If Jony was up there asleep I would wipe it off my hands onto him.

I went up each flight of rungs with deliberation, making no assumptions about the metalwork until I had tested it. I was climbing out of darkness into the moonlight. The windows that I passed were barred and locked. I looked over my shoulder at the buildings behind me. All was dark and silent. When I got to the top I stopped to listen but there was nothing to hear. I popped my head up, and then brought it down as quickly. I had seen nothing but the bare lead-work of the roof so I looked again properly and then climbed over the balustrade. The central dome obscured the seaward side. I leant against the smooth, slightly soft surface and worked carefully round it with the .38 in my right hand.

There was no need for caution; the only other occupant of the roof was very dead. He lay as he had been dropped, with one bare leg stretched out towards me and his soft, slightly downy cheek, pressed hard against the metal. I knelt beside him, Jony presumably, to see what he could tell me. Rigor had set in but wasn't advanced. He was probably dead when I had looked up from the water six, nearly seven, hours earlier. There was a single entry wound from a knife under his right shoulder blade. I imagine that someone had caught hold of him, turned him round and pushed a blade between his ribs and up into his heart, or the major blood vessels near it. Not a difficult thing to do to a slim, young kid like this. No signs of scratches or scuffs in the lead or stonework. His hands and face were undamaged. Whoever had killed him was probably right- handed and had killed this way before, but that was all I could tell.

There were no binoculars on the roof, and when I turned him over they weren't under him either. Theft as well as murder. I got mine out of my bag and had a look at the shed roof at about where I thought I had seen something from the boat. There was nothing that would account for it. No debris, or cowling or anything like that. Either I had imagined it or there had been two watchers watching me, I mean us, load up more than a million pounds worth of hash and take it out to sea. The watcher, or watchers; I had thought I saw two heads, up here; must have seen the one down there, but had he seen them? No way to know.

I looked at the poor lad, staring sightlessly up at the indifferent stars, and accepted that he was my problem now. The sun would be up soon, I could either move him now, or tonight. By tonight he would've had a whole day baking in the sun. Also, Asif would want to bury him before the sun set. It'd better be now.

He was stiff, but not too stiff to manipulate, so I bent him in the middle and carried him over to the top of the fire-escape. The tricky bit was getting him off the parapet and onto my shoulder without dropping him but I did it after a few hairy moments. Once I had him well balanced I started handing myself down and down. It was a long way and my muscles felt like jelly by the time I could let him down onto the bin. Actually I dropped him the last bit but I didn't suppose it mattered.

When I got back from fetching my bag there was a rat looking at him from the top of the nearest bin. I was glad that that was my only company in the alley at the time. I pushed the bin back to its place with its fellows and opened lids, looking for one with enough space to take him. There wasn't one, so I pulled ghastly bags of something or other out of one, and put him in instead, shut the lid and put the bags on top. God, I needed a shower and some breakfast.

No chance of that yet. I shortened the strap of my bag, put it tight across my back and set out running. Running at night in Nador isn't an inconspicuous activity but I was racing the sun and I was sure to lose. The early morning women, heading down to buy fish from the night boats which come in at dawn, looked at me as if I were mad and turned away not to make eye contact.

I passed up through the city, parallel with the streets leading to my flat, and then cut across towards Azooz's yard. There are no gates so the boys sleep in the cars and wake Azooz from his room at the back if he is needed. The Hilux had been filled and sprayed, badly, but that didn't matter, and a sleepy pair of long-lashed eyes looked at me wonderingly from inside it. I smiled encouragingly and held one finger to my lips. The boy recognised me and nodded.

I mimed turning a key and he reached up and pulled down the sun visor. The key fell into his lap and he softly opened the door and gave it to me.

I tousled his head, as one tends to do to boys of a certain age, and pushed him gently towards the Jag, from which two heads were solemnly watching.

The engine started at the second revolution and I backed her round and drove out. A startled Azooz appeared in nothing but underpants and a shotgun from the back. I gave him a casual wave as I went.

The dawn call to prayer began as I stopped alongside the alley on the wrong side of the road. Even in there, the light levels were increasing. I scooped him out, scattering rubbish bags and rats as I did so, carried him to the truck and dumped him in the back. I had nothing to cover him with but I wouldn't stop. The time of the prayer is a good time to be moving a body; I was alone on the street.

I stopped on a deserted bit of the highway and straightened him out and pushed his eyelids down. They didn't want to go but I made them.

Asif was in his place with the nets. He looked old and tired and he didn't realise it was me until I got out.

"I am sorry," I said. "I did not know it, but I was sending your son to his death."

"I felt it. Did he die well?"

I didn't know what dying well was, so I said, "There were two of them and they were trained men. He died as well as it was possible for him to die."

"Where is he?"

"He is here."

"You brought him from the roof of the old library?"

"I knew that you would want to bury him soon."

"That is so. I must take him to his mother now." He looked a bit helpless, not knowing what to do and not wishing to lose his composure in front of me.

"Take this vehicle, I have no need of it at the moment. Go now, I will get Ali to send someone to watch over your things and mine."

"There is no need, Moukhtar will see to it." He held up his hand and beckoned and a young man appeared from behind one of the upturned skiffs on the front. He approached shyly and received his orders from his father.

Asif got into the front of the truck without looking in the back and after a few false starts drove off, heading towards his modest house on the outskirts of town. I heft my bag again and walked off to the Rif.

I went in by the garden gate and sent one of the pool-boys to dig out Ali. He appeared, rubbing his eyes and looking offended.

"My God, you keep some hours, Simon," he said.

"I knew you would be up to pray," I said.

"Prayer be damned. You look, if you don't mind me saying so, as rough as a harbour whore after the Fokin has docked. And you smell worse."

"It's been a long night, Ali. Will you join me for a coffee? Oh, and perhaps someone could find me a car, I should probably go home and have a wash."

"Coffee, Basil," Ali snapped his fingers at the boy.

We sat out by the pool. The water looked very inviting but it would be a crime to get in it in my current state.

"I have very little to tell you, Simon, it has only been a few hours. But I do know that Azooz has a brother who is working for a ferenji at the moment. He has been boasting of it."

"That is interesting. I have something to tell you too. I am trusting you, but you would find out anyway, I know. I set one of Asif's boys to watch the docks last night…"

"Where you called in to pick up bait for your night's fishing trip?"

"…exactly, and somebody neatly dispatched him with a knife."

"Oh, dear, that is bad."

"Our friend?"

"The thin one?"

"Yes."

"Who knows? He wasn't here, or anywhere I know of. I will ask what I can of who I can."

"The others? The ones you worry about?"

"The same. They come and go, usually in pairs or all together. I do not know what they do."

"Thanks, Ali. I think I will go and have a wash now."

"That is a very good idea. I must send to Asif with some food and some white cloths I have."

"That also is a good idea. I should've thought of that."

"Ah, but I feed people. It is what I do. You on the other hand, you kill them. It is what you do. Why would you think of a thing like that?"

"Don't get at me, Ali, I'm tired."

"I'm sorry, so am I."

I took a car from the hotel, through the busy streets, almost to my door. When I opened the door of the flat Soumaiya appeared, looking relieved. She came close to me and might have hugged me but stopped short, wrinkling her nose in a most attractive way.

"Will you take your clothes off there please, Simon. I shall run you a bath and make some coffee." She was smiling.

"Hello, Soumy, God it's good to be home." I was smiling too. I put down my now heavy bag, stripped and dropped my clothes into the washing basket that she put next to me, and then sat on the edge of the bath while the water ran. It wasn't that hot, it never is, but that didn't matter. I soaked and sipped coffee and applied soap and shampoo and became a cleaner, more wholesome version of myself. A thought struck me.

"Soumy," I called.

"Yes, Simon." She put her head round the door.

"Will you wash my back?"

"No, Simon, I will not. I'm making you some food."

"The food can wait, come and scrub my back."

"No. I will get my clothes wet."

"So take them off."

"No, Simon," she began to look a little distressed, "I must not, she would kill me."

"No she wouldn't, anyway how would she know?"

"She would know." She withdrew her head and was gone. I thought about chasing her but she'd seemed pretty serious about it and chasing anyone was a bit too much effort for the moment.

By the time I'd eaten some delicious cold lamb and couscous and salad, I was almost asleep, so I lay down on the bed and must have gone out like a light.

Later that day, some time after lunch, found me sitting up in bed with a tray beside me with coffee and a plate of Soumy's stuffed dates on it, and a lot on my mind.

"You look thoughtful, Simon," Soumy said, taking the tray.

"So do you, Soumy," I said.

"I think that I do not always want to be being afraid you won't come back."

"It's always been like that, you know that."

"I'm also always afraid you will bring her back here again."

"I don't seem to be able to help that," I said.

"It's okay, I'm just trying to be ready for whatever happens."

"You're a good girl, Soumy."

"I'm more than you think I am. I'm only just finding out, myself."

"Soumy?"

"Yes, Simon?"

"Do you know Asif the boatman?"

"I don't think so, no."

"Well, one of his son's was watching out for me last night and someone killed him."

"I'm glad it wasn't you."

"Me too. If I don't come back, it might be best if you were to disappear."

"I have no one to disappear to and no money to disappear with."

"I thought you said there was more to you than I thought?"

"Okay, I will think about that. But it is better if you do come back."

"I'll try. I'm going to go out in the boat now. Just to fish by myself. It means that Asif and his family can all be free to attend the funeral."

"That's thoughtful of you."

"It is, isn't it. If anyone wants me, you can tell them where I am."

I got dressed and walked straight down to the seafront. The sunshine and the water and the boats and the nets drying in the sun were unsatisfactory and ambiguous. I walked along the front feeling burdened with unknowing and with conflicting desires. There was a group of young boys, sons of fishermen, amusing themselves by jumping off the wall into the sea. They hit the water balled up, knees held tight to their chests, and made a happy, laughing, shouting maelstrom of their small bit of the sea. I envied them the simplicity of their day.

The hard, hot concrete and stone of the sea-wall was irrefutably real and walking along it, squinting against the sharp light flicking up from the sea, was comforting after a while. The sun and the light sea-breeze, carrying the smell of the sea and the shore; seaweed rotting in the sun, old fish heads, tar and behind it, subtly, the great astringent, potent, salt-seaness that is the same from pole to pole; drew out some of the poison. In the end, like it or not, the sea is always the sea.

I looked at the Rif and wondered who would be in the bar. I could be certain that several eyes would be watching me from there, even if it were only the staff and Old Henry. I didn't want to go anywhere near it for now, or be with anyone, even Sam.

Mouhktar rose from the pile of nets to greet me. He looked serious and sad and unsure what to say to me in the absence of Asif.

"As-salamu alaykum, Mouhktar," I said, to help him.

"Wa alaykum as-salamu, Mr Ellice. I have kept a good watch for you, sir."

"I'm sure you have. Now, I'm going out on the boat and I will be gone for the rest of the day. Your brother's funeral is before sunset?"

"It is, Mr Ellice."

"Good. Go to your family now, there is no need for anyone to watch until after dark." He looked unsure. His father had told him to watch and I was telling him to go. He was used to obeying his father but not me yet. "Okay. Take me out in the tender and when I have gone then you go, okay?"

"Yes, Mr Ellice." This was better; if there was no boat to watch then he could go.

The little boat put-putted us out and I stepped easily from her onto Nottambulo's transom. It was nice to feel her underneath me, bearing me up. The black paint was hot to the touch and so was the metal plate of the ignition when I put my key into it. I checked what I always check, started number one engine and dropped the mooring buoy. We drifted very slowly backwards in the slight breeze while I got the small boat-rod out of its locker and clipped a rappala onto the line, then I put her into gear and we ghosted through the other moored craft, all of them sleeping in the sun; no signs of life aboard. I took a wide sweep out to the breakwater and then lobbed the lure over the back. I let a hundred yards or so of line out and held it in my fingers so that I could feel the thrum of it working in the water. I put the rod in a holder and clipped it to a lanyard just in case. There was always the possibility of a good trevalley along here though a mackerel was more likely. It didn't matter either way.

I unclipped and folded out the seat beside the binnacle, made myself comfortable on it and put a finger against one spoke of the wheel; with only the starboard prop turning she had a slight tendency to turn to port. The seabirds on the breakwater watched us incuriously as we passed and a lone fisherman with a long beach-caster, fishing the surf on the other side, turned to smile and wave.

As the port and city of Nador shrank and dwindled behind me, I felt less burdened by uncertainty. I had arrived here in this boat and if necessary, when necessary, I could just as easily leave. The blue- mauve hills above the littoral plain were clear and distinct from this distance, unobscured by buildings and palm trees. Somewhere up there Sam would probably be lying by the pool. If she cared to look with glasses I, in my long, black boat, would be clearly visible, stuck on the sea, apparently not moving, like a small black fly. It was likely that someone would be looking out; in that place someone always is.

I took her out of gear and let her drift while I played and landed a strong mackerel. They fight like demons, much more than their size would suggest. The vital, jagging urgency of the fish fighting for its life transmitted itself through the line. I swung it in, blue-green and iridescent, still fighting in the air, caught the line above it in my hand and lowered the rod to the deck. When I'd unhooked it and dispatched it with a crisp, resonant blow to the head from the priest, I put it in a bucket in the scuppers where it continued to quiver. It smelt of fish, surprisingly, and changed the nature of the day by being there.

I lazed about in the lagoon all afternoon; fishing without great intention, happy to catch or not as it fell out, enjoying being out on the water by myself. I went all the way along the narrow strip of land that divides the lagoon from the sea until it turned in to meet the mainland at the very end. Off the village of Kariat Arkmane, which lies at the top of the beach there, I woke the engines up a bit and came alongside a young man and a boy in a brightly painted open boat. They looked at me with fear, which subsided and turned into happy laughter when I hailed them in Arabic and offered them an unreasonably high price for fetching me some cold beer and a box of falafels from the village store.

They looked at Nottambulo with wide eyes and a thousand unspoken questions as they pulled alongside to deliver the goods. The older one pulled the boy back down to his seat to prevent him from leaning over to look inside. What the hell, why not? I laughed for the frivolity of the idea and offered them a ride.

They looked serious and doubtful and shook their heads sadly. I told them that I had enough slaves at the moment and didn't need any more, I would bring them back in ten minutes. That did the trick. They dropped a rock on a rope over the side of their boat and then the older one came aboard carefully. He didn't see anything to be frightened of so he gestured the boy to follow him.

They almost jumped back overboard when I started the other engines. They sat there looking wild eyed, excited and fearful. I gestured them to hold on, put her in gear and moved all four levers up together. The boy screamed with delight and surprise as we accelerated up to sixty knots. The older one turned back to where his village was rapidly disappearing behind us, apparently thinking that he might never see it again.

I backed her down to a safe speed to turn and pointed her back towards the village. "Again?" I asked the boy. "Yes, yes, yes, yes please," he said, so excited he could barely contain himself. I took her up as fast as it was safe to go and still stop in time not to smash their boat, and slewed us round at the last minute, rocking the small craft in the wash of our wake.

"Okay?" I said. They were speechless with delight and relief and adrenaline. "Go on then. I must go now. Thank you for getting the beer for me."

They climbed back into their boat, eager to tell their friends about what had happened to them. I waved and they waved and I left to head back towards Nador.

The sun was getting lower, though it was still hot. I would time my arrival to so that the funeral would be over. Also it was on my mind that I might take an outer mooring and swim in; perhaps surprise that bloody flick in the darkness.

I went slowly back along the inland shore this time. The sea bed was more uneven here and there was more weed about so I didn't let the lure so far out. It danced happily about in the water making the shorter line tremble visibly and scattering water droplets from it. A nice fat bass was a possibility here.

One day, I believe that all this will change; this lagoon is one of the most lovely and probably the largest in the Mediterranean system, yet it's almost undeveloped for tourism and water sports. There are restaurants and cafés for the throngs of Moroccans who take their summer holidays here, and there are more pleasure craft than there used to be, but the water still mainly belongs to the solid, blue painted wooden fishing boats, each one with its noisy Yamaha outboard. Anywhere on the European shore this would be full of jet-skis, water skiers and the like. As it is, it remains an essentially scruffy, North African, place where fishing, smuggling, and the remains of the slave trade continue.

There are a number of gin palaces, which belong to local businessmen and rarely get used, a few speed boats, old Henry's 40 foot wooden sloop and a small but steady trickle of visitors passing through. Of these, the majority are ocean going sailing yachts, and these are the ones I like. They are generally sorted. By which I mean that everything about them is good, tough, clean, neat and ready.

You can always tell the real travellers from the just messing about crowd. For a start, they have more than twice the kit; if you're out for weeks or months you can't afford a flat battery so you have a good wind generator and some solar panels. The same goes for spars and canvas and winches and communication equipment, and every other myriad thing which may save your life out at sea.

The thing about these boats that pulls at me is that they are unbounded; they can go anywhere, more or less, where the sea goes. Nottambulo, superb as she is, is restricted to the quiet waters of the world; I cannot cross the Atlantic or even venture out in a strong Mediterranean blow. These birds of passage are generally pausing briefly here before heading out through the straights and down to catch the trade winds that will carry them to the Caribbean, or on down to the horn and the big south seas.

The men, and usually women, who sail them are tough, lean, tanned people. They have ready smiles and a cheerful word of greeting or a wave but they have steady, appraising eyes and are nobody's fools. By the time they have acquired the look of the real sea voyager, they have dealt with every kind of crooked harbour-master, chandler, and pilot. They've run down waves as high as houses, been winched up the mast in a force nine to free a jammed halyard and held on through countless hours, past exhaustion and on into the numb, surreal world that is bringing a sailing vessel through a storm. Either they've learned to be strong and self-reliant, or they've died or given up.

The sixty footer that I'd seen coming in a few nights ago was anchored off a nice stretch of beach with a café, about half way back to Nador. I passed her at a polite distance so that I could have a look at her; boats have a personal space just as people do.

I couldn't be sure, but I thought she could be an Andre Hoek. She was rigged as a ketch and had classic lines but there was that about her spars and rigging that made me suspect modern technology. There was a rib pulled up on the sand which was probably her tender. She was flying a British flag. More of a Mediterranean bird than an international wanderer I decided; she looked good but not really sorted. I put the glasses on her and read 'Wise Policy' on her stern.

There were three men taking their ease on the seats in the cockpit. One of them raised a hand to me and I returned the gesture. Another one studied me through glasses. There was a line of washing pegged to the handrail and it made a colourful display above her jet-black hull. Her mizzen mast sported a thoroughly modern array of radar pods, aerials and other less easily identifiable electronic equipment. She was a lovely vessel in every way.

I didn't get a bass but the rappala must have been skimming the bottom because I did get a small flounder. I put him back to grow on. I allowed the boat to drift over what I knew to be a deeper hole, most of the lagoon is less than eight meters deep, and cut the engine. It was too early to go in and the complete silence was nice. I changed the lure for a couple of big trebles and hooked one of the mackerel's heads between them and tossed it in. The line sank steadily down through the water as we drifted slowly with the slight breeze. When I felt it hit the bottom I wound it back up a meter or so and flipped the bale arm back over. I would hear the ratchet of the drag sing out if anything took it.

I'd picked up *Moby Dick* as I'd left the house on a whim, and now I made myself comfortable with a beer and the box of falafels and it. I'd been out long enough, essentially doing nothing, to begin to feel an itch to be up and doing again, but I'd set my course so I'd stick to it. The book was a little hard going to start with; it took me a while to get into his way of writing, but after a bit it began to draw me in.

I kept an almost automatic eye on whatever was moving on the water. A pair of fishing boats appeared from the direction of Nador and swept the area of water inshore of me with their net held taut between them. I put the glasses on them when they pulled it in to see what they'd got. It didn't look like much. Nothing showed any interest in the fish-head on the end of my line either.

The sun was getting close to the hills and the light beginning to alter, getting ready to become the brief evening before night fell. I didn't bother to put on any riding lights; the water held the light and there was no one else in my vicinity. A lone fisherman in his blue painted boat made steady progress down the lagoon towards me and passed unusually close. I supposed that Nottambulo must be hard to see against the dark background of the breakwater. I called a polite greeting in Arabic and he raised a hand in reply. He was wearing a keffiyeh so I couldn't tell who he was. I know most of the fishermen who work out of the port and make it my business to be polite to them; they see and hear everything that goes on, on the water so I want them to wish me well. My generosity to Asif is known and stands to my credit with them.

The sun touched the land and the first stars became visible. The lights of the harbour were strong against the black water. I could distinguish the red of the sign above the bar at the Rif and it beckoned me home. I reeled in, started the engine and pointed her at it.

Darkness changes perspective on the water and the jetty became visible sooner than I expected. I was just about to pick an outer mooring to head towards when my stupidity struck me. I spun the wheel, sending us out into the darkness, and then turned back the way I had come. No fisherman, however pale skinned, has white hands; it's just not possible.

The trouble with the blue fishing boats is that they all look alike. They build them to the same design and then paint them the same shade of blue, I don't know why. I pushed along a bit to make up the distance and got my night glasses out of the locker. The flare of light from the bars and restaurants on shore made them less than useful; they only come into their own when there is almost no light, so I went in towards the lights myself so that I would be able to look out into the darkness.

I slid along, little more than a hundred yards out, and, with no lights showing and my dull, black hull, I don't think a single person on shore saw me. The Wise Policy was easy to find, her white superstructure shone in the reflected lights from the land and she had some deck lights on too. I turned the engine off and gently slid the kedge anchor over the stern on a light line. I used the ordinary glasses to have a look at her. There were two men, I think playing cards, on deck. I could still see the rib on the beach and there were four white men at a table in front of the café who might belong to her.

I changed to the night glasses and searched the blackness that was the sea. Sure enough, there was a local fishing boat with only one person in it anchored further out and he wasn't fishing, he was watching the yacht through a very large pair of binoculars. I was watching the watcher; I wondered if anyone was watching me. I switched back to my binoculars in time to see another man aboard the yacht appear in the companionway and speak to the others. He raised a two-way radio and spoke into it. On shore one of the four answered and then they all rose and moved quickly down to the rib. It had a big Mercury outboard and the sound of it starting carried clearly across the water. They pushed it off with practiced skill and headed out to the yacht.

I was starting to get a feeling about all this so I got my one and only MP5 out of the locker and screwed on the long fat suppressor. I would have felt better with an AK but they're very loud. I couldn't be sure at that distance, but it looked to me as though the men in the rib were taking the same approach. They paused on the inshore side of Wise Policy, the side that the man out in the darkness couldn't see, where they received weapons and instructions, and then headed out towards the fishing boat at what must have been a good twenty knots.

Through the night glasses I watched the man put down his glasses in a hurry and start pulling the chord of his small outboard. Not that it would do him much good. It must have fired, I couldn't hear it over the noise of the big Mercury, as he brought the heavy, clumsy vessel about and started to move over the water like a snail being chased by a greyhound.

If I wanted to talk to him, I'd better do something about it, right about now. I started all four engines, pulled in the kedge and joined in.

The sound of their engine covered the sound of mine so when I passed them doing nearly sixty knots, which made them seem effectively stationary, it came as a surprise. I was ready to give them answering fire if they raised a gun, but they just looked stunned and watched me go.

I kept my speed up to give me the maximum time and only slowed when I was right up to the fishing boat. His keffiyeh had come undone and I could see that he didn't know what was going on but he didn't point any guns at me either so I dropped the little kedge into his bows as I came past, where it caught and held. I took the tension in the rope in my hand and let it out until I had him in tow. The rib was closing on us and there were guns in evidence now so I powered up without ceremony.

It was like towing a Reliant Robin with a Ferrari; Nottambulo didn't care, she would have pulled three more as well, but it can't have been much fun for the poor chap. The little boat would try to go its own way and career off to one side, only to be pulled skittering and bucking back into line. At one point I thought he was going to go over and I was amazed that the rope didn't give way, but then I do look after my rope. The rib followed us for a bit and then gave up and turned back.

I took him all the way past Nador and into the quiet end of the lagoon where I could expect to be alone. I stopped the engines so that I would be able to hear anyone coming if there was anyone.

It was suddenly very quiet after all that noise and excitement. He stopped clinging on like a kitten being held over a bathtub and sat on a thwart looking at me. I showed him the MP5 and said, "Hi, Bill, how're you doing?"

"I feel a bit sick, if you want to know."

"I'm sorry about that. Would you care to come aboard?" I pulled him in closer.

"I'm not sure."

"It wasn't really a request."

"Okay, I'll come aboard then."

"That's the spirit."

He nearly fell in but I didn't help him. He made it aboard and sat on a seat looking shaken and incongruous in his jellaba.

"They noticed you on their radar and then probably had a look at you through night glasses. You should have taken two boats and made it look like you were working a net. I take it you and those chaps aren't working together then?"

"I thought there might be a story in them, I think I was right. How did you know it was me?"

"You've got white hands. Bill, I'm a drug smuggler, as you know, and you're police of some kind, not a journalist. Someone killed a man who was working for me yesterday and it may have been you, or something to do with you. You've been hanging about watching me in a rather annoying way. In a minute we're going out there for a boat ride together," I pointed towards the dark Mediterranean beyond the breakwater, "but first I thought we'd have a chat. What do you say?"

"So I have." He held up his hands and they were very pale. "You intend to kill me out there?"

"It's nothing personal. Did you know that there's a family of great whites living off Malta?"

"Can't say I did. Should I ask why?"

"No particular reason. How about you tell me all about it?"

"And if not?"

"If not I'm going to tow you behind the boat for a bit."

"That doesn't sound too bad."

"You hang onto that thought, old son. Now, before we go, I'd rather not have you jumping over the side or anything like that, so you have a choice of a bullet or two in the extremities or cable-ties. Which would you prefer?"

"No chance of dry land and a beer then?"

"Love to, but it's not on, is it. I'll have one for you when I get back, how's that?"

"It's not quite the same. Hang on a minute, let me talk for a bit."

"Isn't that just what I was suggesting? Sit down on the floor and work on looking harmless, will you."

He moved down to the bottom of the boat, crossed his legs and rested his hand on his thighs.

"Okay here it is, you're Simon James Ellice, son of Edmund and Helen Ellice. You work for Guy Wealden delivering bales of kif to, what, a quiet Spanish beach or a trawler, from where it goes on into Europe," he said.

"That's more or less common knowledge around here."

"And knowing it isn't proving it or getting a conviction."

"So you are police, then?"

"Sort of. Do you know the phrase, quis quistodiet ipsos custodes?"

"Who guards the guards?"

"That would be me, sort of."

"So, what're you doing watching me, then?"

"That's complicated."

"Do I look like I'm in a hurry?"

"We have an idea. Well, to be accurate, a young chap in the Met. Vice had an idea, that quite a lot of hash is getting into the country rather too easily. I mean, it's just sort of turning up without due process, if you know what I mean?"

"Not really."

"The usual suspects are selling it, but they don't know where it's coming from. None of the usual smuggling routes seem to be involved. You can buy it easily enough, as long as you buy big enough, and it's always good stuff, which is suspicious in itself. We can't work back up the chain though. God knows, we've tried. Our best undercover guys can't get near them. Even when we use a gang member who owes us, no show. It's frustrating. You can see where that's led me, can't you?"

"Spell it out for me, I'm not from your world."

"So you're not. It means that they're being protected. Someone who has access to our systems is vetting every buy. And I don't just mean the PNC, I mean the Met. Payroll for fuck's sake. It's like the bastards are looking over my shoulder all the time."

"How frustrating for you."

"Yes. Anyway, I decided to try it from the other end. I managed to get hold of some high grade Hash which the lab tells me came from the Rif."

"No great surprise there."

"No. So I'm looking for a shipper with a connection to the UK. I mean more than just a local hood but someone who might know someone, if you know what I mean. The more I find out about the players here, the more often the name of Guy Wealden comes up. I decided to come and have a look at him, which didn't turn out to be very easy, but I found you instead, which is interesting in itself."

"And these other fellows?"

"No idea. Don't they seem like ex-forces to you?"

"Reek of it."

"Yes, anyway, they were watching me watching you so I thought I'd try watching them. It doesn't seem to have gone well."

I looked at him and thought about it all for a moment or two.

"How much of all that is true, Bill?"

"Oh, it's all true."

"But it's not necessarily the whole truth?"

"Pretty nearly. I may have kept a few guesses to myself, that's all. Either you already knew what I've told you, in which case, no harm done. Or you didn't in which case the knowledge is more likely to get you killed than not. That is, unless those men in the yacht get you first."

"Assuming this isn't all bollocks. What've they got against me, I wonder?"

"No idea."

"So why did you kill the kid?"

"I didn't. Who? Killed where? When?"

"On the roof of a building overlooking the docks while we were loading up, or a bit before. A young lad I had keeping watch."

"Not me. I was on the roof of the dock sheds taking photos of you loading up."

"I see. Have you got a chap working for you who's the brother of the mechanic, Azooz?"

"Yes. No, I sacked him. He was talking."

"He certainly was. Ah well, it's time I'm afraid. You ready?"

"I don't suppose you'll let me send a text first?" I couldn't see him very clearly in the weak starlight but I thought I could detect a slight tremor in his voice.

"Bill, I don't care what you do, just so long as you don't get in my way. Now if you'd like to get back in your little boat and pass me my kedge, I'll be on my way."

"Huh?"

"I make it a rule not to kill British policemen unless I really have to. Don't tell anyone that though, will you."

"Fuck. I believed you."

"Good."

"What're you going to do?"

"Now? I'm going to go and have some supper."

"I mean…"

"You mean, about all this? Don't know, I'll think about that over supper, but I'll tell you a couple of things that occur to me."

"What?"

"Firstly, I think those lads back there are going to be looking for you now, and if they find you, you won't be bothering me again. Secondly, if Guy hasn't noticed you yet, he very soon will, and unlike me he's got nothing to lose by killing you. Either way, if you stay here, I think you're going to have your hands pretty full just staying alive, don't you? Now, go and get back to dry land and have that beer before something else happens to you."

"Okay, I will. Simon…"

"Bill?"

"Thanks."

"No problem."

9

LIFE IS WHAT HAPPENS

(WHILE YOU'RE MAKING OTHER PLANS)

"What you up to?" the text said.

"Supper at the Riby?" I sent back.

"Yes!"

"Pick you up 8.30."

"I'll be ready."

I tidied up the boat, nudging the wheel occasionally to keep us heading in the right direction, and rinsed the fish in fresh seawater and put them in a polythene bag. The result was satisfactorily heavy. Asif was waiting at the end of the jetty with one of his sons. They took the painter and stern-line and made Nottambulo fast.

I stepped off and went to greet him and see how he was. He seemed tired but okay.

"Good evening, Simon. This is my son, Imad, he is going to be helping me with Nottambulo, if you approve. Offer Mr Ellice your hand, boy."

"Hi, Imad," I said, taking his hand.

"I will study to deserve the honour, Mr Ellice," he said.

"If you do it half as well as your father you'll be excellent. Are you sure, Asif? I thought you might not wish to expose your sons to danger after what happened to Jony. These are strange times and I don't know what will happen," I said.

"We have spoken of it and decided that the family's welfare should not be in the hands of one old man only. Imad has already survived many things. He has nearly drowned twice, nearly been killed by some drunken sailors once, and he has even been bitten by a red snake and he is still alive. We think that if any of them can survive working for you, he is the one. Also, he is a useless fisherman."

"Are you good with boats, Imad?" I said.

"I love boats, Mr Simon, and yes, I am good with them. Am I not, father? I do not like fish though."

"He is good enough with boats, that is true."

"So be it. I approve."

"Hamdulillah."

"In which case, see that she is clean and full of fuel and put her on her mooring. Then you will watch her and see that no one goes near her. Okay?"

"With my life, Mr Ellice."

"Do you have a phone?"

"Yes, Mr Ellice." He got it out of a pocket in his jellaba. I made him send me a text so that I had the number.

"Good. Now, Asif, have you that white car? The Hilux?"

"It is waiting for you on the road, Simon. My women have cleaned it." He passed me the keys.

I collected the fish, had a last look round her and then walked up to the truck. It was still a very anonymous looking vehicle. I drove into town and parked in a side street near the flat.

Soumaiya took the bag with the fish in it and peered in the top. "You want one for supper?"

"No, you have one though. I'm going out again."

"Okay." She sounded disappointed.

I showered and went to my wardrobe for something to wear. I'm not given to dressing up much but I did have one good pair of trousers and that, with black shoes and a perfectly ironed white shirt, resulted in something that looked fit for company.

"You're dressed up," Soumaiya said, looking at me and walking round me to check that everything was satisfactory.

"Soumy, you remember that you said there was more to you than I knew?"

"Yes?"

"Suppose this was the last night, and suppose I gave you enough money to be able to go anywhere and do anything. What would you do?"

"Is this why you are dressed up?"

"Do you know what you would do?"

"No, but I will think about it if you like."

"Good, but we are being watched. Do nothing unusual, okay?"

"I do not want to think about not seeing you ever again."

"I'm sorry, Soumy. The clouds are gathering and I think perhaps it's time to head for the sun."

I would've had a quick look under the truck just to be sure but that would have spoiled the clothes, so I just got in and drove it. Nothing went bang. The old familiar streets seemed hostile. They'd always been hostile, so there wasn't much in that. I'd not been so bothered before and perhaps I wasn't now.

Guy and Zara were by the pool, like every evening since I'd known them. It was full dark as the late moon was still below the horizon. It wouldn't be up for a couple of hours. The lights and the darkness beyond made the scene intimate. I walked in slowly, appreciating it.

Sam was reading a book on one of the loungers by the pool. She got up and walked round it towards us. She didn't hurry but there was deliberation in her movement. I paused to watch and so did the others. She was wearing a dark emerald dress, with ruby earrings and necklace. I don't know much about dresses, but I can tell you it was very good.

She came straight to me, stood directly in front of me, reached up to pull me down to her and kissed me. When it was time to breathe again she said, "Hello, Simon."

"Hello, Sam," I said.

"Would you like a drink?"

"Yes, I would."

"Come and sit down, I'll get it. We can't stay long though, these two are driving me mad." She put an arm around my waist and led me over to the table.

"Someone seems pleased to see you," Guy said, as Sam sauntered off to the bar, happily swinging her hips.

"I'm not complaining," I said.

"So I see, so I see. I can't remember seeing you looking this smart before, Simon. Is this some occasion?"

"We're off to the Riby. Last time I had to threaten the doorman to get in. I thought I'd make an effort. I'm glad I did."

"Do you realise that your father is still in charge of your life?" Zara said, putting down her magazine and looking at me with interest.

"I rather thought he wasn't. What do you mean?" I said.

"You're here proving him wrong, right?"

"Maybe there was something of that in the beginning. Now, I think I'm earning my living. Isn't that why we're all here, more or less?"

"You do this for money?" Sam said, sitting on the arm of my chair, putting an arm over my shoulders and passing me a glass of scotch with some ice. "I do it because I love it."

"I don't think she has any real concept of money. I've spoilt her," Guy said. "I do it because it's what I do. And also for the money."

"So that means that he's still in charge of your life," Zara said.

"Who's in charge of my life?" I said.

"Your father. If you're doing what you do to prove him wrong. I was just reading about it." She tapped the magazine.

"She's moved on from furniture to psychology," Guy said.

"Do you only do things for one reason?" I said.

"Of course I do things for a reason. Do things, like what?" Zara said.

"I don't know, like live here."

"Oh, that was because Guy told me to."

"You always do what you're told?"

"I always do what Guy tells me to. Otherwise he would kill me."

"No you don't," Guy said. "I told you to cut down drinking and eat something."

"Yes, but you didn't mean it."

"No, I suppose I didn't."

"See."

"I told you not to shag the pool boy."

"No you didn't. Anyway you can't say you didn't want me to."

"Yes I can. Why would I want you to be unfaithful to me?"

"Because you'd had enough of him yourself and wanted to use me as an excuse to shoot him."

"Why would I need an excuse to shoot a pool boy?" he said.

"Because you're projecting your... hang on it says it here." She picked up the magazine and started searching through the pages.

"You two are two of the strangest people I've ever met," I said.

"That's because they never go anywhere or do anything. You're just festering. You two should go out and live a bit," Sam said.

"I like my life," Guy said. "I don't need excitement like you children do."

"I do, though," Zara said.

"Yes, but you don't count," Guy said.

"And off they go again," Sam said.

"Shall we go and eat?" I said.

"See, why don't you ever take me out to eat?" Zara said.

"Because I would probably forget to bring you back, and then I'd have to go to the trouble of replacing you," Guy said.

"If we don't go now, I'm going into the house for a gun," Sam said.

"Unless there's anything we need to talk about, is there, Guy?" I said. "Work-wise, I mean?"

"Nothing, my boy. Go and enjoy yourself and leave all the worrying to me."

"So there are things to worry about?"

"Only how I'm going to get through the evening without being psychoanalysed."

"You could see them as sweet," I said, as we walked to the car.

"Really?"

"Yeah, like some old couple bickering away at each other into their twilight years, but caring for each other really."

"You've been out in the sun too long."

"I have been out in the sun, that's true."

"I know, I saw you. What were you doing?"

"I caught some fish and gave some boys a ride, just for the hell of it."

"You didn't invite me."

"I wanted a little time by myself. It's not a crime, you know."

"Don't worry, I'm not going to pick a fight with you tonight."

"But you might tomorrow?"

"Depends what happens, I suppose."

The doorman at the Riby ushered us in, all smiles. We lingered in the garden, enjoying the lights playing in the water and the leaves, and the scents of jasmine, hoya and acacia. She flicked some water at me from one of the pools so I chased her and caught her under the drooping fronds of a feathery bamboo. We kissed deeply and then she bit me on the cheek, hard enough to make me yelp, and ran off again.

"Save me, Robbie. He's an animal," she said, dancing round behind him as he appeared from the terrace entrance. I rubbed my cheek and advanced, intending to brush him aside.

"Don't…" He tried to get out of the way but she kept backing away, keeping him between us. "… mind me will you. I'll just …" He tripped on a low table, caught himself and descended into a chair. "… Er, sit here then."

I leapt the intervening flowerbed and pounded after her. We walked out onto the terrace a bit later looking slightly dishevelled but with a certain glow about us. Robbie greeted us with a straight face and the hint of an indulgent smile.

"Good evening, Miss Wealden. Good evening, Mr Ellice, I've taken the liberty of ordering drinks for you. If you would care to follow me."

"Hello, Robbie. He caught me," Sam said, taking his arm.

"So I see."

"Well, she bit me," I said.

"She may have done, but I feel that a gentleman wouldn't care to mention it," Robbie said.

"I'm afraid he's not a gentleman, Robbie."

"I had suspected it."

"Does that mean you'd rather not join us for a drink?" I said.

"If the lady wishes it, I could stretch a point."

"Oh, you must, Robbie."

"Very well, I will."

The tables were full, as usual and the staff had added one on the end for us. Robbie called for another chair and glass for himself and we watched while he uncorked a bottle of Ruinart.

"You two looked like you might handle some champagne. Is that okay?" he said.

"Perfect, Robbie. Thank you," Sam said.

"So life isn't too bad at the moment? You look like love's young dream," he said.

"I'm having so much fun. Simon lets me drive Nottambulo and we've been up in the hills walking and riding."

"You should be careful up there, some of the tribes are pretty lawless by all accounts."

"We know," Sam said, with a smile.

"Don't worry, she manages to take care of me," I said.

"What am I saying. I forgot for a moment who you are."

"Don't worry, we're off duty at the moment," I said.

"Oh, good, I'm glad about that. So you'll be restricting any violence to one another then? It's just that it can be off-putting for the other customers."

"Don't look at me," I said. "It's her you need to worry about."

"See. No gentleman," Sam said.

"I know. Did I say that if you ever want, how shall I say, a little more sophistication, I'm entirely at your service?"

"That's very sweet of you, Robbie, but he seems to be able to handle me. Don't you, Si?" She took my hand and looked at me in a rather nice way.

"I'm doing my best," I said, feeling a little self-conscious.

"Oh, my goodness. I think I'd better leave you two alone."

"Don't go, I'm enjoying this," Sam said.

"I must go and do some work in any case, but I will come and find you later if I may? There was something…"

"What's up?" I said.

"Later will do. I'll send you a waiter."

"Food. Yes please," Sam said.

We ate and talked of this and that, ourselves mainly, but also the sea and the Rif and the desert beyond. She was interested in the desert. Over coffee we became quiet and then she said, "Si, you look almost sad."

"I didn't realise."

"What is it?"

"I don't know. It's all beautiful but it passes. Do you know what I mean?"

"Not really."

"Me neither. Perhaps I need a holiday."

"From this? I feel like I'm on holiday right now."

"You're a remarkable girl. I know you've enjoyed the last few days but it's not always like this. We'll just be hanging about for a while now. There's going to be too much moonlight to make any deliveries and the stocks are high, so no need for any trips into the mountains. I think I'll take Nottambulo off for a trip. Would you like to come with me?"

"If you put it like that, yes definitely. Where?"

"What about Corsica to start with and then Sicily, perhaps visit Capri or head up to the Riviera? We could see how we go and just do what we feel. What do you think?"

"Si, that sounds wonderful. When?"

"Why not tomorrow?"

"Okay."

"Shall we go home? Now I've decided, I fancy an early start tomorrow."

"So just sleep then?"

"I didn't say that."

"Back in a minute, I just need the loo." She picked up her small evening bag and sauntered off.

Robbie materialised and sat down. "What did you do to deserve that? That's what I want to know," he said.

"You mean Sam?"

"Of course I mean Sam."

"I don't know; could have been because I was good, or bad. I change my mind on a daily basis. Robbie…"

"What?"

"You're a clam aren't you?"

"I am known for a certain discretion, yes. Are you about to confide your intentions towards that lovely young woman to me?"

"No, but there's a policeman on my tail and possibly some other people too. I think it's time for me to light out while I still can. I'm off tomorrow."

"Bloody hell, Si. I had no idea."

"Hopefully no one else has either. I'll keep in touch with Ali and Asif and you. If it all goes away, I'll be back. If not, not. Sam's coming with me, at least for a bit. She thinks it's just a trip, and maybe it is, so don't say anything to her about it."

"Okay. Look after yourself." He gave me his hand.

"I'll do my best. Try not to get killed by any jealous husbands, won't you."

"Ah, you exaggerate my powers of seduction."

Sam appeared from the hotel. I noticed that we weren't the only ones watching her. Some of the diners on the other tables were too.

"You had something you wanted to say?" I said.

"Oh, nothing. It can wait until I see you again another day."

"Sure?"

"Sure. Go and enjoy the rest of your evening."

He saw us to the door and watched us drive away; perhaps he was feeling the same way about the passing of things as I was.

"He's quite fond of you, isn't he?" Sam said, on the way back.

"He's not a man who has many friends. A thousand acquaintances, but few friends. Bit like me, I suppose."

At Azooz's yard I locked the Hilux and put the key in my pocket. If it was in the way, it was. I planned to be up and about quite early anyway. Sam put her arm around my waist as we walked the short distance to the flat. The streets were quiet. We let ourselves in and went straight to bed. Soumaiya must have heard us but didn't look out of her room.

I think it all must have been creeping up on me a little, as I slept longer than I intended. When I woke I was alone in the big bed but Sam's .32 was on the chest of drawers and I could hear the shower running. The cat came in, jumped up and started kneading my chest. Her eyes were unfocused and she appeared to be going into a trance. I stroked her a bit but she didn't seem to want that, I think it was interrupting her kneading, so I stopped and let her carry on.

Soumy looked in and, seeing that I was awake, came in looking conspiratorial.

"Good morning, Simon. Would you like some coffee?" she said in a whisper.

"Yes please, Soumy. What about the cat?"

"What about the cat?"

"Who will feed her?"

"She will feed herself; she's a cat." She went again.

"Well then, old thing," I said to the cat, "there it is. You're a tough old thing, aren't you?"

"Are you talking to the cat?" Sam said, coming in with a towel wrapped around her.

"I am," I said. The cat jumped off me and left the room.

"Why do people do that?"

"What? Talk to cats?"

"And dogs and horses."

"Have you never had a pet?"

"I prefer people. Come on sleepy, wake up. Aren't we going on holiday then?" She sat on me and put her fingers in my hair and rubbed my head. It was nice. I reached out to pull her down to me but she said, "Ah, ah, no you don't." and pulled away. I got the towel but she got away, laughing and doing a pirouette on her toes. She started dressing and Soumy knocked gently on the doorframe and brought a tray of coffee in and put it on the low table by the bed. She kept her eyes down and left silently.

I sat up, had a big yawn and a stretch and poured two cups of coffee. The motes of dust were dancing in the sunlight again. When Sam moved through them they disappeared in the shadow she cast and then reappeared, swirling about. I started thinking about what I should take and what I should leave.

"I need to get some things from the house," Sam said. She was pulling clothes out of the wardrobe, looking at them and either putting them back or into a holdall on the bed. "I've nothing to wear to swim in and I suppose we might go out in the evening, mightn't we?"

"I suppose we might. Let's go up to the house first, see the old man, then come back here. I'll grab a few things, and we'll go. I think I'll leave the truck with Asif."

"Whatever. If you ever get out of bed."

"Okay, okay." I refilled my cup and took it with me to the bathroom.

Sam was eating toast and marmalade on the balcony when I came out. I made a sandwich of two pieces, with a thick layer of marmalade in between, and took it with me and we went.

We called in at the store on the way. I was pleased that Romeo didn't recognise the Hilux. He sat on his plastic chair with an AK leaning on the wall behind him, staring insolently until I got out and he realised who it was. I made him precede me inside and show me the clipboard with the tally of the last few days' sales, and then sent him back out while I took most of the money out of the safe and dumped it into an old carrier bag. He stood about indecisively, holding the battered old assault rifle, wanting to sit down but not daring to, while I got back into the car, backed round and drove off. He wasn't a problem but I couldn't like the fellow.

"That chap doesn't like you," Sam said.

"I can live with it," I said.

"Yes, but can he?"

"That's another question altogether."

Up at the house I put my pickup next to the one that Happy usually drove and we walked through to the pool. Sure enough the big Nigerian was on a lounger looking massive. Zara was on the one next to his, and even from where I was, I could tell that she was flirting with him outrageously, but that his eyes were on the girl by my side.

"Hello, my boy, hello daughter. Come and join me. Tea, coffee?" Guy was clearly in excellent spirits. He had the papers spread before him as usual and a pot of coffee.

"I called by the store," I said, putting the carrier bag of money down on the table.

"Thanks," he peered inside and then folded the bag over itself and put it to one side. "How're you feeling? Everything all right?"

I looked at him with curiosity. "How'm I feeling?"

"Yes."

"Pretty good. I'd say, I'm feeling pretty good." I sat down and Sam put her bum on the arm of the chair I was in and waved a hand at the boy. "More coffee," she said to him.

"Good. That's what I like to hear," Guy said.

"How are you feeling?" I said.

"How'm I feeling?" he said.

"Yes, how're you feeling," I said.

"Good," he said. "I'm feeling great, actually."

"Good."

"What the fuck are you two on about?" Sam said.

"I don't know," I said. "He asked me how I'm feeling."

"Why shouldn't he?"

"He never has before. Anyway, he's a bloke and I'm a bloke and we don't generally do that."

"Haven't I? I must have," Guy said.

"Not that I recall," I said.

"Well I should have."

"So why are you feeling so good?" I said.

"That's a very good question," Guy said. "I'm glad you asked me that."

I waited. He gathered his thoughts and enumerating the points on his fingers, said, "My lovely daughter, Sam. You know Sam?"

"I know Sam," I said. She put a hand on my arm and squeezed it.

"He knows me," she said.

"Well, yes, my lovely daughter Sam, is happy."

"I am," she said.

"And she's found a vocation as part of my business." He waved a hand airily to indicate his business empire.

"You mean, she likes driving my boat?" I said.

"I do mean that, and the rest of it," he said.

"And the rest of it," Sam said, grinning.

"And that makes me happy."

"I can see it might help," I said.

"And I'm thinking about retiring," he said.

"Seriously?" I said.

"Yes, seriously."

"Will we notice the difference?" I said.

"What do you mean? You think all I do is sit here all day?"

"Well…" I shrugged. "That's what you look like you do."

"You'd be surprised, my boy."

"I *am* surprised. I thought you'd do this for ever. Didn't you say something like that last night?"

"I may have, but we can't do this for ever you know. You do know that, don't you?"

"Well, I never planned to. You know that. I told you so at the beginning."

"So you did, so you did."

"I don't think I'll do more than one more year. That should set me up, I should think, don't you?"

"I should think it would. Especially when you hear what I'm about to tell you."

"What's that then?"

"You, who think I just sit here while you do all the work, don't know this, but I've just done the biggest deal of my life. I'm going to be rich and so are you, my boy."

"I didn't think you were poor."

"I mean really rich. Rich enough to have trouble spending it all. Rich enough to retire. I might even return to the ranks of the respectable and buy a place in the old country. Get a Rolls and go to the old school reunion dinners. That could be fun. I could even take her." He nodded towards where Zara was doing her best to interest Happy in her body. "Maybe not, though I'm not sure she'll travel well."

"You don't think they might give you a retirement home with thick walls, lots of steel bars and no kind of view?" I said.

"Ah, you can always get round that kind of thing. A little money to spread about, dig out the old school tie. Your old man would help."

"I doubt that."

"He would you know. He's a very loyal chap, deep down. And I have been looking after his son and heir."

"Yeah, right. And all this is going to come about, how?"

"Drugs, my boy, drugs. Real ones, I mean. Charlie and horse, and lots of it."

"But…?"

"No buts, my boy. It's all sorted. The H is coming from the fields of Afghanistan and Pakistan across the Arabian sea to Somalia, heading up into Ethiopia where it joins the sub-Saharan route to Timbuktu. The Charlie, which, by the way, is mostly Venezuelan not Colombian, crosses to Nigeria by regular cargo vessel and travels up to meet it. From there it goes by four by four, up through the desert and we're going to meet it somewhere down in that big empty bit south of the N107 and bring it back."

"How much of it? How much horse and how much charlie?"

"Probably more H than C to start with, but we'll see. Quite a bit all told. We're going to start with a couple of hundred kilos of each and go on up from there. Got to consider the cash-flow implications; can't go for the tonne without we build up to it."

"A tonne of the stuff?"

"That's the plan. See what I mean about enough money to retire on?"

"This is because of me and my boat, isn't it?"

"Spot, indeed, on, my boy. It certainly is. You can't go messing about with that much money if it might end up in the wrong hands. You'll get it there, I know you will."

"How long have you been planning this?"

"Since a month or so after you turned up."

"I see."

"Thing is, way I see it, if we get caught with a tonne of kif we're well in the shit, yes?"

"Yes."

"Same goes for the hard stuff, but the payoff is that much greater. In effect the risk is less because you don't have to do nearly so many trips to make the same money. See what I mean?"

"Yes, except that, relatively speaking, no one minds so much about a bit of hash, so the effort to catch us isn't that high. Also, the competition is fierce enough for the trade as it is. There are people about who would send small armies to get hold of what you're talking about."

"I know, I know. So we quietly do a few and then quietly disappear. No one will know that we're doing anything other than what we always do."

"Except of course when it hits the streets the other end."

"By the time any English copper has the chance to track it back this far I intend to be long gone. Not that they can touch me here. Or you for that matter."

"It's not extradition I'm worried about. They might just send some lads to quietly put us away. Save on the paperwork. And unlike those Spanish fuckwits, they probably wouldn't miss."

"You've been reading too much literature again, it's overheated your brain. Even if they do do such things, which I doubt, imagine the trouble they'd be in if it went wrong. British special forces caught killing British subjects without due process on foreign soil, where they're not welcome. What civil servant or politician is ever going to risk his career authorising that one for the sake of a few drugs that are going to get into the country one way or the other anyway? You don't know the official mind like I do, my boy. I do take your point about the competition though."

"I can't imagine you could keep a secret like that round here for long," I said.

"You say that, but apart from the man who's bringing it up from Timbuktu the only people who know you're about to go and fetch it are me, and now you."

"What do you mean, about to go and fetch it?"

"Just what I say, Si. You can finish your coffee first."

10

MIND THAT GOAT

"That's brilliant. You mean out in the desert? Today? Right out into the Sahara?" Sam said.

"Not you, sweetheart," Guy said.

"Supposing I say no?" I said. "I didn't sign up for that."

"You won't," Guy said.

"Why won't I?"

"Because, now I've told you, you have to go. You don't need me to spell out the alternative. Also, by the way, you did sign up for this. Maybe not this specifically but it was always a package deal. You don't get to pick and choose which bits suit you, any more than I do."

"What do you mean, not me? Why not?" Sam said.

"Don't," Guy said, looking at Sam in a way that I'd not seen before. "I don't have time for one of your things right now. Go and have a shower, or something. I need to talk to Simon."

"I see," she said with a controlled, flat sounding voice. She got off the arm of my chair and went swiftly inside.

"So what's the deal?" I said, when she had gone.

"For you, you mean?"

"Yes."

"I'm not messing about: same as it is now. Same straight percentage of everything delivered to Canaillas."

"Okay," I said. That would be a lot of money. A really big lot of money.

"Good."

"Why me to fetch it in from the desert? Who else and why not Sam? Why me, not you?"

"A number of reasons. This isn't going to be for cash. Cash is just a pain in the arse, too bulky, where would we get it, all of that. I'm going to be here with a sat-phone, you're out there with a sat-phone. If you're happy, I send the money, they get a call and hand it over and you bring it back. There's not much trust built up yet, so this time we're doing a relatively small load and you're taking cash as a backup. If there's a problem with communications or whatever, you're to make the deal anyway and bring the stuff back. I can't wire money about from the desert, can I?"

"I'm sure Zara would do it for you," I said.

"Yeah, right."

"Why can't Sam come? She's bloody useful. I'd rather have her than any of the others, and now she's going to be so pissed off I'm not sure you'll be alive when I get back."

"Hah, you have a point. I've an old friend coming for supper and I want her to play hostess."

"And that's more important than this?"

"No. To be frank, she's the only leverage anyone can have over me. She stays here, just in case. If it goes okay, then next time we'll see."

"In case of what? If this is as much a secret as you say, then there shouldn't be any danger, apart from sun-stroke."

"I'm sure you're right, my boy. You'll just have to put it down to a father's weakness for his daughter."

"So I'm going out with, what? The big Toyota and a big bag of 500s?"

"Basically, yes. You can take Happy and Karim and whatever selection of toys you can find in my little arsenal."

"And if there's a problem?"

"Then I'm sure you'll handle it, my boy. You always do."

"Bloody hell."

"Quite."

"So when does all this start?"

"Why, now of course. Why don't you go and sort out the truck. I know you'll want to faff about with it before you go. I'll sort out the comms gear and maps and brief you when you're ready."

"Fuck."

I did, as he put it, faff about with the big Toyota Land Cruiser for an hour or so. It was like preparing Nottambulo for a trip; I needed to know that we were ready and that we had everything that I thought we would need, and that I knew where it was and could lay my hands on it immediately if I wanted it. I'll wing it if I have to, but if I have a chance to be prepared, that's how I prefer it.

I checked all her vital fluids, checked her tyres and her batteries, checked her jack, tyre iron, checked that her wheel nuts were all there and done up tight. The desert can be hard on vehicles, even ones designed for it, like this one. I filled jerry cans with fuel and plastic cans with water, added rope and a shovel and then turned my attention to arms.

Guy has an arsenal that makes mine look thoroughly amateur- ish. Three AKs went in, checked, loaded, spare magazines and two boxes of shells. I took the MAG 60 general purpose maching gun with a couple of belts, just in case. With the extra fuel it all added up to quite a bit of weight but that couldn't be helped. I packed them in the boot wrapped in the mats and blankets that would serve us for bedding.

Some biltong, some chocolate, coffee and a coffee pot, frying pan, a cold-box with a few steaks, an onion and a few beers for the crew, day and night, glasses. That was about it.

Sam came out of the house, wearing a pretty pink top and tight jeans, swinging a bag. I thought she would be furious but she said she was going shopping, kissed me good luck and departed in the little Mercedes roadster with a squeal of tyres.

I joined Guy at the table for a beer and a briefing. He and I looked at maps and debated the merits of this or that route. We checked and marked grid references, played with the sat-phone and GPS receivers and then it was time to go.

"Where's that girl?" Guy said, standing up and looking about.

"Went shopping," I said.

"Really?"

"That's what she said," I said.

"Oh."

"Good. Right, we're gone. I'll phone tomorrow. You ready, Happy?"

"Coming, boss." The big man leapt easily off the lounger and loped over to us.

"You've forgotten something," Guy said.

"What?"

"This." He pulled a holdall out from under the table.

"Oh yes, the money."

"Oh, and by the way, don't worry about your boat while you're away. I've put some extra men on to help Asif look after her, just in case."

"Thanks. Just in case I take that bag and bugger off, you mean."

"I didn't say that."

"No, I did."

We made it down the hill, picked Karim up at the store and took the back roads round the town to join the big road heading south.

There was a bit of traffic madness, as usual, where the road meets the town and we formed a line with the usual pickups, battered cars of all kinds and heavily overloaded lorries, most with endlessly patient passengers riding on top of the load. It's by far the worst bit of road around Nador but if you want to go south you can't avoid it. The heat and the dust and the smell caused me to shut the windows and put the air-con on. Boys darted about, risking death and abuse to sell hot lamb meloui, sticky khringos, cold cans of drink, pre-rolled spliffs, paper cups of mint tea and all kinds of other things. Some of them crowded round the truck and tapped politely on the windows but we ignored them and they moved on.

I was idly watching a man trying to cross the road with two reluctant goats on bits of string when another figure caught my attention. It was Sam in khaki trousers and top, with her hair tied back walking down the line with her usual unconcern for the effect she was having on the rest of the world. The car in front of us stopped to have a look at her and I nearly bumped into it.

She saw us and smiled and waved. Happy jumped out of the front seat, grinning and calling out "Oya, Oya," and scrambled into the back to make room for her. She stepped onto the running board and swung herself in as I moved off. "Mind if I tag along?" she said.

"Glad to have you," I said. "Didn't fancy an evening at home then?"

"Fuck that."

We made it out of the mess and I put my foot down. There was a lot of hard driving ahead and I wanted to break the back of it before dark. The road, like a lot of African roads, wasn't wide enough for two carriageways but had a wide fringe of gravel surface on each side onto which we moved when anything was coming the other way. The big lorries only give way to bigger lorries and overtaking requires nerve and concentration.

I fought the big truck down the road, doing my share of intimidation. It wasn't unlike taking Nottambulo out in a bit of a sea.

Sam tuned the radio to a local station and drummed along to the beat of the music against the dashboard, making occasional remarks about this and that. Happy and Karim were talking about the merits and demerits of women they had known, in the back. The dust rose higher around us as we went south and the mountains dropped behind us and the desert began. The windscreen was splattered with a million dead flies and griffon vultures worked away at the occa- sional roadkill, without paying us even the compliment of a look as we passed.

We filled up at the last place before we would turn off. The atten- dant peered into the top of the filler well, pouring every last drop that he could into the tank. I could see that he was disapp- ointed that it wasn't more. Sam bought some pasties from a vendor beside the road and gave the man a strong mouthful of French when he tried to overcharge her.

When we passed the east-west highway a lot of the traffic dropped away and there were long stretches of road with nothing on it. Ahead, the bulky forms of lorries would appear, often in convoy, and grow until we passed them wide and fast, the gravel battering at the underside of the truck. This was easier driving, in spite of the sometimes dangerously deep potholes, and I got Karim to dig me out a beer to wet my dry throat.

We turned off the road about twenty miles north of the border and took a well used track that was practically an alternate highway. The official border crossing itself is no real problem, but the lazy, self- important border guards demand a toll for letting one through un-molested and there is always the chance that they will prefer to keep a particularly desirable toy rather than accept the requisite bribe. The MAG 60 would be a great temptation if they were to set eyes on it. Anyway, I dislike corruption.

There was a plume of dust on the track ahead of us, coming our way. I moved aside on a bend to let a pickup with trussed up goats in the back pass. The old man driving and his son on the passenger seat looked at us warily. I smiled and called out, "Men fathlek, men fathlek," and waved my hand at him to slow down.

He did and I asked him how the road was. Good, he said, but the local mochadem's men were out. Where? About ten kilo- metres. He looked unhappy about it and said that it had cost him a goat. One whole goat. I thanked him and on we went. We were passing through the last of the foothills of the Rif now and soon the land would open out into the plain that was the beginning of the Sahara.

I took us into a clearing below some sandy yellow cliffs, out of sight of the road, so that we could empty our bladders and make preparations. From here we would be going on on a desert footing. We were beyond the law and there were predators out there.

We dug hardware out of the boot. Sam and Karim took AKs. I gave the MAG 60 to Happy, which made him smile. Actually it was the more recent L7A2 version. Being belt-fed, it should be oper- ated by two but Happy would manage at a push. We were unlikely to need a long period of sustained fire, whatever happened.

"Right, gather round and listen up," I said. "Up ahead there's a few local toughs who will demand toll for the road. I'm going to give them a few dollars to save their faces. When we stop, you three step out wide and make them feel that any kind of nonsense would be unwise. Sam, I want to arrive where we're going with full maga- zines so don't shoot anyone unless you have to. And we may want to come back this way so let's not create a problem. Understood?"

"As if I would."

"Right. If you have to, take the man in your line. Happy, left, Sam middle, Karim right. Happy, if you have to, you start on the left and sweep right, so stand open that way. When I say, take the running boards, guns level, keep your eyes on them until we're out of shot. I'll drive us through. Okay?"

"Okay, boss," they said.

"Where are we going by the way?" Happy said.

"Good question," Karim said.

"I'll tell you all about it later. C'mon let's go." Sure enough, round the last sharp bend, where the hills finally ran out, there was a log across the road. Three men and a goat stood by it, looking at us with appraising eyes. Each one held the ubiquitous AK. Though not the goat. They seemed pleased to see us. Too late I saw a pickup pull out from the cover of a clump of camel thorns behind us.

"Fuck it, I've changed my mind," I said. "Mind the goat. Ready?"

"You bet," Sam said.

"I'm going right," I said, spinning the wheel and putting my foot down.

The firing started as soon as Sam and Happy could bring their guns to bear. First, controlled bursts of four from Sam and almost immediately the belly shaking roar from the machine gun. They barely got to raise their aim towards us before we had cut them to pieces. Behind us the man in the pickup got back in and raced away. He could go.

I eased off the throttle before we accelerated into something hard and passed the end of the log with inches to spare. The plastic table that had been at that end of it was pushed along in front of us for a few feet and then went under us with a nasty sound of breaking plastic.

"Did you miss the goat? I didn't see?" I said.

"Yes, we missed the goat," Sam said.

"Well done. That should be it now, but reload will you."

"Yes, boss."

The empty landscape stretched away into the far distance without even any rising dust to indicate moving people. A small herd of camels plodded their stately way from one place to another for their own reasons. Down there somewhere was the border, but the border was a line on the map, no more than that. There was a track for a while and then it diffused into many or none, as the multitudes who had come before us had each tried to take a different way from those before them. I took a compass heading away to the west of south; it would take us even further from the highways and towards our eventual destination.

The land was not as featureless as it had seemed from the foothills. There were subtle contours and undulations, and here and there groups of camel thorn made a precarious living. For the most part the surface was remarkably even and easy to drive on, but occasionally soft patches of sand gave an intimation of the seas of sand to come. I was always wary for hidden boulders; a broken wishbone or smashed wheel now would be a complete bugger.

"What're we doing tonight?" Sam said.

"There's a hotel just over there," I said, pointing.

"Really?"

"No. We've got sleeping mats and blankets. I'm not sure what you're going to do."

"Perhaps I could share with someone?"

"Just make sure it's me or there'll be more shooting," I said.

"How romantic. A night under the stars."

"Is that the sat-phone I can hear?" I said. It was. Karim dug it out of the bag and passed it over. I pulled up so that I could give it my full attention. It was Guy and he didn't sound happy.

"Have you got my daughter?" he said.

"Hi. We're fine by the way, making good progress. I'll pass you over." I gave the phone to Sam. She took it and listened for a moment, her face looking surprised, then amused and finally angry.

"Boy is he pissed off. He wants to speak to you." She passed it back.

"Hi, what's up?" I said.

"I just got word that the local mochadem has a toll up on the road. I think you should cut out further and go round."

"Not any more he hasn't."

"You're that far south?"

"Not far from the border now."

"Okay, well, take good care won't you. Keep a guard posted at all times."

"Should be only desert from now on. Don't suppose the dassies will bother us much. Don't worry, we'll be fine."

"Okay, phone me tomorrow."

"Will do." I hung up and turned it off.

"Wonder what's eating him?" Sam said.

"Worrying about you getting hurt, I suppose. We'll take a lot of care at the meeting tomorrow."

"But you would anyway."

"But I would anyway. That," I pointed to the bag of money at her feet, "isn't worth getting that het up over. Not if what he's talking about is real anyway."

"I'm sure it is."

"I am pretty sure too."

I drove on, searching the landscape for what I wanted. The sun was getting low over to our right and daylight wouldn't last much longer. There was a group of thorn trees against the dunes to our right that would probably provide some fuel so I headed over to them. It was a nice spot and had the remains of a fire to indicate that others had thought so too. I parked the truck and we got out. The light was already becoming soft and orange. It would be a lovely evening and a clear, starlight night. I told the others to make camp and squatted down to light the fire myself.

Happy fetched a good pile of fire-wood and threw it down in the dust beside me. I pulled a few rocks into a rough circle and nursed a lit match into some dry grass until the smoke was coming thick and strong. The twigs and thin bits that I added caught the flames and passed them about. I put on some split bits of bigger wood and the heart of the fire began to build. I opened a beer and brushed a bit of the ground smooth to sit on.

The acacia grow slowly and their wood is dense and dry and burns like hell. Soon we had a good fire with heat and light and a good crackle and roar. If you think you know what a fire really is, go and light one in the desert, then you'll know.

The others began to gather round and find a place for themselves. The flames reflected on their faces and the darkness beyond deepened. They exchanged gruff comments and friendly insults to keep the intimacy of the situation at bay.

Sam came and leant against me and took my beer from me.

"You cooking then, Karim?" I said.

"That's woman's work," he said, grinning.

"Fuck you, raghead," Sam said, throwing a rock at him.

He ducked, laughing, and went to the truck to get the supper things moving.

"Give me back my beer," I said.

"Happy, will you get me some beer please," she said.

The big man sighed and got up and fetched her and me a new bottle each.

"Thank you, Happy."

"You're welcome, Sam," he said.

"Mind the fire, will you," I said to Sam.

"Where are you going?"

"I'm just going to check the communication equipment and the maps and a few other things."

"You can be a bit OCD sometimes, you know?"

"I know."

"You'll be checking the truck next. You know, those things go on for ever. And then you'll clean and re-load your gun, again."

"Now that you mention it, that's a good idea; the truck I mean."

I put a head torch on so that I could see and lifted the bonnet. The oil was fine, black and shiny. The gearbox oil looked good too. I crawled about underneath her to make sure that everything was straight and no leaks had developed. By this time she had cooled enough for me to get the top off the reservoir. She'd used a little water but that was only to be expected. I topped her up and fiddled about a bit under there and shut the lid. It was all more or less as it should be but not quite.

"Well?" Sam said, when I rejoined the others.

"Truck's fine," I said.

"Told you," she said.

Karim served us up steak onion sandwiches, which were truly delicious. We sat, enjoying the warmth of the fire on our faces as the air cooled. Above us the sky was filled with so many stars that they were like grains of sand on a beach. A night bird flew softly over us, invisible in the dark. The truck ticked as the metal cooled. Apart from the stars above, our world was shrunk only to the pool of firelight. The desert was an unknown thing, out there beyond our small circle of human comfort.

Now and then one of us would push the end of a burning log into the fire with a boot or raise their beer to drink, but apart from that we were immobile, captivated by the flames. It wasn't late by the clock but it was natural to think about sleep now.

"I'll take the first watch," I said. "After that you, Happy. After that you, Karim. Then you, Sam. Two hours each. Make your beds this side of the fire and if you take your boots off, shake them out before you put your feet in again. We don't have any anti-serum for scorpions so we'll just leave you here to die. Okay?"

"Yes, boss."

"Good. Keep the fire up for a bit will you."

"Won't it be visible from a long way off?" Sam said.

"Yes, but that's okay," I said.

I put on a jacket for warmth, hung the night vision glasses round my neck and walked softly back from the fire into the gully between two dunes. As soon as the fire was out of sight round the bend, I was out of its influence and into the desert. My night vision began to improve and I could see to walk from the starlight. The gully ran out so I scrambled up the face of the dune and over the top. I descended a bit so that I would be below the top of it and headed in the direction of the way we had come. It was hard going but eventually I got in a position where I could see a good few miles back the way we had come from the top of a dune. I dug myself down into the sand and pushed the glasses forward; like that I could see but should be impossible to be seen myself.

The only interesting thing that the intensified image showed me was a desert fox stalking a family of dassies, the rock hyrax; an animal a bit like a rabbit, that were living in some rocks not far off. They sensed his presence and stood up on their back legs looking at him. I could almost see him shrug his shoulders, say, 'oh, fuck it,' and walk off. He came across what I guessed was a scorpion instead, as he danced gingerly around it and then bit it and tossed it in the air. He must have decided it was harmless now as I saw him crunching it up with a part of it dangling from one side of his mouth.

All that was entertaining, but beside the point. The desert was quiet and empty of humans and I could go and get some rest. I sat up and yawned and stretched. It had been a busy few days and a long day today and I was close to sleep.

I think I must have heard something, though it should've been too far to do so, as I put the glasses on the track where it issued from the hills. Whatever, what I saw made me lie back down and pay attention. Two four by fours drove slowly out of the cover of the hills with their lights off. Although I studied them intently I couldn't make out anything within them but I could see that they were newish and had spare tyres and fuel cans strapped to their roof racks. They also had the long whip antennae that usually go with short-wave radio communications. They carried on advancing slowly towards us down the track and then pulled up.

I folded my glasses, packed them into a pocket and started running. The soft sand was energy sapping. It kept sliding away from under my feet so that I had no grip. Even so, I'm sure I got back to camp a deal faster than I came out. The fire had burned down to embers and my crew were dark humps near it.

I put more wood on the fire and began speaking to them softly. I knelt beside Happy and carefully put a hand on his shoulder and said his name. Like dogs, it's best to be careful when waking fighting men suddenly. He stirred and opened an eye.

"Trouble," I said, and left him.

Sam was looking at me with both eyes open. "Get up, we have to leave now," I said.

Karim was awake now too. "Get up quietly and move back. Keep behind the fire," I said. I moved back myself so that they could join me by the truck.

"There are men out there with night sights. The light from the fire will blind them until it dies down so we are okay for the moment. Take an AK and spare magazines from the truck. Do not shut the doors. Karim, you take one for me too. Happy, you take the MAG 60. Sam, you take the money. I'm going to get maps and comms. Whatever you do, don't let any metal touch any other; the sound will carry. Go now."

They did as I instructed, moving silently round the vehicle taking what we needed. I groped about in the front, collecting maps, the phone and its charger, my day glasses and a bottle of water just in case. There was no talking and they were quick. We all understood that our lives were in the balance.

I took an AK from Karim, settled it as comfortably as possible over my shoulder and then led them back into the dunes, further than I had gone in. It was quite possible that the men coming, and I was sure that they were coming, would use the cover of the dunes too. We were leaving tracks in the sand but that couldn't be helped. The dunes ran in parallel ridges, not unlike the patterns you find on a beach, so we traversed back towards my view point, one row back as it were. At least our movement was almost silent on the soft sand. I led them as fast as I was able and soon we were all blowing a bit.

When I guessed that we were approaching the place, I gestured them to spread out and lie down and climbed to the top to have a look. The dunes rise as they progress into the pack so the one I was on now was slightly higher than the one I had been on earlier. Through the night glasses I could see the faint tracks that I had made before, but no others. I couldn't see any signs of watchers or movement either. Unfortunately the dune in front of me blocked off the view of the two vehicles, assuming they were still there.

I waved them up to join me, spread them out along the ridge so that they could give covering fire if necessary and plunged down the slope. No one shot at me. I scrambled up to the top and carefully looked over.

The two trucks were where they had been, and a man was sitting idly on the bonnet of one, holding a can of something and having a smoke, the cigarette cupped behind his hand to shield the glow. He lifted his glasses and looked down the track towards our camp. I followed his line of sight and initially didn't see anything. Then a flicker of movement caught my eye and something very interesting was revealed to me. A six man team in desert camouflage was advancing very professionally across the ground. They were all spread out, two would move up one hundred yards or so and then kneel, guns ready. The next two would move up, overlapping them by fifty yards and then the next two would do the same. At any one time, four men were covering the two moving and they all had a good field of fire. They wore helmets, no doubt had short-wave comms and night vision. It was good, but that they hadn't bothered to use the cover provided by the dunes indicated a lot of confidence.

I waved the others up and made them pass the glasses about and look, so that they all knew what was what. They each in turn looked at me with wide eyes as they saw what was approaching the place where we had been sleeping. I took the glasses back and had a better look at the vehicles. The man on guard had got into the front of the lead vehicle and appeared to be having a nap. All to the good.

I slid down behind the dune and beckoned the others to join me.

"What the fuck?" Happy said.

"I second that," Sam said.

"There's a magnetic tracker under our truck," I said.

"You didn't say," Sam said.

"How come?" Karim said.

"Don't know. My first thought was that Guy had put it there, but I'm sure it wasn't there when we left. My guess is that someone stuck it on in the traffic as we left Nador, but that's only a guess. I've no idea who."

"How come you found it?" Happy said.

"Because I looked. I often look for things like that."

"I take it all back, you carry right on being OCD as much as you like," Sam said. "What next?"

"Yes, what next?" Happy said.

"I've been thinking about that. I think we borrow one of their vehicles and leave."

"Sounds sensible," Sam said.

"Hope you're feeling fit, we don't have long before they get to our camp, find we're gone and start coming back. We need to get there before that happens, as one of the first things they will do is alert that idiot they've left on guard."

"Tell us what to do," Sam said.

"You two," I pointed to Sam and Karim, "run, and I mean run, round to the back of their trucks in the dunes. Approach from the back but on this side. That will give you a clear shot. Happy and I will watch the boys move down the track and when they're near the camp we'll walk out to meet you. When you get a shot, take it. We'll take one and disable the other and leave immediately. Okay?"

"Round the back, approach in his blind spot, shoot him. Got it," Sam said.

"Sam, you take the shot. Karim, you back her up if she misses. You can leave that bag with us."

"I won't miss."

"I know. Now go."

"Yes, boss." They went. Sam slipped and slid down the sand and set off at a run along the bottom. Karim followed as fast as he could.

"It's almost like you knew they were there," Happy said.

"I had an idea they would be when I saw that tracker."

"Why didn't you just leave it in the sand and carry on?"

"I'm not sure. I think I wanted to see what it was all about."

"You're as mad as that woman."

"Is she mad?"

"She's definitely mad."

We returned to the top of the dune and carefully had a look at the situation. The assault team approaching our camp was almost out of sight and if I hadn't known they were there I wouldn't have seen them. The guard in the truck was still resting in the driver's seat. I couldn't remember if I'd seen body-armour on him or not.

"Come on then, let's go and do this."

"Right behind you, boss."

We rolled over the top and slid gently down the face of the dune to the bottom. I led the way carefully out into the open towards the vehicles. The starlight was enough to be able to walk without tripping over rocks or stumbling on the uneven ground. If they had posted an observer somewhere, then we could expect bullets in the back any time now.

About half way I held up a hand to halt us and studied the terrain to the rear of the vehicles. Sure enough, two figures were approach- ing from about the same distance as us. They must have made good time. We moved steadily onwards.

The guard was so secure in his understanding of what was what that we got within fifty yards of him before he noticed us. We stood perfectly still and I watched him through the night glasses. In the darkness he couldn't tell what we were or whether he had imagined us, or what. His own glasses were still on the bonnet of the truck so he picked up an assault rifle and stepped out of the vehicle so that he could use the sight on that. Two figures rose from the ground behind the second vehicle and separated so that they both had a clear shot. I gave him a friendly little wave.

There was just long enough for me to see the confused look on his face before a single, shockingly loud, shot smashed the still-ness. His head twitched sideways as if he had been slapped and he crumpled to the ground. We covered the rest of the ground at a trot and so did Sam and Karim.

Her bullet had taken him in the side of the head, an inch below his helmet. It was only the helmet that was keeping what remained of his head together. He was wearing body armour.

"Good shot," I said.

"Thanks," Sam said, joining me.

"Oya," Happy said, grinning with pride.

"I've changed my mind. If we can find the keys we'll take both of these. Happy, look in that one." I pointed to the second truck.

"In the ignition, boss."

"Good, same here. You're with me, Sam. Happy, Karim, you in the other. Let's go."

I took the dead man's gun and put it in the back with the money and the maps and so on, climbed in and turned the key. The engine fired. Sam was in the passenger side so I put it in drive and got it moving. Behind us the other vehicle pulled away too.

I kept us on the track and we raced towards our camp and the men who must be there by now. As we came near to being within range of their guns I turned the headlights on full and turned out into the desert. The lights showed us ground that was thankfully quite flat and free from larger rocks and camel thorn. We flew along, weaving a bit to avoid obstacles. Behind us the lights of the other vehicle danced about. As far as I could remember the land stretched away like this for miles and miles. If I was wrong, life might get a bit tricky again, just for a change.

"Yeeessssss, Go Si," Sam shouted, grinning from ear to ear.

"Having fun?"

"Damn right."

"I'm glad you came," I said, and that was true for more than one reason.

"Me too. Will they come after us? I can't see past the others." She was looking back at the way we had come.

"Shouldn't think so. I've got the main relay to our truck in my bag."

"You tricky bastard. How come you've been so cute on this?"

"You want to know why?"

"Yes, I do."

"I'll tell you. The reason we're alive now is that I didn't like the way your old man sounded when he found out you were with us."

11

AFTERNOON TEA

The moon came up and Sam took over the driving while I studied the map, the GPS, the compass and of course, the stars. What I could see of them; the moon was getting bigger now and as it climbed the sky, it dominated it. At least it made the driving easier. It was so empty here that it was like navigating at sea. We crossed the border at about midnight and pushed on deeper and deeper into the emptiness of the Northern Sahara. The camel thorns ran out and the land became either more sand or less sand. At about four in the morning the fuel gauge was low and it was all sand and we were less than ten miles from the rendezvous. I was tired.

I called a halt and got out of the truck. I was stiff and the air was cold. I stretched out my limbs and shook myself. I sniffed the dry, still air and listened. Nothing. The others joined me, looking weary and bleary and less than fresh.

"Some sleep, I think. Karim, you're on watch. Okay?"

"Yes, boss."

"If anything gets close to us without you waking me up, you walk home."

"Yes, boss." He climbed up onto the top of one of the vehicles and I tossed up the glasses to him.

"I'm going to have a nap in the front seat. You two get some rest as best you can." I climbed into the driver's seat and put it as far back as it would go, which was most of the way. There wasn't anything in the way of covering for me to hand but it wasn't cold inside so I set myself to sleep as I was. Sam got into the other side and did the same. We were facing each other. She put her head down and settled into sleep without any fuss. I watched her for a long moment before I closed my eyes.

I was dreaming of a very big mosquito that was in the room with me, but that I couldn't see, when Sam woke me by speaking my name gently. I was cold and stiff but I had slept well. There was condensation from our breath on the glass so I couldn't see out, but there was the light of early dawn about.

"Morning, Si."

"Morning, Sam."

We lay there for a bit, just looking at each other. I don't know what she felt, but for me it seemed as if I'd known her forever and I would be happy if that carried on forever.

"Ready for another day?" I said.

"I'm ready for another day with you. I have my best days with you."

"Maybe I have mine with you."

"Coffee?"

"If there is any."

"C'mon, let's get up and see what we've got."

We got out into the sunrise. The sun was just a slip of deep orange on the horizon and the desert was a painting of yellows and oranges and reds. The sky went from navy above through blue, through turquoise to pastel pinks in the east and in the answering glow that was rapidly climbing the sky in the west. As we watched, the whole sun came clear of the land and the quality of the light began to lose its softness and to become clear and strong.

Karim, hunched up in his Jellaba, raised a hand to us from the top of the truck, yawned mightily and tossed me the glasses. The door of the other vehicle opened and Happy got out, still partly asleep but grinning at us, or at Sam anyway.

There was nothing to see but sand. Nothing moving, not even a camel or a bird.

"Right then, let's find out what we've got. Karim, you can get some sleep if you want. First prize for the person who finds the coffee," I said.

"Second prize for the toast and marmalade," Sam said.

"I think we'll empty them all out onto the ground and take stock," I said. "Do me a favour, will you. Just go through that lot and make sure it is what it's supposed to be." I tossed the bag of money to her.

"Good idea." She pulled out bundles of 500 Euro notes and started flicking through them.

Happy and I opened all the doors of both vehicles and pulled everything out. We'd done well with them; they were both Toyotas, like ours, but almost brand new; the big V8 version. They had strong luggage racks on the roof, two spare wheels, one on the back and one on the bonnet. There were sand ladders and jerry cans full of fuel. Water too. Each had a shovel and rope.

It wasn't long before we found a neatly packed holdall with primus, coffee, dates, bread, margarine and honey. Happy took charge of this and got the coffee going, spread a blanket out on the ground and laid out breakfast. I did something similar with a collection of, generally heavy, padded bags and cases that I found on the back seats and in the boots of both vehicles.

The assault rifle that I'd taken from the dead guy was an HK416, a good rifle. I'd swap it for my AK if I could find some shells for it. I changed its night sight for a day version from a pack which also contained six spare mags. It was a shame that there was only one of them.

Another bit of good news was a MAG 60 variant and I'd bet that the belts for it would feed ours too. There was also a heavy calibre sniper rifle that I didn't recognise, with day and night sights and ammunition.

An unlocked laptop with attached GPS receiver indicated that a transmitter was broadcasting from a location some way to the north of us. Presumably that was the rugged black plastic box that was currently stuck to the underside of our truck. There was another similar box in the same case. I'd keep that too.

The last and largest case contained a shoulder mounted rocket launcher. I suppose that was their backup plan; if they couldn't get us with stealth and small arms they'd just come up behind us and blow us away with this. I was just closing the case when I noticed that two of the neat row of rockets in the foam slots were actually something else. I pulled out one of those cardboard tubes that expensive bottles of whiskey come in and removed the lid. The inside was neatly packed with bundles of 500 euro notes. The other one was the same. I carefully put it all back and closed the lid. I left my new toys and went to have breakfast with the others.

"So, boss. You were going to tell us what we are doing here?" Karim said, as we sat sharing food and coffee.

"I was. What did Guy tell you?"

"That we were on a buying trip with you," Happy said. "I didn't need to know anything else."

"Yes, but this is a funny place to be buying hash," Karim said.

"Guy didn't tell me not to tell you, so I will. We're here to get a little heroin and a little cocaine. The firm is branching out a bit."

"Then it will be Gerald the nomad. That is good, he is a man of principle," Happy said.

"Who is Gerald the nomad?" Sam said.

"I have heard of him, but I've never met him," I said. "Happy?"

"Indeed, I have met him. I travelled up from Gombe with him. It cost me half my savings at that time but I would not have passed the Hausa without his help. He is a man who does what he says he will do and even the Boko Haram do not trouble him."

"That bag. All there?" I said to Sam.

"Seems right to me," she said. "Gerald is a white man?"

"Depends what you call white. He doesn't live like a white man, or even a decent Yoruba, more like a dirty Tuareg. He drives a battered old six-wheeler with a 50 calibre cannon bolted to the top and travels with his wives and children and some Somalis who make muti men look like little girls. He has a camp out in the desert somewhere, but no one knows where. He goes all over from Khartoum to Dakar to Benghazi. He'll take anything from anywhere to anywhere else, for a price. He talks a bit like Mr Guy, bit like you too," Happy said.

"Well, that sounds better than it could have been," I said. "Can't wait to meet the fellow. Sam, you up for playing with a big gun?"

"Always."

We unpacked the sniper rifle and we both put a few rounds through a cardboard box at 200 yards. It was fine, just as good as the TAC-50.

"Remember, if you shoot anyone, shoot him not me. And don't shoot anyone unless I say," I said.

"Why would I shoot you?"

"Because you could."

"I'm not like that."

211

"Good. Let's sort out some comms."

We played about with earpieces and microphones until we had a comfortable working set each. Happy and Karim had packed up the vehicles. I belatedly crawled about underneath them and searched their engine compartments too, but I didn't find any visible sign of tracking devices. We fuelled up and set off to the rendezvous. Happy with me, and Sam driving with Karim behind.

We travelled in line but spaced out. This meant that if the sand was good the second truck would be okay, and if it wasn't it would be far enough back not to get stuck and to be able to pull the other one out. That's the theory anyway. This wasn't one of the great ergs, the true seas of sand that you get in the Sahara, just one of the lesser, outlying fields, but it was still a lot of sand.

You learn to read the sand like you learn to read the water. Strangely, it seemed harder in the daylight. Last night I must have been so preoccupied with recent events that I'd not thought about it. Now I did, and set about getting myself into desert driving mode. Apart from the sand, there is the whole business of planning your route. You can't go straight, that would mean driving up the sides of the dunes. You have to pay attention to the sand where you are, in case it turns into the fine powder that you just sink through, whether you like it or not, and you have to pay attention to where you're headed because the one thing you don't want to do is stop in a hurry. That only digs you in. It's hard work and the sand can get very hypnotic. Also, it was hot. Very hot.

I kept the windows open rather than put on the aircon. For one thing, the aircon uses juice and we were probably only doing a very few miles to the gallon anyway, and also we'd be out in it soon enough; I didn't want to be struck by the heat when I might need to be sharp.

"You got your aircon on?" I said to Sam over comms.

"Bloody right."

"How are you in the heat? In general, I mean?"

"Fine, why do you ask?"

"If you don't think you can handle it, that's okay. We're saving fuel and getting used to it up here."

"Fuck you, you prick." She put down her window and gave me the finger.

"Thank you, sweetie."

"Stop making so much sand, you bastards, it's getting in my bra."

"I'll bet that's not the only place. Pull back a bit."

"I would but you're going along like a snail. Can't you get on with it?"

"No, I can't. You can lead on the way back and I'll bet you my bodyweight in cold beer that I have to pull you out."

"You're on."

We made it to the GPS coordinates before noon and stopped. If it was hot moving, stopped it was frightening. Happy started to sweat. I rode the heat like water, letting it be, not fighting it. Move slow, drink deep but not too often, stay calm.

I set the vehicles about 200 yards apart, with mine in the direction from which I imagined Gerald would appear. The ground was open, which was probably why Gerald and Guy had chosen it. Sam set up the sniper's rifle on top of her truck and covered it in cloths so that it wouldn't become too hot to touch. Happy checked over his MAG 60 and put it down on a cloth in the shade of the truck. The sun was right above us now and there wasn't much shade. We put blankets over the windscreens and opened the back doors to give shade, and that was all we could do. We each found a place to sit and, with a bottle of water for company, we waited. And waited. And waited.

It's amazing how many beetles and bugs and things live in the sand. When you stop and sit still they appear and scuttle about trying to catch and kill each other. Not unlike us, I suppose.

Anywhere else I would have sat on the top of a truck to get better visibility. Not here; the heat sapped my will and made me indifferent to everything but my own little world of existing between the hammer of the sun and the anvil of the desert. I put a line of small stones, like the minutes on a clock face, on the ground so that I could watch the line of shadow from the door of the truck creep along them. Even through sunglasses looking out was a strain; the glare and the dancing, deceiving heat haze meant that the eye couldn't rest but always de-focused and then the brain followed and before you knew it, you were staring absently into space and a camel could walk up and bite you before you would notice.

The truck was a hot thing; the sand was hot, the air, what there was of it, was hot. Sitting still was unbearable, moving was worse. Eventually, when the line of shadow was approaching the tenth stone, I thought in the back of my mind that there was something out there. I took the binoculars out from under the sand, where I'd put them to keep them cool, and used the eyepieces to push up my sunglasses. There was a pale, sand-coloured shape heaving itself up over the horizon.

I gave Sam and Karim a whistle and said, "Here they come," to Happy, who was suffering silently behind his mirror shades beside me.

The shape slowly made its way out of the heat haze to become a massive six-wheel Russian ex-military lorry. Sure enough I could see the outline of some kind of cannon mounted to the roof. It ground on, slowly but relentlessly on its massive wheels, taking a much more direct route through the dunes than we could have done. When it turned a little in it's path to skirt a particularly steep bit, I could see that its sides were festooned with equipment, including an off-road motorbike, ladders, innumerable jerry cans, what might have been rolled up tents and other things that I couldn't identify.

The behemoth stopped about 100 yards out and six or so men in sand camo with AKs dropped from it and fanned out. A figure in black robes got unhurriedly down from the cab and walked straight towards us. I got to my feet and went to meet him. Behind me Happy stood impassive with the MAG 60 level.

He was a shortish, barrel-chested man with vividly blue eyes, skin the colour of mahogany and a face ravaged by who knows what internal fires. We stopped a few yards apart, looking at each other.

"Colonel T. E. Lawrence, I presume?" I said.

"Hah. A fantasist and a poof. I'm neither." He said in an accent that reminded me of the hunt ball. "You're not Guy Wealdon. Where is he?"

"Sitting by his pool I imagine. Was he supposed to be here?"

"Yes. Who are you? His son?"

"No. Simon Ellice."

"Ah, the go-fast man. Yes, I've heard of you. What are you doing pissing about in the Sahara?"

"I thought I was meeting you to collect a package, but if not I'll go back to my siesta."

"I prefer to meet the people I do business with, not their staff. And I don't like it when people don't do what they say they're going to." He looked at me steadily, giving me a chance to persuade him not to leave.

I had an idea. "I've got an idea," I said.

"What?"

"There's a girl on the top of that other truck under that heap of cloth and she's got the cross-hairs of a 50 cal on your heart at the moment. I'd like you to meet her. How about you get your guys to stay nice and relaxed and I'll call her over?"

"A girl, huh?"

"Yes."

"Okay, why not." He turned and signalled with his hands to the men behind him. They relaxed and grounded their weapons. I motioned Happy to do the same and then looked back at the other truck and said, "Care to join us sweetheart?"

"Love to," a small voice in my ear said.

The cloths moved and her golden head appeared and she slid down gracefully off the vehicle and walked towards us. The man in the black robes watched her with raised eyebrows.

"That's definitely a girl," he said. "Can she shoot? I mean to kill."

"You think I put her there for some other reason?"

"Interesting."

Sam arrived, looking curious to find out what was what, and irritatingly unbothered by the heat.

"Sam, this is Gerald, Gerald this is Samantha Wealdon, daughter of Guy."

"Gerald Ross. Pleased to meet you." He extended a dark, leathery hand.

"I'm so glad to meet you, Mr Ross. I was afraid Si would keep me up there all the time and I wouldn't have the pleasure. You're a legend in our little world, you know."

"So you're Guy's daughter?"

"I am. Honestly. Truly. Cross my heart and hope to die." She laughed. "It's a dubious honour, but it's all mine."

"I believe you really are."

"Can we offer you anything in the way of refreshment, Mr Ross? Would you care for some coffee? I'm afraid I don't think we have any tea with us."

"Call me Gerald, please. Allow me." He turned to his men and began shouting orders in a language that I didn't know; possibly Somali. They started running about and within a few minutes an awning appeared and underneath it a table and three chairs.

"Join me, please. One of my wives will bring us a little repast." He led the way and insisted on holding a chair for Sam. It wasn't exactly cool, but by God it was better than being out in the sun.

"I'm sorry not to have the pleasure of meeting your father," Gerald said, when we were seated.

"I know, he regrets it too. An old school friend arrived at short notice and he felt that he must stay. I hope you don't mind him sending us in his place?"

"Not at all, not at all. His loss is my gain. Do I take it that you partake of the, how shall I put it, family business? You work for your father?"

"Very much so. He made me finish my education first, of course, but now I'm one of the team."

"Quite right."

"I'd been looking forward to joining the business for years. Especially since Simon has been with us."

"I see."

"You have no idea how thrilling it is to drive his boat. It's quite changed everything."

"So I understand. You drive the go-fast boat too, do you?"

"He lets me now and then. I am part of the crew these days." She looked at me with devotion and pride.

"Of course he does. Why wouldn't he."

"She's being modest," I said. "She's my right-hand man. She thinks quicker, shoots straighter and is a whole lot tougher than any of my men."

"I don't doubt it for a moment. Ah, Ayesha, here you are." A pretty young African girl in a black jellaba and headscarf arrived carrying a tray with tea things and a plate of small cakes. She set it down on the ground and ceremonially transferred its contents onto the table, curtsied sweetly, and removed herself.

"Do you have many wives? If it's not an indiscrete question?" Sam said.

"Currently, I have two. You'll meet the other one in a little. I find that any more than that is taxing. I'm not as young as I once was, sad to say. When I was first here it was a different story, but now you see the remnant of the man I was."

"That is clearly not true, Gerald. You travel the length and breadth of the Sahara moving contraband across the most hostile terrain in the world. What other white man can say the same?"

"Not just the Sahara either. I once took a package all the way to Zim for someone who couldn't trust his own men. You can probably guess who."

"We can guess," I said.

"Will you be mother, Sam?" he said.

"Of course." She poured tea for each of us and we helped ourselves to wafer thin slices of lemon with small silver tongs.

"Help yourselves to cakes. They're very good; we make them ourselves."

And very good they were. I sipped tea and ate a couple while Sam and Gerald chatted amicably about the exigencies of desert life and the pros and cons of more or fewer wives. Tall, skinny, wolf-like Somalis stood about smiling and talking amongst themselves and the relatively massive Nigerian stood impassively to one side, not wanting to let the side down by sweating or looking hot.

I gave him a nod to come over and he did.

"Ah, I know this man. Let me think." Gerald drummed his fingers on the table for a moment. "That's it; Yoruba, Okoye, Happiness. That's you isn't it? Never forget a face."

"That's me, sir. You brought me to Tindouf a few years ago."

"Ah, the slave run," an unconscious frown passed over his face. "You've put on weight since then, I see."

"I'm happy to say that life has treated me well since last you saw me, sir."

"Good, good, I'm pleased to hear it."

"Would you get that bag and the phone from the car for me, Happy, and afterwards if you want to reorganise the boot that would be fine."

"Yes, boss," he said, and went.

"They are fine people but they don't survive in the desert I find. You've probably noticed that I prefer Somalis. They do three years with me and then I shoot them. They know this but they don't seem to mind. You just can't underestimate the blind optimism of some people. I believe that they always think that it won't be today and that they'll worry about tomorrow when it comes. Something like that."

"Why do you kill them?" I said.

"Can't help it, dear boy. They get sort of uppity about then; start looking at me in the wrong way; start looking at my women. Don't think they can help it. It just happens."

"And you can't…" I started to say and then realised the stupidity of it.

"… send them home? No, not really." He finished my sentence for me. "Legend has it, and legend is truth for all intents and purposes, that I have a camp, a base, out there somewhere." He gestured over his shoulder with a thumb. "If that were so, then they would have been there, wouldn't they? And then I would have to move, wouldn't I? What a palaver. No, much better to leave them for the birds."

"I imagine you pay them well and they send the money home. Not much to spend it on here," I said.

"You imagine wrong, I'm afraid. If I paid them, they would have rights. No, I own them. They give themselves to me and, if I choose, I accept them. That's all. While they are with me they live hard but well and when they die, they die quickly. For most of them that's better than they would get back home. Besides it's honourable; a fitting life for a man."

Happy returned with the bag, put it down beside me and went thankfully back to the shade of the truck.

"Ah, yes. The deal," Gerald said.

"I believe this is just for back up. We're supposed to be doing this the modern way," I said.

"Right you are." He turned to one of the men and said something. "Luckily my other wife is good at this kind of thing. I'm an unrepentant luddite myself."

A pretty young white girl of no more than twenty appeared in similar robes and headscarf to Ayesha. She was carrying a sat-phone and a ring-bound notepad.

"This is She. Say hello my darling," Gerald said.

"Hello everyone," she said in a home-counties voice, smiling at us shyly.

We said hello back and looked at her with interest.

"You'll be wondering how it is that this pretty young thing is here with me," Gerald said.

"I was, but I wouldn't have asked," Sam said.

"It is no secret, well not a secret as far as I'm concerned anyway. Her father came to owe me a debt that he was having trouble paying, so he offered her to me as payment. I naturally accepted."

"Slavery isn't a career option open only to blacks," I said.

"When was it ever? No, you have it wrong; I've offered her her freedom but she's chosen to remain. Isn't that so my dear?"

"I feel safe here," the girl said, simply.

"And so you are. Would you like to go first, Simon, or shall we? I imagine you'd like to see the package, do some tests and all that?"

"Do you know, if you won't be offended, I won't. It is what it's supposed to be, isn't it?"

"I believe so."

"If you say so, that's good enough for me."

I took the phone out of the bag and turned it on. It thought about it for a minute and then indicated that it was ready and willing to be used. I dialled Guy.

"Hello," a voice said at the other end.

"Afternoon, Guy, here we are with Mr Ross," I said.

"Is that you, Simon?" he said.

"Who else were you expecting?" I said.

"No one. Has…?"

"Excellent line," I said. "You can send some money now if you like."

"Yes, but…"

"Good, see you later." I cut him off and turned the phone off.

"A man of few words, Mr Guy, I see," Gerald said.

"Laconic indeed," I said, Sam was looking at me with interest.

"Our turn then. Will you do the thing, She?"

"Do I take it that you're a fan of H. Rider Haggard?" I said.

"My little joke. I'm impressed that you got it," Gerald said.

"He's an unusually well read drug dealer," Sam said.

"Drug smuggler," I said.

"Ah, yes, the distinction is important, isn't it? I convey gold and drugs and arms and slaves and diamonds and whatever else, but I do not deal in them. That would be beneath me," Gerald said.

"You men are funny, delicate things," Sam said.

"But, aren't we," Gerald said.

"Here you are, sir. The banker is on the line now," the girl said, and passed him the phone.

"Dear boy, how are you?" Gerald said.

Sam and I looked at each other with curiosity.

He chatted politely with someone, enquired about the weather, informed them that the weather here was good. He held his hand over the phone and said to us, "Apparently some money has appeared on his computer." He resumed speaking to the person and then wished them well and passed the phone back to the girl.

"The banker?" Sam said.

"If you don't know, it's not for me to say. You could ask your father," he said.

"I will," she said.

Not the only thing I want to ask him, I thought.

"So that is good," Gerald said. "Now we can forget about all that. Would you like some more tea?"

"I think, if you don't mind, I'd like to get back to the sea," I said. "My native element is calling me and, I don't know if you've noticed this, but I find it a little warm here."

"Dear boy, I quite understand. I'll look forward to meeting you again when we do this properly with a decent load. I don't mind telling you, I shall be charging them more than it is worth to bring this little bit out here to you. But a little caution is a good thing for everyone, I suppose. Will I be seeing you next time, Sam, do you think?"

"I sincerely hope so, Gerald. I'll inform my father that it is your requirement that I do so. And mine also."

"Do that, do that. And if you ever wish for the desert life, I am at your service."

"That is very kind of you. For now, I must serve my father, but if the time comes, I will remember."

"Good. Now, shall we load you up and let you get on your way?"

"Let's do that," I said, rising and taking up the bag of money.

"So be it." He raised a hand and gave orders to his men. They leapt to obey and transferred four heavy, hessian sacks to the back of our truck where Happy took charge of them and saw them well stowed away.

We took our leave like old friends departing from a weekend house-party; Gerald and Sam exchanging kisses and he and I shaking hands. His wives and men lined up to see us go and wave.

Happy rode the running board to the other truck and jumped off to join Karim and they followed on behind us. As they pulled away two more Somalis with AKs appeared at the top of the nearest dune and smiled and waved too.

"Bloody hell," Sam said, when we were alone.

"Yet again, I'm damn glad you were here," I said.

"Me too. What next, I wonder?"

"A lot of driving, I'm afraid. And we're not going back the way we came."

"That's probably a good idea."

"And when we get back, I want a bit of a talk with your father."

12

THE TIES THAT BIND

We crossed the line on the map sometime after the sun had set and were back in Morocco. We picked up a track which eventually took us to the R606 and turned west, away from home, and headed to Taza and then round the Rif and back to Nador. It was a long way but more of it was on roads than the more direct way that we had come. We all took turns driving and the big, powerful vehicles ate up the roads, however good or bad they were, with equal indifference.

I even slept for a while as Sam drove. We were in that place where she was my most capable and dependable partner and I could go to sleep without worrying about what would happen.

Karim had done well. He had kept watch without fail. He hadn't said much, but that's a virtue, and now he did a long spell of good driving while Happy slept. I would look on him with more favour after this.

For all he's a black African, Happy's a big man, and the heat had taken more of a toll on him then the rest of us. It was good to be in the cool of the night and in the healing, comforting darkness.

I had time to think, time to play back the images of the last two days. We had come close to being killed at least once, but a miss is a miss, and that's all that really matters. When we were close enough to civilization to expect a phone signal, I turned mine on and put it on silent, so that it wouldn't disturb the peace of the night drive. There was a message from Guy telling me to ring him. I ignored it.

I watched Sam driving for a bit. Her hands, brown from the sun, slim but strong with fine golden hairs. She was looking ahead through the windscreen, her chin slightly forward, purposeful and certain, a hunter to the very tips of her very lovely toes.

"Hey, Sam."

"What?"

"What d'you think?"

"About what?"

"About everything. About all this."

"I love it. I absolutely love it. This is what I was born for."

"You do, don't you?"

"I feel better now than I ever have. I feel alive, really alive. You know what I mean?"

"I think so, yes."

"If it ever comes to an end I don't know what I'll do. Tell me it won't come to an end, Si."

"It won't come to an end. There will always be the sea and the desert and something someone wants badly enough to pay for. No, I don't think it will ever end."

"That's good. I don't think I'm built for anything else."

"I wouldn't say that."

"Mm. You thinking what I think you're thinking?"

"I'm thinking we should have organised another night under the stars."

"I need a shower. It's amazing where the sand gets."

"Back to mine then?"

"Yes, back to yours."

"We'll send the other two straight to the house with the load. Pull up when you see a good place and we'll sort out the gear."

"Yes, boss."

It was early morning by the time we passed Tiztoutine. We had driven through the night and into the next day. We were heading due east now so the sun came up in front of us, its first rays lancing out down the red, dusty road towards us. I welcomed it. It brought its strength and clarity and made the way seem clearer.

We pulled off the road for fuel and bought strong coffee and food at the nearby makeshift cafe. We were all tired and road- weary, but peaceful and happy. There were other people at the stop too; ordinary Moroccans going about their business. It seemed a bit strange at first to realise that we were back in the normal world. A rather stupid young man came up to us to offer us some dope, which made us all laugh. He looked at us a little more closely and then went away quickly.

I made Happy back the other truck up to the back of the one that Sam and I had been in and had a sort out. When I had finished, the toys that I wanted to keep were in one, and everything else and the cocaine and heroin were in the other. I kept the money too.

"Here you are, Happy," I said, giving him a key. "You have it now. We'll ride shotgun with you until we get to town, then you and Karim take it up to the house. Okay?"

"Me, boss? I thought you would take it to Mr Guy."

"Yes, you. You can take it, why not?"

"If you say so."

"I do. We're going back to mine for a shower and some sleep. You should do the same. I'll catch up with you soon. And you, Karim."

"Okay, boss."

"Not a bad trip eh?"

"Good trip, yes." He smiled like only a big Yoruba can.

"I am a man of the desert now," Karim said.

"You certainly are, Karim. A fine man of the desert. When we go again you will come, if you want to."

"I will want to, boss." He smiled a slow, shy smile.

"Good. Now let's go."

Karim drove with Happy beside him, tired but ready. They took the lead now and we followed them in. There was the usual traffic at the main junction but it was early enough not to hold us up. Perhaps we should have followed them up to the house to make sure, but my store of diligence was empty. I didn't really care anymore. We saw them onto the high road to the houses on the hill and then turned down towards the city and home.

I took my phone out of my pocket and dialled. Guy answered.

"That you, Si? Where are you?"

"It's me. We're back. I've sent Happy and Karim to you with the stuff."

"To the house? No, it's to go to the store."

"We're going back to mine for a wash and some sleep. If anyone disturbs us, I'll shoot first and look to see who it is afterwards."

"Come up to the house. You can use one of the guest rooms. I'll get them to make some food. You both must be tired."

"I'll meet you at the Rif tonight, about eight."

"I don't want to come out. Come up here, whenever you like."

I disconnected and put my phone back on silent.

"Fuck, I need a shower," I said.

"I'll scrub your back if you like," Sam said.

We left the truck in Azooz's yard. He appeared and looked at us with wide eyes. That could have been because of the way we looked or because we were still alive, I couldn't say. I locked it, put

227

the alarm on and put the key in my pocket. Apart from one holdall that I was carrying, all my new toys could stay there for now.

"Azooz, it might be best if you don't let anyone touch that truck. There is a block of C-4 wired to the alarm."

"What is this C-4?"

"You know, plastique. Makes a very loud bang."

"Plastique! No, no, no…"

We ignored his frightened protests and walked, arm in arm, back to the flat.

Soumaiya ran to the door at the sound of my key. Her face registered joy, relief, and then disappointment as she saw Sam.

"Hi, Soumy, we're back," I said.

"I was worried, Simon."

"I know, Soumy, but we are back safe and sound. Weary and dirty. Will you make some coffee and some food and if anyone rings the bell don't answer it, okay?"

"As you say, Simon."

"Thanks. By God, it's good to be home." I began to strip and headed for the shower. Sam did the same and followed me. We lay long and slow and late and lazy as two dogs by the fire through that day. The familiar call of the muezzin floated over us and told us that the day was passing, had passed and was now evening. As fasting makes food wonderful so the desert had made the simple pleasures of comfort and ease wonderful for us. I sat up in bed and stretched and gave my head a good scratch with my fingers. Just being alive was great.

Sam turned over beside me, throwing an arm across me, snuggling into me. I put my fingers in her hair, enjoying its softness, felt the nape of her neck and where it became her back; so slender and fine. The flesh is so weak and vulnerable and yet we endure. The lovely limbs entwined with mine were the same ones that had so recently, and so capably, used a battered old Kalashnikov to smash muscle and bone at my request. Strange to think that, though I'm quite a big man, strong and by no means squeamish, the slight girl there in the bed with me had become my lethal agent. My first choice to kill for me. Sharper, cleverer, more ready, more present than the rest.

"Fancy a beer?" I said.

"Huh?"

"Fancy a beer? I said I'd meet your old man at the Rif."

"Mm." She pulled herself on top of me and kissed me. There was no hurry about that beer.

I spent a little time in my study packing a few things into a holdall and writing a note for Soumy. When I had done, I found her in the kitchen.

"Hey, Soumy, how're you doing?"

"Simon, I do not know how I'm doing. That is the truth."

"Will you give me your phone number please? I may want to send you a text later."

"I didn't know you knew I had a phone."

"It is good that you do, and I don't mind at all if you used the housekeeping money to buy it."

"I knew that you wouldn't mind really, but then I thought you should mind, so I didn't tell you."

"Hurry, I don't have long."

"I will send you a text from my phone as soon as you stop talking to me."

"You know my number?"

"Of course I know your number. It has been in my brain since a long time."

"Okay, now give me two bananas. I must go."

I tucked my .38 into the waistband of my trousers and Sam did the same with her .32. She and I walked down the stairs and out into the sunshine. I offered her a banana but she didn't want one. We picked the big truck up and drove it down to the waterfront, leaving a relieved looking Azooz behind us.

Asif was mending nets, like the eternal fisherman, and Imad was with him. They looked a little worried, but happy to see us.

"Kaifa haloka, Asif? Kaifa haloka, Imad?" I said.

"We are well thank you, Simon, but we have had an anxious time of it since you left us. The thin ferenji has gone but two unpleasant men with guns hidden in a black bag have been sitting on the dock over there. They only went early this morning."

"But they've not been near the boat?"

"They have not. Imad slept aboard her both nights, to be certain that no one swam out to her under the water."

"That's well done. There are several heavy cases in the back of that truck. If you'll wait until it is quiet and then transfer them to the boat and stow them neatly in the lockers, I would be happy."

"It will be done, inshallah."

"Good." I gave him the key and my holdall. "I'll be back for the truck later. Come on then, Sam. Let's get that beer."

"We will watch, we will watch," Asif said.

"You've a talent for inspiring loyalty, I notice," Sam said.

"So do you," I said.

"Do you think we'll see those men from the desert again?"

"Hey, for all I know, they're in the bar now." I held the door for her and followed her in. There were only locals as far as I could see. Old Henry took in our arrival with interest and Ali nodded solemnly to indicate that he'd seen us.

I led the way to a quiet table and pulled out a chair for Sam.

"You're being a gentleman this evening," she said.

"Aren't I always?"

"No."

"Oh. What would you like to drink?"

"A long, cold beer. I can still taste sand in the back of my throat and I think there's some behind my eyeballs." She kicked off her shoes and tucked her legs underneath her.

"How about other places?"

"I didn't notice any. Did you?"

"Can't say I did."

"Well, that's all right then."

Ali joined us. He seemed pleased to see us. "My most beautiful customers, welcome back. What can I get you?"

"Hi, Ali. Have we been somewhere?" I said.

"You have not been seen in your usual haunts for the last three days. I assumed you weren't in bed all the time."

"Ali, what are you saying?" Sam said.

"Nothing, nothing. I observe that is all."

"What do you observe, Ali, apart from us?"

"The man, Smith, has paid his bill and gone away."

"And the others?"

"The others? Oh, you mean them. Yes, no, they have not been here. They went before you did and have not been back since. I hope that is the last of them. And of their captain."

"The one with the wrong haircut?"

"As you say, the one with the wrong haircut."

"Anything else interesting happen while we were away?"

"Mrs Murr has been seen with Mr Robbie."

"Oh dear. Does Mr Murr know?"

"Not yet."

"What does he see in her, I wonder?" Sam said.

"It's something about the way she looks at you," Ali said. "She does it to me too."

"Can't say she does it to me," I said.

"Does she not look at you as if she is in desperate need of being rescued and perhaps you are the man for the job? And if so, all the rewards of heaven are yours for the asking," Ali said.

"Not that I recall. Is that really what she does to you?" I said.

"I think if she asked, I would poison her husband for her."

"You're just an insensitive clod, Si. Don't you know that every woman needs to be protected and looked after?" Sam said.

"Even you?"

"What do you mean, even me. Yes, of course me."

"Protected from what?"

"Myself, of course."

"Oh."

"Here am I standing gossiping when I should be fetching you something. What would you like, Miss Samantha?"

"Beer please, Ali. A long cold beer."

"Me too, please."

"One small moment and I will return."

"Ali likes you," Sam said, when he had gone.

"I like Ali," I said. "He's a good man doing a difficult job."

"Serving beer?"

"Serving beer and keeping the peace. Or at least making sure that we shoot at each other somewhere else."

"I think I'd just let them shoot it out."

"No, I think you'd join in."

Ali returned with tall glasses full of golden liquid and placed them on the table for us.

"Thanks, Ali. Have you seen this lovely girl's father by any chance?"

"Here? I have not seen such a thing for many years. Is it likely to happen?"

"I've no idea."

"Since you have said it, I will go and put on my bullet proof underwear just in case," Ali said, smiling at us and looking worried at the same time as he left.

"I think that's my phone," Sam said, digging in her pocket for it. "Hi, Dad, we've been having such a good time... No, in the Rif with a lovely cold beer... Yes, I suppose I'll be up later. What's up?"

She listened with a frown, "Si? Yes, he's right here, do you… Hang on, I'll tell him. Dad wants us up at the house," she said. I shook my head. "He shook his head," she said into the phone. She listened for a bit and then hung up. "Dad's on his way here."

"Good."

"So…?"

"So?"

"Don't be a prick. What's going on? The last time anyone said no to Dad… well, it was a long time ago."

"Your dad sent me to a meet knowing I'd have company and I'm not entirely happy about it."

"You don't know that."

"Yes I do."

"So what're you going to do?"

"I don't know. Depends on what he says, I suppose. Probably walk out of here, get on the boat and leave."

"You can't do that."

"Oh, yes I can."

"But we're having so much fun."

"They would have killed you too, if they'd caught us, you know."

"But they didn't."

"Okay, fine. You can look at it that way if you like but I'm going to make an effort to stay alive. And don't tell me I worry too much."

"Okay."

We didn't speak for a bit, but just enjoyed our beers and being there, and then she said, "If you go, can I come too? Even if you don't mean to come back, I mean?"

"Yes."

"Okay, you decide what to do and I'll go with you, whatever."

I kissed her. She kissed me back and Guy found us sharing a sofa with her head on my lap and her feet dangling over the arm and kicking about happily in the air.

He walked into the bar, as the song has it, like a man boarding his yacht. Henry looked on and forgot to shut his mouth. Ali cut short what he was doing and came over at a gentle trot. Guy saw us and came to our table. Sam got up to give him a dutiful kiss and then sat down beside me. I watched him notice who was in the bar without seeming to and then fix me with his black eyes. Three men who I recognised as being on his staff from the house, slid in behind him and casually took up positions.

"Ali, how nice to see you," he said, shaking his hand.

"Mr Wealdon, it has been so long. Can I get you a long single malt with soda and two ice cubes?"

"Ali, you are peerless."

"And a couple more beers," I said.

"Coming right up." As he left, Ali adjusted imaginary bullet-proof underpants.

"Evening, Si," Guy said.

"Evening, Guy," I said.

"I haven't been in here for years. It's cleaner than it used to be. It makes me realise that I don't get out much these days."

"You're like an ogre living in his cave on the hill, Daddy," Sam said.

"You're right. I've got into a habit that way."

"That's okay, you have us to take the risks for you," I said.

"The munt said you had a little situation and dealt with it with your usual effectiveness."

"We did, yes."

"And I suppose you're blaming me for it?"

"Perhaps you'd like to tell me again why you sent me instead of going yourself?"

"I told you; that was the plan all along."

"Okay, it's your business. I'll just pack my bags and be on my way. You can send me half my fee and we'll call it quits."

"Dear boy, if that's how you feel, what can I say."

"Daddy, tell him the truth. If you don't I'm going with him," Sam said.

"Very well, if you say so darling. The chap I sell it to in the UK - I haven't told you much about him, have I?"

"You haven't told me anything about him," I said.

"Well, he's an old chum, a bit of a player, if you know what I mean. You won't be offended if I don't name names. His firm have a subsidiary who do refrigerated haulage. There's only so much cold, dead fish that your average customs man will shift before he gives up. Anyway, when I broached the subject of expanding the range he was more than keen, but perhaps he didn't bargain on the price quite as hard as he might have. It did fleetingly occur to me that he might be getting ambitious. In light of the circumstances, I suppose I may have been right."

"You're telling me he decided to shorten the supply chain by removing a link?"

"Yes. The link in question being me. Us."

"Which is why you told Sam that she couldn't come. But were happy to send me."

"I should have realised what she was up to when she didn't tell me to fuck off. I never said I was nice, did I?"

"And I never said I was available to be set up."

"So get over it. Be angry if you want, but get over it."

"Guy, if I were angry, we wouldn't be sitting about talking."

"Fair point. There is something I can do about it however."

"What?"

"This chap. My old chum. There's some photos I have. I might send him a few copies, let him know that they'll hit the papers in the event of anything untoward happening to me or mine."

"You're going to blackmail a drug dealer into not killing you? You think that will work?"

"Not all drug dealers wear the t-shirt, you know. Yes, he'll care all right, I guarantee it."

"Okay, I'm going to take a short break while you sort that out. It's going to be full moon anyway. If you wire me a sufficiently substantial fee for getting it this far, I'll come back and make a delivery at the dark of the moon."

"I'm going with him," Sam said.

"Okay, my children. If that's what you want, so be it."

"I'm glad you see it that way," I said.

"Sure. No point me getting in a tizzy about it. Have another beer and go and get on your boat." He raised his hand to Ali, who was hovering in the middle distance. "You do mean to go now, don't you?"

"Yes."

"Thought so."

I was busy wondering what the old bastard was up to so I didn't immediately notice that the well-dressed woman in her late fifties, who had walked into the bar and was looking about her, was my mother.

13

WITH A LONG SPOON

"Ah, darling, I've found you," she said, coming over.

"Oh, fuck," I said, mainly to myself.

"Who's that?" Sam said.

"Hi, Mum," I said, rising and offering a cheek to be kissed.

"They told me you would be here," she said, giving me the traditional brush of flesh to flesh, touching my sleeve briefly with her hand at the same time, and then stepping back. "Order me a drink will you, dear. Something fairly bloody."

"Sure," I said. Ali was heading our way.

"Well, there you are then, Guy," she said, turning to look at him as if she'd only just noticed him.

"Here I am, Helen," he said, getting to his feet and going to her with his arms open.

"Give me a kiss you old bastard," she said.

They kissed, on the lips, and stood looking at one another.

"You look fine, Helen," Guy said.

"You look old and debauched as usual," Mum said.

"No he doesn't," Sam said.

"My daughter," Guy said, indicating her without taking his eyes off Mum.

"My name is Samantha," Sam said, extending a hand.

"Pleased to meet you, Samantha," Mum said, as if she were conferring a favour. She took the hand with a brief squeeze at arm's length and I had the impression of two female tigers trying to work out which one would kill the other.

"She goes by the name of Helen," I said to Sam. "Sam and I have been working together, Mum."

"Isn't that wonderful, dear. I don't suppose they know how to mix a decent drink around here, do they?"

"We will do our very best, ma'am," Ali said, appearing beside her.

"The lady will have a singapore sling, and so will I," Guy said.

"So I will. What a wonderful memory you have," Mum said.

She took the seat next to the one Guy had been sitting on and the rest of us sat down too. Her gaze rested on me.

"You're looking very well, Si; quite brown. Guy's obviously looking after you."

"Anything for your boy, Helen," Guy said. "You know that. He's made himself quite useful as it happens. I'd almost say I couldn't do without him." He raised a malicious eyebrow in my direction and I was conscious of his men standing at ease, calmly focused on us.

"Who told you I'd be here, Mum?" I said.

"Oh, someone. I forget," she said. "Well, isn't this nice."

"Are you by yourself, Mum?" I said.

"Yes, dear. Your father's off on some bloody conference somewhere so I decided to pop out and see how you were all getting on."

"Where are you staying?"

"With you, I suppose, darling."

"Good. When you've had your sling I'll take you home and you can freshen up and change. I expect you're a little tired after travelling."

"You don't have a spare bedroom, Si," Sam said.

"I'll manage," I said.

"Oh, not a bit of it," Mum said. "I'm a great traveller you know. Of course you know, you were with me on the trans-siberian railway when we went out that way to join your father in Hong Kong. And there was that wonderful tour of the States..."

"Yes, but as I was only four, I don't really remember," I said.

"Talking of travelling: do you remember that safari, Helen?" Guy said.

"Safari?"

"Samburu country."

"Oh, that safari. Yes. We did a lot of driving, didn't we?"

"Even after three weeks and endless miles of bush you looked as fresh as if you had just stepped out of Harrods. I can picture it as if it was yesterday," Guy said.

"Of course I remember. Up by the border with Somalia. That was my honeymoon. My first elephant. You were conceived up there as I remember, darling."

"Was I?" I said. "What was Guy doing there?"

"I arranged it all," he said. "My old man had been in the KAR for a bit and I had contacts. Still do as it happens. Perhaps we should do it again."

"We were quite a threesome in those days," Mum said, "weren't we. Ah, I remember those days."

"These two could do the driving and carry the bags and so on," Guy said.

"Darling, what a wonderful idea. Could we really?" Mum said.

"Of course we could. Just say the word and I'll make it happen," Guy said.

"I'm game," Sam said, looking thoughtful.

"How wonderful. I think I would like that but perhaps this time we'll leave Ed behind. Your father doesn't really like the outdoors you know, Si," Mum said, turning to me.

"I have met him," I said.

"Don't be sarcastic, darling. Ah, here we are. Thank goodness for that."

The drinks arrived on a silver tray. Ali, who was now wearing white gloves, distributed them with some ceremony, starting with my mother.

"Thank you…" she said.

"Ali, ma'am," he said.

"Thank you, Ali. That looks lovely." She tasted it. "It is lovely. Do you think you might have another one on standby, just in case?"

"Make that two," Guy said.

"Oh, fuck," I said, again, so that only Sam would hear.

"D'you know what I think we should do?" Guy said. "Let's all have supper up at my house and we can talk about it. I've got rather a nice place up on the hill with a view across the lagoon and my cook is the second best in Morocco. What do you say, Helen?"

"Only the second best?"

"The king has the best, or so they say."

"You're such a liar."

"He is very good though, isn't he, Si?"

"The bacon he did for me the other day was burnt, and if he's a bacon burner… well, what can I say about the rest. My house girl, on the other hand, cooks the most wonderful local cuisine you can imagine," I said. "Come and have supper with me, Mum. You can catch up with Guy tomorrow."

"Are you two fighting over me?" Mum said. "Isn't that sweet. Darling, if you don't mind I think I'll go with Guy. I simply haven't seen him for years and years. You can have me all to yourself tomorrow."

I didn't look but I thought about the way out and about the three men standing there and then I said, "Sure, if that's what you want, Mum."

"That's a plan then," Guy said. "Si, I expect you'll want to go and do something with your boat but come up for supper at about eight. You can go with him if you want, Sam."

"Can I," she said.

"How lovely," Mum said. "Shall we have that other sling? This one seems to have disappeared."

"If I know Ali, they will be on their way," Guy said. He raised a hand without looking towards the bar and, sure enough, Ali came trotting over with the silver tray. "Thank you Ali. Will you see that this lady's bags are put into my car?" He held out the key.

"Of course, Mr Wealden. Shall I have it brought round to the front?"

"If you would, Ali."

"In which case, if you'll excuse me, I must, as Guy says, go and do something. I'll see you in a bit, Mum," I said, rising and swallowing the last of my beer.

"You go ahead, darling, I'm sure Guy will look after me."

"There's no doubt about it," I said.

"I think I'll come and give you a hand," Sam said.

We left them to it, not that they appeared to notice or care.

"Fuck," I said again, when we were out of earshot.

"Why don't we just go?" Sam said.

"I can't," I said.

"Why not?"

"He'll kill her."

"No he won't, he likes her."

"For that many millions, he'd kill you."

"If he kills her he won't have any leverage over you. He'll just keep her for a bit. You said yourself that there's no work to do for a while. We might as well go and have a little holiday."

"It's tempting but I think I have to try to get her away from him."

"So take her back to your flat tonight. We can go for a boat ride with her tomorrow. What would be more natural than taking her out in Nottambulo? We can drop her off in Spain and then do what we planned."

"It won't happen. You'll see. She'll be staying with Guy while she's here. She's already decided, I can tell."

"For how long?"

"Will she stay? That is a very good question. I don't believe he'll let her out of his sight while he wants me to work for him."

"You mean, I have to share my home with her for the foreseeable future?"

"I believe so."

"Fuck."

"Exactly."

"Ha, ha." She laughed suddenly.

"What?"

"I've just thought of what's going to happen to Zara."

"Oh."

"You have to get her out of there."

"I know."

"Fuck it, let's just go, and leave them to it."

"I can't. And there's something else. I don't know what, but my mother doesn't do things like this. There's something else. She'd have told me she was coming, if only to make sure she had clean sheets or a good hotel room. She could have come out to visit at any time but she hasn't, so why now?"

"I don't care. She's a grown woman and can take care of herself. We should go for a few days at least. She'd rather be with him than you anyhow."

"And she's nervous. She's not usually that..."

"Scary?"

"Intense."

"Come on, let's go."

"I said, I can't. Now leave it."

"If you won't go, I'll go by myself."

"Not in my boat, you won't."

"What's to stop me? One old man?"

"Oh, fuck. Don't start, will you. I've got enough to deal with, without you going off on one."

"She's only an old woman."

"She's my mother."

"Oh, fuck off." She walked away.

"I didn't mean…"

"Just fuck off."

I could have gone after her but I didn't. I went down to the jetty and stood at the end looking at the water. She had a point; I wasn't responsible for my mother's life. I could just drop my phone in the water, get into Nottambulo and leave, but then I wasn't responsible for Sam's every whim either and I didn't want to leave my mother with Guy and not know what was happening to her. Also, I wanted to know what was going on.

Asif coughed gently beside me to indicate his presence and said, "Everything is put away as you said, Simon."

"Thank you. Asif, where would you hide if you didn't want to be found?" I said.

"I don't think it would be easy for you to hide, Simon. You are too big and too well known."

"I don't mean me, I mean someone who might want to be here but not be noticed."

"You mean like one of the unconsidered? Like a woman or a dirty, druggy person, or a black man. Someone like that?"

"Asif, you're a genius. Could you get Imad to go and buy me five big spliffs please, and a lighter?"

"Of course, Simon, but you don't smoke, do you?"

"Perhaps I do tonight."

"As you wish. I will attend to it immediately." He walked away in his stately but inaudible way.

While he was gone I took out my phone and found that Soumy had sent me a text, as she said she would. I saved her number and then called it.

"Hello, Simon," she said, after only one ring.

"Hi, Soumy. Are you in the flat?"

"I am. Where else would I be?"

"I don't know. Do you have to go out for anything?"

"No. I have done the shopping for tomorrow unless you want something special?"

"No. Good. Soumy, listen carefully…"

"I always listen carefully."

"I know, but this is more important than usual. Do you understand?"

"I understand. I will listen more carefully than usual."

"Good. I don't know when I will be home but until I am, I want you to bolt the door. Do you understand? Bolt it, not just lock it. Bolt it so that even I can't get in. Have you got that?"

"I understand. I will wait to let you in when you knock."

"No you won't. You will wait to let me in when I phone. Do you understand?"

"Because it might not be you knocking?"

"Good girl. That's it. You don't go out and no one but me comes in. And that includes Sam. Got it?"

"She will kill me when you let her in afterwards, if I do not let her in."

"No she won't. But do not let her or anyone else in, whatever. Okay?"

"Okay, Simon. I understand."

"Good. I must go now."

"Goodbye, Simon."

"Bye, Soumy."

I hung up and accepted an envelope from Asif who had returned as quietly as before.

"Thank you, Asif. Are you armed?"

"Armed, Simon? I am Asif, I do not need to carry a gun. Everyone knows me."

"Would it be a trouble to you if you and Imad were to take the tender out to Nottambulo and get out two of the Kalashnikov rifles and stay with her?"

"It would be no trouble at all."

"Good. No one is to board her except me. I mean no one. Not Miss Samantha, not Happiness, not even Mr Guy. Okay?"

"We work for you, Simon and no one else. It will be as you say."

"Good. You can use the night glasses to watch out to sea and the day glasses to watch the land and take it in turns to get some sleep."

"We do not need to sleep."

"Well, you're a stronger man than I am. If men in a rib, with a big Mercury outboard come anywhere near you, expect trouble. I'll see you tomorrow. I hope."

I walked thoughtfully along the seafront. It must have been somewhere between eight and nine and my stomach was beginning to rumble. I would go up to the house for supper in a bit but first I had an idea to test.

It was late enough for the drug-addicted derelicts to have come out from the back alleys and taken up their places on the sun-warmed stones of the front. There was a group of them rolling dice for small piles of copper coins about a hundred yards down, where there was a set of steps down to the water.

Some of them had made an attempt to wash their clothes in the sea and the rags were hung on the bollards to dry. I lit one of the cigarettes and took a careful pull to get it going. That made my head swim a bit and I let my gait become unsteady.

When I got to the group I stopped by them and swayed about, waving the spliff gently in the air. They looked up at me with curious, bloodshot eyes. I smiled at them an inane, vacuous smile and offered the nearest one the spliff. He grasped it greedily in fumbling, un- coordinated hands, took a long drag and then looked up at me, questioningly. I nodded happily and he passed it on to the man next to him who did the same. By the time it got back round to me it was a tiny stub. I waved it aside and continued on my way.

The next man was on his own, lying unconscious along the low wall. I used the toe of my boot to push up his keffiyeh. He groaned slightly but that was all. I left him be and carried on.

The group hanging out where the front begins to widen near the docks had been at the bins. Litter, discarded wrappers, bottles and cans were scattered about them. One or two of them were still trying to get the last of whatever was edible from some of the pieces. I went into my routine, which wasn't hard; it's strong stuff nowadays, and kicked at some of the debris in a carefree manner as I arrived. Some of them looked up at me resentfully so I smiled my placatory smile and offered the smoke.

It was taken up with the same enthusiasm and passed around. I watched carefully as each man took his draw with fumbling fingers. One man, huddled beneath his rags, kept his head down and didn't receive the cigarette. They passed it by him without trying to rouse him so I pointed at him and said, "And him, everyone must smoke."

"Summum, Summum. He is deaf, he is deaf," they said.

"Push him. He must smoke," I said, and obligingly they did. Reluctantly a slim brown hand came out from the rags and took the spliff. The man hesitated and then put it under the ragged mess of his keffiyeh to take his pull and then passed it on. I could see nothing of his face.

I wished them goodnight and, scattering a few coins from my pocket, which they almost all bent down quickly to collect, switched to English and said, "I'll be on a bench in the corniche."

I walked back, keeping somewhat in character for a few yards, and then went on more sensibly to the low garden of hibiscus and oleander that the tourists sit in and eat ice-cream in the day. It sits between the front and the one café with pretensions to European standards and the owners of the café pay the gendarmes to keep the beggars away from it most of the time. I chose the most secluded bench and waited. I hoped he wouldn't be long; I was hungry now.

"You bastard," Bill said, sitting down beside me.

"You smell," I said.

"I'm in character," he said.

"Suits you," I said. "What's the point of all this then?"

"I don't know. I just want to know what's going on, that's all."

"Me too. You've dyed your hands."

"I have. You need help?"

"From a smelly man in rags?"

"You want something."

"Is it just you? I mean, have you got any cavalry just over the hill?"

"Might have. Are you trying to cut a deal?"

"There's an innocent Englishwoman got caught up in all this. Thought you might feel duty bound to help her."

"Who?"

"My mother, as it happens."

"Your *mother*?"

"Yes."

"What's she doing here?"

"Visiting me, I suppose. Why did you say 'my mother' like that?"

"If you don't know, I'm not telling you."

"I came here wanting to trust you, not beat you to a pulp."

"Okay, give me something and I'll help. I owe you one."

"So you do. So why am I giving you something?"

"Got to justify the cavalry."

"Have you got them or not? If not, there's no point me talking to you."

"Just trust me, will you. I said, I owe you one."

"Okay. I picked up a sample batch of heroin and cocaine from out in the desert. Just a couple of hundred kilos. We nearly got taken by those lads who nearly got you. At least, I think it was them. How's that?"

"Just a couple of hundred kilos? Bloody hell. That's not bad."

"I didn't sign up for moving tonnes of hard stuff."

"Tonnes?"

"Yes, tonnes. But while my mother is up on the hill I'm not going to have much choice about it."

"On the hill?"

"Yes. With Guy Wealden. What did you think I was talking about?"

"I don't know. Shit."

"Yes, shit."

"Okay. What do you want from me?"

"A chance to get her away. Some kind of distraction, perhaps. And when I go, don't follow me."

"Fair enough. I'll do what I can."

"Just like that?"

"Just like that. Do you know where and when?"

"Where and when what?"

"The tonnes of course."

"No, but probably before the dark of the moon. Either that or we'll have to wait to get it across to Spain for another month."

"That's not long. It's not far from full moon now."

"Is it? I suppose it is."

"I need to know where and when."

"So do I. Later maybe. Do you know who those seven, now six are?"

"Not know, no."

"But you've an idea."

"Possibly."

"Care to share it with me?"

"No."

"Okay, well if you're going to be like that I might as well go and have some supper."

"That's nice for you."

"I doubt it," I said.

"If I've anything to tell you, I'll phone you," Bill said.

"You'll phone me?"

"Sure."

"How did you get my number?"

"We have ways. I'll send you a text in a bit so that if you've anything to tell me, you can phone me too."

"So far, I've told you a lot and you've told me nothing."

"That's my job. Simon…"

"Yes."

"Have you been to the castle on the hill recently?"

"The Riby? No, why?"

"Perhaps you should."

"Okay, I will. Why?"

"No reason."

I left the smelly, annoying, bastard on the bench and went as swiftly back to the big Toyota as I could without running. When I got up to the house the guard waved me in as usual. I parked, locked it, and went through the archway onto the terrace.

It was odd seeing my mother at that table, but also it wasn't. When I saw it, it had a kind of inevitability about it. They're both vain, charming, ruthless, clever, passionate people and together they dominated the place, each making the other seem more. They were sitting together and Zara was on the other side of the table.

"Ah, there he is. Where have you been, Si? We've eaten the first course," my mother said.

I could see what Sam had meant about Zara. She had a glazed, rigid look about her and bright red spots burned at her cheekbones.

"What've I missed? I'm ravenous," I said, pulling up a chair and waving to the house-boy.

"Get your work done, my boy?" Guy said. "All safe and sound out there?"

"I sincerely doubt it, old man, but we do what we can, don't we?"

"You've grown up, Si. Hasn't he, Guy?" my mother said. "If you weren't my son, I'd fancy you."

"Don't bother, Mum, I've been inoculated against that kind of thing by these two. The reason there isn't a pool-boy here at the moment is that they took turns with him, then got bored of that and shot him. Is that the Roederer? Good, that's what I want." I helped myself to a glass of champagne and pulled some of the dishes of fried shellfish, toast and salad towards me.

"That dressing is not bad, by the way," my mother said, passing a jug of melted butter sauce.

"And he doesn't seem to have burnt the toast either. You shouldn't believe everything he says, Helen."

"Whereas I shouldn't believe anything you say. He lies quite well when he wants to but you do it all the time," she said. "As I know very well."

"So you've come all this way just to slander me, have you? That's a fine thing after all these years, and all I've done for you," Guy said.

"I came to see my son, not you. And all you did for us was nearly land us up in the same jail cell as you. The only decent thing you ever did was bugger off, you old bastard," she said.

"Yes, you old bastard," Zara said.

"It speaks," my mother said.

"It'll wish it hadn't," Guy said.

"Can we eat before you all start having a domestic?" I said. "Did Guy tell you he had me go out into the desert the other day to fetch his first consignment of heroin and cocaine? It was bloody hard work and I'm still catching up on my food intake."

"No. Really? Ed told me it was only hash. Maybe I really shouldn't be here after all," my mother said, looking momentarily alarmed.

"When we made camp some ex-forces chaps tried to creep up on us and kill us. They mistook us for Guy. He hadn't mentioned that they might be about. I expect it slipped his mind."

"My goodness. What happened?"

"We killed one of them and carried on anyway."

"Si…" she looked at me without speaking. "I never thought…"

"Don't worry about it, I'm good at it and it doesn't bother me," I said.

"The boy exaggerates. People do occasionally get hurt, but they're only others involved in the same trade. I've never killed someone who didn't deserve it, and neither has Simon."

"You shouldn't tell your mother things like that," Zara said.

"You're quite right, Zara, I shouldn't. Why don't we do this justice instead?" I said. More food was arriving and it smelt excellent. "Boy, my mother would like some of the 96 Medoc, if you can find it."

"Oh, yes, I definitely would," she said.

"Whatever," Guy said, shrugging his shoulders.

I ate, but not so much that it would slow me down, and drank enough of the vintage so that I didn't feel I'd missed out, but no so that the alcohol would affect me. Guy and my mother started a conversation about times past; university, people they had known, balls they had attended. I listened with half an ear. Zara steadily put away a bottle of gin and pushed her food from one side of her plate to the other.

"D'you want to know something interesting, Simon?" my mother said, out of the blue.

"Huh? Yes, always."

"They're going to give him a gong."

"Who, Dad?"

"Yes."

"What for?"

"The same as always; not getting caught."

"Not getting caught doing what?"

"Anything. Making a decision, being the last one standing when they ran out of chairs, taking sides, that kind of thing."

"It'll suit him, he can polish it and wear it at those dinners they have," Guy said.

"I'll be Lady Helen Ellice," my mother said.

"You don't seem that happy about it," I said.

"I am. It's just…"

"Just that it'll be the culmination of his ambition and you don't want something so tawdry to be all there is," Guy said.

"Yes, how did you know?"

"I've known you a long time, Helen. And just because I don't care about all that shit doesn't mean I don't understand it. It's where I came from too after all."

"I'd forgotten," she said.

"Talking of the tawdry and the finite," I said, "I take it that Mum is staying here?"

"Helen, would you care to stay with me for a while? It would give me great pleasure," Guy said.

"I thought I was staying with Simon," she said.

"This would be much more comfortable for you," Guy said.

"No, thank you, I think I'll go home with Simon. There are things we need to talk about," she said.

"Mum, I don't think you've quite got it. You've been a hostage for my continued service since you walked into the Rif bar. You don't want me, do you?" I said to Guy.

"Frankly, dear boy, I'll sleep better with you somewhere else. No, you can go, but be available. I'll have some work for you to do quite soon I believe. And don't talk to any strangers."

"Goodnight, Mum," I said, giving her a dutiful kiss.

"Guy? Really?" she said.

"Sorry, my darling. Needs must and all that," Guy said.

"Well, Lady Helen," Zara said, "welcome to my world."

14

NOTHING IMPORTANT

I went home. I'd forgotten what I'd said to Soumy so I had an uncomfortable moment standing in front of my own front door wondering why I couldn't get in. She answered her phone at the first ring and let me in.

"Hey, Soumy. You okay?"

"I am now that you're here."

"Did Sam come by?"

"Yes, she did. I didn't let her in. I said you had told me not to. It was difficult but I knew she would kill me if I did."

"Well, maybe not kill you…"

She stuck out her bottom lip in a rather charming way.

"…but who knows. Now, I want some coffee and I want to talk to you and then I want some sleep. Okay?"

"Okay. I will make some coffee and bring it to you."

I fetched the letter to her that I'd written and the bag of money that I'd left in a drawer in the study and took them to the sitting room. I burned the letter and let the ashes drift down from the balcony into the street below. She came in with a tray and put it on the low table by the sofa.

"Would you like some coffee?" I said. She looked at me like I'd spoken to her in a language she didn't know. "Soumy," I said.

"Yes, Simon?" she said.

"You said there was more to you than I knew, and more than you knew. You remember?"

"I remember."

"Would that Soumy like some coffee?"

"I don't know."

"Fair enough. I need to talk to her though, if you can find her. I need her help."

"Oh. Okay, I will try."

"Good. You're going to leave here and become a young woman of independent means. I mean a young woman with some money of her own. This is the money." I picked up the cloth bag with bundles of notes in it and passed it to her. She held it carefully and looked inside. It was most of the money that I'd found in the case with the RPG.

"I have never imagined so much money," she said.

"You'll get used to it. Tomorrow you are going to become someone else. Someone that no one knows, or would not recognise. Can you do that?"

"I am a woman. That's easy."

"I thought so. You're going to find a new home somewhere else in the city. You can decide where, but it must be a place where no one knows you and where I can come without causing a scandal. You will buy a new phone and destroy the one you have by hitting it with a stone until it is completely dead. Okay?"

"I think I can do that."

"Good. I will take you from here, with everything you want to take, to a hotel in the morning. You stay at the hotel until you find somewhere and then get a taxi to bring your things. Okay?"

"A hotel?"

"Yes, a hotel. You are a person who has money and stays in hotels now."

"Is this really necessary? I do not know if I can do this."

"You cannot help me as a slave girl."

"I understand that. I will do my best."

"I knew you would. Thanks, Soumy."

"What do I do with this?" she held the bag of money.

"I don't know. Whatever you think best. What do you usually do with money?"

"I have an idea."

"Good. Right, I think I'll go and get some sleep, we need to make an early start."

"Simon, wait a moment."

"Yes?"

"I am going to go and get a coffee cup and my sewing things. I want you to tell me about it, please. You said I have to be the me that is more than I am, and that me wants to know."

"Good for you. I'll tell you all about it," I said, and so I did.

She woke me before dawn with coffee and a serious, but possibly also excited, face. I stood under the shower for a bit and then dressed. When I came out the hall had two piles of bags in it, one for her and one for me. I had a last look round my study, tucked my .38 into the waistband of my trousers and went to fetch the truck.

She was very self-conscious sitting in the front passenger seat but she had her chin up. She was wearing jeans, smart sandals, a top that was flattering but covered her arms, and a headscarf.

"Have you ever been outside the flat wearing anything like that before?" I said, when we had got past the docks and were heading to the Melilla end of town.

"No. I keep thinking everyone is looking at me."

"If they are, it's only because you are beautiful. Now, tell me what you're going to do, Soumy," I said. She told me and it was all right. "Good. What will you say if a man at the bank asks you where you're from?"

"How did you know I was going to the bank?"

"I looked into the top of your bag when you went back for a last look around. You've saved quite a bit."

"You think I stole it from you. It was only what was left over from the housekeeping money. I never touched your money clip." She swallowed and looked away from me, holding her bag tight to herself as if I might take it from her.

"Soumy, it was a damned good idea. Well done." She looked at me from the corner of her eye. "If you intend to put that money in the bank be careful how you do it. Okay? Not all at once."

"Now you think I'm stupid," she said, smiling and holding her head up once more.

"No, but I think you didn't answer my question."

"What question?"

"What will you say to anyone who asks you where you're from, what you're doing here; that kind of thing?"

"Oh, that is easy. I am here to keep house for my brother who is coming to start a business in mobile phone things, which I do not understand. I have been sent to set up a home for him here. We are from Agadir. I know it well enough to be able to answer questions."

"Excellent."

"Though I could always say, none of your business, couldn't I?"

"I suppose you could."

"What are you going to do now?"

"Drop you and your bags outside that hotel and go away quickly before the desk clerk notices me."

"I don't mean that, I mean…"

"I know what you mean, Soumy. I'm not sure. Now get out and go do your thing."

I would've kissed her if I'd had the chance but she got out as I pulled up so it was only left to me to heave her bags out of the back and do as I said. She watched me go for a moment though, before she squared up and went through the doors of the safe, anonymous, tourist hotel.

It was a bit early to go up to the Riby, and truth to tell, I didn't have much of a plan, so I drove all the way along the front and out of town the other way. The call to prayer from the loudspeakers on several competing mosques was both musical and harsh in the stillness of the early morning. Nottambulo was at her mooring and I'm sure Asif and Imad were keeping a good watch, though I couldn't see them.

The ribbon of piecemeal development along the shore isn't exactly squalid, it's too new for that, but it's on the edge of it. Nothing is built with conviction or a sense of pride. Most of the buildings are low sprawls of concrete and red tile; cafés, cheap restaurants with houses that aspire to be villas but fall short, in between.

The blue fishing boats that had gone out before dawn to pull up night lines and lobster pots were coming in, some from the lagoon but most from the Mediterranean beyond. They would join the loud, happy chaos of the morning fish market at one end of the dock. I wondered if Robbie would be there. It seemed unlikely. I thought that he would send one of his two excellent chefs rather than get up that early himself.

In the cafes men were sitting, sipping coffee and watching the smoke curl up from their cigarettes; waking up slowly while their more devout brethren made the ritual prayers. I thought I would never tire of the way the first sunlight gilds even the cheapest plastic and neon, making it for a few minutes, numinous and lovely.

Lovely too was the Wise Policy, sitting in the still water like a black swan, elegant and full of potential. She looked shut up and unused for the moment and the rib wasn't with her or on the beach. There were a few vans and cars in the parking spaces near the café and a few men inside, but only one European. He was sitting at a table near the front with a good view out to sea. He had a laptop open in front of him and a litter of breakfast things around him. On an impulse I backed into one of the spaces and turned off the engine.

I checked my .38. I didn't need to but it gave me a minute to prepare myself. When I got out the scene was unchanged, quiet and full of normality. I walked along in front of the building, climbed the few steps and went inside.

The man had looked up from his computer and was watching me. I went over to his table and said, "Morning. Mind if I join you?"

"Help yourself." He shut his laptop, turned to the approaching waiter, and said, "Waiter, more coffee."

I sat down; at the table but sufficiently to one side so that what he did with his hands wouldn't be hidden from me and forward on my chair so that I could still get at my gun quickly.

"You've some neck, Mr Ellice," he said. He had blue eyes with the warmth of glacial melt water. Close up I could see what Ali meant about his haircut.

"How so, Mr…?" I said.

"You can call me Rupe. You're driving my truck for a start," he said.

"I left you mine," I said.

"Yes, without the fucking relay. And you owe me some money." His eyes narrowed as he remembered.

"You left it lying about. Did I come looking for you?"

"If you do what you do, you can't expect anything else."

"That may be so, but then neither can you. I don't think you can claim the moral high ground here. Were you expecting me or Mr Wealden? Out in the desert?"

He hesitated for a moment and then said, "You should leave. It's not you I want."

"But if I get in the way…?"

"You've already cost me one good man."

"Not that good."

"Okay, not that good. But still, the others would like to get their hands on you, very much."

"Anyway, you killed one of mine."

"When?"

"On a roof by the docks."

"He was yours? You shouldn't have sent a boy to do a man's job."

"I'll try to remember that. But you've got other concerns, apart from a few men here or there. What are they exactly?"

"That's none of your business."

"You've made it my business. You're an unlikely candidate for drug dealer. It's a squalid and mean profession in the end, not in the best traditions of the service at all. Couldn't you do better?"

"What would you know? What makes you think I care about the traditions of the British Army?"

"Apart from your shoes?"

He looked at his shoes. They were clean and well polished.

"You're clearly well funded," I waved in the general direction of Wise Policy, "and half trained, but you're behaving like a bunch of cheap thugs running about killing the wrong people. Can't you find something more useful to do?"

"There are always casualties and war is a messy business." He looked at me. I couldn't read what he was thinking but it didn't seem entirely hostile. "Get on a plane, Mr Ellice and go home. Do it now. You won't get a second chance." He looked at the heavy watch on his wrist. "I'm not going to tell you what this is all about, but take my word for it, it's not for you."

"Okay," I said, rising.

"Okay?" he said.

"I agree. Fuck this. You and Guy can fight it out, I don't want any part of it. Which ever one of you gets it, can keep it as far as I'm concerned."

He looked at me with narrowed eyes again. "You haven't had your coffee," he said.

"That's all right, you can keep that too," I said, and walked out. I got into the truck, headed back towards town and turned in to head up to the top of the hill. I was about to pass the store without stopping but I noticed that Happy was sitting by the door in his massive inscrutable way, so I stopped to say hello.

"Nice truck," he said, grinning when I walked over.

"How're you doing, Happy?" I said.

"Got me some sleep and some food and a nice piece of tail. I'm doing fine apart from I'm doing this boring shit. When's the next thing happening, boss?"

"Good question, Happy. I'll let you know as soon as I know. Be good now."

"Will do, boss."

I left him smiling at the world from behind his mirror shades, sitting on his plastic chair, which would only just hold him up, with his personal AK, waiting for the next thing, and went up the hill. A local taxi driver with more nerve than sense came up a bit close behind me but backed off again when I showed him my brake lights unexpectedly. Sometimes the dope slows them down and sometimes it makes them mad.

It was still early. Early for the house anyway, but I turned in and the guard let me through. There was no one at the table under the pergola but there was a lone figure on a chair at the far end of the pool. I could tell who it was by the big, floppy hat and the long silk dressing gown. I picked up another chair and carried it over.

"Simon," Mum said, when she saw it was me.

"It's a good view, isn't it?" I said, sitting down.

"Yes, it is, isn't it?" Unexpectedly she took my hand and held it.

"How're you doing? You're up early," I said.

"I'm a fool, aren't I?"

"Why are you here, Mum?"

"Your father…"

"Yes?"

"I don't know. They phoned me. Looking for him…"

"Not at a conference then?"

"Apparently not."

"And you think he's here?"

"No. Not really. I just thought…"

"Does he know I'm here? That I'm working for Guy?"

"I don't know. He might."

"How could he know? Have you told him?"

"No, darling. But he finds things out you know… Sometimes he finds things out."

"What kind of things do you mean, Mum?"

"Things that people do. He wouldn't be happy about you working for Guy."

"I know they fell out, but is it really such a big deal?"

"He's a more passionate man than you might think, darling."

"If you say so. I was about to leave. Right then, when you walked into the bar. This is madness, all this," I said. "I doubt if Guy will let me leave. Alive, I mean. If he can help it anyway."

"Don't think that, darling. That can't be true."

"How well do you know him, Mum?"

"Guy? Oh, I've known him forever."

"I know. What I mean is, the Guy I know, he kills people when it suits him. I'm not at all comfortable with you being here. Not that there's anything I can do about it."

"Oh, darling. Guy and I, well we get on, you know. Always have. We're pretty much family, you, me and Ed. He won't hurt us. You're probably just seeing him in his, well, his professional capacity. Everyone has to do things sometimes, you know, that they wouldn't do otherwise. I'm sure he wouldn't hurt me, or you, darling."

"Mum, you do think Dad might be here, don't you?"

"No, darling, I just thought... I just thought it was time you came home, that's all. I came to get you."

"Not to see Guy?"

"No."

"No?"

"Well, perhaps a bit."

"I don't suppose it matters now. I must go, but, Mum, promise me something."

"What, darling?"

"If anything happens, keep your head down. Right down."

"Like what, darling?"

"Guns, explosions, things like that."

"Oh, I'm sure there won't be anything like that. Guy, and you, have everything very well organised. Anyone can see that."

"Just promise me, Mum."

"Okay, if it makes you happy, I promise."

I kissed her on the cheek and left her looking at the view.

The guard let me back out again and I drove on up to the Riby. There were a few cars in the car park but not many. Someone's chauffeur looked at me briefly from the front of a Merc and turned back to his paper. This early there was no one at the door so I walked through the gardens and out onto the terrace. Sam was having breakfast with Robbie at one of the tables.

He saw me first and looked like a dog caught with the Christmas turkey still in its jaws.

"Si. There you are. Would you like some coffee?" he said.

"Morning," I said.

"Morning, Si," Sam said, looking up at me with her clear blue-grey eyes. She looked perfectly calm and composed, happy if anything, as if everything was perfectly normal. If there was any kind of normal.

"What I'd like is some breakfast, if you can manage that?" I said.

"Si, we, I…" he trailed off.

"Robbie…"

"Si?"

"Shut up and get me some breakfast, will you." I sat down at the table with them.

"Right away." He whistled to a waiter and waved him over.

"Have you been to the house?" Sam said.

"Just came from there."

"I suppose that woman is still there?"

"I suppose she probably is."

"What woman?" Robbie said.

"I think she means my mother," I said.

"Oh, really?"

"I'm afraid so."

"She and my dad seem to be having a bit of a thing," Sam said.

"Or at least he's holding onto her as leverage to make me run tonnes of cocaine and heroin into Europe," I said.

"You shouldn't be telling me things like that, surely?" Robbie said.

"I'm past giving a fuck about anyone else's secrets," I said.

"I see," he said.

"So tell me now, what you were going to tell me the other day," I said.

"Ah, yes. Well, the thing is I assumed it was just a coincidence at first, then, well… Why don't I just show you?" He looked at Sam.

"Show me what?" I said.

"Er…"

"Don't mind me," Sam said. "Just take him and show him whatever. I'm fine here."

"Okay, yes. Come with me, Si. Just for a moment, while they're cooking your breakfast."

"Come on then. I'm hungry."

"This way." He led me into the building but instead of passing into the gardens or turning left into the hall that received guests on the rare occasions when it was nicer to be inside, we turned right and passed through the kitchens and servants' quarters. I followed him into what appeared to be a pantry. There were shelves of tablecloths, napkins, cutlery, glasses and other paraphernalia of serving at table.

"Mind your head," he said, opening what I had taken for a cupboard door, flicking a switch on the wall, and stepping through. "Distrustful lot, whoever built this."

"Very important thing, trust," I said, following him into a low passage which turned right and then left and became stairs.

"We're in the main wall of the keep now," he said.

It was so low and narrow that my shoulders brushed the wall on either side and I couldn't stand up straight. I'm not particularly claustrophobic, but I can't say I was enjoying it. I had to duck even lower each time we passed one of the intermittent low level lights hanging from the cable snaking up the stonework.

I couldn't see anything apart from Robbie's backside going on before me, and little enough of that as either he was casting shadow from the bulb ahead or I was from the one behind, but then he disappeared and I found myself on a tiny landing with a slim arrow-slit window before me. I looked out. As far as I could tell we were about halfway up. I could see part of the car park and the walls of the adjacent section of the castle, which had been the harem and which now housed the hotel's bedrooms.

The stairs had turned back on themselves and continued up. I followed on and, after what was presumably the same distance, it doubled back for a few more steps and let us out through a small but massively constructed door onto the parapet itself. I held onto the stonework and looked about. If the view from the terrace was good, from here it was fantastic. Africa one way and the Mediterranean the other, laid out at our feet. I could see why they'd built it in that spot. It wasn't that high really, but it was high enough that the cars in the car park seemed like small things. I could see the tiny figure of the chauffeur in the Merc turn the pages of his paper.

I thought I heard a sound, and then another. Not shooting but something like it. Someone scaring birds perhaps. It wasn't repeated. I was about to say something about it but as I turned Robbie had his finger to his lips. I nodded and followed him along the parapet to the landward edge. Here we were looking down a story or so onto the roofs of the harem section of the castle.

In hindsight I shouldn't have been surprised, but at the time I was. Instead of bare roofs I was looking down into a hidden garden. There was even a lovely tile-lined pool with fat koi circulating slowly round it. There was room for three sets of tables and chairs in the open spaces and at one, by a bed of bright red cannas, a man was sitting reading a paper. It looked like The Times. He wore a wide-brimmed straw hat and a well-starched white shirt, had polished brown shoes and neatly pressed khaki trousers. I couldn't see anything of his face but there was something familiar about him.

"We make this available to customers who wish to stay here but not be seen. That chap," Robbie said, standing near me and speaking in a low voice, "goes by the name of Robinson and has a passport in the name of Robinson, but his luggage has the initials E.E. on it and I think I overheard him answer his phone with something that sounded like 'Ellice'. I just wondered, that's all."

I looked again. He was right. No wonder he'd seemed familiar, it was my father reading a paper down there.

"Fuck," I said.

"Is it?" Robbie said.

"Yes. How long has he been here?"

"Just over a fortnight."

"Does he have visitors?"

"No. Uses his phone quite a lot though."

"Has he been out at all?"

"Not so far. Seems to be getting a bit impatient if you ask me." There was the familiar signet ring on his left hand, clearly visible as he used it to hold up his paper. So bloody typical that he would be wearing immaculate clothes even here, even when there was no one to appreciate them. I could easily have lobbed a brick onto his head if there had been one to hand.

"So, that's…?"

"My father. Yes."

"And you mentioned earlier that your mother was here too?"

"Apparently we've all moved to Morocco."

"Sweet of them to come and find the prodigal, I suppose."

"If only. No, there's more to this than that."

Down in the garden below us my father's phone rang. He picked it up quickly, spoke a word and then listened. He stiffened, got up and began pacing about the space. Robbie and I ducked down in case he should look up.

"…Damn. You must…" I could only catch the most emphatically spoken words. "…No. Now, dammit. We've…" He turned away and I couldn't distinguish any more words before he disconnected.

"I need to think and I need some food," I said in Robbie's ear.

"Right oh. Come on then."

I followed him back down to the table, grasped a coffee cup and stared over it at the middle distance.

"What's up?" Sam said.

"I'm thinking," I said.

"I can see that."

I ate something, I can't remember what, and let it all swirl about in my brain.

"We once went on holiday to Crete. It was a bit like this as I remember," I said.

"How do you mean?" Robbie said.

"Her over there with someone else, him over there with a paper and a phone and me…"

"Sitting at a table ignoring a beautiful girl," Sam said, ruffling my hair.

"Something like that, yes."

My phone buzzed briefly in my pocket. It was a text from Soumy, 'no name house on no name street behind Olad Boutaib'

"I've got to go see a man about a dog," I said.

"Not coming out to play then?" Sam said, stretching her arms above her head and wriggling her bottom on the chair.

"I expect Robbie will," I said.

"He doesn't play the kind of games you do."

"He's very sensible."

"I wouldn't say that. Can I have a lift home?"

"I'm going that way. Ready now?"

"Yes."

"Come on then."

When we got to the car park I stopped and looked at the few cars in it. "Hang on, I'll be back in a second," I said, and retraced my steps.

"Are you going to hit me now?" Robbie said, when I caught up with him on the terrace.

"No, later. Have you been out into the car park yet today?"

"No, why? I'll be going down to town in a minute. I always do on a Wednesday."

"There's a Merc in the car park with MUR in the number plate and I think there are three men in it. They've been there a while."

"Oh, fuck."

I gave him a sunny smile and left him to it.

Driving down the hill I said, "I suppose I'd better come in for a moment and say good morning to Mum."

"I can do that for you, if you like," Sam said.

"Probably best not."

When we got there, there was a battered old Nissan abandoned by the gates, which were open. I stopped and looked at Sam.

"Oh, fuck," she said.

I backed the big truck up to the open gate so that it obscured the entrance and so that it was pointing the right way to leave quickly. Sam and I got out, me with my .38 and her with her little .32 at the ready. There was no need to speak. We stayed apart and approached carefully. She kept watch while I went into the little guard's hut to have a look.

There were two men dumped in a heap on the floor. One was the guard and the other was certainly a taxi driver. The upper portions of each of them was a bloody pulp, there were splinters and rends in the wooden structure of the hut and pieces of brown paper had fluttered about and landed here and there across the tarmac.

I went back out so that she could have a look. She came out and nodded.

We went inside, guns up. There was the acrid smell of the aftermath of tear-gas and explosive about, but no movement. The door of Guy's office had been removed with small charges at the hinges. We glanced inside and then moved on, checking that the outside areas were clear. The boy who usually hovered near the house, ready to fetch and carry, was face down across the path so we stepped over him and went through the house, room by room, entering one at a time and moving left or right so that we weren't silhouetted against the doorway and didn't block each other's fire. There was no need.

The chef had managed to open a cupboard at the back of the kitchen which contained an AK but was lying slumped against it, shot twice in the back and then ignored. Other staff had been killed further back in the building as they ran for cover. There were more than I'd expected and I realised that I'd not generally bothered to distinguish between them and hadn't any real idea how many there were. None of the bodies were my mother, or Guy, or Zara.

At the back of the compound someone had strung long jumper cables across sections of the electrified fence and then cut out a panel. There were a number of empty shell cases about here and there.

We found no one alive so we walked back, looking into all the rooms again, with a more considering eye. Guy's arsenal, a room off the main hall with a ridiculously flimsy door, had been ransacked. The main bedrooms and guest quarters were empty. We returned to the area by the pool and considered that. Apart from a couple of empty gas canisters and the dead boy, there was nothing unusual to see.

I went behind the bar, pulled two beers out of the fridge, took the tops off and handed one to Sam.

"Thanks, Si. Good idea."

"I think they waited until Guy was at the table, away from the house. Where'd he go?" I said.

"Come see," she said, and led me into the office.

The big filing cabinet that was usually against the side wall had been moved aside. It was on rollers, which I'd never noticed before. Where it had been was a small, strong looking, steel door.

"That fence behind the cars, the one with all that bougainvillea on it, is a double one. The space between leads to the back of the mayor's garages. He keeps the other Range Rover there."

"The other Range Rover?"

"You know Dad; if it matters, have two." She pulled her phone out of her back pocket.

The two computers on the desk were interesting. Each one seemed to have been the scene of a small fire. Presumably their hard drives would be beyond being read. I poked one experimentally. It was still warm.

"Answerphone," she said, hanging up.

"I think you should go and pack anything you might want," I said.

"I expect we'll be back quite soon, but I will anyway." She put her gun away and went back into the house.

"I'll just look about and see if there's anything interesting to see," I said.

I wandered thoughtfully out to the pool and remembered what I hadn't seen. I walked round the pool looking at the loungers. Coffee things but no gin bottle there, none at the table either. I tried the door of the small room that houses the pumps and whatnot for the pool. It was locked but it wasn't much of a door so I opened it with a kick.

Zara was sitting on a plastic chair. Her arms were hanging down like she was a rag doll. Her head hung down too but not as far as it might. The haft of the long knife that had been pushed through her throat was getting in the way. She seemed smaller than she had in life and disconcertingly naked in her bikini. I pulled the door shut and left her be.

"Find anything?" Sam said, dragging a big suitcase on wheels out of the house.

"Nothing important," I said.

15

A RUG AND SOME CUSHIONS

"What next, Si?" Sam said, when we'd got back into the truck.

"I suppose I'd better go and have a chat with my father."

"Really? Is he about then?"

"Yes, he's staying at the Riby."

"Oh, that's what you meant a minute ago. How interesting, I'd like to meet him."

"I don't see why not. Let's go back and have a beer. We can invite him to join us."

The Merc was still in the car park.

"Shall we get rid of them?" I said, motioning towards it.

"It'd be more fun to leave it," she said.

"I know, but this isn't the time, come on."

I walked up behind it on one side and Sam took the other. The driver saw us in his mirror and wound down his window. We could see two figures in the back through the tinted glass, but not clearly.

"You waiting for Robbie?" I said to the driver, squatting slightly and leaning in, in a friendly way.

"None of your business ferenji," the man said. He was overweight and the gap between the steering wheel and his stomach wasn't very big. He pulled aside his jacket with his right hand to expose an old revolver tucked into the top of his trousers. "Now piss off."

I hit him on the nose with my right hand, which made him put his hands up to his face, and lifted the gun out. I jiggled the locking button on the car door with my left. This unlocked the back doors and Sam and I opened one each, stepping back so that we were behind the occupants and they would have to turn a long way to get a gun in line with us.

There was another renta-thug on Sam's side and she stamped on the instep of the foot he foolishly put outside, guided the barrel of a luger away from her and hit him on the wrist with the butt of her .32. He yelped and dropped it and she kicked it under the car.

On my side, Mr Murr was looking at me as if he wasn't sure whether to be more angry or more frightened.

"Afternoon, Mr Murr," I said.

"Hello, Mr Ellice."

"You want to kill Mr Robbie?"

"He has dishonoured me."

"I know. You want the woman?"

"She is nothing to me. I have divorced her."

"Where is she?"

"I have no idea." He shrugged.

"Have your men find her and bring her here. That will be punishment enough."

"I do not think it will."

"That is a shame. I need him alive at the moment so I will have to kill you instead. I apologise for the unfairness of this." I let him look down the barrel of my .38. "Do you want me to kill these two men also, or shall I leave them alive to take your body back to your family?"

"Yes, no, I mean I suppose that you are right. Now that I think about it I see that your idea is a good one. I will do as you suggest."

"You are very wise. Allah favours the compassionate. Goodbye, Mr Murr." I handed him his driver's revolver and shut the door. Sam and I walked off towards the castle.

"That was a bit sneaky," Sam said.

"It just sort of came to me."

"Do you think he will?"

"Bring her up here? I don't know, he might."

"Well?" Robbie said, appearing from behind the wall holding an AK as if it were a snake.

"We had a word. They're going away." I took the gun off him and put the safety on.

"Bloody hell, Si. That's amazing. And after I…"

"I'll take a cold beer on the terrace if you can find one," I said.

"And me," Sam said.

"I think I was just putting off doing this," I said, when we'd sat down. I took out my phone and hunted for a number that I hadn't used for a long time. I dialled it and listened to it ring for a bit.

A voice said, "Simon, what can I do for you?"

"I'm on the terrace. You need to come down and talk to me," I said.

"How did you… Never mind. That's out of the question I'm afraid. Perhaps you could join me up here. I'm sure your friend Mr Anderson will show you the way."

"You know Mum's here?"

"What? Where?" His voice was no longer so studiedly calm.

"I'm sure you can guess. I'll be here while I finish my beer and then I'm off," I said, and hung up.

"He'll know I told you," Robbie said, joining us and putting down a tray with beers and glasses.

"Tough," I said.

"It's none of my business, of course, but that didn't sound entirely cordial," he said.

"We've never got on. I think he sees me as a... I don't know, as a retrogression or something. And probably a threat to all that he's done so much brown-nosing to get."

"Where has he got?"

"Hard for me to say, he never talks about it directly, but if you believe him, he's something big in the civil service back home. Mum says he's up for a knighthood of some kind so there must be some truth to it. When I was a boy I'd always rather go shooting or fishing with Grandad than be with him. We got disconnected when I went to school and we've never got connected again."

"Your schools have a lot to answer for if you ask me," Robbie said.

"You may be right about that. Then, after basically ignoring me for years, he starts having opinions about what I should do with my life."

"I take it what you've done isn't quite what he had in mind?" Robbie said.

"Anything respectable and well paid would have done. Something that would lead to the phrase, 'my son the...' would have been good."

"And not end in drug dealer?" Robbie said.

"Smuggler. Exactly."

"You didn't say what he's doing here," Sam said.

"I don't know. Or at least I don't think I know. I'll ask him when he comes down."

"You sure he will?" Robbie said.

"Pretty sure. It'll be easier than phoning me back and risking getting hung up on again."

I was right. A tall figure in a wide brimmed straw hat came out of the shadow of the big doorway from the courtyard garden and walked towards us. I had a momentary urge to stand up and pull out a chair for him but I suppressed it. He stood over us, looking at me with curiosity and then at Sam. Robbie did the business with the chair.

"Dad, this is Sam," I said. "Have a seat. Sam, this is my father, Edmund Ellice."

"Pleased to meet you, Miss... er, Sam." He still had the same presence he always had, a man most people naturally defer to. I thought that there were lines of tension around his eyes that hadn't been there last time I'd seen him, but I could have been wrong about that.

"Pleased to meet you too, Ed. Would you like some beer?" she said. Whatever effect he had on others wasn't working on Sam.

"Simon, we should talk."

"We should. Have a seat."

"Forgive me... Sam, there are things I need to say to Simon which are..."

"Have you tried ringing her?" I said.

"She's not answering," he said. "She seldom does, however."

"That's true. Okay. Sam, will you take this idiot out the back and show him which end of an AK is which, or something?"

"Yes, boss." She got up and saluted.

"Can I get you anything, Mr Ellice?" Robbie said.

"No thank you, Mr Anderson. You've done quite enough," my father said.

Robbie and Sam left.

"That girl called you boss?" my father said, when they were out of earshot.

"She's one of my crew," I said. "I also have a big, black Nigerian."

"On your boat?"

"Yes, on my boat. The one I use for running drugs for Guy Wealden."

"I see."

"So you know all about that then?"

"This is all your fault, you know. If you hadn't done this thing with that boat, none of this would have happened. Why do you never listen to me?"

"Because you never listen to me. What has happened? Why are you here, Dad? Why are you and Mum both here?"

"I didn't know she was here."

"I think she came looking for you. What are you doing here? Come on, tell me."

"I… If you must know, I came to tell Guy to sack you. This can't go on. Your mother is worrying about you."

"She hides it well. So you can tell Guy what to do, can you?"

"Yes. No. We're old friends; he'll listen to me."

"So you are. What's Rupert here for then?"

"Where's your mother? Is she staying with you?"

"No, she's with Guy. I think they got away from his place when it was taken by Rupe and his team a bit over an hour ago. Who is he, by the way?"

My father's hand reached towards his pocket and then stopped. "She's with him? With Guy?"

"That's what I'm telling you. Who's this guy called Rupert?"

"I don't know anyone called Rupert. What are you going to do?" he said, instead.

"Right now, I'm telling you. What are you going to do?"

"Do you know where he's gone?"

"Guy?"

"Yes, Guy."

"No, I don't. He'll have a contingency though. Could be a flat in town or a camp in the desert."

"Can't you find out? You work for him."

"Unfortunately we've had a difference of opinion. Mum is a hostage to make me run cocaine and heroin in Nottambulo. Or at least she was, I'm not sure what's happening at the moment."

"This is your fault. If you hadn't gone off like that none of this would have happened. You should go home now and leave this to me."

"What are you going to do?"

"Find him and talk to him."

"How?"

"There are ways."

"Okay, I'll get in my boat and bugger off."

"No… Take a plane."

"Why? I can't just leave her here."

"They'll be watching it."

"Who'll be watching it?"

"Guy of course. He'll want it."

"But Guy's on the run from Rupe and his gang."

"Doesn't matter. Just go away will you, and leave this to me."

"Okay, Dad. If you aren't going to treat me like an adult and tell me what's going on, then I might as well."

"That's exactly why I can't. You always refuse to trust me and do what I tell you to."

"But you keep lying to me."

"No I don't."

"You've lied to me more than once in the last few minutes."

"No I haven't. I never lie."

"You lied about Grandad."

"That was different."

"Was it? And what can you do anyway? You're here by yourself. You've no staff to run errands for you here. Have you?"

"I'm not going to tell you what I'm going to do. I will get your mother out of this situation and bring her home. All you have to do is leave it to me and go home."

"Okay, Dad. This isn't doing much good. As usual." I got up. "I might as well go home for all the good I'm doing here."

"Finally we understand each other." He got his phone out of his pocket. "I'll phone you when I have some news."

"That would be a first." I walked away, through the arch and into the garden. Sam and Robbie were sitting on cane chairs looking at me with interest.

"Bloody hell, Si. I'd forgotten what you look like when you're angry," Sam said.

"If I didn't know you to be such a nice chap I'd go and stand behind Sam," Robbie said.

"Ugh." I shook myself, trying to get out of the place I'd got into. I'd known that would happen; that's why I'd put it off. "I'm going into town now. Let me know if Guy gets in touch will you, Sam?"

"Sure, but give me a lift, will you? I'm bored here already."

"What're you going to do in town?"

"I want some wheels. I don't suppose you'd lend me yours right now, would you?"

"After the last time, you suppose right. Anyway, I need it. What's wrong with the cars at the house?"

"No, I mean desert wheels. I'll buy something in town, or steal it. It'll give me something to do."

"Come on then. I'll drop you off at the Rif. Ali's bound to know who's the best dealer in town."

"Or, if there's something nice outside I could help the owner get a little drunk and lift the keys, couldn't I?"

"I'm quite sure you could."

"I'm going to go and have a nice cup of tea and hope the day gets back to normal when you're gone," Robbie said. "I just didn't know when I was well off, did I?"

"We never do," I said.

There was a small Vauxhall car with a green stripe along it parked at the gate of the house as we passed, the Gendarmerie had turned up.

"Do you want to have a word with them?" I said.

"Not really. If Dad's alive and well he'll have phoned the mayor, if not it doesn't matter," she said.

"Fair enough."

"What Robbie said was right, wasn't it?"

"How's that?"

"About appreciating what we have."

"Oh, that. What are you appreciating? Me?" I said.

"No, Dad. Seeing you with yours made me appreciate mine. He might piss me off sometimes, but at least I don't usually look like you looked earlier when he's about."

"So you're saying that you're better off than me because your father is Guy Wealden? Fuck me, I suppose you may have a point."

"You're not having a good day, are you, Si?"

"No, not really."

The store was open for business as usual and Romeo was serving a small queue of customers. Karim was occupying the place by the door. He'd acquired some mirror shades. There didn't seem any point calling in so we passed without drawing attention to ourselves.

The sea was still there, blue and sparkly and uncomplicated, and the boats, Nottambulo amongst them, nodded gently in the small waves from the onshore breeze. I slowed down as we approached the Rif.

"Actually, I think I might go into town first." Sam said. "I don't suppose the staff are going to be doing much work for a while so I'd better assume the role of domestic goddess."

"I thought you would be staying at the Riby?"

"Oh, I am, but Dad'll be on the phone soon enough wanting scotch and soda, I'll bet you."

"RPGs and heavy calibre automatic weaponry, more likely."

"Well, possibly, but he may already have those. You know what he's like about that sort of thing. But I'll bet he's forgotten the scotch."

"You may be right. If anyone can look after himself, it's Guy. I just hope the same thing applies to my mother. I'm just going to go out to the boat and see the boys. Do you want to get a beer or something?" I stopped in a space near the end of the pontoon.

"I'll wait in the car. I might see if I can find any news on the radio."

"Ali will have all the news. Won't be a minute." I jumped out, stuffed the keys into my pocket and ran down the jetty. It was nice to run on the springy planks. It was good to be back with the sea too.

I would have liked to swim out to her but that would have meant putting my phone in a waterproof bag, which I'd left in the flat, and I didn't have any other clothes either. Asif answered my hail and soon Imad was motoring towards me in the little tender.

I got him to get out and hand her over to me and turned the handle on the little seagull motor as far as it would go, which wasn't far. I trailed my right hand in the sea on my way out to her and the water felt wonderful on my skin; cool and tingly. Asif looked weary, sitting on the thwart with an AK propped carefully beside him.

"What am I doing to you, old friend?" I said, passing him the painter.

"Hello, Simon, it is good to see you," he said.

"And you, Asif. Tell me, has anyone been looking at my girl?"

"Not that I can tell you, no. All has been very quiet. We have not seen any of the men from up that way," he pointed down the lagoon towards Wise Policy, "or that skinny fellow, or anyone at all."

"That's good. Now help me pack a bag, will you."

We opened several lockers and I hunted about for the things I wanted. It added up to quite a bag-full.

"Are you going to war, Simon?"

"I think the war has come to me. Let's hope I survive it," I said.

"If Allah wills it, I hope so too."

"Asif, I have changed my mind. I still think that someone will take my beautiful boat from me, but that cannot be helped now. I do not want you to stay aboard her anymore."

"That must not be. We will stay and kill anyone who comes near her."

"No, Asif, it will not do. You will go and get some sleep now. Imad will watch her from the shore and keep any water rats away from her. Otherwise, if any ferenji come he must keep low and let them take her. You understand?"

"I do not understand. How can you wish this? We have guarded her for so long and now you wish that any dog can have her without a fight. It is not like you, Simon, if I may say so."

"I'm sorry, Asif. It must be so. Will you believe me if I say that it is my strategy? If I say that I have a plan in my head and that I must appear to go backwards in order it go forwards later?"

"If you say that I must believe it. Is it so?"

"Who knows, Asif."

"Allahu A'lam. Have you all you want?"

"I do, old friend. Come on, take me back and go home."

"As you say, Simon."

He looked back wistfully at the long black, deadly looking shape of Nottambulo as I went up the pontoon with my heavy bag on my shoulder. I waved him a cheerful wave and threw the bag in the back seat.

"What're you up to now?" Sam said, seeing the bag. "That looks heavy."

"Just a few useful things I think I might leave at the flat. Give me options," I said. "Shall I meet you there later? I'm not exactly sure what I'm doing but I might give you a lift back up the hill if you like. Where do you want me to drop you?"

"Don't mind much. Where are you going? I'll get out there."

"Okay, let's go into town."

I drove us down the front a bit, turned in and skirted the old centre, keeping to the wider, newer roads.

"This'll do," I said, when I found a space on the Avenue Du Mars, "I don't trust Azooz anymore. I'll get a taxi to take me and the bag and walk back later."

"You could just leave that bag in the boot. I'm sure it would be quite safe," Sam said.

"I know. Call me paranoid if you like," I said, pulling the bag out, locking the car and putting the keys in my pocket.

"Well, Si." She put her arms around me. "I hope you have a nice afternoon. Try not to worry about your mum. I'm sure she'll be okay." She held me tight and kissed me. "You be careful. You're not yourself today. Okay? I'll see you later."

"Okay. You be careful too, Sam."

"Don't worry about me, I'm Guy's daughter, remember?" She gave me her characteristic waggle of the bum as she walked happily away. I watched her go down the street for nearly a hundred yards and turn into a department store. The car keys were no longer in my pocket. I took the small, but heavy, black lump of the tracker out of the bag, bent down and reached under the truck and let it attach itself to one of the suspension mountings.

Ten minutes later I slung the bag under a table in a café a few corners away. While they were bringing me coffee, I phoned Soumy.

"Hey, Soumy. How's independent life?" I said, when she answered at the first ring.

"I am independent for a few hours and what am I doing?"

"I don't know, what're you doing?"

"I am sitting here waiting to find out if you are still alive, as usual. So much for independence."

"I am alive."

"I know that now."

"You've found a safe place?"

"Not clean, but safe, yes. Are you coming to visit me?"

"Yes. Where shall I meet you?"

"Okay. I will sit on a bench in Ichomay Park. When you come you can walk behind me and I will lead you to the place."

"Good girl, Soumy. I'll see you there."

I took the battery out of my phone, paid for the coffee, slung the heavy bag over my shoulder and went out into the bright sunshine. It was after lunch and there was a somewhat sleepy tone to the city. Here, away from the old centre and the hubbub of the market, the working people worked, or didn't work, at a pace which always had time for one more coffee, one more pipe. Only the ever-present young men who live by theft had quick, alert eyes. An unprepared newcomer, of any colour or race, could lose their bag to a snatch or their wallet to a knifepoint robbery at any time of day or night. They would be looking at me and my bag and wondering what was in it. If only they knew.

I crossed the Avenue Du Mars. It's one of those dividing lines that you find in cities; the town side has pretensions, the other side hasn't. It's not as bad as the badlands where the store is but it's teetering on the brink. The residents of the cemetery, crowded together under brightly tiled head and foot stones, wouldn't care though. I ran my hand along the tops of the railings, looking at the symbols of our common mortality. To me they looked like stones and tiles, things of simple matter, not evidence of death itself. That comes to us in the air, suddenly, in my experience, and it is the shock of the change from person to thing that seems real. That tear in the fabric of life that we quickly look away from and forget.

I swung in through the wrought iron gates, into the patch of scrubby grass and bushes that had presumably been intended as a tranquil adjunct to the graveyard, where mourners could meditate on the wisdom of the Almighty and find solace in the beauty of His world. As it was, a few women in various forms of hijab sat on the benches, loosely supervising a rout of small boys who were kicking two footballs about in the dust, in a game that looked more like warfare than football.

They looked at me with questioning eyes. Not exactly hostility but tending towards disapproval. The streets belong to men and the houses to women, so in theory I had more right to be there than they. In practise it was bad manners of me to intrude. I passed along, resisting the urge to put down my bag and join in the game, and headed for the other exit.

Soumy, in full penguin suit, black jilbab and headscarf, left the group of women, passed me with a little skip of her heels and I followed on at a discreet distance.

A few streets and a few corners later she turned into the yawning stairwell of an ugly concrete block of cheap apartments. The balconies, which gave access to the rooms, ran along the back, overshadowed by the blank wall of the side of a mosque. She flitted ahead of me along the one on the second floor and disappeared into the last door. I followed and put my bag down gratefully in the hallway of small, basic, unfurnished apartment.

"Hello, Simon," Soumy said, stripping off her headscarf and jilbab to reveal shorts and a t-shirt. "What do you think? Will it do? It's not very nice but I think it's quite safe."

"Soumy, you're brilliant. It's perfect." I reached for her but she danced out of the way.

"I expect you would like something to eat."

"That's true, and a shower and a rest. Is there a bed of some kind?"

"Of some kind, yes. Come and see." She led me into the bedroom. There being no bed she had laid out a rug on the floor and arranged cushions and quilts to make a charming and very comfortable nest.

"Soumy, you didn't go back to the flat?" I said.

"No. I bought these in the medina. I made two men carry them for me and I wore my modest garments and was bossy with them. They were glad to go away."

"Good girl, Soumy. Does the plumbing work?"

"Yes, if you are patient. Shall I take your clothes for washing?"

"No, I must put them back on when I go out again, but you could come and scrub my back for me."

"I will go and make you some food."

"Well, at least you're dressed like yourself."

"I'm in my own home. I can dress how I like."

"That's true."

When I woke, later, she was sitting next to me, looking down at me. She looked serene and beautiful. I had a big stretch and a big yawn and felt the feeling of being comfortable and rested and, for the moment anyway, safe.

"Hey, Soumy. You look happy," I said.

"Actually, I am," she said. "You look happy too."

"Strange isn't it?"

"Yes, it is strange, but it doesn't feel strange. Do you know, I love this little house but I don't think I will feel sad when I leave it. Isn't that strange?"

"You've only been here for a few hours."

"I know, but those hours have been. This has happened and it cannot unhappen. That is how I feel anyway."

"Hm, there are a few things I wish I could make unhappen. What time is it?"

"It is the time you said. Six o'clock."

"Has it ever happened that I've asked you to do something and you've not done it?" I said.

"No, why should it?" she said.

"You know, I can be an idiot sometimes."

"Yes."

"Soumy, go and make us some coffee, will you. I've got some unhappening to do."

I splashed some water on my face and put my clothes on. Soumy sat with me and drank a cup of coffee. I put my phone back together and turned it on. When it came alive I wrote numbers from it onto a small piece of paper and put that, folded up, under the insole of my left boot.

When the coffee was finished I said, "Right, I must go and see a man about a dog."

"You want a dog?"

"It's a saying." I dialled the number I'd saved under 'Bill'.

"Simon," he said, after the third ring.

"Bill," I said.

"Fancy a coffee?"

"Could do. Where are you?"

"I'm in town at the moment, where are you?"

"I'm in town too."

"Excellent. Corner of Massira and Des Far in fifteen?"

"Deal. Are you still in character?"

"I'm always in character." He hung up.

I slipped the small, flat pocket knife that I carry down into my sock inside my boot. I left my wallet and my .38 on top of my bag. Soumy let me kiss her briefly at the door. I went quickly; there was no one in front of the building, and took a more southerly route back towards where I'd parked the Toyota. It wasn't there.

I walked past the four pillars of water of the Fountain Nador at the corner of Mars and Taouima. The white, foaming water sparkled in the fierce light and the hiss of it falling endlessly back into itself was hypnotic. Here, in the newer part of the city, where most of the buildings were hard, white concrete and glass, and the spaces were wider, they had planted palms and acacia. It wasn't too bad in its way but I much preferred the old city. I crossed the small square and traversed the narrower streets to the Avenue Massira.

There was a girl in khaki shorts and a smartly pressed shirt with some kind of logo on it standing on the corner of Massira and Des Far. She had round glasses and her hair was done up in a bun. She had the earnest, hopeful look of someone who, given half a chance, will pounce on you and start talking to you about God. She did, in fact, appear to be holding a bible. I looked past her with the intention of avoiding eye contact and carried on.

"Simon Ellice?" she said.

I stopped and looked at her doubtfully. She opened the bible and showed me a photo of myself, standing on the deck of Nottambulo, caught in the act of receiving a bale of hash.

"If you'd like to come with me, Bill is expecting you."

"He's a tricky bastard, isn't he?" I said, indicating that she should lead the way.

"So they say, sir," she said.

I followed her round a couple of corners and up three flights of stairs to a door in a shabby apartment block labelled 'Church of the Evangelical Shepherd'. There was a pause, presumably while we were inspected, and then the door was opened by a young man with a ponytail and a beard. His shirt had the same insignia as the girl and I could see that it bore the same words as the door and included a cross. He also happened to have what looked like a 9ml Sig in a holster at his hip.

"Welcome, Mr Ellice. Come this way. Bill's in the comms room."

I seemed to be in a fairly spacious flat. There was a central hallway from which rooms radiated off in all directions. There was a small kitchen, a sitting room which contained a TV and several bedrooms with bunk beds. The room with the TV also contained at least six men who forcefully reminded me of Rupert's boys. They didn't bother to look up from their card games or playstations as I passed. The man led me to a small room at the back.

"Simon, come in and have a pew." Bill was cradling a mug and sitting on an old office chair that was losing its foam stuffing. In front of him was a bank of computer screens, laptops and other electrical equipment that was less easy to identify. Another young man with big, padded headphones over his ears, was gazing abstractedly into the middle distance and occasionally typing at a keyboard. The young man with the ponytail and the Sig leant against the doorway in the casual way that is meant to indicate that he just happened to be there. Not that he was guarding me at all.

"How long have you been here?" I said, taking the third chair, carefully.

"About three weeks now."

"Do you do much missionary work?"

"Hah. Clever, isn't it. It's a universal phenomenon that everyone will cross the street to avoid an evangelical Christian and no one will suspect him or her of being anything other than annoying and harmless."

"You seem to have brought the cavalry," I said, jerking my thumb in the direction of the TV room.

"Well, you did ask. Speaking of which, what news?"

"I had a chat with Rupert this morning."

"Yes."

"What do you mean, yes?"

"I mean, yes I know." He pointed to one of the screens which showed a partial image of the café near Wise Policy. "What did he say?"

"He said he has a higher purpose and that I should bugger off before I get hurt. I said I would."

"Is that all?"

"I thought about asking him about his plan of action but decided he probably wouldn't tell me. As it happens I know now anyway."

"Oh?"

"At about ten this morning they stormed Guy's compound and killed everyone they found inside. But perhaps you knew that?"

"Oh dear. No, I didn't know that."

"You don't have cameras up there?"

"We tried but…" he shrugged his shoulders. "So, are you telling me… What exactly are you telling me?" He looked at me, possibly with some genuine concern.

"I believe that Guy and my mother got away in the spare Range Rover that he keeps, kept, next door at the Mayor's place."

"Spare Range Rover?"

"If it matters, have two," I said.

"Quite so. Actually, I suppose it doesn't entirely surprise me. I take it you've not been to your flat recently?"

"Not since very early this morning."

"Lucky for you I'd say. Someone has kicked the door in. Took a bit of effort. Apparently, it has a steel lining, but you probably knew that?"

"It's possible," I said.

"Ransacked the place. More or less empty. Shame, nice place," he said.

"Thanks. I assume you just called by out of neighbourly concern?"

"Something like that. You were telling me about what happened to Mr Wealden's compound?"

"Not much to say. The computers in his office are all very dead and Rupert and his boys cleared out most of his arsenal. Who is Rupert, by the way?"

"Here." He passed me a file from the desk. "John Seymour Grant, lately of the SAS and currently employed by something called Scitan Ltd."

I looked at a familiar face with a much more sensible haircut, under a pale olive beret with the familiar winged dagger motif on it.

"He doesn't strike me as a crook exactly, but he is a ruthless bastard. He killed the poor lad I sent to watch out for me when you took that photo of me loading the boat," I said.

"Which explains why they are hunting me too. Must have seen me up on the shed roof and thought I was competition."

"Well, you are, aren't you?"

"No, I'm the law."

"There is no law in Morocco."

"Don't tell the Sûreté. They'll put you in prison for saying that."

"Exactly."

"Anyway, I'm glad you popped in. You'd like us to rescue your mum, I suppose?"

"Do you think you can find her?"

"No, probably not, but with your help we might be able to find Guy, which is the same thing."

"Guy will have a bolt hole somewhere and it will be well hidden. How are you going to find him?"

"I don't suppose he'll just quietly slip away, will he?" Bill said.

"The Guy I know is more likely to quietly turn up when you're looking the other way and kill everyone in sight," I said.

"That's what I thought. Let me tell you something else I think."

"What?"

"It's full moon tonight."

"So?"

"So, not long now to the dark of the moon. What happens at the dark of the moon round here?"

"I make a delivery."

"So you do, and I suspect that if Guy is back on top he's going to want you to do the same this month. Or, if Mr Grant has the day; I assume he's here to take what Guy has from him; if he can, he'll want to do the same. Do you agree?"

"I can't say I don't."

"Good. So they both want your damn boat, and, given what you've just told me, I don't think Mr Grant is likely to let the grass grow, do you?"

"You think he'll make an attempt to get hold of Nottambulo?"

"Yes. I also imagine they'd quite like to get hold of you or the girl right now and ask you where to find him too, but we'll get to using you as bait later."

"I'll look forward to it," I said. "And I imagine that the next thing you're going to tell me is that you have a plan."

"I do, or rather Freddy does. Ben, would you ask Freddy to join us please."

The young man disappeared and then a much larger individual blocked the doorway.

"Come in, Freddy. Sorry there's nowhere to sit. This is Simon Ellice, Captain Tom Fredrickson."

He was a bit older than me, in his early thirties. He had good humoured eyes and seemed pleased to meet me.

"Glad to know you, Mr Ellice. Heard a lot about you." He didn't make it sound as if that was a particularly bad thing.

"Call me Simon." I took the offered hand. If he squeezed quite hard I may have done the same.

"Call me Freddy. Everyone does. Don't worry, Bill, I've been sitting on my arse for long enough anyway." He perched on the edge of the desk beside me. "Are we up for tonight then, Bill?"

"We are. Have a look at this, Simon." he pointed to one of the screens, "From earlier today, you'll see that Captain Grant has called for reinforcements." It was a frozen video image of two men unloading kit bags from a van. In the background four more were standing round Rupe, who was pointing towards what I took to be the stern of Wise Policy. "So that's a lot of men to kill."

"Guy won't mind," I said.

"Neither do I," Freddy said.

"We think that if you were to call off your guard dogs, the men you have guarding your boat I mean, we might take over the job for you. What do you think?" Bill said.

"I already have. What I think is, it doesn't help my mum very much."

"I know, but we have to do what we can, and we'll do this first."

"You're saying that in the tone of voice of someone who's telling me, not asking me," I said.

"Sorry. Didn't mean to. But you see what I mean don't you? Here," he didn't wait for me to reply, "we've also got this." He pulled what looked like a tracking device from a drawer. "This is a tracking device. We're going to install this too, so that if the worst comes to the worst…"

"He means if we get killed," Freddy said.

"… if anyone gets hold of the boat, we can follow them. I thought we'd begin more or less now, if that's all right with you?"

"And if I say no?"

"Ah, well, the thing is…"

Another big man stepped smoothly through the door and took hold of my left arm in his hands. Freddy had already done the same to my right. They lifted me up with no trouble at all and Bill calmly began emptying my pockets.

"… the thing is, we really do think you should."

"You only had to ask," I said.

16

EVERY DOG HIS DAY

When it was dark they put me in the back of an old Mercedes estate, Freddy and Mike, the other big chap, one each side of me with Bill in the front and the thin young man, driving. We drove down to the waterfront road and along to the parking by the jetty. Nottambulo was riding peacefully at her mooring. There were some boys fishing but no obvious sign of Asif or Imad.

"I'll just have a recce," Bill said, getting out.

"Where are your men? The old fellow and the young one, who always guard the boat?" Bill said, sticking his head back in.

"I told you I stood them down," I said. "I had a feeling that someone serious might try to take her so I told them to go home. Didn't seem worth getting them killed to no purpose. Probably lead to more holes in the hull anyway."

"Very thoughtful of you. Over to you, Freddy."

"Right then, Simon. Here's the thing. I'm a simple soldier, right?"

"You shouldn't put yourself down. I'm sure you're not that simple really," I said.

"Very funny. As I was saying, I'm a soldier and you and your drug running enterprise is an enemy of my country. Do you understand?"

"I think you're a bit confused, but go on."

"And from now on this is a military operation. If I feel the need to kill you, I will."

"Are you trying to tell me that I'd better behave, or else you'll get a bit cross?" I said.

"Give the man a doughnut. You and me are going to get out of this car. I'm going to cut that zip-tie and then we're going out to your fancy boat. Like we're two pals going fishing. Got it?"

"I think I'm keeping up with you so far."

"We take her down the lagoon a bit, nice and easy, and pick up the lads and some kit and come back again. They'll be keeping their heads down and then you and me come ashore, like we've had our little trip, and go away. You with me?"

"Leaving anyone watching with the impression that she's empty but in fact there's a surprise waiting for anyone who goes to have a look?" I said.

"You're not as dumb as you look. Any questions?"

"You driving, or me?"

"Better be you, but anything I don't like and I'll put a bullet in you and prop you up beside the wheel. Come on, let's get on with this."

They more or less lifted me out of the car and cut the tie that bound my wrists. Mike pulled an HK416 with a fat suppressor fitted to it, out of the back and sat along the back seat of the car, with his feet up and the barrel propped on them. He had a clear field of fire down the pontoon. Freddy unzipped his light wind-proof jacket and let me see the butt of a holstered automatic.

"See you shortly, Bill," Freddy said.

"Be careful, Freddy," Bill said.

"Don't worry, I do this for a living," Freddy said.

"So does he," Bill said.

"No he doesn't, he just moves things about. He's an overpaid delivery driver."

I set off down the pontoon at my usual amble, got in the back of the tender and pulled the little seagull outboard into life. Freddy came along beside me, looking no more anxious or keyed up than the water itself. He untied the painter and then the stern rope.

"Up to the front, you. I'll drive," he said. "Keep your hands where I can see them."

"We usually call it the bow," I said, doing as instructed. "I just mention it because if you say, 'go left' or something like that I may not know whether you mean my left, or your left, or in fact, port. I don't want to get shot over a misunderstanding."

"Don't worry, Simon, you'll only get shot if I intend to shoot you."

"That's a relief."

He got into the stern - the boat was quite low in the water with both of us in her - and took us in a confident sweep which avoided passing behind any of the other boats, out to Nottambulo. I stepped aboard her with the painter like a docile little lamb, tied her to a cleat and moved away so that he felt comfortable coming aboard.

"If it's okay with you, I'd like to do my pre-flight checks, oil, cooling fluid, fuel, things like that," I said.

"Go ahead, but if you pull a gun out of a locker it'll be the last thing you do." He unholstered a Sig, screwed on a silencer and pointed it at my belly. "You can put that against the block of one of them. Under the outlet manifold probably." He handed me the tracker, which he'd pulled from another pocket of his coat.

"D'you know what, Freddy, I don't think I want to shoot you, even if I could," I said. I got on with my checks. "I don't mind admitting I've got in a bit over my head here. Delivering a bit of hash is one thing but killing agents of the British Government is the kind of thing that makes enemies."

"You're not wrong about that. You saying you're intending to be a witness for the prosecution?"

"I doubt there'll be any prosecutions, will there?"

"Not if I have anything to do with it."

"Thought so. How about that?" I put the tracker against the underside of the steel coolant reservoir where it attached itself with a solid clunk. It was almost invisible.

"That'll do fine," Freddy said.

"Good." I lowered the engine cowling and secured its clips. "I'm going to start the engines now. Then I expect you'd like me to go and unhook us, wouldn't you?"

"Don't think being helpful is going to make me lower my guard," he said.

I started all four. He looked interested when he heard the low rumble. In spite of having seen the engines I don't think he'd any real idea what he was standing on. He carefully supervised me leading the tender up to the bow, pulling in the rope to the buoy, releasing Nottambulo and attaching the little boat instead. We began to drift backwards in the breeze.

"I'd better catch her before we bump something," I said, moving aft. Freddy kept to one side as I passed him and stood on the deck of the aft end of the cargo bay where he could see what I was up to. I engaged starboard number one engine only and let her move forward on tick-over, spinning the wheel to take her out without passing behind the gin palace at the next mooring. Already we were moving out of range of the shore. "I'll take her out clear of the sandbanks over there," I said, pointing vaguely to starboard.

"I didn't know there were any sandbanks in the lagoon," Freddy said.

"Not many and not a problem. They move about a bit when we have a big blow from the north west. They gave up charting them long ago. We're not tidal here so the worst you get is the embarrassment of having to be pulled off. You going to tell me where to go then?"

"It's a way down. This thing's supposed to shift, isn't it, so go on, open her up a bit."

"Okay, hang on," I said.

I pushed the lever up a bit, but still only on one engine. She rose up in the water and we were doing a bit more than twenty knots. Freddy didn't look very impressed.

"The lagoon isn't as big as you think it is," I said, over the sound of the engine. "That's the lights of the café near where Mr Grant is anchored." I pointed.

"No it isn't," he said, pulling a map from an inside pocket. He stood with the gun in one hand and the map in the other looking at the shore, but with me still in his line of sight.

"Okay." I shrugged and under cover of the movement engaged the port two. Now both props were turning. "I'll just push her up a bit, shall I?"

"Whatever." He was still trying to figure out where we were.

I put one leg out behind me, raised the revolutions on starboard number two and engaged the clutch so that it was online too. I engaged the lock to hold the wheel where it was, took a firm hold of the binnacle and pushed all four levers up as far as they would go.

The roar of the engines and the sudden acceleration came as a complete surprise to Freddy. He didn't have a free hand to catch himself with and didn't want to drop his gun or his map so he was forced to step forward to keep his balance. The massive props gained more and more grip, pushing us on faster and faster and turning his step into a stumbling run.

As he came level with me I straight-armed him over the side. He managed to catch onto a cleat with his finger tips, and they showed whitely there for a moment before the force of the water on his feet tore him free and he was gone.

I backed the engines down a bit and looked over the stern. There was no sign of him. Presumably he could swim.

I unlocked the wheel and turned her towards the entrance to the lagoon. Ten minutes later I had crossed the bar and disappeared into the enfolding darkness of the Mediterranean sea.

Damn it was good to feel the old girl under me again. That and the fresh eternal salt sea, and the howl of those beautiful engines, and the speed of us made me feel positively cheerful. The thought of Freddy's face as he realised he was going over the side didn't hurt either.

I didn't turn right for the Cote D'Azure or Monte Carlo, or even Capri or Sicily, I went out and, after a while of running at full speed, turned left round the Cap du Trois Fourches instead. A while later still I came gently back into the coast and put her back on the beach where I'd hidden that load of hash little more than a fortnight ago.

I took her as far to one side of the beach as I dared, praying that there were no sharp rocks under the placid surface. The sound of the engines beat back at me from the rocks and I pushed her in at shocking pace, so that she rode almost a third of her length up onto the sand. If I ever came back for her, and she was still there, I would have to winch her off. When I stopped the engines the silence was deafening.

I rummaged about in the lockers and found a disposable phone still in its packaging and a battery for it that was supposed to be charged, some chocolate and an old jersey that I'd forgotten I had. I checked that she was as locked up as she could be, which wasn't much, and jumped down off the bow onto the sand.

Then I thought better of it and went back for some light rope. I coiled this over my shoulders and stood at the bottom of the cliff looking up. I didn't much like what I saw, not that I could see much except the black mass of it outlined by the stars.

I was about to start up when I stopped, called myself a hard name and scrambled back aboard. I'd forgotten the damn tracker. I got it out and looked at it. I should have dropped it overboard out at sea. I jumped back down and started looking for a suitable rock to hit it with when another thought struck me. I tucked it into my shirt and addressed myself to the rock face again.

I don't like heights much but I do quite like climbing. You soon learn as a kid that if you only go a few limbs up a tree, the adults will walk about underneath you completely oblivious of your curious ears only a few feet above them.

The end of the peninsula is made of some very hard, pale rock; some kind of basalt I think. It makes for very steep cliffs but at least it's strong and you can trust it with your weight. I picked the same side that I'd parked Nottambulo, scrambled over the mess of jagged boulders at the bottom and got onto a ledge that was running up at an angle. This was taking me up but also out along the arm of the bay, away from the land. It wasn't very wide and the rock-face above it was too smooth to have any real hand-holds, but it leant back enough for me to be able to keep my balance. Pretty soon I was looking down on the boat from a height that would break bones if I fell.

The ledge got narrower. I was moving along sideways with only the balls of my feet on it now, and the face was more and more vertical. I didn't want to go back but I would have to if I didn't find something better soon. I put my hands up the face as far as I could reach and thought I detected the beginning of a parallel ledge above. I couldn't get my fingers onto it enough to grip but I might if I went on. It was no fun feeling only the toes of my boots having any purchase. I moved in inches, pushing my foot as hard against the rock as it would go and applying my weight very carefully. I was rewarded though, by the ledge above becoming definite and useful. If I had been only an inch shorter it would have been impossible. I moved along like a flat thing, pasted to the rock at full stretch.

The ledge was threatening to give out completely but the corner was only a few feet away and it seemed to be at a much less steep slope than the face. I nerved myself, went along swinging myself on my hands only, my muscles screaming and my feet over nothing but space, and finally got my leg over the sloping ridge of stone.

It cut into my leg cruelly but took a lot of my weight and I was able to get one hand round too and straddle the spine of rock. Now it cut into my groin but its ragged sharpness was my salvation. I could find hand and foot holds now and work my way upwards.

There was another tricky bit where the rock faded up to the very top and went smooth and empty of holds, but a trailing root from a tamarind gave me the probably illusory confidence of its support and I scrambled up with my boots scrabbling and slipping and got a hand to its trunk. I pulled myself up and sat with an arm around the blessed plant, scratched and bruised and bleeding a bit, but safe.

When I felt a bit more functional I got up and had a look about me. A chap in the Rif bar once told me that the Cap was an important wildlife refuge but to me it looked like a lot of scrubby tamarind and acacia and sandy soil on top of a big lump of rock. One thing it was though, was quiet; even the cicadas were silent. There was the faint loom of the lights of Melilla and Nador in the distance, and in the far east the possibility of the moonrise but otherwise the stars had the sky to themselves.

I checked my pockets and found that I hadn't lost anything, had some chocolate and wished for water instead, and then put the phone together. It came to life and its pale glow intensified the darkness without illuminating anything. It showed one bar of signal and nearly half a charge on the battery, which was pretty good all things considered. I dialled Soumy's number from memory.

"Hello," she said, sleepy and doubtful.

"Hi, Soumy, it's me," I said.

"Simon…"

"Everything okay?"

"Yes, but I'm not awake. What time is it?"

"You could say it was late or you could say it was early. Will you come and get me please Soumy, I'm on the Cap?"

"How will I do that, Simon?"

"I'm going to give you the phone number of a nice young man called Imad. I will call him first and get him to borrow his father's car and then you can call him and tell him where to meet you. Then you tell him where to go. Okay?"

"You want me to drive about in the middle of the night with a man I've never met?"

"Yes."

"Okay. Where are you again?"

"I'm somewhere on the road out to the lighthouse on the Cap des Trois Fourches, you know, the Cap. Got it?"

"But that's a long, long way."

"I know, and I'd rather not walk back, so get up and get going, okay?"

"Okay, Simon."

"Good girl." I hung up and phoned Imad. Happily he answered and after managing to wake up enough to understand that it was me, readily agreed to do what I asked.

That done, it was time I found the road so I tucked the rope under a bush and pointed myself at Mars, which was hanging in the south east, and started walking as fast as I could without breaking my neck on the uneven ground. After a while I took my jersey off - it had had a bad time on the cliff - and hung it on a tree. I wished I'd thought of bringing some water. In one way it was quite nice being out and about at night in such a lonely place, but I'd had quite enough of banging into trees and scrambling up and down gullies and low hills by the time I found the road.

The pale ribbon of dust snaked off around a corner. I decided that I wanted to be able to see the car coming, when it came, so I set off down it. I'd not gone far before a nightjar rose up from under my feet, making me jump. Generally it takes quite a lot to make me jump, so that meant I was getting a bit ragged. I followed the road until I had a clear view for a hundred yards or more and then sat down with my back to a rock and waited.

I must have closed my eyes for a minute because the next thing I remember is Soumy gently shaking my shoulder.

"Wakey, wakey, Simon." She looked very pleased with herself. Imad was standing behind her, looking a bit worried.

"Soumy. Is it… what's the… have you got any water?"

"Yes, Simon. And some food and some clean trousers and a shirt." She turned to Imad and said, "water, quick you fool. In the back in the green bag."

She snatched the bottle from him as he brought it, took the top off and passed it to me. I drank a good deal of it, which made me feel much better and made it a lot easier to speak.

"Bloody hell, Soumy, you're completely bloody marvellous, do you know that?"

"Am I?"

"Yes, you are." I got to my feet and let her brush some of the dust off me.

"You're in a mess, Simon. You must come home and let me wash those cuts. Here, boy, open the door for Mr Ellice."

"Hi, Imad. How're you doing?" I said. There was a battered old Peugeot behind him.

"I'm fine thank you, Mr Ellice, how're you?"

"Pretty good, thanks. If you wouldn't mind driving, I think we should get going. Soumy, you and I'll get in the back and you can do whatever you like to me while we're driving. Okay?"

"Okay, Simon."

The moon rose while we were driving back down the long peninsula and looked perfectly full. As it climbed, it got so bright that it competed with the car headlights. It was a moon bright enough to read by. By the time we were approaching Nador I was a new man. I'd eaten a picnic of bread and olives and cheese and Soumy's wonderful stuffed dates and drunk another litre of water. She'd worked at bits of me with a damp cloth and I'd wriggled into clean trousers and shirt. We sat close, side by side. She leant her head against my shoulder and held my hand. I didn't mind.

"What happens next, Simon?" she said.

"I'm going out into the desert to find my mother," I said.

"I suppose you should do that if she's in trouble."

"I'm not completely sure that I should, or that she's really in trouble, but I think I have to try to find out."

"Will you be gone for long?"

I just squeezed her hand for answer.

"I know, it was a stupid question," she said.

"I must get my bag," I said. "We'll stop a few streets away so that Imad will be unable to tell anyone where you are. Just in case."

"You're very thoughtful, Simon."

"We both know that's not true," I said.

This time it was her turn to squeeze my hand.

It was well into the small hours of the night now. There were cats about on the roads but little else. Imad was getting used to driving me and was driving well and quickly. I was glad to save my strength; if all went well I'd be driving myself very soon. I made him pull up near the mosque that Soumy's building backed onto and almost ran to the flat with her.

I kissed her, and she let me, and there she was again, looking at me in that sad way, as I left in the dead of night once more.

"You've done well tonight, Imad. I'm grateful. Drop me near the old market and then keep going and don't stop until you get home. Give my regards to your father and tell him I hope to see him soon," I said, getting in the front this time.

"It is my great pleasure, Mr Ellice. I just remember, we were watching when you went out with that man. His friends fetched him from the water in the little tender. My father said you would put your beautiful boat somewhere safe. Is she safe, Mr Ellice?"

"She's as safe as I can make her, Imad. Did the man live?"

"I think so. We did not really look to make sure. We were worrying about the boat. And you, of course."

"Here'll do nicely. Goodnight, Imad." I shook his hand. He held my hand and looked at me for a moment with serious eyes, perhaps wondering at my mad rushings about, or what kind of thing I was, and then let in the clutch and drove quickly out of sight.

I was alone on the road with the dark buildings crowding above me, and a heavy bag full of interesting things. I took my .38 out of the bag, checked that it was ready and put it into the waistband of my trousers. That done, I shouldered the bag and went as quickly and quietly as I could to Azooz's yard.

There was an interesting selection of 4x4s there. An old Land Rover, which I passed over, two Hiluxes, which I briefly considered and one of the old 70 series Land Cruisers, which would do nicely. The big, curious eyes of the yard boys looked at me from various vehicles. I smiled at them and gave them a friendly wave but they didn't smile back.

I opened the door of the Land Cruiser and had a look inside. A boy had been asleep under a blanket along the back seat. He sat up and looked at me uncomprehendingly. It smelt mustily of the boy. I put my bag on the front passenger seat and pulled down the sun-visor, but no key fell down. I tried the other, but it wasn't there either.

"Where is the key?" I asked the boy in Arabic.

He pointed mutely towards the office and looked frightened.

"Okay, we'd better go and wake the old bastard up," I said.

A group of them followed me through the path between the vehicles to the workshop. It was a dark cave lit by shafts of moonlight streaming in through the side windows. I walked in slowly. There was a pit there somewhere and I didn't want to fall into it. There was a strong smell of engine oil and the benches and cupboards around me were covered in heaps of spare parts. It was a shocking mess. I was standing there in the middle of it, wondering what it was that was different about it, when Azooz himself stepped out of the office at the back. He was holding his old double barrelled shotgun and it was pointing at my belly.

"Hey, Azooz. I need to borrow a car again I'm afraid," I said. "Sorry to disturb you at this time of night."

"You filthy, ferenji dog. If you move even one muscle I will blow you to kingdom come," he said.

"Wake up, Azooz, it's me, Simon Ellice," I said.

"I know exactly who you are and exactly what you're worth. Keep your hands where I can see them or I will shoot them off. Stay where you are, don't come any closer."

"Okay, if you feel like that, I will. Do I take it that there's a bounty on my head and you intend to collect it?"

"There has always been ticket for you. You know that very well. But now it has gone up to twenty thousand Dirham and your precious Mr Guy Wealden is gone to the devil where he belongs. I shall be the one to collect it, which is only fitting after all the service I have done you, isn't it?"

"I seem to remember that you've been paid for that, but let's not quibble. Is that dead or alive, by the way?"

"Only ten if you're dead, but ten is better than nothing so don't think I won't kill you if you do anything stupid. You think I'm not a dangerous man, but I am, as you are about to find out. You, who have looked down on me for so many years."

"I've not even been here a year, Azooz. Relax will you? Do I look like I'm giving you any trouble? You've got a shotgun pointed at my guts for goodness sake. If that goes off it'll make a hole right through me and probably through that boy behind me too."

"The boy does not matter."

"I think the boy may matter to the boy, but perhaps we should let that one go. What would you like me to do, Azooz?"

"I am thinking about that. You just wait now, okay."

He moved forward a bit, bringing his head into the light. It looked to me as if his fat, bald head was sweating a bit. I yawned and automatically put my hand up to cover my mouth. The shotgun twitched in the direction of the movement.

"Sorry," I said, "it's been a long day and I'm pretty tired."

"Boy, get closer behind him. Lift his shirt up at the back and see if he has a gun there."

I felt tentative, gentle fingers do that. I think the boy must have nodded as he made no sound.

"Lift it out then, carefully, and bring it to me here. Put it on the bench there. You there, go round and get the handcuffs from upstairs. You know where."

One slim, young figure carefully and very deliberately lifted out my .38 and took it over to him and put it down just as gently, the other went round the other side of the bench near which I was standing and up the stairs beside the office. I watched him go.

"You didn't see the cameras, did you? Clever Mr Simon Ellice, who no one can touch."

"No, I didn't see the cameras. Is there an infrared alarm too?"

"You broke the beam when you came through the gate. No good knowing that now, is it?"

"No, it isn't. What can I say? I've underestimated you, Azooz. You..." I narrowed my eyes and concentrated on the stairs behind him.

"What?" he said.

"Nothing," I said bringing my eyes back to him.

"Boy, where are you?" Azooz said.

There was the sound of movement from above but no reply. I don't think the boy had heard him.

"What are you looking at?" Azooz said. My eyes had returned to the stairs.

"Nothing," I said, bringing my eyes back to him.

"No funny tricks now. I'm ready to shoot you."

"No tricks," I said, keeping eye contact with him and raising my hands slightly, palms towards him to show that I was harmless.

"Go and see what's keeping him," he said to the boy beside him. As the boy moved behind him my eyes, apparently involuntarily, flicked back to the stairs and widened in shock.

"What?" he half turned, looking towards the stairs and away from me. The gun followed. I scooped up the alternator lying on the bench by my right hand and threw it at his head. He saw the movement in his peripheral vision and began to turn back towards me. The alternator struck him solidly in the forehead with an audible 'thunk'. The gun swinging back towards me went off with a deafening thump but I was under it and diving for his legs. He was falling backwards, taken off balance by the blow to his head. I locked my arms around his legs and we crashed down onto the greasy, black floor in an ungainly mess.

I could hear things falling down behind me from whatever the shot had hit. I knocked the barrel of the gun up and away from me, got one of my knees under me and raised myself up off the fat, smelly body, my fist ready to strike for his throat. There was no need, he was still stunned by the blow to his head and was floundering about, moaning.

I pulled the gun out of his hand and stood up. The boys, one on the staircase holding a pair of handcuffs, stood looking at us with great interest.

"Fuck," I said, loudly. Then I broke the gun and took out the remaining cartridge, closed it again and struck him hard on the head with the butt. He stopped moving. So much for the clean clothes Soumy had given me.

"That's better, isn't it?" I said to the boys. "I hope you don't mind me hurting Azooz?" They shook their heads enthusiastically and began a slow smile. "Do you think you could find the key to the Land Cruiser for me?" I said to the older looking boy. He nodded and went into the office. "And I think you should fetch the others, don't you?" I said to the remaining lad. He nodded too and went out into the yard. I put my .38 back where it belonged.

Six of them gathered round him, looking at the lump of him on the dirty, greasy floor, in the jagged pattern of moonlight and shadows. They made me think of a pack of underfed dogs.

"He's yours now," I said. "He doesn't need to hurt you again if you decide. You can do with him whatever you like." One of the boys picked up a hammer from the bench. "There will be a box of money somewhere about here. You can probably find it. You have until the daylight and then you should probably go."

"Thank you, Mr Ellice," the taller one said, giving me a key.

"I didn't do anything you couldn't have done. One thing…" I paused and they all looked at me. "Look after each other, all of you. Okay?" They nodded solemnly. "Good. Good luck then, I'm off."

The yard was deserted under the moonlight. People don't get out of bed in the middle of the night to investigate a shot in Nador. The Land Cruiser started at the first turn of the key. I tucked the .38 into the seat beside me, backed her round, drove her out of the yard and set out into the sleeping, moonlit city.

17

FATHER AND SON

It rattled and squeaked a bit but the old truck seemed okay. The steering didn't wobble too much, the gears changed without hesitation and the four litre straight-four pulled nicely. According to the gauges she had oil pressure and was charging.

I drove past the store but it was locked up and deserted so I carried on up the hill, driving through patches of shadow and light up towards the moon. The temperature gauge stayed steady.

There was blue police tape across the entrance to the drive but I just ignored that and drove through it. I parked in my usual spot, though I could have chosen any, all of the small stable of cars had gone, and had a quick scout about. Whoever had taken the cars had also taken the bodies, including Zara's, and apart from its emptiness, the place seemed very much its same, lovely, tranquil self.

I fetched my heavy bag from the back of the truck and put it on the table under the pergola. For a short while this was my headquarters, not Guy's. I fetched myself an orange juice from the bar and got out the laptop that I'd taken from Rupert out in the desert. I plugged it into the outside socket that Guy had had fitted for the purpose and turned it on. While it was doing that I connected the GPS antennae and hooked it over one of the beams of the pergola.

Sure enough, when the thing had got going and I'd navigated my way around the software, I found myself looking at a pulsing dot, way out in the empty space north of the small desert town of Merceria. Seemed like I'd be going back to Algeria again. I memorised the GPS coordinates and dialled a number on my new phone. It went to answer-phone so I disconnected and tried again, and again. Eventually a sleepy, disgruntled voice said, "Who is this? Do you know what time it is?"

"Morning, Dad. I think it's about four in the morning. Sunrise in two hours."

"Simon. What do you want? I thought you'd gone home."

"Who says I haven't."

"Why are you calling me?"

"So, have you got Mum to safety yet?"

"I told you, I'm handling that. No, not yet, but it's only a matter of time."

"Okay. I'm off to pay her a visit. Thought you might like to come along for the ride."

"You know where she is?"

"You don't?"

"If you know where she is, just tell me."

"No chance, but I'll take you there if you want. I'm leaving shortly, I'll give you an hour to get ready."

"Where are you?"

"Right now? I'm in an all-night café down by the docks. I take it you're still up at the Riby?"

"You know where she is?"

"As I say. I'm off to pay her a visit in a minute. Do you want to come with me or not?"

"What are you going to do? What do you mean pay her a visit?"

"She's at a camp out in the desert. I assume she's with Guy. I'm going to go and visit them, have a coffee, see what's going on. You want to talk to him, don't you?"

"What do you mean a camp in the desert? Whereabouts exactly?"

"We've been round that one already. Do you want to come with me or not?"

"All right. Yes, I do."

"Good. I'll pick you up in one hour from now. Bring a hat, some warm clothes and a sleeping bag if you can find one. Oh, you can wake Robbie up and get him to make up a picnic too. Walking boots if you have them. I'll pass by the end of the lane up to the Riby at 05.14 and if you're there you are, if not, not. I won't wait."

"That's not…"

I hung up on him.

The GPS coordinates of the dot hadn't changed since I'd remembered them so I powered the laptop down and packed it back in its case. From the bag I got out a simple, hand-held GPS receiver and set it to charge. After that I took out the HK416, inserted a mag and worked one into the chamber. From then on it went with me while I worked. I went out to the front and tied the two ends of the police tape together so it looked as it had before, and then did my best to prepare the truck for desert travel.

In the garage I found a couple of jerry cans, one of them half full, behind the bar; a big pack of unopened mineral water bottles, and, in the kitchen; stale bread, dates, a length of cured sausage and a net of oranges. Now that she had cooled sufficiently, I topped up the oil in the engine and checked the water in the radiator. I used the compressor to top up the tyres; they weren't new but they would do and the spare was holding pressure.

I stuck the tracker that Bill had intended for Nottambulo onto the bulkhead inside the engine bay.

While I was working, an old Peugeot passed up the road. I watched it through the rifle's sights from behind a handy bougainvillea. It looked like the profile of Mr Grant driving. He seemed to be alone.

When I was as happy with my transport as I could be, I turned my attention to myself. Soumy, thoughtful as ever, had tucked some chocolate and a clean shirt and trousers into the top of my bag. I ate half the chocolate, washed myself at the outside tap, with the HK propped up near me, and put on the clothes. It was really nice to be rid of the smell of oil and Azooz.

By the time I'd done everything I could and carefully packed the truck, it was nearly time. I went back to the front of the house. The water in the pool was dark and mysterious under the moonlight. I stood looking out over the bay. My boat was gone from her place, my flat was no longer a home, this place where I stood, was, for now at least, the residence only of ghosts. I wondered how Sam was. I was looking forward to seeing her again. If I was honest with myself I'd been pretty much a passenger in events up to now. That was true for far longer than I'd understood, until recently. It was time for that to change. I got my phone out and dialled Bill.

"Hi, Bill."

"Is that Simon?"

"You seem to be awake."

"I told you, I'm always awake. Freddy's alive by the way. Not happy, but alive."

"It's sweet that you think I care. That wasn't very sporting of you was it, old boy?"

"I leave the sportsmanship to people like you, old man. Doesn't seem to have done me much good in this case though, does it?"

"We might be able to put that right. Apart from keeping my family alive, well my mother at least, I'd quite like a clean slate. How do you feel about that?"

"Not really up to me, is it. What're you suggesting?"

"I was thinking I might do your job for you, how about that?"

"You want to write reports and lick some highly polished boots?"

"No, but I could lead you and your friend Freddy to some nasty drug smugglers, if you like. Would that get me a free pass?"

"It might help I suppose. Can you do that?"

"Do you know where I am?"

"Can't say I do. Should I?"

"You're not paying attention, Bill. Have you looked at your GPS tracking system lately?"

"Can't say I… Oh, is that you?"

"Should be. I'm off for a little road trip. If you care to follow me you might end up somewhere interesting."

"Knowing you the little I do, that wouldn't surprise me. Any idea where we're going?"

"Big sandy place, they call it the Sahara. You should tell Freddy to pack his biggest gun."

"I see."

"Do you? That's more than I do. And, Bill, you should probably hang back quite a bit. I don't think you'll be the only one following me."

"You're organising a party, are you?"

"Could well be."

"Well, thanks for the invite. I owe you one."

"That's what you said last time."

"I know."

I disconnected, and got going. The HK416 was resting on my

lap as I drove through the tape again and turned left.

There was a tall figure in a straw hat and windbreaker standing by the turning for the Riby. His face was in shadow but I recognised the upright stance of my father. There was a black hold-all at his feet. The spot was the best I could think of at the time and now I saw it, there was altogether too much cover nearby to make me feel comfortable, but then, in life you have to take chances. I pulled up beside him.

"Get in, Dad. You can throw that bag in the back," I said.

"You said you were going to go home and leave this to me," he said, getting in. I held the HK up out of his way.

"Yes, but I was lying."

"This is all very unfortunate. Is that really necessary?" he said, looking at the rifle.

"Usually, in my experience. Do you know what to do with it?"

"Of course I know what to do with it. I did my service too."

"I'd forgotten. Good, then take it and get familiar with it," I said, passing it to him.

"Supposing we get stopped or have to pass a border crossing?" he said.

"Its purpose is to prevent us getting stopped, and we won't be using any border crossings."

"So we're not going far then?"

"I wouldn't say that."

We stopped at the first fuel station on the road and filled up the tank and the jerry cans as full as they would go. The sleepy attendant shook his head when I asked for coffee but bought us cans of soft drinks and Mars bars.

There was almost no traffic at the main junction. Out on the N19 a few road trains were visible in the distance, making an early start to beat the congestion, or just driving in shifts through the day and night. The moon had passed its zenith and as the landscape opened out into the first stretch of plain we could see the beginning of the dawn in the east. Ahead of us, to the south and east, lay the barrier of the Rif mountains.

"It's going to be a beautiful morning," I said.

"Isn't it always here?" Dad said.

"It's one reason I like it," I said.

"So you've enjoyed your holiday here then?"

"No, this has been a job for me, not a holiday. We've a long drive ahead of us so we might as well try to get on with each other."

"I take your point. I just don't understand how you can see this kind of thing as a career, that's all."

"I know you don't." I put my foot down hard and swung out to pass a lorry laden with huge bales of something or other. Men, women and children looked down on us from on top of the load. There were two more lorries ahead of it. The stones of the gravel skirt flew up and battered against the underside of the vehicle. My father gripped the door handle and concentrated ahead.

"You can tell it's Africa, not Europe, can't you?" he said.

"That's another reason I like it. So, go on then, what's your job got that mine hasn't?"

"I'm sure I've explained that before."

"Probably, but I may not have been listening."

"What a surprise that would be."

"Well?" I passed the final lorry and pulled back in sharply to let the oncoming pickup have the road and returned the wave from the men in the back of it.

"Okay," he said, taking his hand off the handle and flexing his fingers. "I said, career not job. I started, well not at the bottom exactly, but as an executive officer, which is pretty near it, and now I'm a deputy director in the Home Office, which is where most of the real power lies."

"And you like power, do you?"

"Who doesn't? Yes, I like power. And influence."

"Power to do what?"

"Whatever needs to be done."

"Done in what context?"

"Done for the good of the country, I suppose. For all of us. We, the Home Office, are the central point where all branches of the UK government meet, executive, analytical, scientific, everything. If it's deemed that this or that needs to be done I can pull together a team from any department I like to get it done."

"For example?"

"Suppose there was the threat of a new disease being brought into the country by aid workers returning from the Sahel, one that wasn't widely known about. I would put together a team who could identify the individuals most likely to be concerned, access their medical files, track their movements, intercept them at the point of re-entry into the UK, or preferably at a suitable foreign location. Have them tested, inoculated or treated if possible, and if necessary quarantined, without the individuals concerned or the wider public knowing anything about it."

"Why?"

"Why what?"

"Why the secrecy?"

"Because sometimes the information is wrong and there's no point causing alarm, and when people know about potential threats to themselves they tend to act in self-interest, which makes it harder for us to act in the general interest."

"So that's the kind of thing you do? Prevent us all getting bird-flu?"

"That's an example of something I might be involved in. I'm not allowed to talk about my work as such. You know that. It's just not done."

"Interesting, I can tell you all about running drugs from Africa into Europe, which is supposed to be an antisocial activity…"

"It's illegal, certainly. And that's only because I'm your father and I won't turn you in."

"… but you can't tell me about all these good things that you do."

"That, Simon, is rather my point. You've chosen to be an outsider. I've chosen to be an insider, that's all. Your line of work, if you can call it that, leads nowhere, except money and probably an early death. Mine is interesting, rewarding and carries with it the approbation and respect of my peers. You, on the other hand, are in danger of spending the rest of your life behind bars, or as a hunted criminal. I don't really care what you do as such, but if you decide to do it on the wrong side of the fence, I'm telling you it won't end well. And I do care about that."

"I'll end up like Guy, you mean? Assuming I survive."

"Yes, like Guy. Right now he's out in the desert, according to you anyway, with every man's hand against him."

"Every man, like who?"

"Like whom. I don't know specifically of course, but I assume everyone who would like to take what he has from him, and everyone who has any interest in law and order. I don't know about the second half of the list but I imagine the first half is long and varied."

"That's true. I'm still not convinced though. I've had more fun and earned more money this side of the fence than I ever have the other. And I'm acting on my own responsibility. I'm not hiding behind some bureaucracy."

"I don't suppose I thought you would be. It must be in the genes."

"You mean Grandad?"

"If we're to get on, we shouldn't talk about him now."

"Agreed. Your turn to drive," I said, pulling into the side of the road.

"What do you mean, my turn?"

"Just what I say. I need some sleep if I'm going to be any use later on. You can drive, can't you?"

"Of course I can drive."

"Good." I got out and went round to the passenger side door and opened it. "You can leave that with me." I took the HK from him. "Stay on the N19. If you see a gendarme, wake me; if anyone tries to get you to stop for any reason, wake me; if the car plays up in any way, wake me; if we get to the fuel stop and café before Tendrara, wake me. Got it?"

"I think I can manage that." He got out stiffly and went round to the driver's side.

I settled into the passenger's seat and waited until he'd found a gear and pulled away. When we were up to cruising speed I told my unconscious to wake me if the motion stopped and set myself to sleep.

When I woke the sun had rather burned the side of my face. It felt a little tender to the touch and would probably peel. My father was at the wheel, driving with concentration but looking relaxed and quite comfortable. It was a long time since I'd seen him doing anything like that, and in the hinterland of neither wake nor sleep, it took me back to childhood holiday trips for a moment.

"Ah, Simon, you're awake. Good."

"Where are we?"

"Ten kilometres from Tendrara, according to the last sign."

"That's excellent." I had a big stretch and rubbed my fingers through my hair to help myself wake up. "I want some breakfast and I want some coffee."

"I'd forgotten your capacity to sleep anywhere."

"What do they say, I sleep the sleep of the just."

"No pangs of conscience then? All this drug dealing and killing."

"It's smuggling. And what killing?"

"You must've had to kill to get where you are. You and Guy."

"And I didn't in Afghanistan?"

"That's different."

"Maybe. Maybe not."

"Well?"

"Guy mainly but yes, a few. Only those who intended to kill me, if that helps. I find that when they shoot at you, it's quite natural to shoot back."

"So you're really telling me that none of this bothers you? None of this dirty business. I still find that hard to believe."

"Oh, I didn't say that. There's a boy I sent up a building to watch out for me. Just a young chap. He was killed by Rupert or one of his men. I didn't do it and I couldn't have known it was going to happen, but I still don't feel good about it."

"By Rupert?"

"Yes, you know. The chap I was asking you about yesterday. John Seymour Grant. Special forces chap with twelve, or is it eleven buddies. Presumably calls himself Rupert because it's forces' slang for officer."

"Oh."

"His main intention seems to be to kill Guy, as far as I can tell anyway. He's not particular though; he'll kill anyone who gets in his way, I think. He told me to leave before it happened to me."

"He told you… how can he have told you?"

"We had a coffee together yesterday morning. Pull in here, let's get some breakfast." I reached into the back and tucked the HK away out of sight.

We stopped at one of the busy, litter strewn fuel and refreshment stops and my father sat on a plastic chair drinking coffee and absentmindedly eating lamb meloui at a table outside the roadside café. He didn't say anything. I put my food away pretty quickly; now that I was awake I wanted to be up and at it, and went round the truck carrying my coffee in one hand. All her vital signs were okay. I was developing more confidence in her.

I wandered over to the pumps and had a word with the lad who worked them. I showed him the roll of Dirham that I was carrying and quietly asked him if he could find me another jerry can. He thought about it and then nodded. I went back to the truck and not long after he appeared from behind one of the several parked lorries and other vehicles with one. I put it in the back and drove over to the pumps. I made him rinse it out with fuel, just in case, and then fill it and the tank to the very brim. He went back to his chair, grinning, with a fat bundle of notes in his pocket.

I looked over to where my father was sitting and saw that he was using his mobile phone. He had his back to me and was banging the table with his fist.

"Come on then, Dad. Let's get this going on, shall we?" I called over to him.

At the sound of my voice he looked quickly towards me and the expression on his face was one of fear. He saw that I was looking at him and rearranged his face. He spoke a few more emphatic words and put the phone away.

"Trouble with your broker?" I said, as he got into the passenger side.

"Just a work thing."

"Bit like this for me then. Hang onto your hat, we're going to get off the road in a minute and it's going to get rough and it's going to get hot." I pulled out and put my foot down.

"As far as I'm concerned, this *is* hot." He fanned his face with his hat to make the point.

Before we got to the small desert town of Tendrar we took a lane off the main highway, which ran between a fold in the low hills. A few miles on we passed a herder feeding his flock of tough, skinny sheep from the back of his pickup and then the track faded away and the real driving began. This was neither the desert pavement of relatively flat land with a covering of smaller or larger rocks, nor the dunes of the Saharan heartland but a broken mixture of low hills, dry wadis and occasional banks of sand. It was disorienting, so I got out the compass and noted the position of the sun.

The driving wasn't difficult in itself, but I had to constantly gauge the terrain and prevent myself from being forced off my path. I could have slowed right down and taken a more direct route but speed was important now so I pushed hard at it, choosing the faster going and weaving to one side or the other as my feeling for the country dictated.

"Do we have to go so fast?" my father said.

"This isn't fast," I said.

As we went on the land became more barren and lunar. The small scrubby bushes in the bottom of wadis became fewer and fewer and then disappeared. The rocks that often lay like a spine along the tops of ridges were black and, in contrast to the increasingly common patches of fine golden sand, gave the place a stark, bi- tonal look. The sun was right up in the sky now and we were both drinking regularly from plastic bottles of water.

"I wish you'd chosen a vehicle with air conditioning," my father said, wiping his brow with a silk handkerchief for the second time in a few minutes.

"She seems to be a pretty good old girl," I said, patting the dashboard encouragingly, "but I am missing the big 100 series that I had before. Easy come, easy go, I suppose."

"How do you mean?"

"A few days ago I was out here, well, a bit further west and south actually, but out in the desert, and we ran into Rupe and his boys. Guy sent us to fetch an initial delivery of cocaine and heroin and they thought it was him. I think they got a local kid to pop a tracker on our vehicle at the junction with the N19 and then followed us out, but they must have known that we were going, more or less when we were going and, in general terms, where. That's interesting isn't it?"

"What makes you say they were out to kill Guy?"

"I sat on the top of a dune watching them go at it. Believe me, they weren't just paying a social call. And they'd brought along an RPG."

"An RPG?"

"A rocket propelled grenade."

"I know what an RPG is."

"Then you'll know that it's not a subtle option. If you send one off at a vehicle, and it hits it, you don't expect prisoners."

"Did you learn all this in The Rifles?"

"Some of it, but I've been trained by Guy too. He likes to be prepared, as you know. He keeps a farm, well a couple of thousand acres, a few awful buildings and a herd of horses, out near lake Afret, and he and an ex-military chap called Andy would take me, and some others, out there and give us lessons in all kinds of things. He's a good teacher, Guy. We get on, though I recognise what a complete bastard he is."

"I imagine you do."

"I like to think I have a reasonable aptitude for it."

"I'm sure you do. What were you saying about taking a something series from this person called Rupert?"

"Oh, yes. When we stopped for the night, I found the tracker that they'd put on our vehicle and went back up our trail to see what turned up. What did turn up was Rupert in two nice big four by fours. We disabled ours and made off in theirs. It was a pretty fair swap."

"And where are they now then?"

"They got one back from Guy's compound when they took it yesterday and Sam stole the one I was driving later on. Like I say, easy come, easy go."

"Sam? The girl?"

"That's the one."

"I thought you said she works for you?"

"That's sort of true. It depends on the situation. She's also Guy's daughter."

"My God. I thought… I didn't know…"

"I don't think there's much doubt about it."

"Where is she now?"

"Unless I'm mistaken, about a hundred and twenty miles that way."
I pointed in the direction we were driving. "I put a tracker on the truck
she stole from me. Very useful things these GPS trackers, aren't they?"

"I wouldn't know. You're saying she's gone to meet Guy?"

"I'm betting on it. She's not one to miss out on the fun if she can
help it."

"So she'll be there when…"

"When?"

"When we get there."

"I hope so. I'm looking forward to seeing her and she's the most
useful person in a fight you can imagine."

"I think I've wandered down a rabbit hole. She's the most useful…?"

"Yes, absolutely lethal. Makes me look like a pansy. No offence."

"Fucking hell," he said. That was quite strong, for him.

"I'll get out the laptop and make sure they're still where I think
they are once we're over the border," I said.

"What border?"

"That border." I pointed to the low escarpment ahead. "Once
we're up on that, we're in Algeria."

The border, as borders often do, followed a handy geographic
feature. In this case it was a change from the broken land that we
had been travelling over to a slightly higher plateau of much flatter
land. I had to traverse a bit before I found a place where I thought
we could get up, and when I did, I had a look on foot first. It was
steep and the last bit of it would require a bit of nerve, but I thought
I detected signs that others had been this way before.

I got back into the truck and said, "This is going to be a bit of a
ride. I won't be offended if you choose to walk up."

"I'll be fine, just get us up in one piece." He was holding onto
the door handle already, which was odd, considering that we were
stationary.

"Here we go then."

I put my foot down and got us over the skirt of soft sand at the bottom by momentum. After that it wasn't too bad for a bit. We were rock hopping, but those trucks are very good at that. As long as you don't get hung up over a rock or break something, it's amazing what they'll go up. There was one sticky bit where a gully threatened to widen beyond what our wheels could straddle and drop us in, but sometimes, on hard dry rock, an inch of grip will do.

I let her sit on a small level patch just under the very top. Sand had collected above us, sculpted by the wind into almost an overhang.

"You can't be serious," my father said, looking up at it through the windscreen.

"I think it looks worse than it is," I said, letting in the clutch slowly. We moved into the sand, the bonnet rising and rising in front of us. I felt the back wheels begin to spin and then the front. We were digging in. I gave her more throttle and then more and more, moving the wheel gently from side to side. Above us the ledge of sand collapsed and slid down onto us. For a moment we seemed to be sinking, almost upright, into a sea of sand and then the sand falling past our back wheels began to pack down beneath them and we started to move ahead.

Almost at once our nose began to drop as a gap in the crest of the ridge of sand appeared ahead of us. Then our front wheels were not on sand but on rock and we pulled ourselves out with our rear wheels still scrabbling for grip almost until we were level. I went on a few meters so that we were off the skyline and stopped.

"I need a drink," my father said. "And a quiet sit down in my favourite chair at home."

"Move about a bit and drink some water. It'll make you feel better," I said, suiting my actions to my words. It did too.

All four wheels were still attached so I emptied a jerry can of fuel into the tank and made Dad produce the food Robbie had provided. I ate a warm, limp sandwich. He looked at his dubiously but ate it anyway.

"The next bit should be a picnic. Ready?"

"Whatever this is, it's definitely not my idea of a picnic."

"Come on, this is fun, isn't it?"

"Ask me later, if we survive it."

"You can drive for a bit," I said. I found the compass and consulted it. "About there should do. See that middle hump?" I pointed to the hills in the distant haze. He nodded, swallowing water. "Good. Come on then, lets get going."

I got the laptop out of the back, stuck the GPS antennae on the roof and got in the passenger side.

"This is a strange place," my father said. "What did you call it?"

"Desert pavement. It's like this all the way to those hills. Easy driving but rather boring. It's a layer, a crust of quite small stones, sitting on, well, dust, dirt, sand, that kind of thing. It's a place where nothing has happened, or will happen, for a very, very long time. As long as you don't break the crust."

"And if you do that?"

"In this case, what's underneath would start blowing about in the wind and join the Great Western Erg. You can go a bit faster, by the way."

"The what?"

"The great inland sand-sea that's just over those hills," I said. "Where we're going. At least, that's where I think we're going." I booted the laptop up and waited while it found a satellite and asked its questions. The flashing dot was in the same place. "Yes, that's where we're going."

We picked up a track that led us over the low hills and joined the N6 highway heading south.

"Have you got a visa for Algeria?" I said.

"I wasn't intending to visit Algeria," my father said.

"Me neither," I said.

"What happens if we get stopped?"

"We pay someone, or we shoot someone, or we go to prison. Conceivably all three," I said. "Pull in if you see a fuel stop."

We saw one so we stopped and bought fuel and coffee and garantita, a kind of chickpea bread that is full of oil and keeps well. They may have noticed our Moroccan plates but why should they care? About ten kilometres further on we took another track and headed out into the desert again. There was an hour or more of winding through the hills which became lower and lower and faded into a rolling, landscape dotted with low scrub. There was a dry wadi over to our left with acacia and tamarind and occasionally a palm, and ahead of us only more of the same undulating scrub and sand as far as the eye could see. The sun was still fierce but it was driving in through the right hand windows now, slipping towards evening.

The wall of the erg, when it lifted itself from the desert floor, was a dark orange with sinuous curves and stark, black shadows thrown by the lowering sun. We stopped before it and I let the tyres down to about 15 PSI.

"You ready then, Dad?" I said, getting into the driving seat.

"I've no idea, Simon, but we've got this far. I suppose you'll get us further."

"Probably, but you never know."

I built up what I guessed would be enough momentum and put us into the slope of sand. We swung smoothly up to the lowest point of the ridge and stopped. The far side was much steeper, as they usually are. It was a little heart-stopping going over but I kept her straight and the power slightly on and we swooped down, through the trough and up the far side. The next dune was higher than the first and the one to come higher still.

"How far have we got to go?" my father said, looking a little pale in spite of the golden evening light.

"For now, no further than the light will let us," I said.

Three dunes further in we stopped in a trough, which I thought we could get out of without the momentum gained from the previous slope. I turned the engine off and got out. The sand, when I put my fingers in it, was warm to the touch but in the dark shadow of the hollow the temperature of the air was already beginning to fall. The sun retreated off the top of the far slope, hung invisible in the air for a moment and then was gone.

"I'd forgotten how many stars there are," my father said, leaning on the bonnet of the truck and looking up into the black bowl of the night sky.

As we stood there together the afterglow faded and the carpet of stars became complete. Stars in a multitude beyond comprehension from rim to rim.

"Supper and then rest. You're on first watch," I said.

"Who put you in charge anyway?"

"You're feeling better then, Dad?"

"I've been worse I suppose. Where's the scotch and soda by the way?"

"About ten miles that way," I pointed into the interior of the erg.

"Bugger," he said, with feeling.

I looked at him in surprise and smiled.

We sat on an old blanket and made a pretty decent meal of the last of the sandwiches, some more garantita, some spicy cured sausage, and followed that with dates.

When we'd put the remains away I shook the crumbs off the blanket, arranged a bit of sand to my satisfaction and lay down to sleep.

"Fuck," I said.

"What?" Dad said.

"I haven't filled up the fuel tank or checked the oil and water," I said.

"Leave it to me, Simon."

"Okay, thanks. Wake me in three hours, Dad."

"Okay, Si."

As I went to sleep, my father was moving quietly about the vehicle doing the chores.

18

ALL IN A GOOD CAUSE

When I woke up about five hours later, he was sitting above me, leaning against the wheel of the truck, the HK propped beside him and his hat tilted back on his head. He was snoring gently.

There was no point disturbing him so I got up quietly, got the binoculars out of the truck and climbed the highest bit of dune I could see, which was high enough to let me look over its lesser brethren, back along our track. The moon was just rising out of the sand in the east but it's light was only throwing shadows, not yet illuminating the land. The peaks of the dunes were touched by it, leaving the troughs in deeper darkness.

I needn't have bothered with the glasses; I could see the headlights out in the darkness easily. Three sets, racing towards us, less than a mile from the edge of the erg.

I ran down the face of the dune, all sleepiness gone, calling to him to wake up.

I got in and started her up. Dad got in the passenger side looking confused. I got back out and grabbed the HK from where it had fallen on the sand and the blanket too.

"Sorry, I …." he said. "What's…?"

"Wait a bit, Dad. Let me just do this," I said.

I backed her up the slope behind us as far as she would go and sent her at the shoulder of the dune ahead, up into the silver moonlight. It seemed okay but as we got within the last few meters the wheels began to spin and we were losing way. I gave her more power and twitched the wheel from side to side and she just made it. I didn't like to linger on the top as we were beginning to slip sideways, so I sent her straight back over into the darkness.

I took us over the next few on adrenaline and bravado and then collected myself and did a little thinking. I paused on a lower crest to consult the GPS and the compass, and find a smock from my bag, as it was cold. After that we went on in a more considered way, weaving our way through as best we could, sometimes traversing the troughs as our destination was at an angle to the set of the dunes. Driving on sand you generally have to go up or down. If you try to go too diagonally you risk getting stuck or even turned over.

"You can get some sleep if you like, Dad," I said.

"That may be possible for you in conditions like this, Simon, but for me it's not. Anyway, I seem to have already had some. Sorry."

"No harm done. I didn't intend to get going again until the moon rose anyway." The pools of darkness were already perceptibly shrinking and the driving getting easier.

"Why are we rushing about like this? Why don't you put your headlights on?"

"There are three vehicles coming along behind us at speed. I saw them from the top of a dune earlier. I can only imagine that they're heading for the same place we are. I don't know who they are but I'd like to get there ahead of them, don't you think?"

"We could just…."

"Yes?"

"They might be friendly."

"And they might be Martians for all I know. I'm not sure I have any friends round here right now, and if I do, I'm not sure which ones they are. How about you?"

"I suppose you're right. Is there anything I can do?"

"I'd kill for coffee but I suppose water will have to do. Oh, and some chocolate if you can find some."

In simple distance it was no more than ten kilometres. This wasn't simple distance though, it was dune distance, which is another thing entirely. Dad was looking a little seasick. Not for the first time I blessed my strong stomach and pushed on.

The late moon was high in the sky and the dawn barely an hour away when I checked the GPS for the dozenth time and decided it would do. I stopped in the moon-shadow of a particularly big dune, took the key out of the ignition and pushed it into a split in the upholstery of the passenger's seat.

"Right then, time for a short walk," I said.

"Walk? In this? Why?" my father said, getting out and holding onto the side of the vehicle like a man who might fall down.

"I thought we'd leave this here. In case we want it later."

"Oh. I see."

"Get your things together. I'm just going to have a look under the bonnet," I said, heaving out the big bag in which I'd brought all my gear.

While my father was fumbling about in the back of the truck looking for his bag, I managed to transfer the tracker that I'd put on the engine bay bulkhead to mine. From there it went into a smaller holdall with some spare mags for the HK, the GPS receiver, my .38, some chocolate and a bottle of water. The small plastic compass I stuffed into the back pocket of my trousers. I put the laptop in the big bag, zipped it up and buried it in the sand two paces north east of the offside rear wheel.

"Ready?" I said. I slung the HK over one shoulder on its strap and followed it with the strap of the holdall over the other. It was a poor combination; I should have thought to bring a rucksack. Then I took them off again and put the holdall on first so that I could get the HK into action if I needed to.

"You ready then?" my father said, standing there at ease with the light holdall resting easily against his side.

"If you're going to be sarcastic you can carry some of this," I said. "It's going to be hard going."

And it was. The sand moves under your feet. When it gets steep it seems as if you're walking on a treadmill that moves under you; you expend effort and make no progress. And the sand gets into your boots. I took off my smock and tied it round my waist. Dad did the same with his coat.

"I'm sure this wasn't necessary," he said. "I'm sure we could just have driven there. Isn't it that way? You've turned right a bit. That star was in front of us a while ago." He pointed to Sirius low in the sky, a bit north of east.

"I was just getting us round that big dune," I said. "Trust me, I'm an ace navigator."

"If you say so," he said.

"Another half a K and let's go up a dune and see if we can see it. Sun should be rising by then."

"See what?"

"The Waaha Bint. The oasis of the girls. The place we're going."

"I didn't know. Why the name?"

"Chap called Ibn Battuta once left six hundred slave girls there while he went off to fight some Tuaregs. Or so the story goes."

"Recently?"

"About six hundred years ago I think. The sand moves about so it may have been a lot easier to get to then. No one bothers to go there much now."

"I'm not surprised."

When we had ploughed our way to the top of a high peak of sand a while later, we discovered that my navigation had indeed been spot on. Less than a kilometre further on a lump of red sandstone lit by the first rays of the new sun shouldered its way out of the sand. On its top we could see the remains of walls and towers and at the base of it the vivid wonderful green of date palms.

"How about that then?" I said.

"Let's hope they've got the coffee on," he said.

The last bit of trudging through the sand seemed longer than it should have and the sun was beginning to be warm when we made it over the last ridge and looked down into the camp.

"Bear with me a minute, I just need a pee," I said, turning to one side. "No point taking a full bladder into camp." I surreptitiously flipped the tracker out of my holdall, nudged it into the sand and peed on the spot.

"Good idea," my father said, turning to the other side and putting his bag down with a thump.

"Ready?" I said, doing up my flies and resuming my burden.

"Ready," he said, doing the same.

There was a faint haze of smoke rising from a fire and the coffee was on. Happy was arranging breakfast things on a table under an awning and my mother was watching him appreciatively from a deckchair near by.

Sam was the first to see us. She was coming back from the pool of water at the base of the sandstone cliff, her hair wet, a towel round her shoulders.

"Si. How wonderful," she shouted and ran up to me and flung her arms around me. I caught her up and swung her round, kissed her and put her down.

"I thought you might be missing me," I said.

"Si. And Edmund. Well I never," Guy said, appearing from behind the flap of one of the tents. He had an AK resting casually over one arm.

"Good morning, Guy," my father said, a little stiffly.

"Darling, how wonderful of you to come and rescue me," Mum said, getting up and giving him a decorous kiss.

"Hi, boss," Happy said, grinning like only he can. "Now you're here, everything's going to be okay." Karim raised a hand to me shyly from where he was chopping onions.

"Hi, Mum. How's life?" I said.

"Dear, sweet boy. Did you come to rescue me too?"

"Do you need rescuing?"

"I will if we run out of gin."

"Guy, I brought you an old friend," I said, dropping my rifle and bag to the sand and stepping away from them.

"So I see. And how did you find us, pray?"

"I knew Sam was about to steal my truck so I put a tracker on it," I said, pointing to the very vehicle parked behind the tents.

"Say that again," Sam said, standing in front of me.

"I could tell you were going to steal my truck," I said. "You asked for it and I said no. What else were you going to do?"

"He's right you know," Sam said, punching me in the chest in a playful way.

"And then walked, I suppose?" Guy said.

"We had a disagreement with a dune on the way. We were close so I decided that we'd come and join you for coffee and dig it out later," I said.

"Daughter, you brought them here, so you can search them," Guy said. "No offence, gentlemen."

I held my arms up theatrically while Sam did a quite unnecessarily complete search of my person. Happy fetched the HK and my bag and laid its contents out on the sand.

My father submitted to the same fate with a rigid face, saying nothing while Sam's hands patted him down with professional thoroughness. The contents of his bag, when spread on the sand, revealed some clothes, washing and shaving things, a book of Anglo Saxon poetry and a mobile phone.

That done, Guy leant his AK against the table and went to stand in front of Dad. "Hello, Ed, how are you?" he said, offering his hand.

"Well, thank you, Guy. How are you?" my father said. He took the hand but gave it back quickly.

"Bloody hell, you two," my mother said. "Let's have some coffee for goodness sake."

Sam was looking from one to the other with interest. Come to that, so was I.

"Good idea, let's do that," Guy said. "Karim, will you go up and keep a watch. I don't want any more unexpected guests walking in."

"I'm surprised at you, Guy," I said.

"I'm surprised at myself," he said.

We sat at a low table under an awning and Happy served us coffee. It was excellent. Guy was looking at Ed over steepled fingers. My mother seemed amused and exasperated and sat looking mainly at her husband, though physically closer to Guy. Sam sat next to me and punched me again.

"You're right, I have missed you, you bastard," she said.

"Have you left the boat unguarded, Si?" Guy said, switching his attention to me.

"No, hidden," I said.

"Well done, where?"

"Up a tree," I said.

"Fair enough," he said.

"Si, perhaps you should take your father home," my mother said.

"Or perhaps you should," I said.

"I don't need taking anywhere by anyone, thank you," my father said.

"No one is going anywhere just at the moment. I have some business to transact and then we shall see," Guy said.

"So you're not too bothered by our friend the Rupert?" I said.

"You mean the men who disturbed my breakfast the other day?" Guy said.

"And Zara's," I said.

"Oh?" He looked at me curiously. "No, I'll deal with them later."

"It was quite exciting. All that shooting and fleeing down a secret tunnel to a waiting Range Rover," my mother said. "Well it seems like it now anyway."

"Do you have any idea how much danger you and Simon are in?" my father said. It was the first time he'd spoken to her since we'd arrived.

"I don't imagine we're in any more danger than you are, darling. If anything, Simon seems to thrive on it. Don't you, sweetie?"

"Dad has a point, Mum. I'm not quite sure how we're all going to get home in one piece," I said.

"Don't worry, my darling, Guy and your father will work it out. They always do. Don't you, darlings?"

"Tell me why you're here again?" Guy said, looking at me.

"In Nador I've got people trying to kill me, or take my boat from me. I could leave, but if I do my parents may come to a bad end in my absence, which would be annoying. I thought I'd bring Dad to you in the hope that you'd work it out, whatever it is. If not…" I shrugged, "… something might turn up."

"You might get a chance to kill me you mean?"

"You never know," I said, smiling at him.

"Right, bugger off you lot. I need to talk to Ed," he said. "Sam, you're responsible for this one and yes, Helen, that does include you."

"Well, if you're going to be like that I'll get that rather fine black gentleman to help me with my tan," she said, rising and walking off with the coffee pot.

"Come on, Si. Let's go and explore the old fort," Sam said, taking my hand and pulling me away.

We picked up a blanket and a bottle of water and left them to it. I wanted to see the water so we went there first. It seemed impossible in that landscape but yet there it was, a pool of dark water under the cliff of porous, red sandstone that had conducted it here over thousands of miles. There was a fringe of tall grasses along most of its edge and date palms crowded together from the water and continuing along the cliff, where I suposed their roots could still get down to it.

At its edge I found that it was perfectly clear and looked as clean as water from a tap, cleaner probably. I scooped some up and splashed it over my head and then put my head into it to drink. It was surprisingly cold. I'm not saying there aren't better feelings, but cold water in a hot desert is right up there.

Sam tried a judo throw on me but I'd been expecting her and caught her up and threw her into the deeper water. She landed with a scream of anger and delight and disappeared under the surface, already trying to swim back towards me. I smiled and waved at her emerging head, grabbed the blanket and water and ran for it.

She caught me in the ruins of the old fort. We found a good spot, under a broken vault of supporting masonry, with deep shade and a view over the tops of the palms towards the south, and settled down on the blanket to reconnect with each other. I'd missed her and she'd missed me and it was very good indeed.

I must have slept as the sun had moved round quite a long way. She was thoughtfully juggling with some of the old AK 47 shell casings that littered the ground. Every now and then she tossed them higher, giving her time to throw one at my right foot and then scoop up another from the pile on her lap.

"Wake up, sleepy head. I'm hungry," she said.

"What for?" I said, putting an arm round her and attempting to pull her down to me.

"Food, you idiot." She managed to elbow me in the ribs without dropping any.

"Ouch," I said.

"Serves you right for knowing what I was thinking," she said.

"I'm sure you know what I'm thinking," I said.

"Any idiot can know what you're thinking," she said.

"I am a simple sort of chap," I said, trying to pull her towards me again.

"Simple Simon," she said, letting all the shell casings fall, moving on top of me and leaning down so that the curtain of her hair hung down around my head, "tell me what you want."

"Right now, Samantha Wealden, I want you," I said.

"Do you?" She gently rubbed herself up and down me, "Well..." she wriggled about a bit more, "... you can't have me." She leapt off me, grabbed her clothes and boots and vanished round the buttress of rock.

"Cow!" I went after her, but the fierce heat of the direct sunshine and the imminent probability of being exposed to the observation of the entire camp defeated me. I'm not a shy man but even I balk at some things.

When I walked across the sand from the ruined buildings to the camp, dressed but not entirely composed, she was sitting demurely on a deckchair next to my mother sipping a long drink through a straw. I gave her a look which said what I thought of her and she grinned happily back at me.

"They've gone for a walk," my mother said.

"In this heat?" I said.

"It's just Guy being a bastard as usual and your dad not having any common sense. They're under the palms over there," she waved a languid arm in the direction from which I'd just come.

"Karim's making lunch. We missed breakfast," Sam said.

"Are we expecting guests?" I said. Karim had one of those massive round-bottomed pans over the fire and it seemed to be full of stew. Goat probably. It smelt wonderful.

"Couldn't say," Sam said.

"Well, darling, what do you think?" my mother said.

"About what?" I took a deckchair from where I could see them both.

"About the price of vodka. What do you think I mean?"

"The more I think about it, and that isn't much, the more I think I should have left you three to it."

"That's a bit naïve darling. It's about you after all. About you and your boat, which I still haven't seen, by the way."

"Of course it's about me, isn't everything? What do you mean, it's about me? There are other men and other boats."

"Yes, but…"

She was interrupted by a loud cry of, "Hey, the camp. Strangers coming from the south." It was Happy on the rocks high above us.

"From the south?" I said.

"Why not?" Sam said.

"No reason I suppose. There's not a lot down there for a long way. You don't suppose it's Gerald, do you?"

"I couldn't possibly say," she said.

"When I can be bothered, I'm going to give you a good hard spanking," I said.

"Feel free to try at any time," she said.

"He's still pretty fit, isn't he?" my mother said. She was watching Guy run out of the shadows of the palms and climb swiftly up the path to the top of the hill.

"All this has woken him up a bit," Sam said. "He was kind of asleep for a few years I think."

My father walked out of the palms and joined us under the shade of the awning. He was sweating and looked tired.

"Come and sit next to me, darling," Mum said, indicating the chair next to her. "It really was very sweet of you to come."

"I wish I hadn't. For all the good it's doing I might as well have gone home. Thank goodness it will all be over soon," he said.

"Will it? How come?" Sam said.

"Your father will have done what he came here to do, whatever that is, and we can get out of this damn desert."

"You should get some sleep after lunch. This heat can be a bugger until you get used to it," I said.

"I'm sure you're right," he said, wiping his face with a limp and dirty handkerchief.

Guy and Happy returned. Guy was looking pleased.

"Better get your toy out, Happy. Just in case," he said. "Karim, you can feed the belt."

"Yes, boss." The big man went to the back of the Range Rover and came back with his MAG 60 over his shoulder and a heavy metal box of ammunition in one hand. They went inside a tent and got on with checking and loading.

"Daughter, would you care to take that rather nice Heckler and Koch that Simon brought us, and assume the position?"

"Love to, Dad." Sam came to life.

"But for God's sake don't start anything. We need these people."

"Yes, Dad." She slipped away behind the tent and was gone from sight.

"What's happening?" my father said.

"Look there," I said.

Two white pickups had come into sight over a dune. They were both full of men.

"It was something you said, Si. You said that people with small armies would try to muscle in on what we're up to. You're right of course, so I decided to get myself a small army, and here it is. Cost me a bit, but should be worth it."

"Are they what I think they are?" I said.

"Probably. Gerald fixed me up. Very obliging chap," Guy said.

"Get him to make tea for you if you ever meet him," I said.

"I'll do that tomorrow. He'll be here with the first proper load, all being well."

"You haven't delivered the first one yet," I said.

"You mean, you haven't," Guy said.

The approaching men were well wrapped up against the sun but the features I could see had the lean, wolfish look of Somalis. The vehicles pulled up on flat ground about fifty yards from us and the men got down off them. They stood patiently, looking at us with mild curiosity and holding their AKs with the perfect, unconscious familiarity of those who handle them most of their waking lives. They looked calm and enduring under the fierce sun. Battle hardened, ready to kill, ready to die, and in the meantime, ready to watch and wait, and see which it would be. I counted sixteen in all.

Guy walked out to meet them, keeping out of the line of the tent, of course. A man got out of the passenger side of one of the pickups and came to meet him. He was the only one not carrying a weapon.

The two stood talking for a few minutes, each with an intense concentration on the other, and then their body language relaxed.

They shook hands. The black man was smiling, showing his teeth. He spoke to his men and the smile spread to the rest of them.

Guy spoke again, pointing to the area to one side of the camp. Then the man gave orders, pointing in the same way that Guy had. The pickups moved, the men walking beside them, to the spot. They began to make camp.

Guy and the man walked over to the rest of us.

"This is Liibaan. These are my friends," he said.

"I am very pleased to meet you," he said, studying us each in turn with a direct and unashamed appraisal.

"Hello Liibaan, welcome to the party," my mother said. "You certainly look the part."

"I do not understand," he said.

"She means that you look like real men, not like a bunch of girls," I said.

"Ah, no, we are not a bunch of girls," he said, grinning. "I'm glad that you have noticed that."

"Right, Liibaan, if you will take charge of your camp now, we will have lunch and then rest. After that we will have small arms drill. Pick a man to take sentry duty up there," Guy pointed to the top of the hill, "they can wash over there. But not in the water, beside it." Liibaan nodded, understanding. "Good. No arms carried in camp but stacked ready for use. Okay?"

"Okay, Mr Guy. I will see to it now." Liibaan gave Guy a salute, which Guy returned, and stepped off smartly to carry out his instructions.

"Well, Captain Wealden, get you," my mother said, giving him an exaggerated salute as he sat down.

"I think of myself as a general, not a captain, thank you," he said, grinning. He made an unobtrusive beckoning gesture and sat down. Sam, Happy and Karim reappeared from their positions. "Let's eat. Helen, you can make yourself useful and lend a hand."

"Really?" she said.

"Yes, really," he said.

I couldn't remember when I'd last seen my mother serving anyone else in a domestic capacity, but that's what happened. She and Karim served us bowls of lamb stew with rice. It was excellent. Happy, Sam and I had seconds. My father ate little and retired to try to sleep in one of the tents. The awning above us was radiating heat now and it was bloody hot.

When we'd eaten, the big bowl of stew was passed to the Somalis, who received it with smiles of appreciation and took it to their part of the camp. Helen went to join Dad, Guy went off into a different tent and the rest of us made ourselves as comfortable as we could on mats and blankets under the awning, each of us with a water bottle beside us.

I slept again. Sam slept beside me.

Happy was snoring when I woke. Guy was sitting on a chair gazing thoughtfully into the middle distance. The sun was low in the sky. He looked at me and winked.

"Come on then, Si. Get up and let's see what we've got, shall we?" he said.

"Might as well I suppose," I said, and gave Sam a nudge.

"What?" she said, not really waking up.

"I think your old man wants us to go and play with the staff," I said.

"That I do. I'm feeling strangely competitive today. We'll divvy them up, do an hour's weapons check and training and then have a competition, shall we?"

"What's the prize?" I said.

"In your case, perhaps your life," he said.

"I can't promise you the same, I'm afraid," I said.

"Very funny, come on."

We walked over to the Somalis. They were resting under a tarpaulin stretched over their two vehicles but were more than ready to get to work, getting up with ready smiles and lithe, quick movement. Guy had them line up, including Liibaan, and we chose one each in turn, just like picking teams at school. Guy went first and chose Liibaan for his first pick. The men who fell to Sam looked a bit confused.

We took a case of ammunition each from the back of one of the pickups and led our teams to the base of the fort. I found an old, tyre-less metal wheel and jammed it between rocks at about fifty yards. I made the men line up facing me and took the AK from the first man. He was unsure about letting me have it but when I stripped it in front of him, checked and cleaned the bore and the action, and put it back together he started to smile. When I followed that by making the target ring with a burst of four they all grinned and clapped.

I passed it back to him and indicated that he should take four shots at the target. He did, and hit it four times with speed and confidence. I took the rifle back off him and told him in Arabic that the target was clearly too close and would he please go and put it in a better place. This caused laughter and a lot of chatter in Somali, which I didn't understand. He put it at about a hundred and twenty yards but they shouted at him and he shrugged and walked back to about eighty yards. In other parts of the area shooting broke out as the other teams started firing too.

I repeated my drill with the next man but failed to completely contain the rise of the gun and missed with the last of the four. He didn't though. The mood became concentrated and professional. I corrected my error with the final two and they also hit the target. Their weapons were old but perfectly serviceable and well maintained.

We were already a slightly different group of men than we had been, when we rejoined the others. The men in Sam's team no longer looked confused but were smiling and making big eyes at their friends. Karim was on watch at the top of the hill but Happy and my parents, who had come over to see what all the noise was, were watching us with interest.

"Okay, Si," Guy said, beckoning Happy over and tossing an AK to him. "You set up a short assault course over there somewhere. Better be quick, the light is going. You three go first to demonstrate and then each team in turn. I'm going to time it, so don't be surprised if I win."

"Don't you want to take part?" I said.

"Don't be silly, I'm an old man now," he said.

I called my team to me and we scouted about until we'd found four decent sized pieces of date palm trunk. These I set up standing in strategic places amongst the ruins, propped up by stones. Everyone watched me while I did this and moved into a position from where they could see them clearly.

I trotted back and said, "All logs down. Firing only from cover. One log per team member, except us. Sam, you get two. Next member to move forward while the other is firing. Got it?"

"Got it, Si," Sam said.

"Ready, boss," Happy said.

"Ready, Guy?" I said.

"Ready," he said, with his phone in his hand.

"Go."

I ran for the nearest cover. The others were with me. Sam threw herself prone behind the first heap of boulders and started hammering rounds into the top of the nearest post. By the time it had fallen Happy and I were in cover forward and he was firing. I ran on with Sam hard at my heels and took the next post while she passed me. She slid into the dust with her gun up and firing on automatic and the last post went down. My ears were ringing with the noise and I'd got a stone in one of my boots. We walked back to the others to the sound of applause.

"Fifty eight seconds is the time to beat," Guy said. Some of the Somalis nodded, holding up their phones. There would be no cheating after all. I sent my men off to put the posts back up.

Guy's team went next, naturally, it would get more difficult as the light softened, and found it a little harder than we had to get the posts down, putting in a time of over a minute twenty. I could see that they weren't as used to finding their aim after hard running as we were. Mine did well, beating his by five seconds and Sam's came closest to ours, missing by only a couple of seconds. I could see that they were desperate to live up to her performance; so much for their doubts about being led by a girl. The brief twilight came and went and it was dark.

"Did someone say something about a drink?" my mother said, coming up to me and putting her arm through mine.

"I suppose I could use something to wash the dust away," I said.

"Why didn't I know that about you?" she said.

"Why didn't you know what about me?"

"That you can be like that."

"Like what?"

"All grown up. I've not really noticed before that you're a man now."

"I'm usually like that. You just haven't spent much time around me, that's all."

"How did that happen?"

"I've wondered myself. You've seemed to be a bit busy with other things."

"I've been selfish and self-absorbed, you mean. I know, you don't have to tell me. Ed has, often enough."

"I didn't notice at the time, but this was all your idea, wasn't it?"

"What was?"

"Me being here."

"Oh, that. No, not really."

"Hey, Si," Sam said, coming up on the other side of me and claiming that arm. "That was fun. I'm so glad you're back."

"I wasn't really gone. Just looking for a new truck," I said. "You know you can't manage without me."

"Prick," she said, trying to stamp on my instep.

"Which reminds me…" I said.

"What?" my mother said.

"That it's time to light a fire and pour a drink," I said.

"Ed's talking to Guy again. It's like old times, being out here with them both. Except you're here too now. I like it," my mother said, "it makes me feel young again."

"That must take some doing," Sam said, under her breath.

"What's that, dear? You're mumbling," my mother said.

"Sorry, I forgot that it gets harder to hear as you get older. I'll speak up," Sam said.

"Probably your diction, sweetie. Your generation seem to have given up on speaking properly," my mother said.

"Let's open a bottle and find somewhere comfortable to sit," I said, releasing them and looking round for the men I considered my team.

I needn't have bothered. Happy had collared a few of the Somalis and they were coming up with arms full of what little firewood could be gathered. Happy and Karim settled down by the fire and got it going merrily, the wood giving off cracks and bangs as it burnt, loud in the utter silence of the desert. Mum and I sat down on the comfortable mats under the awning. The Somalis went off to their part of the camp with a crate of beer bottles that Sam fetched from the back of my truck. She really had been shopping for supplies. She threw beers at the men by the fire and they caught them grinning. They popped the tops and caught the foaming liquid in their mouths.

"And me," I said, holding up a hand."

"Catch," she said, lobbing one hard at me.

"You two are two of a kind, aren't you?" my mother said.

"Yeah, but I can shoot," I said. Sam raised a finger in my direction from where she was loading bottles and glasses onto a tray.

"Edmund never had that. His father did, but him, never. It's a shame."

"I never had what?" my father said, walking out of the darkness with Guy.

"An aptitude for all this outdoors stuff, darling."

"It's all right for a bit but I have to say I'm longing for a decent hotel right now," my father said.

"Never mind, Ed," Guy said, putting a friendly hand on his shoulder, "you've got the rest of us to do it for you, eh? Ah, well done daughter. That's the idea."

They found places to sit and accepted drinks from Sam. She sat next to me with a beer. No one spoke for a bit; we savoured our drinks and thought our thoughts. The crackling fire deepened the silence and the darkness. My father and Guy were lit by the firelight, their faces dramatic angles and planes of light and shadow. Mum was watching them, her back to the fire and her face in enigmatic darkness. They were each very aware of the other and Sam and I were just an audience. I sipped my beer and looked at them until it was time for me to say something.

"When did all this start, then?" I said.

"When did what start?" my father said.

"Scitan," I said. "That is you two, isn't it? You and Guy."

"Hah," Guy said. "So much for keeping him in the dark then."

"I've been a bit slow, haven't I?" I said.

"You seem to be catching up," Mum said.

"What are you talking about?" Sam said.

"Do you remember that I told you I had the idea for Nottambulo and for using her in the Med, for working for Guy, all of it, myself? Well I didn't. It came from Mum. Didn't it, Mum? A word dropped here and there. The picture on the table that day, all of it."

"I could see you were going to do something a bit wild anyway. I thought it would be better to keep it in the family."

"Only it didn't originate with you did it?"

"Of course it did," she said.

"No it didn't. It was Guy's idea. Which, of course, is why he didn't exactly look surprised when I turned up. Only you didn't mention any of this to your business partner did you, Guy?" I said.

"He would've had a fit. Well, actually he has had a fit," Guy said. "Haven't you, Ed?" He put his hand on my father's shoulder. He shrugged it off.

"Hang on. Come that again?" Sam said.

"I don't know this for a fact," I said, "but I think that these two did a deal, quite a long time ago, probably about when Guy fell from grace. Is that right?" I looked at Guy, who nodded, grinning. "It was probably his idea and he probably used some kind of leverage because that's his style. Is that right?"

"Pictures. Sordid pictures of what I thought was love," my father said.

"I had nothing to lose, but Ed did. I needed some help and he didn't want to give it to me so I made him, that's all. And since then I've been largely responsible for your rise to power, haven't I, Teddy?"

"That's a lie. More accurate to say that I've been responsible for you still being alive," my father said.

"That's not fair. I would've found a way. I always do, haven't you noticed?"

"And once it was going it worked out so well that it's kept going ever since and got bigger and bigger. And then you thought you'd get me involved and that changed everything didn't it, Guy?" I said.

"I only found out two months ago," my father said.

"I appreciate that, Dad. I appreciate the thought, but if you'd just told me," I said.

"We've been a bit slow to realise he's grown up, Ed," my mother said.

"What the fuck did you think you were sending me into, Mum?" I said.

"I don't know. I suppose I didn't really take it seriously. It's all worked out though, hasn't it," she said.

"Not yet, it hasn't," I said.

"I never seem to get it right," my father said.

"You never did, old boy," Guy said.

"I still don't…" Sam said.

"I think it's like this," I said. "Dad was in the Home Office, trying to make a name for himself. Guy had just been kicked out of the army in disgrace but still had plenty of contacts. They cooked up Scitan, which is Anglo Saxon for shit, isn't it?"

"It seemed appropriate," my father said.

"Dad's an Anglo Saxon scholar," I said. "Your military service was in intelligence, wasn't it?" I said.

"As it happens," he said.

"When you say civil servant, you mean spook. Don't you?" I said.

"That's a foolish term," he said.

"Well, anyway, Scitan. Guy's end of the business is to get the product and get it to Europe. From there a group of ex-forces chaps, all of whom no doubt get paid a lot more for it than anything else they could conceivably do, take over and distribute it. The income, and it's a pretty huge one, goes to fund Rupert and his crew, doesn't it, Dad?"

"Yes," he nodded.

"And Rupert and his boys quietly and efficiently dispose of anyone who might be a threat, or an embarrassment, to the UK. Or at least that's the idea, isn't it, Dad?"

"More or less. None of you will ever know how many lives I've saved. If I get my K, I will have earned it. And a lot more than most," my father said. "And I've never taken a penny from it, apart from my salary."

"More fool you," Guy said.

"So Rupert and his colleagues are doing their patriotic duty, at least by their lights - I imagine some people might not agree - and Dad's department soon gets a reputation for being able to sort out problems that others just can't handle. I imagine that no one ever wants to know what you do, but they're perfectly happy for you to go on doing it, as long as you don't get caught, right?"

"Damn right, they are. Which is why these two bringing you into it was insanely stupid," Dad said. "Sooner or later it was going to lead some plod back to me and bring the whole thing down."

"You have a self-destructive streak, Guy, don't you?" I said.

"I know, I can't help it. I get bored," Guy said.

"I know the feeling," I said. "And so does Sam."

"So this Rupert works for your father and he's here to kill us?" Sam said.

"Well, Guy, certainly," I said. "He became too much of a risk to stay alive and without him I'd be unemployed, and would go away, and hopefully stop being a potential embarrassment. That's the way Dad saw it. He's more ruthless than he usually gets the credit for being."

"As long as he doesn't have to actually witness what he's caused," Guy said.

"I don't think you can claim the moral high-ground here," I said. "Any of you. However, I have an idea that Rupert's a man on a mission. There's a messianic gleam in that man's eye that worries me. What are his instructions, Dad?"

"What do you mean?"

"The reason I gave you an hour to get ready was to give you time. It was Rupert following us earlier, wasn't it? What are his instructions? What is he planning to do?"

Guy was very still, looking at me intently. "What do you mean, following you?" he said.

"I couldn't say," Dad said.

"Won't, you mean," I said. "As usual. I strongly suspect that he's out there right now," I waved a thumb in the general direction of the darkness that was the desert, "Perhaps we should take some precautions?"

There was the sound of a sharp buzz, twice but so close as to be almost indistinguishable, and the wet smack of Happy's skull shattering. Karim folded forward, exsanguinating in gouts from his neck onto the fire, which hissed.

I should have spoken sooner.

19

THE PARTY

Everyone started moving except my parents. I scooped Mum up with an arm under her ribcage and dragged her behind the nearest tent and then to one of the vehicles. There was shouting and then automatic fire from the direction of the Somalis.

"Get under and dig yourself into the sand. Dig yourself in. Understand?" She nodded so I left her to it.

Sam and Guy had disappeared but Dad was still sitting where he'd been. There was movement at the periphery of the camp; men running. I threw myself on the ground beside him and pulled him down. "Crawl to the vehicles as fast as you can," I said.

"They won't shoot me," he said.

"Don't be stupid. Anyone might shoot anyone right now. Move."

"Okay, okay." He started crawling awkwardly, and appallingly slowly, away. I left him to it and went to see what I could do to help.

Over to my right the sharper sound of the HK started. Tap, tap. Tap, tap. Disciplined firing. Someone was finding targets. I got up and ran to the Somalis. They didn't mistake me for the enemy and shoot me, which was a minor miracle and showed just how experienced they were. They had dug in between their vehicles, throwing up sand and the bodies of the dead to give them some cover. Liibaan was among the dead.

I slid down amongst them calling out, "It is me, Simon," in English and Arabic. One of the dead received a couple of rounds from the darkness that were no doubt intended for me. One of the Somalis put his head up a little and sent a quick burst of fire at the pinpricks of light out in the darkness that were the muzzle flash from the shots. I hoped he got the bastard.

"We know, Simon. We see you," a voice said, in English.

There seemed to be six still alive but one of those was holding his stomach and moaning. Given that the attack had been a complete surprise, it could've been worse. I took an AK from one of the dead and slid back the action to check that there was a round in the chamber. The dull brass gleamed at me in the faint starlight. "We must go," I said. "They will have mortars or RPG."

They nodded gravely. They understood but none of them wanted to go out into the open with the unseen enemy able to pick them off from the cover of darkness. I didn't want to myself.

I was considering trying to get out under one of the pickups when there was a whooshing sound from somewhere near the other fire and then a star-shell burst above us. The intense magnesium light revealed the enemy, frozen for an instant in their firing positions, spread out on the slopes of the sand dunes all around us. Then they began to roll, get to their feet and run. The roar of the MAG opened up and the HK was tapping away too. Three of the Somalis were joining in with their AKs.

"Come," I shouted. "Behind them. We must get behind them. Come with me." They nodded, grinning. This was more like it.

I led them straight out into the desert. The enemy would be too busy, for the moment, to attend to us. So it proved. We crossed the next gully and rise and slid down into the sand behind the crest as the star-shell fell back to earth and the darkness returned.

"You, you and you." I tapped shoulders. "Go round that way. Like this." I motioned with my hands, demonstrating them staying apart so that they wouldn't present one target and moving forward in turn. They nodded, understanding. "Go that far," I said, pointing, "and wait for the next light. Okay?"

"Yes, yes, Simon. We understand," one who spoke English said. They all grinned at me, their eyes alight. "We know what to do."

"Good, so go." I gave him a friendly shove and led my team around the other way.

The next star-shell came before we had got to where I wanted to be, so we cut in anyway, running as hard as we could in the sand. Over the crest of the next dune we came on a party of four grouped round a field mortar. They had anticipated our flanking, or were just well trained, and each man was in firing position, weapon up.

Bullets tore into the man ahead of me and to my right and he went down. From behind me a sustained burst knocked the shooter backwards, his gun still firing. I managed to get some stability in the sliding sand, get my aim and join in. It was a brutal business as there was no hiding or taking cover for any of us, but we were spread out and they were in a tight group. I remembered that they would be in body armour and tried to aim high and low for heads and legs as they writhed about, trying to get their weapons to bear.

The man in the centre, who had been about to drop a mortar into the tube, arched backwards as his body went into spasm from the bullets hitting his armoured torso and then collapsed like a punctured balloon as one of them went through his neck.

I concentrated on the one returning fire from the right side of the group and there was a terrible moment as I saw his aim shift from the man to my left, who had gone silent, towards me. Sand was flying up in my face and the air was full of bullets, it was inevitable that I would be hit. I was looking over the now hot barrel of my AK, desperately concentrating my aim, and the mag must be about to give out when I saw him twitch and then fall forwards, his gun still firing, but now into the sand.

My gun was empty so I rolled to one side, lay as low as I could on the slope and swapped out the mag. Before I had done so, it was over. The silence was ringing from the storm of fire and thin grey propellant smoke was drifting in the lurid light from the flare. It can only have been three, four seconds in all. The flare finished its slow fall and we were back in darkness.

I eased myself down the slope, alert for the slightest movement from the huddled mass of bodies. There was none. One of the Somalis joined me, his arm hanging useless and dripping blood into the sand. The other two were darker shapes on the starlit slope.

One of the men moved, lifting his head and trying to look at me, saying something I couldn't hear. I shot him point blank in the head. I regretted it almost at once because it was in anger and fear that I did it, though it was probably the kindest thing I could have done.

"Is that you, Si?" Sam's voice said from the darkness towards the camp.

"More or less," I said, and my voice sounded a bit strange. I could feel the onset of hysterical laughter welling up in me.

"Glad you got to these in time. That mortar might have dented my truck. I'm just having a scout round to see if there's any clearing up to do."

"Okay," I said weakly. I sat down on the sand and put my fingers in it and made myself take a long slow breath, count to four and breathe out again. And then again, and again. The Somali was looking at me with a glazed expression, also in shock.

I noticed the blood running down his arm and cut a section of cloth from one of the dead men's uniforms to bind it. The action made me feel better, and him too, possibly. There were a few single shots here and there but I knew that it was only Sam making sure. We got up and walked over the dune back to the camp.

My mother had her arms around my father who was sitting on the sand by the fire holding his leg and rocking back and forth.

"Si, thank God," she said, when she saw me.

"What is it?" I said, going down on my knees beside him.

"It's his knee. I've put a tourniquet on it but I don't know what else to do."

"Hang on, I'll be back in a minute," I said, and went back to my pile of corpses. It didn't take me long to pull a head torch from one of them and, with its help, to find the pack containing field dressings and morphine.

I started up the big Toyota and carefully drove it around so that its powerful headlights illuminated the area.

Now that I had a working light I released the tourniquet, dusted the wound with antibiotic powder and bound it up as well as I could. I think he had lost quite a bit of blood and the knee was going to need surgery. I stuck a needle full of morphine into his thigh and that was all I could do. Mum sat with him, holding him as he rocked back and forth. Her face had a quality I'd not seen before, as if she'd finally taken something seriously.

A Somali staggered into the pool of light, carrying one of his friends. With his help I did the same for his friend and for the one who had been with me. The one who had been with me would live and probably keep his arm, but I wasn't so sure about the other. I suspected that he had a shattered pelvis and needed to find himself on an operating table pretty quickly. That wasn't about to happen.

Guy walked out of the darkness and put the MAG 60 down on the sand. He looked alert and more awake than usual, but also a bit pissed off.

"So much for my small army," he said, looking at the one remaining fully functional Somali. "Ed, if you hadn't already been shot, I'd shoot you, you fucking idiot."

"Leave him alone," Mum said.

Sam joined us, looking at the scene with interest. "That was a bit close, Dad," she said. "If Si hadn't got the mortar when he did, we'd be toast now." She propped her HK against the truck and picked up a beer.

"Good shooting yourself," I said. "You're a one woman army."

"I am, aren't I." She grinned at me and did her little dance of pleasure.

"Ah, yes. Simon." Guy turned to me. "You knew that was about to happen didn't you? That's what you were saying, wasn't it?"

"Don't look at me. You've known Dad's been trying to kill you for longer than I have. You didn't need me to tell you that he might have brought his boys along with him. Did you?"

"That's a fair point, Dad," Sam said, laughing. "He's got you there. You've been a bit slack by your standards."

A red spot appeared on his chest, and then another. The same thing happened to Sam and the Somali, and me.

Guy and Sam both stood very still and looked at me.

"What the fuck?" Guy said.

"What I didn't tell you, though, was that I brought some friends along too," I said.

Stealthy figures with assault rifles walked out of the darkness and surrounded us.

20

WHAT MUST BE DONE

(MUST BE DONE)

"Why didn't I just shoot you when Sam told me to?" Guy said.

"Just a bit soft, I suppose," I said.

"Evening all," a voice said, from behind me.

"Is that you, Bill?" I said.

"Indeed," he said.

"Well, don't piss about. We've got some seriously injured people here. You must have a medic in your lot. Get him on the case and get them loaded up and on their way to hospital."

"Fair point. Freddy, will you take sensible precautions with this lot? With all of them."

"It'll be a pleasure," one of the men behind an assault rifle said.

Bill wandered away having a conversation with a radio and the men put zip ties on our ankles and wrists and sat us in a line in the sand. Me, then Guy, then Sam and finally the poor Somali, who was now looking scared. One of them stood over us, moving the red dot of the laser sight of his weapon from each of our foreheads in turn and then back again.

"I'm going to kill you," Guy said, conversationally.

"You started it," I said.

"No, I mean, I'm going to kill you," he said.

"Yes, I understand what you mean. I'm just saying that all this is your fault, not mine, and you should take it like a man and not blame me," I said.

"I know that, and the best way for me to make myself feel better is to kill you," he said.

"Fair enough, if that's the way you want it," I said.

"I think we should get out of this first, Dad," Sam said.

"I'm leaving that to you, daughter," Guy said.

"I'm starting to think I do most of the work around here," she said.

"Shush," I said.

"What?"

"I think I can hear a helicopter," I said.

I was right. A Sea King in desert camo came in fast and low over the dunes, circled once and was waved in to land in the clear area.

They loaded Dad first, Mum sticking close to him and helping the medic with the drip. Then they manhandled us into the simple metal and canvas seats and strapped us to them with webbing straps that weren't going to be breakable. It was bloody uncomfortable.

Bill and the skinny young man with the beard came too. He looked perfectly at home in his combat fatigues. The bird was only on the ground for a few minutes and then we were airborne and away. Apart from the straps, the journey back was going to be a lot more comfortable than the journey there. And a lot quicker.

I managed to catch the medic's eye and look the question. He nodded encouragingly. Apparently Dad wasn't doing too badly. It occurred to me that they hadn't bothered to bring the wounded Somalis.

It was too loud to talk and there was nothing useful I could do so I settled myself as comfortably as I could against my restraints and had a doze.

I tried to make Happy sit up and pay attention so that I could tell him something, but he kept letting his head fall apart. I tried holding it together for him but the insides of it kept running through my fingers and the white edges of the bone wouldn't fit together properly. The stuff running out of his head was sand. Someone was shouting at me.

Bill and my mother were standing over me, looking at me with concern. My arms ached and I was in a horrible muck-sweat. She wiped my face with a cloth and put a bottle of water to my lips.

"Thanks," I said. The water, and saying the word, made me more present in the chopper and less in the dream. It was very loud in there. I made myself relax my arms.

I must have looked okay as Bill sat back down and Mum went back to Dad. Sam was looking at me with interest. Guy gave me a nasty, knowing look and I was glad that he was as tightly restrained as I was.

The sun came up and made squares of light on the roof of the chopper. They began to creep slowly downwards.

We landed somewhere and Dad was taken out. There were men in green hospital-looking uniforms waiting to receive him as he was loaded onto a gurney. Mum went with him. They shut the door and we were off again.

We landed in some wasteland behind a disused warehouse. I didn't recognise it but it must have been on the outskirts of Nador. They zip tied us and lifted us into the back of a transit which smelled unpleasantly of meat, and drove off. When the doors opened we were at the home of the Evangelical Shepherds. There was more manhandling and I ended up in a room by myself. I say room, I mean kitchen, if you could call it that. There was a sink, a row of dilapidated cupboards and a small gas ring. They sat me on a chair and left me.

Happily they shut the door on me so when they'd gone I snapped the ties on my wrists, which isn't hard to do if you know how, and reached a rather blunt little knife out of a drawer to cut my ankles free.

I quietly put a pan of water on to boil and hunted about for some coffee.

I offered some to Bill when he put his head in a bit later. He went back out and started shouting. I heard the word handcuffs mentioned. He came back in and accepted the mug of coffee.

"Fuck," he said, with feeling.

"How's my father?" I said.

"Stable. They're flying in an orthopaedic surgeon from London. He may need a new knee but that's about the worst of it."

"So that could have ended worse, all things considered. I'm glad you brought that chopper."

"Me too. Borrowed it from the Spanish."

"What did you do with all the bodies?"

"What bodies?"

"The dead ones over the border."

"Oh, them. I imagine Freddy will have thought of something."

"Our Rupe?"

"Sadly, amongst the fallen."

"Shame."

"Quite. The question is, what am I going to do with those live bodies in there?"

"Not planning a trial then?"

"For what? My boss has made it very clear that if I bring any of this home, I'll be transferring myself to traffic duty at the same time. In Bradford. On nights. Why did I bring them back?"

"I don't know. Why did you bring them back?"

"Because I'm a policeman, not a bloody executioner."

"Speaking of police work, if you were to have a look into a firm that transports seafood and belongs, however distantly to Scitan, I suspect you'd find a lot of hash," I said. "You'll probably find that a lot of its staff are ex UK armed forces."

"Why didn't I think of that?"

"You were waiting for me to think of it for you, I expect."

"Wait there." He left the room for a bit and I finished the coffee.

When he came back in he said, "You're right, you bastard. We've found them. They're organising something as we speak."

"Might help to keep you off traffic duty then?" I said.

"Yes, but it doesn't help me with what to do with those two though," he said, indicating the other room.

"If you won't be offended, I think I might leave that one with you. May I go? I could do with a shower and some breakfast and some sleep."

"Do you realise you're the only one of us who's had any sleep. I'm hanging." He looked pretty rough. I expect I did too. "Yes, you may. When you've told me everything that happened and everything you know, without evasion."

"You've made promises like that before," I said.

"You should still trust me. I'm the best hope you've got."

"No, you should trust me. I've just done your job for you, in spite of you trying to hold me against my will. Illegally, I might add. I was going to let that go, but if you try anything like it again, I'll get very pissed off with you."

"Now you're threatening me?"

"Yes."

"Fuck, you've got a nerve."

"I've been being shot at, a lot, and I've been killing people. A lot. Have you?"

"No."

"Then you'll understand that I'm not completely in my normal state of mind, and that if you piss me about, I'm very liable to post you out of that window." He looked at the one window in the room. It was about big enough for a cat to fit through it. "I did a very stupid thing coming to Morocco and running hash, but I'm not the only one round here who's been doing stupid things, and I'm doing my best to get back on your side of the fence. I've never been your problem but if you treat me like one, I'll become one. Are we clear?"

"What the fuck," he said, getting some glasses out and pouring us both a shot from a bottle of brandy. "I don't even have a case against them, never mind you. You're right. I'm sorry." He held out his hand.

"You're sorry?" I said.

"Yes. One gets into habits of distrust, being a policeman. That was pretty crap of me."

"You should try being a drug smuggler," I said, taking his hand. "Where do you want me to start?"

"At the beginning, please."

"Okay, I'll start at the beginning. It was about a year and a half ago. I'd just got back from a year's ocean racing and I was completely broke. I was sitting in the kitchen at home reading an article about go-fast boats in the Caribbean, that I'd found lying there on the table, and Mum came in carrying an old family photo album…"

We made more coffee and he asked occasional questions; he was interested in my service in the British Army and my post-graduate education by Guy in the arts of war, and in my facility for languages.

When we had finished Bill said, "I think I'll give them to the Sûreté."

"Sam and Guy?"

"Yes."

"Give him to them. Sam's just his daughter. You can't give a girl to those animals."

"Some girl. I'll think about it."

"Don't let her kill you, will you."

"I'll try not to."

I left without saying goodbye to anyone. It seemed unlikely, somehow, that I wouldn't see them again. Anyway, I'd had more than enough of all of them for the time being.

Soumy cried when she saw me. Then she hugged me. Then she told me how smelly I was through her tears. Then she got cross with herself for standing there crying when there were things to do. Then she got cross with me for making her cry. Then she hugged me again, even though I was so smelly.

I had a shower and she tenderly washed me, and then shaved me, which was good as, now that I was safe and home, I seemed to be losing all ability to do anything much at all.

I lay down in the nest of cushions and rugs to rest while she prepared food, but what my body needed was sleep, so that is what happened. I went out like a light and slept the sleep that is a long swim down into clear, warm, blue water, and that washes away all troubles. If I dreamt they were good dreams, watched over as I was by my slight, doe-eyed protectress.

When I woke, the rest of that day and a whole night had passed and it was late morning and I was very, very hungry.

Soumy ate with me, which seemed perfectly natural to both of us now, and then I phoned my mother. Dad was in hospital in Melilla, where the chopper had left him. The surgeon who'd been flown out had screwed the bits of his shattered knee back together and said that he would be fit to be moved back to the UK in a few days. Mum sounded subdued. I said I'd come and see them later.

I didn't mean to tell Soumy about what had happened in the desert, but I did anyway. It made me breathe hard and hold her hand too hard, but I told her about what had happened and how it had felt. How is it she, who has seen so little of such things, seems to understand so well? I don't know.

We lay down together in the nest of cushions and I might have slept again but she was no longer unavailable to me. We made love. Very gently and slowly and it was different from the way it had been before. Better. Afterwards we lay together, her head on my shoulder, contained in my arms.

After quite a long time of just being there she gave a big sigh and said, "What will happen to Mr Guy and the woman?"

"The policeman, Bill, was talking about giving them to the Sûreté," I said.

"That's bad. I would not wish that to happen to anyone. But I do not believe we will be safe until they are dead."

"I can't say you're wrong about that."

"What will you do now, Simon?"

"I think I'll go and see Ali at the Rif, and maybe Asif, and maybe Robbie. Then maybe I'll go and fetch Nottambulo back from where I've hidden her."

"No, don't do that, Si. Leave it where it is. Or you could sell it, or give it to someone or, I don't know, sink it. It's trouble. You know it is." She sat up and pulled away from me.

"But she's my boat, I made her. I cannot do that."

"If you are going to do the drug business again you must go." She pointed to the door and her lower lip trembled. "I will not have that again in my life again. Never."

"Soumy, you are right. I'm not thinking much yet. I promise," I took hold of her hands and made her look at me, "I promise, no more drug smuggling. At all. None. Okay?"

"You promise?"

"I promise."

"Okay, I believe you."

My phone rang. It was my mother asking if I would fetch my father's things from the Riby. I said I would and got dressed.

"Soumy, don't go out."

"I have to get things for supper. You've eaten every bit of food in the house."

"Okay, but be a penguin. Promise?"

"I promise."

"Good. See you later."

I went down to the street and walked along the front and into the Rif bar. Ali was polishing a glass and staring into the middle distance.

"Hi, Ali. How's life?" I said.

"Simon." He looked at me strangely. "You truly are hard to kill. I did not believe that I would see you again."

"I'll drink a beer if that'll help to convince you," I said.

"Your boat is gone and Mr Guy is gone and there have been people of all kinds, and the wrong kinds at that, looking for you. There have been wild rumours of all kinds flying about. Where have you been? Perhaps you should not tell me." He gave me a beer.

"Perhaps I shouldn't. But I am alive, as you see, and most of the people who were looking for me are not, so it could be worse."

"And Mr Guy? Is he alive too?"

"Yes, but I don't believe we'll see him again. I hope not anyway. His reign is over now."

"There will soon be a new king of Nador. Will it be you, Simon?"

"No, Ali. It will not."

"I think I am glad about that."

"I'm not sure how to take that," I said.

"I'm not quite sure how I meant it, either," Ali said. "Did you hear about Azooz?"

"No?"

"His boys turned on him and beat him to death. Slowly. No one blames them. I have two of them working here now, as it happens."

"Good for you, Ali. Good for you."

My phone rang. It was Bill. "Hi, Bill," I said.

"We've had a bit of an accident," he said. "The one you warned me about. Are you busy?"

"Are you asking for my help?"

"I said I was sorry. Yes, I am."

"So you did. Shall I come now?"

"If you wouldn't mind."

"I'm on my way." I hung up.

"Apparently I've given up drug smuggling and taken up working for the British police," I said.

"Really? I don't think you should say that, even in jest."

"I'm sorry, Ali. I take it back. It was a bad joke."

"Okay. Would you like another beer? You seem to have finished that one."

"No, Ali. I really must go, but hopefully I will come back for it later."

I took a taxi back into town and had him drop me near my destination. I knocked and Bill let me in.

"I went out to get some more coffee and some food," he said.

I followed him into the flat. The thin young man with the beard was lying slumped against the wall outside the toilet. There was what looked like the end of a pair of tweezers sticking out of his neck, over where the carotid artery is. The holster at his hip was empty. In the sitting room the two soldiers who had escorted us back sat staring, empty eyed, at the TV. Both had taken two rounds through the chest, over their hearts, an inch or two apart. Their body armour was stacked neatly at the end of the sofa on which they sat. Their weapons were missing.

"Sam persuaded him to let her go to the loo," I said.

"And then she stabbed him through the neck with a pair of tweezers she found there. I know," he said.

"Where's Freddy?"

"Still a few hours away. They've tidied up and they're back over the border, but it's a long drive yet."

"Have you talked to the Sûreté?" I said.

"Yes. They weren't too happy."

"Phone them back and tell them that he's escaped and he's got two hundred kilos of cocaine and heroin with him."

"He hasn't. Freddy found that in his Range Rover and burnt it."

"So lie to them. We want them to want to catch him, don't we? They would eat their grandmothers for that much money. They'll have road blocks up in the whole area within half an hour, so warn Freddy."

"Okay. That sounds good."

"And don't mention Sam."

"She's just killed three people."

"I know. And she'll probably be with him and whatever happens to him will probably happen to her too. I can't help that, but I owe her a sporting chance, that's all."

"I don't."

"No, but you do owe me, so go and make those calls. I'm going to have a think."

I sat on the other sofa and stared at the TV. I don't know what was on it. Bill came back in.

"You were right about the Sûreté," he said.

"What do you want to do with these poor chaps?" I said, indicating the dead men.

"I can't take them home. They'll have to be lost in action, I suppose. Fuck knows how I'm going to get rid of them, poor sods. And I was doing so well."

"Would you like a permanent agent in Nador to tell you what's moving in the port, and who's moving it?"

"Of course I would."

"Will you pay for it? A remittance every month."

"Yes, that's no problem."

"Good. I'll get this sorted out for you then."

"Really?"

"Sure. Can you borrow that helicopter and pilot again?"

"Should be able to. Why?"

"I have an idea. Get it to meet us at the place where it dropped us off in about two hours."

"Okay. If you say so."

I phoned Imad. He sounded pleased to hear from me. I told him where to come and to bring the pickup and some tarpaulins.

Half an hour later we loaded three heavy, well wrapped bundles into the back of the pickup. Bill shook hands with a grave and thoughtful Asif and a cheerful, smiling Imad over the beginning of an understanding between them. I had a quiet word with them out of his hearing and off they went. The bodies would disappear, well wrapped in chains, into the still deep beyond the inshore shelf.

"I brought those men out here. I'll have to tell their families," Bill said, shutting the door.

"You'll get over it," I said.

"Thanks."

"Put the coffee on then. Did I hear you say you bought some food? There should be plenty to go around now."

"You seem to be feeling better."

"I've had some excellent sleep."

"I wish I had."

Half an hour later we stood on the wasteland behind the warehouse, which turned out to be on the road to Melilla, waiting for the chopper. I'd bought my .38 and an HK I'd found, and Bill hadn't objected.

"Well?" Bill said. "Tell me what we're doing."

"It was a conversation Sam and I had right at the beginning," I said. "I told her that when I'd had enough of working for her dad, I would probably take off round the Med for a bit. Keep out of the way and work up a sensible story to tell when I got back to the UK. I thought she might come with me, and so did she. Though of course, in reality, there was never any question of me being able to leave."

"You think they'll try to get away by sea?"

"I do. They may have already. Guy's always got an eye on the main chance and if there's one person who can guess where I've hidden Nottambulo, he's the man. We're on the way there now."

"And if we find him?"

"The funny thing about Guy is that although he lies all the time, he doesn't say anything he doesn't mean. I crossed a line when I bought you lot to his camp out in the desert. It's him or me now. Sometime, somewhere. I think it had better be now."

"You're going to kill him?"

"If I can find him. Unless you've a better idea?"

"No, I don't."

"But you're a policeman not an executioner. I know."

"I'm finding that line a little blurred today."

"It may not be a problem; first catch your hare."

The chopper clattered its way out of the sky at the appointed time, just as the sun was setting, and we climbed in. This time there were headphones and microphones so that we could hear and be heard, each other and the two pilots. I went up front with them to navigate.

They were cheerful, amenable chaps, as pilots often seem to be, ready to enter into the spirit of the hunt. I guessed that a rotation of duty to Melilla was a pretty boring option, and that we'd brought a little colour into their lives.

Helicopters may be loud and rather vulnerable, but when you want one, they're brilliant. We went straight where we were going at over a hundred miles an hour and what had taken me hours on land a few days before, took a few minutes. I had them fly along inland of the coast, taking an occasional peek out over the edge, until I got my bearings and started to recognise the geology.

When I looked down on what I'd climbed it looked bloody horrible. As we moved out a bit I could see the dark line of the rope against the pale rock, like a crack all the way down. Someone had abseiled down. There was no black arrow on the sand. Nottambulo had gone.

"What now?" Bill said over the comms.

"We should have come sooner. I thought he would wait 'til dark but he didn't." I looked down at the sea. It looked pretty flat, but then it always does from a height.

We had a bit of a look out to sea, but what there was, was black water, nothing else, nothing visible anyway.

"I'm starting to see why no one ever caught me," I said. "We'll have to just take a guess. Due east, please pilot, and give her all she's got."

We crossed the peninsula, rocketing out over the sea and gaining height. I did calculations in my head about how long it would have taken Guy and Sam to get to her and get her out, assuming that they'd gone straight to it as soon as they were at liberty.

"Where do you think they're headed?" Bill said.

"My gut says east. There's the whole North African coast to hide in and beyond that the islands and the Black Sea. That's what I'd do. The question is, are they behind us, or ahead of us?"

"Your call, Si. I haven't a clue."

"Take us north please, driver. Then we'll zigzag a bit. Eyes skinned, everyone."

There was nothing on the radar. I didn't know whether to be disappointed or pleased by that. We swept the water, taking a quadrant each and swapping night glasses for day glasses in turn, as we only had one pair of each. It was hard work. We were travelling at the Sea King's maximum speed of 112 knots and, at our height, had a horizon of over a hundred miles. In that light though, or lack of it, the moon still had hours before it would rise, it was only the lights of even small tankers that made them visible to us at much less distance than that. A small black boat with no lights showing would have to be within a few miles for us to see it and, as I knew well, the sea, even the Western Med, is a big place. We quartered the sea up to the Cap and turned to the west again without seeing anything apart from cargo vessels and a few local fishing boats.

On one of our turns I noticed the co-pilot, who was doing his best with his naked eyes to help, stop in his sweep and concentrate on a point.

"What do you see?" I said.

"Nothing. I thought a pale mark for a second, but it is nothing."

"Point," I said. "We'll go and look."

The mark was back on our track and we had seen nothing there, but we were clutching at straws now, so back we went. Again, there it was for a second, a pale mark on the sea, right at the edge of sight. I understood; it was easier to see looking back; it was the short wake of a light boat travelling at speed, high speed. It was Nottambulo.

They must have been doing a good eighty knots as, after slowing to make the turn, we were not gaining on them. The pilot put her nose down and pushed the throttle levers against their stops. I re-checked the HK that I'd taken from the house, went back and slid the bay door open. The rushing air and the yawning drop tried to make me throw myself out into oblivion, but I held on to the roof strap with white knuckles and the feeling subsided a bit. Bill appeared beside me looking pale and tense.

"I don't want to do this," I said.

"If you're right, he'll kill you if you don't," he said.

"I was thinking of my boat," I said, giving him a rather fixed grin.

The pilot, who was definitely enjoying himself, put us a bit sideways and she appeared in the opening, closer than I'd expected; my boat, that I had made. Long like a javelin, flying over the water like nothing on earth. I wished I'd seen her like this before. She was, for a moment, the most beautiful thing that I'd ever seen.

Then I noticed that there was only one person aboard her, and that he, and it was Guy, had locked the wheel, was bracing against the movement and swinging something up towards us.

There was the thudding sound, felt as well as heard, of rounds hitting the underside of the chopper and we swung suddenly away, banking as hard as the rotors would grip the air. Bill and I hung on like death, his face white, mine too probably.

When we levelled out I said over comms, "Sorry about that. He's found the MAG I left on board. Any important damage?"

"Only to Manuel's underpants," the pilot said, laughing.

"If we were to do that again, may I use your cannon?" I said.

"If we do that again, I think you better had. And please don't miss," the pilot said.

"I'll do my best," I said.

Bill watched while I unlocked the armature that carried the fifty-calibre box-fed cannon and swung it out and round. In spite of its weight it moved smoothly on its bearings. I traversed it experimentally and then swung it back in to remove the muzzle cap and work the action, loading the first round. I unlocked the safety and checked that the thumb pads would depress, rested my fingers on the levers and said, "Okay, fuck it, I'm ready. Let's do it."

"I'll count you in. Here we go," the pilot said.

He took us back up to speed, but low this time. There was a pause that may have been a few seconds, but felt like a year, then, "Diez, nueve, ocho, siete, seis." I swung the muzzle to the forward edge of my sight and lowered my head. "Cinco, cuatro, tres, dos, uno, ahora." The square transom of Nottambulo appeared in the opening and I pulled against the firm spring of the levers with my fingers.

The roar of more than a thousand rounds per second is like nothing else. It took the whole helicopter in its grip and held it tight. Time stopped and I followed the glow of the tracers curving down, willing them at the target. I was swinging now, not to over-shoot and for a brief interval I was locked on. I knew I was on it, just for a half a second or so. Then it was past.

I let go of the levers and the shaking stopped. Shell casings were dancing about on the floor in their hundreds, and being whipped out into the void by the wind. The pilot banked us hard right and then back left, making the sea disappear and then reappear, almost under us.

The long black shape was still racing away below us but some-thing had changed. The back of the boat was torn and ragged. Something was slumped over the binnacle, white stuffing was showing everywhere from the ripped up seats.

We hung over her, no longer in danger, watching her, now a hearse, bearing her cargo blindly across the face of the water.

There was a flicker of flame at the back of the port engine cowling, not extinguished by the rushing air, and I was shouting, "Up. Up." And then we were punched by a hot, white fist from below and everyone was shouting.

Even our sanguine young pilot had had enough now. When he had regained his composure and caught the aircraft in its wild lurch, we hovered for a moment as the black smoke was dispersed by the wash from the rotors. There were a few bits of burning debris, but very little. She was gone.

In silence, we turned for home.

21

OUT AND DOWN

It should have been later, but it wasn't. Less than three hours had passed since the chopper had picked us up at nightfall. They put us back where they found us, brushing off our thanks, their minds on home and getting away from us, wanting the healing camaraderie of the mess and their own kind. Tomorrow they would tell stories about it, but for now, they were sick of it.

Bill looked a bit sick too. I was feeling rather quiet myself.

"That's solved a few problems, hasn't it?" I said.

"I'm not used to solving problems like that."

"You feeling like a policeman again?"

"What I feel like is a lot of sleep. What I've got is telling Freddy that two of his men, and one of mine, got killed by a girl, and are now at the bottom of the sea. He should be back by now."

"I might not stop by to say hello. Can I drop you off and use your car?" We'd come in the old Mercedes estate.

"I suppose so. What are you going to do now?" He got in the passenger side and I drove.

"Mum asked me to get Dad's things from the Riby. I might have a bite to eat there and then go see them. I suppose I should tell them, well Mum anyway, that Guy is dead."

"Yes, of course. I'm sorry. I wonder where his daughter is."

"Waiting for him at Ras Kebdana, perhaps. That's the direction he was headed."

"I'm glad she wasn't on the boat. I shouldn't ask but, you and her?"

"It's complicated."

"I'll bet. And you lost your boat today too. I hadn't really realised what she was until I saw her like that."

"Me too, but there will be other boats."

"Not go-fast ones, I hope."

"No, I don't think I'll do that again."

"What will you do? When this is over, I mean?"

"I've no idea. Have a holiday, do a bit of fishing."

"I'll give you a job, if you like."

"Being a policeman? You're joking."

"Not exactly. Just give me a call if you get bored. I'll find you something interesting to do."

"Like what?"

"Like, wait and see. This isn't the time to talk about it."

"You can be a bugger sometimes. If I get that bored, which I doubt, you can buy me a beer and tell me about it." I pulled up at the end of his street.

"You should," he said.

"Hang on. So, what you're telling me is - I've been working undercover all this time? I haven't done anything illegal after all."

"That's a story that could be told, I suppose."

"Working under the auspices of my old man, of course? He's the one who put you onto the dead fish network, isn't he?"

"Is he?"

"Definitely. You'll make a good team, you and him. When he's back at the Home Office. It'll be good for you to have him at your back."

"You've got a lot of nerve."

"You know it makes sense. Quite apart from the fact that you owe me one. Or two."

"Good night, Simon. I'll think about it and catch up with you tomorrow."

"No problem. Just phone me if you want me."

I took the long way up the hill. I'd had enough of heights for one day and there was no hurry. The old castle looked like an oasis of comfort and tranquillity. The cicadas were singing in the date palms and the moon was just about to rise out in the desert. The doorman waved me in with a smile and I wandered through the garden, enjoying the scents and the contained quiet of the place. Being in it made me think of Sam. Of her smell and the feel of her body and the way she was so alive. I hadn't connected with anyone in quite the same way since Grandad had died. Knowing what she was thinking, feeling, being able to anticipate her actions and rely on them without a word spoken. A precious thing, usually hard won, that had come to us so easily, so naturally.

I wondered if I would have swung that cannon with such accuracy if she had been on Nottambulo. Perhaps, but I was glad I hadn't had to find out.

Robbie walked into the garden from the terrace. He was looking spruce and cheerful.

"Si, there you are," he said. He took my hand, slapping me on the shoulder affectionately.

"Hey, Robbie. Here I am," I said.

We walked out into the moonlight of the terrace. There was a sliver missing from it now but it was bright. There were diners at all the tables, apart from one on the end. We sat down.

"Oh, thanks for the present, by the way," he said.

"Mrs Murr?" I said.

"No longer Mrs Murr."

"Mrs Anderson?"

"God save me, no. I call her Gina. She's got all the chamber-maids terrified of her, I don't know how."

"Careful what you wish for," I said.

"Huh?"

"You said you wanted to settle down with just one woman."

"Did I? Really?"

"Sort of."

"Was I drunk?"

"As I remember, yes."

"Well, that doesn't count then. Would you like a drink?" He raised a hand for a waiter.

"A scotch I think. Better make it three glasses."

"Oh, why?"

"Robbie, you're a crap liar, even when you don't say anything. You haven't asked me where I've been, or what's been happening."

"I knew I couldn't carry it off." He gave the order to the waiter.

"Don't worry, it's an endearing trait. If you don't believe me, ask Gina."

"So, where have you been and what's been happening?"

"Apart from what you know, I've just sunk Nottambulo with 50 calibre cannon fire from a helicopter."

"You mean that?"

"Yes."

"Bloody hell, Si."

"Guy was driving her at the time."

"Oh my God."

The waiter brought a silver tray with crystal glasses, a bottle of the 63 Glenlivet and a jug of water. I poured three good shots into the glasses.

"Cheers, Robbie," I said.

"Cheers." We gently touched glasses and drank.

Sam walked out of the archway and across the terrace towards us. She was wearing the long black evening dress again and she looked heart-stoppingly beautiful.

"Hello, Si, you're here at last," she said, sitting down and putting her evening bag on the table.

"Hi, Sam." I passed her a glass. "Sorry I'm a bit late."

She sniffed it, wrinkling her nose appreciatively and taking a sip. "That's very nice," she said, looking at me over the top of it.

"Robbie's idea. A valedictory malt," I said.

"He's a good man."

"But a bad liar."

"He's under the thumb, you know."

"I know. Are you hungry?"

"Bloody hungry."

"I'll go and see to it," Robbie said, rising. "Anything in particular…?"

"No, we trust you," I said.

"Whatever you think, Robbie," Sam said.

"I knew you'd get away. I told them but they wouldn't listen," I said, when he had gone.

"People don't, do they. I told Dad you would be trouble, but he wouldn't listen. He thought he would always be one step ahead of you."

"He was, most of the way. It was Dad he didn't reckon with really."

"He said that Ed would always do the thing that would protect his reputation. That that mattered more to him than anything else."

"He was wrong. He came out here with Rupert and all those men, to kill Guy, to get me back. I think it was personal."

"Dad's not possessive like that. What's it like to have someone care about you like that?"

"I'm not sure. I haven't really thought about it yet. He had other reasons too, though."

"I'm bored with drugs and money now."

"Me too. I'm not sure why we all bothered."

"Dad's very bothered. He intends to get it all going again."

"Rupert was like that: an ambitious man."

"Not any more."

"No, not any more."

"We were good, weren't we?"

"If I had to do it all again, I'd want to do it with you."

"That's a nice thing to say."

"But you still told Guy to kill me."

"Yes, of course."

We looked at each other for a bit, not talking but understanding. Her eyes were still iron grey and without pity for herself or anyone else, but I didn't mind that in the least.

"You weren't at finishing school, were you?" I said.

"Dad wanted them to cure me."

"But they couldn't?"

"They were about to find the bodies, so I left."

"And Guy thought, if you couldn't be fixed, he might as well put you to work?"

"Which I'd been telling him for ages."

"I kept telling mine that he should stop being in control and tell me the truth," I said.

"They don't listen."

"No, they don't. Zara was you?"

"Yes." She smiled at the memory. "I'd been looking forward to that for months. Dad wouldn't give me the chance. Kept her where he could see her all the time."

"Until Mum distracted him?"

"Yes."

"Thought so."

The food came, and with it a cold bottle of Quincy. We ate marinated strips of tuna with salad and bread still warm from the oven, followed by dates stuffed with delicately spiced marzipan.

"Robbie's in the zone tonight," She said, wiping her mouth with a napkin.

"Do you remember the last time we were here?" I said.

"Yes, and the time before too. You were falling in love with me then."

"I was, wasn't I."

"I'm glad you got over it."

"I haven't entirely."

"It didn't stop you setting off Armageddon."

"I'd had enough of being used. You didn't mind though, did you?"

"Hell no, I enjoyed it." She smiled at the thought.

"I knew you would."

"You haven't asked me what I'm going to do now."

"Neither have you."

"No, I haven't." She put a hand on her evening bag.

"I killed Guy earlier this evening," I said.

"How?" she didn't miss a beat.

"I sank Nottambulo from a helicopter. On the way to pick you up at Ras Kebdana, I imagine," I said.

"Yes."

"After you'd killed me," I said. "That is why you're here, aren't you?"

"Yes. You sank your boat? You sank Nottambulo?"

"50cal cannon. Nearly full tanks. Big bang. No chance I'm afraid."

"I told him to let it go."

"I knew he wouldn't."

"So did I. So did he."

"Sorry."

"No matter."

"What will you do?"

"I think…" she poured us both a little more from the whiskey bottle, "… I think I'll take up that invitation from Gerald. What about you?"

"I might take a cruise. If I'm alive to take it. I'm not armed."

"I know. Strangely I don't want to. Didn't anyway."

"I decided that if you were going to, I'd let you."

"How strange."

"I know."

"I must get going." She got up and tucked her evening bag under her arm. "I've a long hard road full of enemies ahead of me."

"You'll make it," I said, getting up too.

"I know. I'll see you, Si."

"See you, Sam."

We put our arms around each other for a moment and then she was gone.

I sat there for a bit with my glass of scotch, looking at the endless sea stretching away under the silver moon.

Robbie bought a pot of coffee and two cups and joined me.

"I've had your father's things packed up," he said.

"Thanks, I'd better go and see them now."

"I lent her my car."

"Saved her stealing mine. I don't think you'll see it again."

"Who cares. Will she make it?"

"She's got the Sûreté after her now. And anyone who knows Guy's day is over and fancies their chances. Yes, I think she'll make it."

"What about you?"

"They'll be after me too, soon. I don't plan to be here for long."

"I'll miss you."

"I'll keep in touch. I suppose I should pay my bill sometime."

"I don't feel owed."

"Good. Come on then, give me a hand with the bags."

"Okay."

We went out to the car park together. I gave him a hug, because that's what seemed right, and drove away.

It was a bit of driving to get to Melilla, but I didn't notice it. They let me in to the private ward without any trouble and a porter helped me with the bags. We put them quietly by the door and I walked into the small room with floral curtains and a hospital bed.

Mum was asleep on a chair beside the bed but Dad was awake. He smiled a sweet, unconscious smile when he saw me and lifted a hand.

I took the hand and said, "Hi, Dad. How're you feeling?"

"Pretty crap, Si, but I'll live. I'll live. Apparently I'll walk again too. So they tell me. I can't say it feels like it…" His face had sunk in on itself a bit and the stubble on his chin was white.

"You'll be fine, Dad. Back home soon."

"I'm dreading it. What will they say? I've made such a mess."

"No you haven't. Wounded whilst overseeing the biggest drugs bust in years. That's all."

"How can you say that?"

"My friend Bill. The copper who rounded us up in the desert, if you remember?"

"Not really."

"No problem. Trust me, it'll be okay."

"Simon." Mum had woken up at the sound of our voices.

"Hi, Mum. I brought Dad's stuff."

"Thank you, darling." She tried to look her light, carefree self but it didn't work. She looked tired; more than tired; bereft.

"Shall we leave Dad to rest and go and look for a coffee or something?" I said.

"Okay, darling, that's a great idea." She got up, smoothed down her skirt and checked that the bag of the drip was full and dripping. "How's the pain, sweetie?"

"Oh, you know," he said, holding up the button that activated the morphine driver. "I push this every now and then, and it backs off a bit."

"See you later, Dad." I led the way to the end of the ward and held the door for her. She turned left and I followed her to a room with chairs and a TV. The lights were subdued and there were only the faint background sounds of nurses moving quietly in the distance and the hum of the air-conditioning.

We sat on two chairs that were close together and she took hold of one of my hands and held it hard.

"How're you doing, Mum? You look a little tired," I said.

"I don't know what happened, Si."

"How do you mean?"

"It was all such fun and I was feeling like myself again… and now…" she waved a hand in the direction from which we'd come, "… we've come to this."

"Dad will have a limp but otherwise he'll be okay, won't he?"

"He needs me now."

"Why, Mum?"

"Why what?"

"You've been in contact with Guy all along, haven't you? It didn't end when he left in disgrace did it?"

"Of course not. We were never like that. I was never like that."

"But Dad's work. You had to pretend?"

"Yes, and that was horrible but it wasn't that. I felt left out. They had their thing and that was okay in its way, but then they carried on without telling me. He would go out once or twice a year, but he never told me. Guy told me of course."

"So when Guy asked you to send me to him it seemed only fair?"

"I didn't understand. I didn't understand what I was doing, or what your father would do. I'm sorry."

"I didn't understand either, Mum. You didn't make me do anything. I thought it would be fun. I had no idea what it really was, or where it would lead."

"Your father cares so much. He can never seem to say the right thing, but he cares. More than I do, most of the time."

"It feels like the thing with Dad and me was always coming, wasn't it? We're so different, I don't know, I don't understand it. I don't know why he always seems to want to control me and would never trust me."

"You don't know why?"

"No. You do? Tell me."

"I thought you knew."

"Knew what?"

"I assumed you'd worked it out when you decided to come here. I'm sure you said…"

"What?"

"Maybe not. I can't remember. Guy's your father, dear. Not Ed. You must have known that."

I left her in that room and walked out of the building. I don't remember driving back to Nador but I must have done so. The waterfront, the buildings and the docks, they all looked familiar and full of memories, and at the same time strange and as if they belonged to another world. As I drove past where I would turn up towards my old flat I wondered how the cat was doing. She was a pretty tough cat, so hopefully okay.

The Rif bar was lit up and full of people. I had meant to go in and say hello to Ali, have a beer for one last time, but I passed it, and the jetty from which I'd taken Nottambulo out so many times, with scarcely a glance.

The road east along the lagoon had its usual share of taxi drivers taking people to and from the bars, but it didn't bother me that I had to follow one, weaving this way and that, for a mile or so. I pulled in by the restaurant, put the key under the mat out of habit, and walked down to the sea.

Asif was waiting for me with a little tender. He must have spoken to me but I don't remember what he said. We pushed off and he took me out to Wise Policy.

When I came up over the side, Soumy's sweet little face, with such gentle eyes, was peeping out of the companion way. She came out shyly and put her arms around me.

I pushed the button to start the diesel engine and Imad got in and stowed the kedge. He ran agilely up to the bow and brought the main anchor up and down. "Ready, boss?" he said.

"Ready," I said.

He brought it all the way up and lashed it, and then slipped over the side and down into the tender. I put her into gear and we began to move forward.

We were going out and down. Down to the trade winds and the big, clean Atlantic Ocean. After that, we would see.

The End

Need more Si in your life?

Get your next next Simon Ellice story from the Rat's Tales website:

www.ratstales.co.uk

Visit the Simon Ellice Website for exclusive content,
straight from the brain of his creator.

www.simonellice.co.uk

You can also find Rat's Tales and Simon Ellice on social media.